"You can smell the cordite, hear the explosions, and feel the fight in this one. Action jumps from every page."
— Steve Berry, *New York Times* bestselling author of *The Malta Exchange*

"Weaves adrenaline and angst, intrigue and insight, onto every page. In a crowded field, Bentley just raised the bar and vaulted over it."
— Andrews & Wilson, US Navy veterans and authors of the *Wall Street Journal* bestselling Tier One series

"Destined to be the best debut of the year. Bentley writes with the precision of Lee Child and the wit of Nelson DeMille."
— Brigadier General Anthony J. Tata, US Army (ret.), national bestselling author of *Dark Winter*

"Matt Drake has to fight two wars, maybe more, and he has to save himself before he can save everyone else. An intense, deeply personal story written by someone who has been there."
— Larry Bond, bestselling author of *Arctic Gambit*

"Don Bentley has lived this life, and he writes with deep authenticity. This is one hell of a book."
— Nick Petrie, national bestselling author of *Tear It Down*

"An unflinching dive into the soul of the modern warrior that is so beautifully written and expertly executed that I cannot believe it is a debut novel."

—Joshua Hood, author of *Clear by Fire*

"Realistic, gritty, and hard-hitting—an incendiary debut."

—K. J. Howe, international bestselling author of *Skyjack*

"An adrenaline-soaked rocket ship of a debut novel with fascinating characters and off-the-charts action. It's hard to reach the level of Brad Taylor the first time out of the box, but Don Bentley does just that."

—Simon Gervais, international bestselling author of *Hunt Them Down*

"This is a novel with an emotional core, and that may be what makes it stand out from other thrillers of a similar ilk. A page-turner with the kind of small details that lend unquestionable authenticity." —*Kirkus Reviews*

THE OUTSIDE MAN

"A fresh and worthy entrant into the top tier of military-political thriller authors" —BookTrib

"Bentley adds brains to the traditional brawn of yesteryear in crafting a thinking man's shoot-'em-up that keeps us on the edge of our seat from beginning to end."

—*The Providence Journal*

"Another super-charged, action-packed adventure that's tailor-made for fans of Mark Greaney and Brad Taylor. . . . Gritty, timely, and packed with nonstop, heart-thumping action, Don Bentley's *The Outside Man* is a must-read for fans of propulsive, unputdownable thrillers."

—Ryan Steck, The Real Book Spy

HOSTILE INTENT

"The intricate level of who's-doing-what-to-whom adds twists. Readers who enjoy the world of special ops should add Bentley to their reading pile."   —*Library Journal*

"An excellent, fast-paced plot will keep readers engaged."
—*Mystery & Suspense Magazine*

FORGOTTEN WAR

"*Forgotten War* is as good as it gets. Intense. Explosive. Riveting. Absolutely unforgettable."

—Joel C. Rosenberg, *New York Times* bestselling author of
The Libyan Diversion

"With his trademark combination of loyalty, lethality, and sardonic wit, Drake is a hero with soul. . . . *Forgotten War* is the kind of inspired adventure you stay up all night reading."

—Tosca Lee, *New York Times* bestselling author of
The Line Between

"This fourth book in the Matt Drake thriller series has an intensity that few writers can achieve. . . . Fluid writing, great characterization, and fantastic world building."

—*Mystery & Suspense Magazine*

TOM CLANCY'S JACK RYAN JR. NOVELS WRITTEN BY DON BENTLEY

"Exciting. . . . The action builds to a terrific, multiple-point-of-view battle scene. . . . Bentley proves himself a worthy successor to Tom Clancy." —*Publishers Weekly*

"Bentley is at his best with witty inner dialogue and edge-of-your-seat action scenes that feel creative and authentic." —BookTrib

"Bentley keeps Jack Ryan Jr.'s life exciting in this latest grand-scale Tom Clancy adventure. . . . Fast, furious Clancy fare, fun even though you already know who wins." —*Kirkus Reviews*

"Since taking the reins of the Ryanverse, Don Bentley has shown to be a masterful storyteller, adept at crafting intricate plots that intertwine global politics, cutting-edge technology, and heart-stopping action."

—The Real Book Spy

TITLES BY DON BENTLEY

The Matt Drake Novels
Without Sanction

The Outside Man

Hostile Intent

Forgotten War

Tom Clancy Target Acquired

Tom Clancy Zero Hour

Tom Clancy Flash Point

FORGOTTEN WAR

DON BENTLEY

BERKLEY
New York

BERKLEY

An imprint of Penguin Random House LLC

penguinrandomhouse.com

Copyright © 2023 by Donald Burton Bentley II

ISBN: 9780593333570

Berkley hardcover edition / April 2023
Berkley premium edition / April 2024

Printed in the United States of America
1   3   5   7   9   10   8   6   4   2

Book design by Kristin del Rosario

To the eleven Marines, one sailor, and one soldier who gave their lives on August 26th, 2021, at Kabul International Airport's Abbey Gate. You are the very best of us. May we who remain prove worthy of your sacrifice.

Fortes fortuna adiuvat.

(Fortune favors the brave.)

—**PUBLIUS TERENTIUS AFER**

PROLOGUE

B rother—you are free."

Mullah Qari Wasiq blinked in the bright sunlight, his tired eyes watering as they struggled to adjust to the unexpected brilliance. Ten years. He'd waited ten years to hear those words, but at the moment when his freedom was finally realized, Qari found himself consumed with thoughts of something else.

The will of Allah.

Qari looked from the cloudless blue sky to the five mountaintops that surrounded Bagram Air Base. Though Bāgh Darē Ghar stood the highest at nearly twenty-four hundred meters, Kōh-e Tōp was by far the most prominent. These two peaks had kept Qari company for almost a decade, but the glimpses he'd stolen from the tiny window in his cell had not done them justice. Seeing the summits in their full unfiltered glory took his breath away.

"Brother?"

With a sigh, Qari turned from the mountains to the man standing before him.

The young man standing before him.

Ten years ago, Qari had been young too. But captivity in Parwan Detention Facility, Afghanistan's most notorious prison, had aged him. His once luxurious beard was scraggly and streaked with gray. His hair was a patchy mess, his back feeble, and his eyesight poor, but Qari now had strength in a place that had once been a dwelling for weakness.

His spirit.

"What is the time?" Qari said, his voice raspy from disuse.

"Brother?"

"The time, boy," Qari said. "What is the time?"

The fighter shook his head, but he pulled out a cell phone all the same.

"Ten a.m., brother."

"Thank you," Qari said with a nod.

Two hours before *Dhuhr*, or noon, prayers.

That was fine.

With a groan, Qari removed his outer tunic, revealing the emaciated flesh beneath.

The fighter sucked in a breath.

Qari wondered which affliction had caused the young Talib the greatest surprise—Qari's protruding ribs or the puckered flesh from the gunshot wound sustained during his capture? Or perhaps it was the faint web of lines that spidered across his abdomen? Maybe even the collection of shiny burns on his forearm. Scars delivered by guards who'd used his body as an ashtray.

Qari could mark the passage of time by the scars that now dotted his body.

Bending on wobbly knees, Qari arranged his tunic on

the ground facing west, brushing away the dirt as he fashioned a makeshift *sajjada*, or prayer rug. Then he lowered himself to the fabric and began to pray. Each time his forehead brushed the cloth, he praised Allah for granting him a second chance. For purging his soul. For burning away his pride. For giving him new purpose in his humility. In many ways, Qari considered himself fortunate. Historically, Allah often used periods of isolation to shape his followers. Qari could have spent forty years wandering the desert like Moses, but he had not.

After the final *salat*, Qari stood and reclaimed his tunic.

Where there once had been but a single fighter, now a gaggle of ten stood. Ten warriors, one for each year of his imprisonment.

Allah was faithful and merciful.

"Are you Mullah Wasiq?"

This time the question came from one of the new arrivals. Unlike his boyish companions, the speaker had an air of gravitas. His beard was thick and stretched to the middle of his chest. His face was weather-beaten and his dark eyes glowed with intelligence.

This was a commander, not just another foot soldier.

"I am," Qari said, his voice already stronger.

"Praise Allah," the commander said. "I am called Abdul. We've been searching for you."

Qari nodded.

The guard had told him the truth.

Like all nonbelievers, the man had been weak, but as Qari had learned the hard way, Allah transformed weakness into strength. Many of the prison guards had grown friendlier as the fighting between the Taliban and pro-government forces drifted ever closer to Kabul. But this man had shown mercy long before his brethren. When the sound of artillery fire had rolled over the jail's walls, Qari had taken the man into his confidence and given him a message.

A message for his Talib brethren who, Allah willing, would be his liberators.

"The guard found you?" Qari said.

"He did," Abdul said. "We discovered the building just as you described."

The commander pointed toward one of the men, and for the first time, Qari realized that his former captor was standing among his liberators.

Qari stared at the man, taking in his frightened features and lack of a weapon.

"Did they mistreat you?" Qari said.

The jailer shook his head. "No, sir," the man said. "They honored our agreement."

"Good," Qari said. "And the technician . . . he is still here?"

"Yes, brother," the jailer said.

"Find this man and bring him to me," Qari said, turning his attention back to the Taliban commander. "The knowledge he carries in his head is vital."

Already his confidence was returning as the crushing helplessness of the last ten years faded like a mist burned away by the rising sun. Qari pushed back against this feeling. He was no longer the arrogant commander he'd once been. Allah had reformed him, reshaped his life's purpose.

He would not forget his transformation so quickly.

"The brothers have finished loading the equipment," the commander said. "We took appropriate precautions, but you may inspect our work if you please."

Qari shook his head.

He was probably the least qualified to judge the quality of their work. Qari hadn't been the most technologically savvy before his imprisonment. He could only imagine how much things had changed since. While he understood the value of the information housed in the building, the electronic medium on which it was stored might as well have been taken from another planet. This was why he needed the technician. Besides, Qari's faith did not rest with electronic boxes or flashing lights. Allah had brought this moment to fruition. Surely he would not let it be undone by the very men he'd enlisted to his purpose.

"No," Qari said, "but I require a phone."

The commander reached into his pocket, withdrew his cell, and handed it to Qari.

"Thank you," Qari said, even as he began punching in the number he'd carefully memorized. He'd recited the digits daily, each time he finished his prayers. He'd been uncertain that he'd ever have the opportunity to dial them, but neither could he abandon the hope they'd represented.

No, Qari mentally corrected himself. That wasn't right. His hope, like his salvation, was in Allah. The phone number, as with the computers in the building, was a tool.

Nothing more.

Victory did not reside in flesh and blood or the things they created.

"Pardon, brother," the commander said, interrupting Qari's efforts. "What should be done with him?"

He pointed a dirty fingernail at the cowering jailer.

Qari studied the man's face even as he hit the dial button.

"Kill him," Qari said.

"Wait," the jailer said, his voice pitiful. "You said you'd be merciful."

"Mercy belongs to Allah," Qari said, "not men. But you are correct. Allah has seen fit to grant you mercy. Your family will not also bear the cost of your sins, unlike your fellow jailers."

The man let loose with a pitiful scream, which was quickly silenced by a gunshot.

Qari didn't pay attention to either sound.

He was too busy listening to the ringing phone.

ONE

Today was supposed to be a good day.

A day for celebrating new beginnings and old friendships. Few places in the world were better suited for celebration than my home city of Austin, Texas. While the self-proclaimed home of the weird wasn't anyone's idea of paradise in August, the city offered many ways to mitigate the stifling heat and suffocating humidity. It was four o'clock in the afternoon on a Thursday, and by now the three-acre Barton Springs Pool was undoubtedly crammed full of swimmers. The spring-fed water offered both refuge from the sun and a chance to meet the elusive and federally protected Barton Springs salamander, which lived in the pool's rock-lined bottom.

If the spring's year-round sixty-eight-degree water wasn't your cup of tea, the good folks over at Deep Eddy Pool would probably let you in a little early while they prepared for another nightly showing of *Jaws*. You read that right. Hundreds of people would soon be floating in inner tubes as they watched the scariest shark movie ever made. If experience was any guide, an illicit flask or two filled to the brim with the Austin-based Deep Eddy Vodka would be circulating among the audience.

I was partial to the Ruby Red variant.

This was Austin at her eccentric finest.

Though I loved my home city's eclectic summer offerings, I was seeking sanctuary somewhere more befitting a man of my low stature.

A bar.

But not just any bar.

The establishment in which my two companions and I found ourselves had no equal.

At least no modern equal.

The bar was small, dimly lit, and adhered to strict rules. Rule number one—booths must be reserved. Reservations were for a minimum of one hour and a maximum of three. Rule number two—no mobile devices and no obnoxious behavior. Despite, or perhaps maybe because of, its prime location, the bar's capacity probably topped out at about fifty. The customers sat in a row of booths that flanked a single walkway that led from the entrance to the employee area in the rear. Obnoxious behavior in the form of drunken carousing or endless electronic scrolling detracted from the bar's atmosphere.

And atmosphere was king.

The bar's history was both sordid and long. At different points it had served as a brothel and a speakeasy among other equally less reputable businesses. Now the establishment was a fixture on Austin's infamous Sixth Street. An island of calm in which the Austinites who actually paid for the city's expenses via ever-increasing property taxes could enjoy an evening apart from the throngs of college students who regularly mobbed the street. If there was an establishment in Austin custom-made for private celebrations, the Twilight Wrangler was it.

And we were here to celebrate.

Assuming our missing party eventually joined us.

"You sure you told her the right place?"

The question came from a slightly built African American man seated across the table from me. When we'd first met, he'd been one of the deadliest human beings I'd ever encountered. His physique had always skewed more toward endurance than strength, but his ropy muscles and prominent tendons could have been crafted from steel cables and iron ingots rather than flesh and blood.

Now he was a shadow of the fearsome warrior he'd once been. While we were operating together in Syria, an explosively formed penetrator had sheared off his left arm at the elbow and ruined his left leg. He'd recently had the mutilated leg amputated just below the knee so that he could be fitted with a prosthesis. Rehab had gone well, and the procedure had given him an exponential quality-of-life improvement.

Even so, I couldn't look at him without seeing the man he'd once been.

Though his given name was Frederick Tyler Cates, everyone called him Frodo, including his fiancée, Katherine, who was seated beside him. Their recently announced engagement was one of the reasons we were here to celebrate. I was ecstatically happy for the couple. I knew Katherine well, but my relationship with Frodo ran much deeper. He was my confidant, coworker, and, most important, best friend.

I treated him accordingly.

"Of course I'm sure, ya jack wagon," I said. "She's my wife."

While the girl in question was most assuredly my wife, I was less certain about the first part of my statement. My wife wasn't late. Ever. Since it was now fifteen minutes past the time we'd agreed to meet, there was a better-than-even chance I'd given her the wrong address.

But I wasn't about to admit this to Frodo.

"Maybe she's looking for parking." Katherine's statement was infinitely reasonable.

Like Frodo and me, Katherine had spent time in the military before taking her current role in the NSA, but she'd inhabited an utterly different world. The slim African American woman with warm eyes, shoulder-length hair, and a contagious laugh had been an aviator—a Black Hawk pilot, to be precise. And while helicopter pilots were a breed unto themselves, Katherine and her fellow aviators could on occasion admit when they were wrong.

This was not the case for men like Frodo and me. We hailed from organizations within Special Operations Command that viewed being wrong as only slightly better than being last.

Or maybe that was just me.

In any case, there was no way I could acknowledge the slim possibility that I'd texted my wife the address of our favorite watering hole on Rainey Street rather than that of the Twilight Wrangler. But I was beginning to get worried. Laila was not looking for parking because she wasn't driving. My wife excelled at a good many things. Battling Austin's homicidal motorists for the one remaining parking spot this side of Lady Bird Lake was not one of them. Laila was Ubering, which meant that her tardiness was not due to parking.

This was concerning.

"Everything okay, Matty?" Frodo said.

His earlier levity had vanished.

I'd organized this meeting at Laila's request, and she'd been adamant that its true purpose remain a secret. Katherine had taken this condition in stride, but Frodo had done everything he could to worm the topic of discussion out of me ahead of time. He'd grown more and more annoyed the closer we'd come to the appointed hour as his attempts to interrogate me continued to fail. Now his concern had a different target. Unlike our fellow patrons, Frodo and I did not have vocations in which a wife's absence could be taken lightly.

Frodo had not earned his nickname because he resembled a hobbit or had a penchant for second breakfasts. Prior to becoming a double amputee, Frodo had been a member of an organization known as the Unit to the special operators skillful enough to be listed among its members. As was the custom with newly minted assaulters, Frodo had been awarded a call sign.

Whether or not he liked it was immaterial.

I, on the other hand, had spent my last military assignment as a company commander in the vaunted Ranger Regiment. Jumping out of airplanes and kicking in doors alongside the finest infantrymen God had ever created had been a fine way to earn a paycheck. Those years did not hold a candle to my current vocation. Case in point, I'd once engaged in a shoot-out with a team of Iraqi hitters just a few blocks from where we currently sat.

Unexplained absences made me nervous.

"She's Ubering," I said, fishing my phone from my pocket. "Should be here by now."

The change in Frodo was subtle but recognizable. At least to me. One moment the fingertips of his remaining hand were resting on the stem of his fancy cocktail glass. The next, the calloused brown digits were nowhere to be seen, which probably meant they were hovering in the vicinity of his concealed SIG Sauer.

But it was more than just the location of his hand that signified a change in my best friend. Frodo's narrow shoulders now presented sharp edges against his button-down shirt, and his eyes projected hyperalertness. Frodo might have been a double amputee who walked with the aid of a cane, but dismissing him because of his injuries would have been a mistake.

A lamed wolf did not somehow become a sheep.

"Y'all need something?"

Our waitress had approached with a broad smile—after all, who wasn't happy to be working at a gourmet cocktail bar—but her grin had steadily evaporated the closer she came to our table. She had the bleached blond hair and requisite septum ring and sleeve tattoo required of a hip Austin waitress, but now her laughing eyes communicated something else.

Concern.

"We're fine," Katherine said, trying to warm up the sudden chill. "Right, guys?"

I was about to agree when my phone vibrated.

After reaching into my pocket, I pulled out the offending device.

The waitress took a step backward.

Maybe Frodo wasn't the only one who looked ready to brawl.

At six feet and one hundred eighty-five pounds, I wasn't physically insignificant, but neither did I inspire an automatic *Oh, shit* when someone drunkenly spilled beer on my boots. This was by intention. In my line of work, it was better to go unnoticed. To be the proverbial gray man. Accordingly, I was sporting what Laila playfully termed my ragamuffin look.

At least I hoped it was playfully.

My hair was long and my beard scruffy, but my Wrangler pearly-snap shirt framed the wide shoulders and broad back of a person for whom physical fitness was more than just a passing fancy. Even so, I still worked to project the just-another-guy-enjoying-a-drink vibe.

Except that, like Frodo, sometimes the real me peeked through.

"Right," I said, trying to add a reassurance to my voice I didn't feel.

The Glock 23 tucked into my Don Hume inside the waistband holster pressed comfortingly against my right hip even as the pulsing phone reminded me that there were some problems that a trusty .40-caliber pistol couldn't solve. Yet another reason I missed having Frodo watching my back with his eye pressed to a SIG Sauer

TANGO6T optic mounted to his HK 417. A 7.62mm projectile traveling at a speed of twenty-six hundred feet per second wasn't the answer to all of life's problems, but it certainly solved many of them.

I unlocked the phone to see a text message. The originating number consisted of the digits 911 repeated over and over. The person responsible for sending the text was a former master sergeant from 10th Special Forces Group named James Scott Glass. He was also my boss. Subtlety wasn't his thing. Across the table, Frodo reached for his own phone. I had a feeling that not all was well in our world.

The text confirmed my suspicion.

CHECK OUT THE NEWS. NOW.

"Can you turn that to a news station?" I said to the waitress, pointing at the flat-screen mounted to the wall above the bar.

She slowly shook her head.

"I'm sorry," the waitress said. "The manager says it ruins the ambience."

"Please," I said even as I peeled a couple of twenties from my money clip. "It's important."

"No need for that," the waitress said, refusing the offered bills. "I'll see if I can find the remote. But only for a minute or two. Okay?"

"Sure," I said.

"What's this mean?" Frodo said, flashing me his phone. The same message glared from his screen.

"We're about to find out," I said.

The waitress pointed a black remote at the TV and the display glowed to life. It was tuned to MSNBC—we were in Austin—but I didn't care about the station's political leanings. I was too busy focused on the video playing over the anchor's shoulder.

"Holy shit," Frodo said.

"Can you turn it up?" I said. "Please."

The waitress shot me a look but obliged.

A moment later, a cultured voice flooded the room.

"This is unprecedented," the newscaster said. "The Taliban now control Bagram Air Base."

"Holy shit," Frodo said again.

Mom loved to remind me that foul language was evidence of low intelligence. That might be true, but in this case I didn't agree. Though he'd joined the Army straight out of high school and had never darkened the doorway of an institution of higher learning, Frodo was one of the most intelligent people I knew and he had a vocabulary to match. He wasn't swearing because he was too lazy to think of better words. He was cursing because he was shell-shocked.

So was I.

"Why is that on, Hannah?"

The tone carried just enough indignation to indicate that the man asking the question was the bar's manager. He was standing at the far end of the room, hands on his hips and glaring at our waitress. Like Hannah, the manager was dressed in black slacks and a white dress shirt. The top several buttons were undone and his shirtsleeves were rolled, exposing portions of a tattoo that seemed to traverse his entire torso. While Hannah's nose ring and ink seemed somehow charming, the effect wasn't nearly so endearing on this joker. My assessment probably had something to do with the tone of voice he was using with Hannah.

"Hey," I said, waving to get his attention, "my fault. I asked her to turn it on."

The manager could have taken the off-ramp I'd provided.

He didn't.

"Thank you for apologizing, sir," the manager said, "but Hannah should have known better."

Crossing the bar in three quick strides, the manager snatched the remote from Hannah and pointed it at the TV.

"Stop," Frodo said.

My commando friend didn't shout, but the manager still jerked.

I understood why.

Authority radiated from Frodo's voice.

"I'm sorry?" the manager said, turning toward Frodo.

"Don't be sorry," Frodo said, speaking with a drill sergeant's crisp cadence. "Just leave it on."

"Until the station break," I said. "Please. We're Afghanistan vets."

"I'm grateful for your service," the manager said in a tone suggesting otherwise, "but our policy is clear."

He extended the remote toward the TV.

"Don't. Touch. It."

Frodo's words cracked through the air, each one landing like Rocky Marciano's mighty right hand. Images of carnage and rioting shone from the screen, but at that moment, Afghanistan didn't have anything on the violence Frodo's tone promised.

"We don't mind if you leave it on."

The comment came from a couple seated at the table catty-corner to ours. The man was the one who spoke, but his date vigorously nodded. The man's earnest expression suggested that he genuinely wanted to help, but I was betting he would have the opposite effect. Maybe the manager might have backed down before, but now his face-saving off-ramp was gone. Petty tyrants are the same the world over whether they run a bar or a country. A man who isn't secure in his own authority will always view differing opinions as attacks.

"Sorry," the manager said, stabbing the remote.

The TV winked off.

The manager turned from the TV to Frodo, a self-satisfied smirk stretched across his face. Like the television, the manager's smile died a quick death. The average person's concept of violence is formed by action movies or schoolyard shoving matches. This naivety leaves them wholly unprepared for the visceral nature of actual combat.

To be fair, few human beings have meted out violence on the scale practiced by Frodo. Comparing the squabbles of day-to-day American life with the world that Frodo and I inhabited was the equivalent of calling a house cat a mountain lion. Sure, the two felines shared similar qualities, but someone who'd seen both would never confuse one for the other. The look on the manager's face suggested that he'd just stumbled upon his first lion.

I made a grab for my best friend but needn't have bothered. A half second earlier, I'd been convinced that Frodo was a heartbeat away from thrashing the arrogant manager with his prosthesis. Now something else demanded our collective attention.

The door to the bar slammed open, and two people entered.

People with guns.

TWO

Encountering people with guns is not a novel experience for me. Like Frodo, I am an operative for DIA, or the Defense Intelligence Agency. My job title is deliberately both long and misleading. The short version is this: I am a spy. I persuade men and women to betray their countries by providing me with sensitive information.

With black hair and a dark complexion, an aptitude for languages, and a history of operating overseas, I have the ability to work nearly anywhere in southwest Asia. Over the last decade, I'd probably spent more time on foreign soil than American. The secrets I tried to steal were protected by counterintelligence officers, sheepdogs trained to protect their herd from predators like me.

I was no stranger to people who carried guns.

But the bar's newest occupants didn't look like the Iranian Quds Force members I'd dodged in Iraq or the Russian GRU, SVR, and Wagner Group thugs I'd gone to war against in Europe. These two looked as American as baseball and apple pie.

But that didn't make the pistols printing through their clothing any less deadly.

Because I'd arrived at the bar first, Frodo had his back to the door. He shouldn't have known about the new arrivals. He still did. Like most operators, he had a preternatural ability to sense pending violence. Agency shrinks throw around words like *hyperawareness*, but to me the explanation is much simpler.

Frodo was a predator.

Even though the bar's door was a good twenty-five feet behind us, and the fracas with the manager and the TV covered up the sound of their entrance, Frodo had still reacted to the pair's presence. One moment he was focused on the manager with a disquieting intensity. The next, he was turning in his seat toward the greater threat. I don't know whether it was the look on my face, a breeze blowing through the opening door, or some other supernatural sixth sense that had alerted Frodo.

All I knew was that my friend was ready to go to war.

By the look on the newcomers' faces, that feeling was mutual.

To be fair, the pair wasn't going out of their way to be jack wagons, and they hadn't dressed like roided-up bounty hunters. The woman was wearing a blue blazer, white blouse, dark slacks, and flats. Her partner was dressed in the male equivalent—a dark sport coat, a button-down shirt, khakis, and dress shoes that tied. A bit more formal than the Austin bar crowd, but not terribly out of character.

The woman was in charge.

She was Hispanic and in her early thirties, and her

black hair was pulled into a ponytail. Her brown eyes found mine and hardened. She said something to her partner and then moved our way. Her male counterpart paused to show his creds to the hostess before falling in behind.

That was a mistake.

Not a huge one, but a mistake nonetheless. He should have either ignored the hostess or asked his partner to wait for him. Now a good five feet separated them. If I'd harbored less-than-noble intentions, I could have gone kinetic before the man was in a position to lend a hand. The woman might have been Bruce Lee, but I outweighed her by almost eighty pounds, enjoyed a six-inch height advantage, and was not a stranger to persuasion via fisticuffs.

In the noncinematic world, these details mattered.

Luckily, my intentions were completely noble.

Mostly.

"Can I help you?" I said, sliding out of the booth.

I stepped forward, interposing myself between Frodo and the pair. This was not because I thought Frodo needed protecting. I just wanted to buffer my former bodyguard from anything physical. Frodo was still a pretty good shot one-handed, but his grappling days were over.

The woman answered. "We're not here for you," the woman said, her eyes sliding from me to Frodo.

"But I'm Drake," I said.

"And he's Frodo," the woman said. "Out of the booth please, Mr. Cates."

"What's going on?" Katherine said.

The question was a perfectly warranted response to what was happening. The volume at which Katherine asked it was not. Then again, Frodo had nearly been killed on our last operation, and Katherine had helped me rescue him. Though she wasn't an operator, Frodo's girlfriend was an NSA analyst, not a shoe saleswoman. For her, violence was not an abstract concept.

"Out of the booth. Now."

The woman's partner joined her and was apparently attempting to compensate for his tardiness with testosterone.

Never a wise choice.

"Go sit in the corner," I said, eyeing the muscle-bound bruiser. "Mom and Dad are talking."

A flush swept up the man's bull neck, and he moved closer, his meaty hands rising to chest level. Far from making the encounter better, the man's predictable response forced the Hispanic woman to take her eyes off me so she could put her partner in check.

"Stand fast, Fred," the woman said. "I've got this."

I used the woman's momentary distraction honorably, meaning I edged into her personal space, sandwiching her between me and her partner, as I moved to the left, placing my hip against the bar.

That single motion accomplished several things.

One, I negated the two-on-one advantage she and her partner should have enjoyed by orienting them into a single-file stack. Two, my position against the bar made it impossible for them to flank me to the left. Three, by moving forward, I opened up space for Frodo to climb out of the booth.

Which he did.

It was almost like we'd done this before.

The same could not be said of the woman and her partner. To her credit, the Hispanic woman realized her mistake almost immediately. Her lips compressed into a thin line, and her hand drifted toward her waist.

"I'm here for Frodo," she said, "not you."

"If you buy a ticket, you get the whole ride," I said.

"I'm calling the police," the manager said.

The manager's tone made the statement sound more like a question, but I liked where he was headed. I'd already garnered several useful data points during the interaction. The pair was armed, and judging by the fact that the woman hadn't referred to her partner by his last name, they were not traditional law enforcement. Since they were alone, I was also betting that they hadn't coordinated this meeting with the locals.

That was an angle I intended to exploit.

"Great idea," I said to the manager. "Allow me."

I dipped my hand into my back pocket.

Meathead's fingers darted beneath his sport coat.

"Easy, jack wagon," I said, removing my phone with exaggerated smooth motions.

I thumbed speed dial, activated speakerphone, and rotated the device toward the Hispanic woman. Her expression suggested that I was onto something. She was still plenty mad, but I saw something else in her face now.

Worry.

The phone rang three times, long enough for me to consider how stupid I was going to look if no one picked up, when a male voice answered.

"Tell me you're not standing over another dead body."

"Good evening, Special Agent Rawlings," I said. "No one's dead. Yet."

Terror replaced worry on the Latina's face. Her partner wrapped his fingers around the butt of his holstered pistol, but he made no move to draw the weapon or clear his partner from his gun line. He'd never win the spelling bee, but that didn't make him any less dangerous. At the moment, it was his partner he was placing in danger. The Hispanic woman seemed to understand this even if he did not.

"Stand down, Fred," she said.

"Seriously, Drake," Rawlings said, "can't you do your killing in Syria or Iraq? Maybe the Mossad needs your help. Again."

If the room had been quiet before, you could have heard a pin drop now. The manager had forgotten all about the TV. Right about now he was probably wishing he had something more lethal than seltzer lurking beneath the bar. Fred still hadn't drawn his weapon, but he'd crowded behind his partner, further decreasing her options.

The animal part of your brain could be helpful if harnessed correctly, but meathead's fight-or-flight instincts were becoming a liability. Because he was physically powerful, his default action was to close ground and prepare to grapple. This was exactly the wrong response. Instead, he should have created space and angles for his pistol and options for his partner. I had a feeling he'd be receiving some pointed feedback once this little fiasco concluded.

"Great thoughts, Agent Rawlings," I said, "but first I need your help to resolve a Mexican standoff. Two chuckleheads with pistols and attitudes just interrupted what was shaping up to be a peaceful night of drinking. As my designated liaison with the Federal Bureau of Investigation, I thought you might want to have a word with them."

"You called me *before* you killed anyone? It's a Christmas miracle."

"You gonna talk or not?" I said. "Makes no difference to me."

A long sigh echoed from the cell.

"Sure," Rawlings said. "Hand them the phone."

"No need," I said. "You're on speaker. I did mention that, right?"

"I want a face-to-face after this is over, Drake," Rawlings said. "If you ghost me again, I'll send the SWAT team. Clear?"

"Crystal," I said.

"Excellent. Now let me introduce myself to the dipshits with pistols. I am FBI Special Agent Rawlings from the Austin Resident Agency. You've got sixty seconds to identify yourselves and explain why you're arresting someone in my city without my knowledge. If your answer isn't satisfactory, I'll be sending SWAT for a different reason."

The Hispanic woman's face flushed.

"Fuck this," Fred said. "Let's just grab him and go."

"Not a smart play, shit bird," I said.

Fred pushed past his partner and tried to do the same to me. I snapped a palm strike into his solar plexus with enough force to get his attention, but not so much that it hurt.

Much.

"Final warning," I said.

"I'm not going to say this again, Fred," the Hispanic woman said. "Stand the fuck down or go sit in the car. Your choice."

Fred's eyes said he wanted to argue, but he didn't. He clamped his lips shut, but the look he shot me promised that this wasn't over.

Fine.

If he wanted to circle back later, I'd oblige him, but he'd have to get in line. The list of people who wanted to smack yours truly in the mouth was both long and distinguished.

Well, long anyway.

"My name is Julie Soto," the woman said. "I'm an Army CID special agent. I'm here to arrest Fredrick Tyler Cates also known as Frodo."

"On what charge?" I said.

Julie looked back for a long moment.

This time hers were the eyes that were glittering.

"Murder."

THREE

"Bullshit," I said at the same time Katherine said, "I don't believe it."

"I have a warrant for Frodo's arrest," Julie said. "He's coming with us. How that happens is up to you."

"Let me see the warrant," I said.

"Fuck off," Fred said. "You're not the subject of the warrant or his lawyer. We don't have to show you shit."

"That's correct. You don't," Rawlings said, his disembodied voice ringing through the bar, "but I'm asking you to share it with me, as a professional courtesy."

"Why?" Fred said.

"Because you're in my city," Rawlings said, "and that's how things are done. Or I can ask my friends at Austin PD to pull you over for a traffic violation and develop probable cause for a body cavity search while I make some calls. Choose wisely."

"This is bullshit," Meathead said.

"Welcome to the big leagues, kid," Rawlings said. "Read me the warrant or one of Austin's finest checks you for a hernia."

The flush that had begun in Fred's thick neck had now

reached his jowly cheeks. He opened his mouth, but Julie's smooth alto cut through whatever he'd planned to say.

"We're happy to extend professional courtesy," Julie said, even though the look she gave me suggested otherwise. "I'll send you a copy of the warrant once we've taken the prisoner into custody. He's being arrested for a murder that took place in Afghanistan in 2011."

Afghanistan?

I hadn't seen that coming.

"Bullshit," I said. "We're not going anywhere."

"Matty," Frodo said.

"I don't know how else to say this," Julie said, "but we're not here for you, Mr. Drake."

"We were in Afghanistan together," I said. "He didn't murder anyone."

"Matty," Frodo said, his voice more forceful.

"The warrant sounds legit, Matt," Rawlings said. "I can take a look when I get there, but—"

"Not happening," Julie said. "You asked for professional courtesy, and I gave it. Now my partner and I are walking out of here with Mr. Cates. End of story."

"Don't take this the wrong way," I said, squaring off with Julie, "but unless you've got five more friends waiting outside, Frodo's not going anywhere."

Julie's eyes blazed.

Whatever.

Frodo and I weren't just friends. I'd been in the seat next to him when an explosively formed penetrator had ended his career as a commando and nearly his life. He was my brother. No way was he leaving here in handcuffs.

"Matty!"

I turned to see Frodo standing beside me.

"I'll go with them," Frodo said.

"You can't—" I said.

"I love you, man, but you make a mule look compliant. We both know I'm going with them."

"Not happening."

"Damn it, boy," Frodo said. "Think. What good will you be sitting in the jail cell next to mine? Let me go, and do your thing."

Frodo squeezed my shoulder and then slipped past me.

"I've got only one hand," Frodo said, offering his right arm to Julie. "Not sure how your cuffs are going to work."

"We've got that covered," Fred said, grabbing Frodo by the shoulder and spinning him around.

The CID agent took a pair of specialty restraints from his pocket. He fastened one on Frodo's wrist and the other to the stump just above his prosthesis. "Don't expect any special treatment because of your injury. You're a war criminal. Period."

Frodo.

A war criminal.

If there were any two sentences in the English language more incongruent, I couldn't think of them. Though he never talked about it, Frodo had been awarded the Silver Star for an operation in Afghanistan during which he and another Unit sniper had saved the lives of four SEALs. What he had done that day was legendary in the special operations community.

Frodo had never seen fit to mention it to me, even though we'd been running and gunning together for more than a decade. The information had come to light only when a SEAL had asked him about it in my presence. I'm not saying that Frodo was perfect, but war criminals were by and large cowards, thugs who preyed on the helpless.

Frodo was no coward.

"Check it out, stud," I said to Fred. "You're walking out of this bar because that's what my partner wants. But our justice system says that my friend is innocent until proven guilty. He has done more for the cause of freedom than you will ever know. Call him a war criminal again, and I will reach down your throat and rip out your spleen. Tracking?"

Fred was tracking. His dress shirt tightened across his chest as his muscles flexed.

"Point taken, Mr. Drake," Julie said. "Fred—take Mr. Cates to the car. Now."

Though she was all of five foot nothing and probably a buck ten soaking wet, Julie spoke with unmistakable authority. Fred's eyes told me that this was far from over, but his mouth said, "Yes, ma'am." Putting his hand on Frodo, the CID agent guided my best friend out of the bar and into the street. Once the door slammed behind her partner, Julie's features softened. Her brown eyes shone with more than just determination.

"Fred is still learning the ropes," Julie said. "We're going to have a long discussion once we get back to post.

For what it's worth, I know who Frodo is and what he's done. Most days I love my job. Not today."

She didn't offer a handshake, but she did nod, a gesture of respect from one professional to another.

"He didn't do it," I said as she turned to go. "Whatever y'all think you know, you're wrong. Frodo is the most honorable man I know. He's not a murderer."

"You still don't get it, Mr. Drake," Julie said. "I'm not the one you have to convince."

Then she followed her partner.

FOUR

"What was that?" Katherine said.

"I don't know," I said, which was true.

Mostly.

Frodo and I had deployed as a team to Afghanistan at least half a dozen times. None of the deployments had been walks in the park, but 2011 had been one of the toughest. As Katherine and I stood on a nondescript Sixth Street sidewalk, it was hard to reconcile that this world and 2011 Afghanistan existed in the same universe.

Even though it was August and the University of Texas was still officially out of session, the streets teemed with life. College kids in T-shirts, shorts, and flip-flops mingled with tech workers dressed in trendier vintage T-shirts, jeans, and the obligatory Chuck Taylors. The Twilight Wrangler prided itself on zero signage in a nod to its speakeasy roots, but the establishment was still chic enough to attract a line of women wearing sundresses and heels accompanied by men in sport coats and designer jeans.

A pretty brunette confidentially stepped up to the

door and pressed the second button down from the top. A buzzer sounded, she gave the correct pass phrase, and the steel door swung open. A funny throwback to the prohibition era one hundred years previous when this game was played for keeps.

Kind of like 2011 Afghanistan.

"You must have some idea," Katherine said.

Her brown eyes bored into mine as I thought through what I should or could say. My reticence to speak wasn't because I was worried about Katherine's trustworthiness. She'd been working with us informally for some time. Her assistance had morphed into an official relationship with DIA during our previous operation in Europe. Katherine's analytical skills and calmness under fire had kept Frodo from a shallow Ukrainian grave with a Russian bullet in his skull.

But we were no longer facing a foreign adversary. The Army's Criminal Investigation Division had arrested Frodo. Katherine would be criminally liable for any help she provided to me and any information she withheld from the investigators. I knew she'd be willing to go to the mat for Frodo, but I also wanted to shield her from the fallout that was bound to accompany whatever happened next. As Frodo had intimated, I was pretty good at doing my thing, but once I started making the sausage, life got messy.

Fast.

"I might," I said, staring into Katherine's soft eyes, "but I won't know for sure until I make a couple of calls."

"Until *we* make a couple of calls," Katherine said.

I shook my head. "That's not how this is going to work."

"Are you kidding me? Frodo's my fiancé. Besides, I earned a spot on this team."

"Yes, you did," I said, resting my hand on her shoulder. "If I was going into harm's way, I'd want you in my corner. That's no bullshit."

"But?" Katherine said.

"But we're not going up against terrorists or homicidal Russians—those I know how to handle. This fight is against lawyers. I'm not an attorney, but I do know this—anything we discuss is fair game for the folks who arrested Frodo. I'm not going to put you in a position where you might have to lie to federal investigators."

"That's not for you to decide," Katherine said, her eyes flashing.

"Yes, it is," I said. Her shoulder muscles tensed beneath my hand. "Frodo trusted me enough to walk out of that bar in handcuffs. You have to do the same. At some point I'll need your help. Until then, you're on the team, but you're not on the field. Not yet."

Katherine looked at me for a long moment before slowly nodding her head.

"Okay," Katherine said with a sigh. "I'll play it your way."

"Thank you," I said. "Catch a flight back to DC and be ready for my call."

Left unsaid was the reason I wanted Katherine in DC—her NSA terminal. She didn't voice this and neither did I. But I saw understanding in her face all the same.

"Get him back, Matty," Katherine said.

Standing on her tiptoes, she kissed my cheek. Then she hailed a taxi with a whistle that would have done a New Yorker proud. A cab pulled over and Katherine climbed in without a backward glance.

She was on a mission.

So was I.

I pulled out my cell.

Branch Chief James Scott Glass might now be a member of the DIA's rarified Senior Executive Service, but he was not a bureaucrat. If anybody could help me navigate the current quagmire, it was the former 10th Group team sergeant who'd once broken a Taliban fighter's neck with his bare hands. My phone began to vibrate before I'd finished typing in his number.

This was not surprising.

James had a sixth sense when it came to his operators in the field.

I keyed the answer button and held the cell to my ear.

"James?"

"Matt, it's me."

The voice was low-pitched and carried a hint of a rasp. It did not belong to my boss. It belonged to my wife. My wife who was now almost twenty minutes late.

Shit.

"Laila—are you okay?" I said.

"Yes. Well, no."

"What's going on?"

I kept my voice even and my reply light, but my heart was thundering. Like seemingly everyone I loved, Laila had not escaped unscathed from the violence that swirled around me. I often felt like the eye of a hurricane made of death and destruction. Laila had once been captured and nearly killed by a madman looking for leverage over me. When my wife said that she was not okay, I started looking for someone to kill.

"I'm not going to make it for drinks. I need you to come home. Now."

I was already in motion toward the parking garage where I'd stashed my truck.

"Be there in fifteen," I said, careening down the sidewalk like a runaway freight train. Austin might have had a deservedly laid-back reputation, but even drunk college kids knew when to get out of the way. "Is the baby okay?"

Laila was carrying our girl, Virginia, named for another colleague who had not escaped Hurricane Matt. She was just beginning to show, and I loved having heart-to-heart conversations with our daughter as I rested my head on Laila's swelling belly. Those two were my life.

My whole life.

"Little girl's fine," Laila said. "So am I. I'm sorry—I should have said that in the beginning. No one's in danger."

"No worries," I said, suppressing a shudder. "What's up?"

"My parents. They're here."

"I didn't know they were coming over," I said.

"Neither did I. This isn't a social call. Mom's in tears and Dad will barely say two words."

That got my attention.

Laila's Afghan mom and Pakistani dad were a study in contradictions. Her mother, Fatemah, was one of the most stoic people I knew. Laila's dad, Kashif, could talk to a houseplant. In the ten or so years I'd been in their lives, we'd weathered our share of tragedies and hardships. Laila's sister's eldest child had been stillborn. Her father's brother had passed unexpectedly of a heart attack. Her parents were solid stock, as my mom would say. Immigrants of the kind who had been making America great since her founding. Laila's folks were not easily shaken. This was serious.

"What's going on?" I said, sliding into the cab of my Dodge Ram.

"I don't know," Laila said, frustration evident in her voice. "They won't talk to me."

"Then why are they here?" I said, spooling out of the parking garage.

"You," Laila said. "They're here to talk to you."

I hammered the accelerator.

I couldn't explain my premonition, but I knew I had to get home. Now. The work I did was complicated and only Laila understood its full significance. My parents knew that I worked for the government, but they believed I was a natural resource specialist for the Department of the Interior.

Laila and I had decided not to tell her parents even that much. I had no reason to doubt their patriotism, but the majority of their family still lived in Afghanistan and Pakistan. Even a casual comment could prove damning if heard by the wrong ears. As such, we'd explained that I worked for one of the legions of defense contractors that populated the greater DC area. Her parents were astute folks, and I didn't know how much of my legend they actually believed. Either way, they had been kind enough not to push.

Until now.

FIVE

Hey, baby," I said, sliding my arms around Laila.

She hugged me back, the muscles in her shoulders and back hard with tension.

Though she claimed to be five feet three, Laila was off by an inch or so. And while she dreamed of being taller, I loved that her height meant that her head nestled just beneath my chin. I buried my face in a mound of raven hair smelling of vanilla and something more exotic—an intoxicating fragrance that could calm my heart or set it to racing depending on her mood.

She was dressed for cocktails in a sleeveless white blouse paired with a khaki pencil skirt. The outfit showed off miles of smooth brown skin in the form of toned arms and athletic legs. Her growing baby bump meant that the skirt was probably making its last appearance for a while, and I was all for giving it a proper send-off. But first I had to see to the two people seated in our living room.

"Hey, guys," I said, smiling at my in-laws over Laila's shoulder. "Good to see you."

It was good to see them. I genuinely enjoyed spending time with Laila's parents and loved listening to them talk about their pre-American lives in Afghanistan and Pakistan. Fatemah was in her late fifties. She was plumper than her daughter and her midnight hair was streaked with gray. Even so, Fatemah still garnered admiring glances from men half her age.

Her husband, Kashif, was mostly bald and his midsection reflected a fondness for Dairy Queen. He was happiest when putting his mechanical skills to use whittling down Laila's never-ending list of improvements to our fixer-upper. As his laugh lines attested, Kashif lived life with a smile on his face.

His wife was a different matter.

"Hello, Matthew," Fatemah said, setting her cup of chai delicately on its saucer.

Fatemah and Kashif's differences complemented one another. While Kashif had readily adapted to the American ideal of beers with friends after a hard day's work, Fatemah retained the formality of her upbringing. I often joked with Laila that her mother seemed more British than Afghan. Fatemah had never addressed me as anything but Matthew.

Tonight was no exception.

But there was something distant about her this evening—a stiffness I hadn't seen since I'd asked Fatemah for permission to marry her daughter. To be fair, I'd intended to speak with just Kashif, but as I soon came to realize, nothing happened in this family without the permission of its matriarch. Fatemah ruled her household as a benevolent dictator.

Or perhaps not always so benevolent, based on Laila's account of her teenage years.

Then again, my strong-willed wife was a reflection of the woman who'd raised her. Though they loved each other dearly, I suspected that Laila's time as an adolescent had been difficult for both women. I'd once mentioned as much to Kashif. He didn't outright confirm my suspicions, but he'd made a point of describing how much more hair he'd had on Laila's thirteenth birthday than her eighteenth. And now the formidable presence that had once been able to bring my wife to tears with a single disapproving glance was focused on me.

"Laila said y'all needed to talk," I said.

Though we were in my living room, I still felt like a petitioner seeking an audience with a queen. As always, Laila's mom was dressed impeccably. Though she'd finally come to terms with Austin's casual vibe, Fatemah's truce was an uneasy one. Laila's father was dressed in a short-sleeved polo shirt, cargo shorts, and boat shoes. Not so his wife. In deference to the August heat, she'd forgone her usual dress but was still wearing a short-sleeved blouse, black jeans, and heels.

For my mother-in-law, this was casual.

But Fatemah's regal air was a product of more than just her clothing. She had a presence. A force of personality that was as intrinsic to her as her caramel-colored eyes.

But understanding who Fatemah was did not make her any less intimidating.

"Yes, we do," Fatemah said. "Please, sit."

I seated Laila, kissed Fatemah's offered cheek, gave Kashif a quick hug, and pulled up a chair for myself. Was being invited to take a seat in my own house a bit strange? Sure. But in this family, it's how things were done.

"Matthew," Fatemah said after I'd settled in, "we've never asked what you do."

I froze with a coffee cup partway to my lips. I'd wargamed how the conversation with Laila's parents could go several times during the fifteen-minute drive from Sixth Street. I'd arrived at our house confident that I'd be able to handle anything they threw at me.

My confidence had been misplaced.

"Mother," Laila said, her face a thundercloud.

"It's okay," I said, smiling at my bride before turning my attention to my mother-in-law. "No, Fatemah, you haven't."

There didn't seem to be any harm in acknowledging the obvious. From the look on Laila's face, she didn't agree. Normally, I'd have deferred to Laila in matters concerning her family, but this felt different. Almost as if her mom was about to ask for a boon from her knight-errant. Or maybe this had something to do with the little Drake growing in Laila's belly.

In that moment I realized my mistake.

Laila had wanted to wait until the first trimester was over before telling her family about Virginia. Her mother and sister had both lost children in pregnancy, and Laila was worried that she had inherited a propensity for miscarriages. As such, we'd only just shared the fantastic news with her parents. In fact, this was their first visit since we'd surprised them a week ago, which meant that if there was some strange family ritual concerning grandchildren, this was when we'd hear about it.

When I'd hear about it.

Laila knew what was coming even if I didn't, which

went a long way toward explaining the uncharacteristically unhappy look she was shooting my way. For a guy who wormed his way into other people's heads for a living, I really could be an idiot.

My inner monologue couldn't have lasted for more than a second, but Fatemah seemed to understand that something had changed. Or that something inside me had changed. She gave a tiny nod as she met my gaze.

Then she went somewhere unexpected.

"Do you work for the CIA?"

"Mo-ther," Laila said, breaking the syllables into two words.

I thought Laila might lapse into Pashto, but she didn't, probably because she intended for me to understand exactly what she was going to say to her mother on my behalf.

I loved that woman.

"Matt cannot talk about his job," Laila said. "Not now, not ever."

"Not even to family?" Fatemah said.

"Especially not to family," Laila said. "Family understands that certain subjects are off-limits. This is one of them."

My wife's eyes are amazing. They're a vibrant shade of emerald highlighted by her dark complexion. But their color wasn't the only reason I was infatuated with them. Laila's eyes were a window into her disposition. When she was happy, they sparkled. Sad, and they resembled deep jade-colored pools. But it was when she was angry that her eyes underwent their biggest transformation.

They shimmered.

Like listening for a rattlesnake's rattle, I'd long ago learned to judge Laila's moods through her eyes. Her intentions were sometimes hard to decipher through words alone, but to paraphrase the Eagles, my wife couldn't hide her shimmering eyes.

At this moment, they weren't just shimmering.

They were incandescent.

"Forgive me," Fatemah said, "but this is important, perhaps even a matter of life or death."

Even though I was the subject, the apology was not directed toward me. Laila locked gazes with her mother, refusing to wilt under the force of Fatemah's presence. For a moment, I thought I was about to witness a power struggle for the ages. The exact instant when an unstoppable force encounters an immovable object. Even Kashif recognized the gravity of the situation. He studied his boat shoes like the scuffed leather held the key to world peace. In a first, his ever-present smile was nowhere to be found.

The looming clash might just shake our little house to its foundation.

Then something amazing happened.

Fatemah dipped her head a fraction of an inch.

The gesture was minuscule, unnoticeable to anyone who didn't study body language for a living. I understood its significance. With that tiny motion, Fatemah had recognized her daughter's standing. Laila was too gracious to gloat, but she met her mother halfway with a tiny nod of her own.

Maybe world peace really was achievable.

My wife turned her beautiful eyes my way.

They were no longer shimmering.

"Tell her what you can, Matt. Please."

Were it not for the *please*, I would had been tempted to think that when it came to family matriarchs, the apple did not fall far from the tree. But that wasn't right. Where Fatemah was a typhoon, bending everyone to her will, Laila was a mountain stream, slowly eroding away obstacles with a gentle yet firm presence.

"Let's do it this way," I said, smiling at Fatemah. "Walk me through your problem. I'll try to help."

I thought this a completely reasonable request. My mother-in-law did not. Her answering huff announced her displeasure while remaining within the confines of the newly established family dynamic. Fatemah might now view her daughter as something approaching an equal, but this distinction did not extend to me. Though he was still studying his shoes, Kashif's trademark grin had returned. Sometimes I thought my family life would have been far less complicated if I'd married into the Sopranos.

"Laila has a cousin who may be in trouble," Fatemah said.

"Who?" Laila said.

"Ferhana," Fatemah said.

"Never heard of her," Laila said.

"More like a distant cousin," Kashif said. "In Afghanistan, everyone is family."

"The point is," Fatemah said, shooting her husband a withering look, "Ferhana is the daughter of family friends. She's just nineteen. She traveled back to Afghanistan to attend a wedding."

"Why would she do that?" Laila said.

Fatemah elegantly shrugged. "She did so against her family's wishes. Sometimes daughters can be difficult."

So much for world peace.

"Where is the wedding?" I said, stepping into the breach before hostilities could resume.

I glanced at Laila as I spoke and saw gratitude reflected in her eyes.

Maybe I was getting the hang of this husband thing after all.

"Wazir Akbar Khan," Fatemah said. "It's in northern Kabul."

I knew the neighborhood quite well, but there was no reason to reveal this to Laila's parents. Wazir Akbar Khan was an affluent suburb that served as home to the US and Canadian embassies, among others. A number of foreign expats lived in the Western-style dwellings, but perhaps more important, the neighborhood was less than forty miles from Bagram Air Base.

The same facility the Taliban had overrun just a few hours ago.

I knew where this conversation was headed.

"Is Ferhana still in communication with her parents?" I said.

"As much as any girl these days," Fatemah said.

Fatemah didn't quite sniff, and neither did she look at her daughter. Even so, the comment's undertone wasn't exactly subtle.

"Ferhana posts on Instagram," Kashif said, taking a turn at playing peacekeeper. The ease with which he defused the tension between two of the most important women in his life was impressive. Perhaps my husband skills still had a way to go. "She claims she's not in danger, but . . ."

But nineteen-year-old girls weren't always the best judges of danger.

"When is Ferhana scheduled to return?"

"Not for another three days," Fatemah said, "but the wedding's tomorrow. She told her mom that she might be willing to fly home early, but the girl refuses to even consider leaving before the ceremony."

Spoken like a true child of summer.

I didn't claim to be any wiser than my stockbroker neighbor, but I'd experienced a world bereft of the protections offered by civilization—a world where the strong preyed upon the weak and might made right. I knew firsthand how close to the surface our baser instincts lurked. I didn't wish my knowledge on anyone, but when it came to the depravity of humankind, I was uniquely qualified. If the images of Taliban crawling across Bagram were any indication, Afghanistan was teetering on the edge of darkness.

"How does Ferhana stay in touch with her parents?" I said.

Fatemah looked to her husband.

"WhatsApp mostly," Kashif said. "I can get you her username."

"Is she a US citizen?" I said.

"What difference does that make?" Fatemah said.

"To me, nothing," I said, ignoring the disgust in Fatemah's voice. "Ferhana is important to you, so she's important to me. But to the American government, it matters a great deal. Is she a citizen?"

"No," Kashif said, shooting his wife a look of disapproval. "But she is a green card holder."

The topic of citizenship was a thorny one to Laila's parents. While they both had acclimated to America, her father had gone about the process with an engineer's precision. Kashif had waited the allotted time after obtaining his green card to take and pass the citizenship test. That he'd needed to renounce his Pakistani citizenship as part of the process was unimportant. In his mind he was becoming an American in every way, and he fully embraced a burn-the-ships mentality.

Fatemah had not.

While Laila's mother was no less patriotic, she maintained an unbreakable connection to her birth country. While she despised the rise of the Taliban in Afghanistan and the sway that Islamic fundamentalists held over the government in Pakistan, this did nothing to dampen her love for her countrymen. Fatemah still believed that her nation would someday rid itself of the joint stumbling blocks of Islamic terrorism and government corruption. If becoming an American meant renouncing her homeland, Fatemah was content to remain a permanent green card holder.

Which would be fine if that's where she left things. But Fatemah was not content to make a choice of such magnitude in quiet or permit others to do the same. It offended her even more that her progeny had followed in their father's footsteps by renouncing their birth citizenships in favor of America.

"Well," Fatemah said with a huff, "it seems odd to make a big deal of such things."

"Odd or not, it's the world we live in," I said, determined not to plow already tilled soil. "Give me everything you have on Ferhana—WhatsApp info, cell number, passport, current photo, social media accounts, and email. Everything. I'll see what I can do. But I need to level set expectations—Ferhana is nineteen. She's an adult. If she doesn't want help, I can't force her to accept it."

"Understood," Kashif said. "I'm familiar with the notion of strong-willed women."

Kashif spoke completely deadpan, and it was all I could do not to laugh. Fortunately, Laila's shimmering eyes helped me temper my chuckle into a well-camouflaged cough.

"What is this *adult* nonsense?" Fatemah said. "The girl is barely old enough to drive. Besides, you and your comrades have been black-bagging men and whisking them off foreign streets for twenty years. Surely, you can help a wayward girl find her way back to her parents?"

This time Laila didn't even bother with English. The torrent of words spilling from my wife's mouth was as impressive as it was undecipherable. At least to me. I speak Arabic and can get by with Pashto and some of the other tribal dialects, but as near as I could tell, Laila was reaming her mother in at least three different languages.

But while I couldn't make heads or tails of what Laila was saying, Fatemah certainly did. The family's matriarch seemed to diminish before my eyes. She weathered the initial volley well enough, even attempting a few comebacks of her own before Laila crushed her mother's objections like an avalanche burying an unwary skier. After no more than a handful of seconds, Fatemah ducked her head twice, then turned to me.

"I'm sorry, Matthew," Fatemah said. "That was uncalled-for."

"No problem," I said with a smile I didn't feel. "Afghanistan has us all a little tense. I'll do what I can for Ferhana, but I need you to understand something—I don't work for the CIA."

"Of course you don't," Fatemah said, getting to her feet. "How absolutely silly of me to think otherwise. Come, Kashif. I believe we've overstayed our welcome."

Even I knew better than to wade into that one.

I looked at Laila, fully expecting my wife to extend her mother an olive branch.

She didn't.

"Thank you for entrusting us with this, Mother," Laila said. "Have a good evening."

Once again I couldn't help but think that the order of things had just changed. For the first time in memory, Laila was dismissing her mother rather than the other way around. There was surely more subtext than what I was understanding, but this was not the time for clarifications. Instead of asking questions, I did something at which I excel—played the goofy American. I shook Kashif's hand and slapped him on the back and then enveloped Fatemah in a bone-crushing hug.

For an instant she hugged me back with equal vigor.

"I'm sorry," Fatemah whispered.

Then the hug was over, and she was walking out the door.

Kashif shot me a half smile as he followed—a kind of welcome-to-the-asylum look.

Then it was just Laila and me.

"She drives me crazy," Laila said.

Laila was standing in front of the closed door with her hands on her hips as if she could see her mother lurking on the other side. I sidled in behind Laila, slipped my arms around her, and rested my hands on her belly.

"It's not her fault," I whispered.

"How can you say that?" Laila said, turning to face me. "She insulted my husband in my own house and you're sticking up for her?"

"Have you seen the news?" I said.

Laila shook her head.

"The Taliban just took Bagram. Kabul won't be far behind."

Laila looked at me like I was speaking another language.

"Afghanistan's going to fall? After twenty years?"

"That's the way it looks," I said, "unless the administration drastically changes course, I'm afraid we're going to piss away the last two decades."

Laila's green eyes burned through me. Then she stepped closer, resting her cheek against my chest.

"I'm sorry," Laila said. "How are you doing?"

"I haven't really had time to process it. I've been too focused on something else."

"What?"

"Frodo," I said.

SIX

Frodo?" Laila said. "Why?"

"He was just arrested," I said, "by Army CID."

"On what charge?"

"Murder."

Laila looked at me in silence. Going to war with her domineering mother wasn't something Laila relished, but it was a moment for which she'd prepared. My wife was on the path to partnership at one of the nation's largest accounting firms. There wasn't much she was afraid to face head-on, but a friend accused of murder was definitely new territory.

Though Laila was born in Taliban-controlled Afghanistan, those memories were faint compared to her American childhood. Even when she'd still lived under one of the earth's most tyrannical regimes, her parents had done an admirable job of shielding their children from the madness. Her father had found work as an engineer after arriving in the States, and Laila had grown up like most American kids—comfortable and safe. Her relationship with violence had been abstract in nature. A learned concept rather than something derived from personal experience.

Then she met me.

Laila and I had begun dating while I was a company commander in the Army's Ranger Regiment. She watched action movies like anyone else, but the sanitized version of violence portrayed on films was a far cry from the real thing. Because of me, Laila had come face-to-face with evil. The mass of puckered brown skin that encircled her triceps muscle had come from a sniper's bullet. A sniper's bullet that had nicked her brachial artery and nearly killed her.

The scar on her arm could be hidden beneath long sleeves.

The ones on her psyche were invisible but no less potent.

Her brush with death had also changed Laila's beliefs. My wife had never been a peacenik, but neither had she understood her fellow citizens' desire to carry a concealed weapon.

This was true no longer.

Laila's attitude toward death had also become more practical. Where before she would have said that it was wrong to kill outside the sanction afforded the military or law enforcement, now her opinion was more nuanced. This was why she was waiting for me to speak instead of asking the obvious question.

The question that haunted me.

Was Frodo a murderer?

No. My best friend had a rigid set of morals. He did

not kill frivolously or because his emotions had gotten the better of him. Before losing two of his appendages, Frodo had laid waste to countless enemies.

But he was not a murderer.

This was not to say that all of our operations had been accomplished flawlessly. As much as we, and the men and women who sent us to deal death on their behalf, wanted to believe otherwise, the work we did was messy. Just as the world's most accomplished vascular surgeon can still accidentally nick an artery, the battlefield Frodo and I inhabited was not a sterile place, and we were not robots.

Operators were human.

We made mistakes.

And then there was our adversary.

Military tacticians were fond of parroting the truism *the enemy has a vote*. Unlike a doctor whose opponent was an inanimate tumor, Frodo and I fought against intelligent, skilled warriors who wanted to survive just as badly as we wanted them dead. Of the countless operations I'd helmed as either a paramilitary operative or Ranger, few had gone as planned. This wasn't to say that I never achieved my desired outcome. The opposite was true. Most of the time, my side emerged from the arena victorious, but that didn't negate the fact that at some point during nearly every operation, I'd had to call an audible.

The enemy had a vote.

In 2011 Afghanistan, they'd certainly cast it.

"Frodo's not a murderer," I said, staring into space, "but neither is he an angel. Shit goes sideways sometimes. Most times if I'm being honest. Skill, training, and the men to your left and right are enough to mitigate most dumpster fires but not all."

"What are you saying?" Laila said.

I sighed as I tried to put my feelings into words.

"Twenty-eleven Afghanistan was a bad time. A real bad time. There are things about that deployment I'll never forget. Things I don't want to relive. I'm afraid Frodo's arrest is going to unearth them."

Laila gave a slow nod like she understood.

She didn't.

I had been there and I barely understood.

"Want to talk about it?" Laila said.

I did.

But my buzzing phone had other plans.

SEVEN

"Drake," I said, holding the phone to my ear.

"Sorry about the wait, Matthew. As you can imagine, underwear is spontaneously igniting all up and down SES row. This shit with Bagram is bad news. Word is that quite a bit of the equipment we left for the Afghans is now in Taliban hands."

As was often the case, I found myself devoting precious mental energy trying to unravel one of my boss's colorful metaphors. James was every bit as eccentric as his patterns of speech. Though James's operational career had ended when a Taliban RPG robbed him of his right eye, he was still a door kicker at heart. He spoke with a blunt manner that was more at home on the battlefield than in DIA conference rooms. His unique attitude also extended to his wardrobe.

James might have traded his MultiCams for office attire, but he'd refused to adopt the button-up attire expected of Senior Executive Service–level civilians. Instead, he wore his dress shirts open at the collar and rolled up at the cuffs, exposing tattooed forearms. James didn't own a tie, and when the occasion mandated a sport coat, the fabric strained to contain his massive chest and thick neck. A black eye patch, which sharply contrasted with the gray stubble that remained of his hair, completed his look.

Even so, James was one of the best bosses I'd ever worked for. Though never one to shy away from giving his subordinates the rough side of his tongue when he thought their actions merited it, James was fiercely protective of those in his charge. An affront to Frodo or me was an affront to him. If anyone could cut through the noise to find the signal with regard to Frodo's arrest, it would be James.

"So what's the plan?" I said as the earlier images of black-turbaned Taliban fighters strolling down the Bagram flight line came to mind. "Are we surging folks into country?"

"Nope," James said. "So far we're just wringing our hands and worrying."

"Is that a joke?"

"Yep," James said, "but not in the way that you mean. The head shed believes—and I quote—that this is a problem for the duly elected Afghan government to solve."

"Unreal," I said. "Bagram is only seventy kilometers from Kabul. If we don't stop the hemorrhaging, the duly elected Afghan government will be nothing but a memory."

"Buckle up, Matthew. The worst is yet to come."

James's sobering comment felt like being doused with ice water. It was hard to imagine what could be worse than the Taliban rummaging through the countless storage containers scattered across Bagram. Containers piled high with hastily abandoned American and coalition gear. Still, as bad as that sounded, it paled in comparison with the reason I'd actually called—Frodo.

"Chief, I need help," I said. "Frodo's been arrested."

"Goddamn it, Matt," James said. "If I've told you once, I've told you a thousand times: Do not antagonize the hipsters."

"I'm serious, Chief," I said. "Frodo's been taken into custody."

"By who?" James said. "Locals or Feds?"

"Feds."

"I thought you and Agent What's-his-name had an understanding?"

"His name is Rawlings," I said, "and we do. Army CID picked Frodo up, not the FBI."

"Why?"

"Murder."

I'd expected my answer to elicit another outburst.

It didn't.

"Chief—you there?" I said, convinced the connection had dropped.

I'd weathered a James Glass storm many times. While the decibel levels were quite high at the storm's apex, the violence quotient trended toward the milder end of the scale. Or at least milder from an ex-Ranger's perspective. Like a beachfront dweller, I'd become adept at riding out the hurricane and rebuilding after. James expressed his displeasure in a number of inventive ways, ranging from profanity-laced tirades to pummeling his distressed-wood desk with ham-hock-sized fists. This was my first experience with silence.

It was terrifying.

"Listen to me very carefully, Matthew," James said in a whisper.

Even at lower volumes, James's tone usually reminded me of steel wool abrading metal. Not today. At this moment, James Scott Glass sounded like a normal human being.

A concerned human being.

"You don't have much time," James said, enunciating each word. "CID will eventually transport him to an Army facility. Somewhere beyond our reach. But I'm willing to bet that hasn't happened yet, which means you have an opportunity. A window."

"A window for what?" I said.

"Use your head, boy! Do you think it's a coincidence that Frodo was picked up for murder just as Afghanistan is going to shit? The amount of CYA going on at headquarters is mind-boggling. Afghanistan's collapse is shaping up to be the biggest intelligence failure since 9/11. Frodo plays into it all somehow. I can feel it."

"What do we do?"

"Not we," James said. "You. Frodo's beyond my reach, but not yours. Not if you move fast anyway. Figure out where he's being held and get in to see him. Get some answers. That's the only way we're gonna understand what we're up against."

"How am I supposed to do that?" I said.

"Now I have to spoon-feed you?" James said. "You're a Ranger—make shit happen. Christ—that's the Director calling on the other line. I've gotta take it. Out here."

Normally I find my boss's use of radio protocol on the telephone amusing.

Not today.

"What was that?" Laila said.

She was looking at me like I'd lost my mind.

I wasn't entirely certain I hadn't.

"Not really sure," I said. "Never seen James like this."

"Like what? Angry?"

"No," I said. "Scared."

Laila's green eyes bored into mine.

"What are you going to do?"

"Follow my boss's advice—make shit happen."

EIGHT

"Didn't I once compare you to syphilis?"

"Herpes," I said. "Syphilis doesn't keep coming back."

"No," Special Agent Rawlings said. "It just kills you."

"Apparently you've never had herpes."

I was standing on the front porch of Rawlings's home. He didn't seemed inclined to let me in.

"Nice place," I said, surveying his neat little yard. "Supervisory Special Agent must have been a pretty nice pay bump."

Rawlings still didn't invite me inside, but his lips twisted from a frown into a look I knew well.

Resignation.

Rawlings and I weren't exactly pals, but we did have a history. A history in which information I'd provided him had helped to uncover a traitor who had almost been appointed as the Director of the Central Intelligence Agency. Rawlings's work with yours truly gave the Agency one hell of a shiner, which had the effect of instantly endearing him to the accountants and lawyers who ran the FBI. His promotion to SSA, or Supervisory Special Agent, happened shortly thereafter.

"Look, Drake," Rawlings said, closing the door behind him as he joined me on the porch, "I'm not ungrateful for your help."

Even without his customary Bureau garb of a sport coat, slacks, a button-down shirt, and lace-up dress shoes, Rawlings still looked like a federal agent. He had the earnest face of someone you wanted to trust, and his brown hair was short but stylish. He'd answered the door in a polo shirt and khakis, and even at this late hour, his cheeks seemed freshly shaven. Agent Rawlings could have been a poster boy for the Federal Bureau of Investigation.

Which meant that he instinctively distrusted spies like me.

"But," I said, drawing out the word.

"But I already went out on a limb for you with those CID agents. I don't want them thinking the Bureau's involved."

"Strange," I said. "Usually, the Bureau can't wait to stick its nose into another agency's business. What gives?"

I am not an architecture aficionado, but even I could tell Rawlings's new house had set him back a pretty penny. As was common in Austin, Rawlings had bought a lot featuring an older house and promptly demolished the dwelling. While his neighbors had the kind of late-1950s houses typical of *Leave It to Beaver*, Rawlings's ultramodern domicile was all funky angles and floor-to-ceiling windows. I thought it looked like something you'd see in an art film, but in the home of the weird, the house fit right in.

The price tag had to have been in the couple-of-million range. Just the designer tin roof probably cost more than what Laila and I had spent on our fixer-upper, albeit in a far-less-desirable neighborhood. Don't get me wrong. I'm all for capitalism. If Rawlings wanted to build hip new digs in one of the nation's most desirable zip codes, more power to him. I was just wondering how he swung the mortgage on a government paycheck.

"You're what gives," Rawlings said. "Working with you can be career ending."

"Not from where I'm sitting," I said. "How much does this set you back in property taxes?"

"Lay off about the house," Rawlings said, his usual gruffness returning. "Not that it's any of your business, but this is from my wife's income."

Rawlings stooped down as he was speaking, turning over what looked like a rock situated in the perfect landscaping to the right of the porch. It wasn't a rock. Though the faux granite perfectly accented the bush it lay beside, the chunk of ceramic was actually a hollow container meant to store a spare key or an additional garage door opener. In Rawlings's case, the dry void revealed a pack of Marlboros and a lighter wrapped in a ziplock bag.

"I told my wife I quit," Rawlings said as he retrieved the pack and lighter, "and I did. Except when I'm around you."

He stuck a cigarette in his mouth and incinerated the tip before offering me the pack.

I declined.

I'm all for the occasional cigar, but Laila's sense of smell had reached superhero levels, thanks to her pregnancy. If I had any hopes of sleeping in her bed tonight, I needed to abstain.

"Not the most clandestine hiding place," I said, pointing at the rock. "I take it your wife isn't a PI?"

Rawlings exhaled a lungful of smoke.

Most of it hit my face.

I'm sure it was accidental.

"My wife is a novelist," Rawlings said, pointing at me with the burning ember.

"Is her protagonist a handsome DIA officer?" I said.

"She doesn't write comedies."

"Detective books?"

"No."

"True crime?" I said.

"No."

"Fantasy? Orcs and hobbits?"

"Will you please stop?"

"What does she write, Rawlings?" I said.

"You're like a dog with a bone," Rawlings said, taking another drag. "Historical romance, okay? Her pen name is Sarah Walton."

"Seriously?" I said. "That's your wife?"

"You read historical romance?"

"Nope, but Laila's a huge fan. Would your wife sign a book for her?"

"If it gets you off my front porch."

"No reason to get testy," I said. "I'm just asking for a little help."

"What kind of help?" Rawlings said.

With the cigarette now dangling from his lips, my FBI friend looked every bit the gumshoe detective.

"The guy the CID agents pinched is my best friend," I said, staring at Rawlings in the tombstones. "He's watched my back in shitholes the world over. Before that, he was a sniper in a special mission unit. One that spent a hell of a lot of time in Afghanistan."

I made the last comment instinctively, a kind of throwaway I hadn't expected to stick.

But stick it did.

Rawlings took the cigarette out of his mouth and ashed it on the landscaping.

"Was he part of ODA 3324?" Rawlings said.

The change in my companion was pronounced. No longer were we two pseudo friends standing on his front porch. His entire demeanor shifted. His posture became more erect, his face blank. I recognized the transformation because I'd seen it before.

This was his interview persona.

"No," I said, shaking my head. "Frodo was in the Unit, but he was never part of an ODA. Why?"

ODA stood for Operational Detachment Alpha, the formal name for the organization under which Green Berets were grouped. Though there was something familiar about ODA 3324, nothing about the Unit's operational history came to mind. Maybe I'd rubbed shoulders with them during my time in the Regiment.

Rawlings beckoned me closer before he spoke, as if we really were in a Humphrey Bogart remake.

"I'm seeing some weird shit from headquarters,"

Rawlings said. "Scuttlebutt says that Washington Field Office sent out a slew of high-priority leads concerning ODA 3324. The case file has been grouped under an Afghanistan identifier, but it's restricted. I've got a buddy on a TDY at WFO, but even he doesn't know what this is about."

"What do you think?" I said.

Rawlings shook his head. "I don't know for sure, but here's my guess—Afghanistan is dominating the news cycle. Networks are recycling old stories, they're so desperate for content. With popular opinion swinging against the President's handling of the withdrawal, the cynic in me thinks that maybe someone's anxious to make sure a certain story doesn't get unearthed or resurrected."

"And Frodo's somehow caught up in this?" I said.

Rawlings lit another cigarette. "I'd have to see the arrest warrant to be sure, and before you ask, no, I can't get it. That CID special agent wasn't exaggerating—everything Afghanistan-related is restricted access. Here's what I do know—a murder charge is great for keeping a potential witness away from people you don't want him to talk to."

For a long moment I didn't get it.

Then I did.

"Bail," I said, the wheels turning faster. "A murder charge makes it more likely a judge will grant a motion to deny bail."

"Exactly," Rawlings said. "It pains me to say it, but just because someone's a prosecutor doesn't automatically put them on the side of the angels. I've seen plenty of folks use the old ends-justifies-the-means argument to do some squirrelly shit."

"Which is exactly why I need your help," I said. "I've got one chance to talk to Frodo before he disappears into the system. One."

"Have you listened to a word I've said?" Rawlings said. "Anything to do with Afghanistan is radioactive."

"My mistake," I said. "I thought I was talking to a federal law enforcement officer. The kind of crazy son of a bitch who runs into a bank as it's being robbed. I guess that's not you."

"Fuck off," Rawlings said, crowding my personal space. "I've looked down my Glock at plenty of bad guys."

"Then start acting like a warrior instead of a paper pusher," I said. "'Fidelity, Bravery, Integrity'—that's y'all's motto, right?"

Rawlings puffed on his cigarette while surveying his recently mowed yard.

"Three weeks and not a single smoke," Rawlings said. "Ten minutes with you, and I'm on my second. Thank God I'm not an alcoholic."

He didn't even try to make it look accidental as he exhaled into my face.

"I can't get your friend out of jail," Rawlings said.

"Just get me inside to talk with him," I said. "Alone."

"The facility's interview rooms will be wired for sound."

"That's my problem," I said.

"Do you have a set of credentials?"

"I was hoping to borrow yours," I said.

"I'm going to pretend I didn't hear that."

"Joking," I said.

I was, mostly, but I figured it was worth a try.

"Will these work?" I said, handing my DIA credentials to Rawlings.

Rawlings eyed them for a minute before passing them back.

"They'll have to," Rawlings said. "If your buddy's still in town, he'll be at the federal detention center just west of here. No promises, but I'll make some calls. Give me an hour."

"Thirty minutes," I said, "and you've got a deal."

Rawlings called me something decidedly out of place in his bougie neighborhood, but he didn't say no.

Progress.

NINE

Prison was not designed to be an enjoyable experience. Imagine an environment in which everything pleasant, everything uplifting, everything meant to bring comfort has been purposely removed, exchanged for the minimum accoutrements necessary to sustain life.

And not much of a life at that.

Prison was like a weathered skeleton of the real world. Bleached bones, hard edges, and discolored metal that smelled of industrial cleaner and despair. It was a place devoid of hope and heavy with sorrow where fear lurked around every corner. If hell wasn't a lake of fire, it was probably a prison.

And my best friend was now a resident.

Though he'd been in custody for less than three hours, Frodo wore the obligatory orange jumpsuit and paper slipper shoes. His normally vibrant skin looked pale and faded beneath the sterile lighting, as if he were beginning to wither.

But it wasn't his clothing or pallor that most alarmed me.

It was his eyes.

Frodo had the eyes of a dead man.

"Hey, buddy," I said, wearing a smile I didn't feel. "Did ya start digging your escape tunnel yet?"

Frodo did not smile.

At first, I didn't think he was even going to respond. Then he let out a long sigh.

"Why did you come?" Frodo said.

"Because you don't belong here," I said.

"That's the thing, Matty. I do."

I stared at my best friend, trying to make sense of what he'd just said.

I'd known Frodo for more than a decade. Ours was a deep, unshakable friendship. A bond forged in combat. One that had weathered the very worst life had to offer. I knew Frodo better than any other human being, including my wife.

The man seated across from me in the cheap plastic chair was not Frodo.

"Give me a sec," I said as I reached into the messenger bag at my feet.

I wasn't sure what Rawlings had said to the detention center's administrators, but he'd done the trick. Though I still had to put my stuff into the X-ray machine and walk through the metal detector, there were no invasive pat downs or searches. The workers had been courteous and efficient, which made me think that Rawlings hadn't been truthful about my affiliation. And while I appreciated all the *Yes, sir*s and the expedited processing, what I really cared about was getting the little piece of magic in my bag through the gauntlet unscathed.

The device was about the size of a deck of cards and

looked just as interesting. If asked, I would have told the Department of Corrections folks that it was a digital recorder. This was true, after a fashion. The device did in fact record sound if the microphone was working. Alas it was not. Fortunately, I hadn't brought the device along to record my conversation with Frodo.

In fact, I wanted to do the opposite.

After placing the device on the table between us, I pushed the prominent red button located dead center. Since there was only one button, I didn't have to worry about pressing the wrong one. In the parlance of my profession, the recorder was operator proof.

A green LED light located above the button illuminated. I waited for a second to see if I heard anything. I didn't. Then again, I wasn't the target for the high-frequency sound waves emanating from the device. As of this moment, the microphones situated throughout the room were all experiencing a regrettable technical failure. Nothing so obvious as electronic static. Were the guards to play a recording of this meeting later, they would hear our voices, but words would be muffled and unintelligible.

"We're good to speak freely," I said, "so run that last part by me again, the bit about you belonging here."

"It's true," Frodo said.

"You're not a murderer," I said.

"What do you remember about Afghanistan in 2011?"

I'd already done some thinking on this subject, so my answers came easy.

"It was our first operational assignment," I said. "We recruited three high-level assets. One Taliban, one from the Haqqani network, and one who was a member of the Pakistani ISI. Not bad work."

"What about the beginning of the tour?" Frodo said.

"You talking about the Bagram raid?" I said.

"Yes."

"What's that have to do with this?" I said.

"Everything."

I looked at Frodo, waiting for him to continue.

He stared back.

After a moment, I took the bait.

"Care to be more specific?"

Frodo shook his head.

Another long silence.

"I don't understand," I said, my frustration spilling out. "Talk to me."

"No," Frodo said.

"Then how am I supposed to help you?"

"You're not," Frodo said. "I don't know how else to say this, Matty. I belong here. They'll move me tomorrow to Bragg, where I'll meet my court-appointed JAG attorney. I'll tell them that I want to plead guilty. That's it."

I looked at Frodo in stunned silence, waiting for the punch line.

It didn't come.

The silence stretched for one minute.

Two.

Ten.

After a quarter of an hour, the guard stuck his head in the door.

"I'm sorry, Mr. Drake, but you're out of time. Are y'all through?"

"Yes," Frodo said.

But we weren't.

Not by a long shot.

TEN

I sat in the detention center's parking lot. My truck was idling and my blood was boiling. The first tentative drops of rain from a brewing thunderstorm exploded across my windshield, each impact turning the road grime into a muddy crater. The radio provided a soundtrack that mirrored my mood as a disembodied voice gave updates on the latest from Afghanistan.

The Taliban were closing in on Kabul.

I'd never felt so helpless.

I was sitting in a dusty pickup, listening to a growling Hemi that was begging to be set free, but I had no idea where to point the brush guard. I did not normally struggle with indecision. Early on in my Army career, I'd learned the value of the oft-repeated maxim attributed to Thomas Paine but championed by General George S. Patton—lead, follow, or get the hell out of the way. As trivial as it sounded, there was something to be said for the concept of inertia. Forward motion. In absence of orders from their higher headquarters, American military units were expected to attack rather than defend. I'd lived by this philosophy, and it had served me well.

Until now.

For the first time in memory, I had nothing to attack.

The news that the announcer was so calmly conveying twisted my stomach into knots, magnifying the feeling of helplessness. Almost eight thousand miles away, a nation I'd poured my life into was fraying at the seams. Less than one hundred yards distant, the man I loved like a brother was unrecognizable. In the course of three hours, Frodo had become despondent. Lethargic. Ready to spend the rest of his life behind bars.

What was happening?

Lightning flared and the pitter-patter of raindrops became a downpour, and I triggered the windshield wipers. Frodo was not a murderer—on this I would stake my life. Even if everything else seemed to be shifting sand, I knew that my best friend would never take another's life without cause. If this was true, then reason dictated that someone was forcing Frodo to confess to a crime he hadn't committed.

Men like Frodo didn't quit.

Ever.

His decision to rot in prison rather than go toe-to-toe with whoever was falsely accusing him could only mean one thing—he was protecting someone.

Like a match tossed into a pool of gasoline, this thought turned my malaise to rage. I always valued a good rage. Channeled correctly, the emotion was like rocket fuel and I had enough right now to send me into orbit. If Frodo couldn't fight for himself, then I would go into battle on his behalf.

Digging my cell from my pocket, I thumbed a number and waited. The sound of a ringing phone broadcast from the truck's speakers, thankfully drowning out the radio announcer's voice.

"What?" Rawlings said.

"One more thing," I said.

"Exactly what every criminal always says. Before this conversation goes any further, I want you to confirm that Frodo is still in protective custody."

"Are you serious?" I said.

"Don't play coy. A yes-or-no answer or I'm hanging up."

"Frodo is still in federal custody," I said.

"And you have no plans to break him out."

"And I have no plans to break him out."

Rawlings sighed.

"Thank God. Maybe now I can get some sleep."

"One more thing and you'll be sleeping like a baby," I said.

"What do I get?"

"My undying gratitude," I said.

"I'm hanging up."

"I'm serious," I said. "I'll owe you one, and that is not a trivial promise. I honor my debts. Always."

I heard a rustling followed by the tinkling of cellophane.

"Those things are going to kill you," I said.

"You're going to kill me. Besides, I'm not even smoking this one. I'm just holding it in my mouth."

"Said every criminal everywhere."

"What do you want?" Rawlings said.

"A copy of the warrant."

"I get you the warrant, and we're done?"

"Scout's honor," I said.

Another long sigh.

"Let me see what I can do," Rawlings said.

My phone vibrated.

A text from Rawlings with an attachment.

The warrant.

"You had this the whole time?" I said. "And you still made me beg?"

"I am a trained investigator," Rawlings said. "I figured you'd want it."

"I thought you said the case file was marked *restricted access*?" I said.

"I don't ask how you do spy shit," Rawlings said. "Don't ask how I do my job. Besides, most of the warrant is redacted."

"I still can't believe you already had the warrant," I said.

"Karma's a bitch," Rawlings said. "Don't come around here no more."

He hung up before I could even acknowledge his brilliant ode to Mr. Petty.

I thought about calling him back but didn't. I began to read instead. It didn't take long since most of the document was blacked out. Even so, I found the words I was looking for.

. . . the murder of Staff Sergeant Tommy Ledbetter . . .

The Bagram raid.

It all came back to the Bagram raid.

ELEVEN

BAGRAM, AFGHANISTAN
TEN YEARS EARLIER

You see our ride?" Frodo said, shouldering his duffel.

"Nope," I said, falling in beside him. "But we're definitely not in Kansas anymore."

"You have got to update your movie repertoire," Frodo said.

"You don't like the classics?"

"I love the classics. But if it wasn't filmed in the eighties, it's not a classic."

We were standing to the left side of a C-17's open ramp, watching the rain bounce off the concrete as a column of forlorn-looking soldiers streamed by. The clouds obscured the view of the mountains normally visible from the airfield, but that was fine by me. The way the sun sparkled off their snowcapped peaks in the winter always reminded me of my home outside of Salt Lake City, Utah.

Summertime was different.

This time of year, the rocky formations looked forlorn.

Desolate.

A fitting representation of this country.

The loadmaster coughed from the other side of the cabin. Loudly. He'd given us the evil eye once already, but he had yet to order us off his airplane. This was probably because he didn't know what to make of us.

I understood.

I wasn't sure what to make of us either.

Unlike the camouflage-wearing men and women trudging past us, Frodo and I were dressed in contractor casual. REI provided most of our outerwear with the rest coming from a more specialized outdoor store. We both wore beards and neither of our haircuts would have made it past a sergeant major's steely-eyed stare. If found standing at the baggage claim at the Denver airport, Frodo and I would have passed for outdoorsmen headed for Colorado's backcountry.

We were not in the Denver airport.

We were on our first joint operational assignment to Afghanistan. Unlike the C-17's other passengers, who'd probably spent most of the last forty-eight hours living the military's infamous mantra of *hurry up and wait*, Frodo and I had flown commercial from Washington, DC, to Germany. We'd boarded the C-17 in Ramstein, nodded to the loadmaster, and generally kept to ourselves for the seven-hour flight. This was not because we were too cool to mix with the soldiers resting in the faux airline seats bolted to the cargo jet's bulkhead or sprawled across the spacious floor, wrapped in camouflage poncho liners.

Far from it.

The older I got, the more I believed that the wide-eyed kids who looked at the two cool dudes with envious expressions were the real heroes in this never-ending war. Frodo and I might have finished our military careers as part of SOF, but that didn't make my admiration for the average joes any less. This conflict wasn't going to be won by special operations teams or intelligence officers with duffel bags of cash.

Don't get me wrong. I fully support making the world a better place by decapitating terrorist organizations. Bad guys who live in fear are less effective commanders. Less effective commanders make mistakes, and enemy mistakes save friendly and civilian lives.

But Iraq had revealed the limitations of this strategy in stark detail. The last six months had been a shakeout tour of sorts for Frodo and me, and it was not an exaggeration to characterize our relationship as hell on wheels. With the former Unit sniper watching my back, I'd run a string of assets who had pointed me toward countless insurgent and militia commanders, each of whom had met a grisly end at the hands of Frodo's old comrades.

But our efforts hadn't been enough.

Not by a long shot.

Like the mythological Hydra, the organizations we targeted sprouted new heads almost as fast as we could chop off the old ones. Were the new commanders as effective as the old? For the most part, no. Then again, you didn't have to be a particularly brilliant tactician to order a twentysomething kid to detonate his suicide vest in a crowded market. We were slaying bad guys like it was going out of style, but we'd still lose the war unless soldiers like the kids on this flight massed in great enough numbers to hold and dominate the terrain.

This lesson dated back to the Roman Empire, but modern militaries constantly had to relearn it. Killing his generals would set an enemy back on his heels, but to defeat him, the opposing force had to seize and hold his battle space. Even with our lopsided technological advantage, seizing and holding terrain still required planeloads of soldiers and Marines.

These kids would always be the real heroes.

"You two getting off?"

The loadmaster's question had caught me woolgathering, and I jerked in surprise.

Frodo did not.

This was why I ran the agents, and he kept us alive.

"Keep your pants on," Frodo said. "We'll be out of here soon."

I turned to see the loadmaster eyeing Frodo, a rather unkind expression on his face. Wisely, the airman said nothing. The long snake of disembarking soldiers loaded down with rucksacks and weapons had queued up in front of waiting buses. With no other passengers aboard, the loadmaster was well within his rights to throw Frodo and me off his jet. Like a captain's authority on his ship, the loadmaster owned his aircraft. His edicts were law.

In theory.

On the other hand, something about Frodo urged caution, even to the uninformed. Though he had the iron-forged build of an endurance athlete, Frodo was slighter in stature than many hulking operators. He also didn't do steely-eyed death stares or employ a cooler-than-thou attitude. Frodo was reserved and polite, and he could employ his dry wit to devastating consequences when the mood struck him.

He was also lethal.

Frodo radiated violence like a puma lounging on the far side of a zoo's enclosure. A sense of tightly bridled aggression that could erupt at a moment's notice. My companion didn't project menace. That would ascribe a malicious intent to his capabilities. Frodo wasn't a hyped-up killer. He was an extremely skillful craftsman whose craft happened to be the death and destruction of his nation's enemies.

I likened it to the difference between a coiled viper and a loaded handgun.

One would lash out in anger at anything that happened by.

The other was a tool.

"I need to get the plane refueled and reloaded," the loadmaster said. "Got another run tonight."

"Don't let us stop you," Frodo said.

My bodyguard's reply was even and without anger. Frodo's gaze never left the falling rain, but the loadmaster seemed to hear the unspoken message. With a final huff, he wandered back into the aircraft's cavernous interior.

"Not buying what he's selling?" I said.

Frodo shrugged. "Sometimes it's worth reminding the support folks exactly who they work for and why. Besides, that jackass is a bully, and I hate bullies."

"What do you mean?" I said.

"Did you see him on final approach?"

I shook my head.

"As the plane began its final descent, he started kicking the sleeping soldiers awake. Some of those kids might be coming home in body bags. They deserve better than that."

I turned, intending to engage the loadmaster in a more intimate discussion, but Frodo grabbed my shoulder.

"Relax, Matty. I handled it. Douchebag wanted everyone off his bird so he could grab some chicken nuggets before the trip home. Chow hall closes in two minutes, and I just made sure he's not going to make it in time. Justice has been served. Besides, I think that's our ride."

A beat-up pickup truck rolled onto the flight line, waddling from side to side as its worn-out suspension tried to mitigate the transition from gravel to pavement. From the truck's faded paint to its dinged hood, the vehicle certainly looked like it belonged on Bagram Air Base. At greater than thirty square miles, the sprawling complex was difficult to navigate on foot, especially if you were carrying kit. Between us, Frodo and I had four Pelican cases, two kit bags, our rucks, and other miscellaneous baggage.

My days as a light fighter were over.

The pickup's headlights played across us as the vehicle drove up to the C-17's ramp. I stepped back, in case the driver intended to roll the truck up the ramp, but the vehicle stopped just short of the metal grating.

"Guess he doesn't like the rain," Frodo said.

"Makes two of us," I said.

The door opened and the driver leaped out, jumping

from the truck to the protection of the C-17's overhang like the raindrops were made of acid.

In Afghanistan, that wasn't such a far-fetched notion.

The driver was dressed in civilian clothes of the sort that suggested he shared our tailor—knit hat, black fleece, hiking pants, and solid boots. Only the Glock holstered at his waist suggested that he wasn't just another civilian contractor. That and his wide chest and heavy shoulders. He triggered the headlamp strapped to the front of his hat, hitting me in the face with a flood of red light.

"You guys Peluso and Halas?" the man said, his crimson eye moving from me to Frodo.

"'Fraid not," Frodo said.

"Anyone else left on board?"

"Nope," I said, "unless you're counting the pissed-off loadmaster."

"Hell's bells," the driver said as his headlamp played across the empty aircraft. "Guess I'm shit out of luck."

Something about the man's Southern accent and bowlegged walk seemed familiar.

Then I had it.

"You've always been shit out of luck, Sergeant Brown," I said.

The red light snapped back to my face.

"Well, I'll be," Sergeant Brown said, "if it isn't the worst commander I ever served with. I knew I should have stayed in my hooch. Come here, sir, and give me a hug."

I wasn't much of a hugger, but when Sergeant Jason

Brown wanted a hug, you didn't have much say in the matter. Jason and I had been Rangers together. He was the senior squad leader from first platoon and had often filled in as platoon sergeant. The soldier from North Carolina was everything you wanted in a Ranger—smart, fit, and deadly.

Even back then I'd figured that Jason was not long for the Regiment. Some Rangers were content to spend their entire lives as Batt Boys, but many long for more than just kicking in doors and shooting bad guys in the face. These folks typically gravitate toward one of two paths—the Unit or Special Forces.

Since Jason didn't recognize Frodo, he must have chosen the latter.

After an uncomfortably long period of time, Jason released me. His arms still felt like pythons, but he'd lost a little of the muscle-bound look common in Regiment. This wasn't so much a play on vanity as a job necessity. Prior to 9/11, Rangers had been built like endurance athletes. But as their mission set transitioned in the ensuing years, that changed. The days of arduous overland infiltration marches were gone, replaced by fast-roping directly onto the target from a hovering helicopter. Rangers today more resembled bouncers than distance runners.

Not so for the Army's Green Berets. These soldiers embedded with the local nationals they led and often mirrored their forms of transportation. In Afghanistan, this could take the form of long foot marches or even travel by horseback. Accordingly, Green Berets tended to be leaner than their Ranger brethren. But just because Jason's physical transformation made sense didn't mean I couldn't rib him about it.

"You like tofu now?" I said.

"Why?" Jason said.

"Because you sure as shit aren't built like a carnivore anymore."

"Please," Jason said. "I can bulk back up, but you'll always be ugly."

I didn't think the joke was very original, but Frodo laughed.

Loudly.

"Who's your friend?" Jason said, focusing on the Unit sniper.

"This is Frodo," I said. "He's my—"

"Good Lord," Jason said, grabbing Frodo in a bone-crushing handshake. "Everyone knows Frodo. What in hell are you doing slumming with Captain Drake?"

"I ask myself that question every single day," Frodo said. "We worked together before?"

"Nah," Jason said, "but we've got mutual friends. Real friends. Not like your running buddy here."

Then Jason turned to me, his smile growing wider. "Hell's bells, if you took the Long Walk, then I don't have to call you sir anymore."

"As usual, you're half right," I said, "but mostly wrong. You don't have to call me sir, but not because I joined the Unit. I'm a civilian now. Frodo and I are here with DIA."

"How about that?" Jason said. "Captain Drake's a spook. I never thought you'd amount to much, sir, but you still managed to fall below my already low expectations."

Once again I didn't think the joke was that funny.

Once again Frodo seemed to disagree.

"If you're done busting balls, can you give us a ride?" I said. "I melt in the rain."

"Don't I know it, sir."

"Matt," I said.

"That's going to take some getting used to," Jason said. "How about fuck head instead?"

"How about I show Frodo how fast I can make a Ranger-turned–Green Beret tap out?"

"His sense of humor was always for shit," Jason said, directing the comment to Frodo. "Throw your kit in the truck. I'll run you guys in. Two replacements for my team were supposed to be on this flight. I guess they didn't make it."

"A team or B team guys?" Frodo said.

"A team," Jason said as he grabbed one of our Pelican cases, "which puts me in a pickle. I'm down a couple of assaulters, and we've got an imminent Op. Maybe I can borrow some SOF guys from across the street."

I understood Jason's predicament. While manning shortages to the B teams were problematic, missing A team members could make the entire organization combat ineffective. It was akin to the difference between a sports team being short a couple of trainers versus missing part of their starting lineup. If Jason had an imminent operation, he needed every rifle he could get.

"Who's here from SOF?" I said, climbing into the passenger's seat.

"Usual suspects," Jason said. "A company plus of Rangers and a squadron of SEALs. Unfortunately, all of Frodo's friends are getting their jihad on in Iraq."

In a nod to the practicality of attempting to maintain ongoing conflicts in two very different theaters, the Army's elite SOF had largely ceded Afghanistan to the SEALs, reasoning that the Unit's man-hunting expertise was critically needed in Iraq. Whether or not this strategy was tactically sound would be a topic for future historians. Bottom line was that Jason was left with two choices. He could ask to borrow some Rangers, knowing that incorporating a highly motivated but very inexperienced nineteen-year-old kid into his tactical formation would be an operational chore. His second option would be to cede the operation to the frogmen since the SEALs would not willingly loan two operators to an Army SF team.

Neither course of action was particularly attractive.

"What's the Op?" I said.

Jason shot me a glance before returning his attention to the road. The rain was coming down in buckets, and the sickly yellow light from the pickup truck's aging headlights wasn't doing much to banish the darkness. Jason had to be driving by muscle memory, or maybe the truck just knew where it was going. Either way, we rolled off the flight line and onto the airfield proper without adding any more dings to the truck's battle-scarred bumper.

I'd take that as a win.

"It's a hit," Jason said. "Intel folks have identified a bomb-making cell. Believe it or not, the jihadis are set up just a couple of kilometers from Bagram's front gate."

"I believe it," Frodo said. "Sometimes it's better to hide in plain sight."

"Exactly," Jason said, nodding at Frodo in the rearview mirror. "Our Fox has an asset who says a high-value target is coming to check out the operation sometime in the next seventy-two hours. Could happen as soon as tomorrow."

Fox was a reference to an 18F MOS designation. Every member of an A team received an 18 series designator while attending the *Q*, or qualification course. An 18D, or Delta, was a medic, while an 18E, or Echo, was a communications sergeant. An 18F, or Fox, was an intelligence sergeant. In addition to the traditional tasks associated with IPB, or intelligence preparation of the battlefield, 18Fs were also taught to run and recruit assets, a topic I happened to know a thing or two about.

"You've got an asset providing you real-world intelligence, a high-value target, and a bomb-making cell," I said, "but you can't prosecute the target because you're down two shooters. Do I have that right?"

"Yep," Jason said.

"Sounds like the makings of a joint operation," I said. "What do you think, Frodo?"

"I think that was a foregone conclusion the moment we got into this rattletrap," Frodo said.

"You guys can just attach yourselves to my team?" Jason said.

"We're from the government," I said. "We're here to help."

"Hot damn," Jason said. "How do you feel about bunking with us?"

"Would you happen to have a bottle of Listerine that tastes suspiciously like Johnnie Walker Black?" Frodo asked.

"For the record, I have no idea what you're talking about," Jason said.

"And off the record?" I said.

"Off the record, y'all should pick out a rack, drop your kit, and mosey over to the team room. It might just be Tequila Tuesday."

"My man," Frodo said.

One part of me thought that I could get used to a spook's life. The other part wondered what my new boss was going to think when I told him what I'd just done. But that was a problem for tomorrow.

Today was Tequila Tuesday.

TWELVE

I put the truck in gear and motored out of the parking lot, my thoughts still on Afghanistan. Austin weather was pretty mild if you discounted the oppressive summer heat and the occasional winter Snowmageddon. Okay, so San Diego it wasn't, but compared to North Dakota, the climate in Bat City wasn't so bad. But mild or not, there was one severe-weather phenomenon common to Austin that would give even the frozen plains a run for their money.

Thunderstorms.

Especially summer thunderstorms.

The rain was coming down sideways, pinging off the truck's frame. I looked at the digital thermometer. Eighty-five degrees Fahrenheit. Still plenty warm, but the temperature had already dropped ten degrees. In addition to torrential rain and some serious lightning, Austin thunderstorms had another endearing quality.

Hail.

And not just the cute ice pellets that danced on sidewalks and made kids laugh. Austin hail destroyed roofs and left golf-ball-sized indentations on unprotected cars.

There was nothing fun about getting hit with a ball of ice that packed the punch of a Nolan Ryan fastball. Right now only water was detonating against the windshield.

But that could change in a hurry.

I followed the meandering service road and watched the detention facility's bright lights fade in my rearview mirror. The jail was about an hour's drive west from Austin in the area of Texas known as Hill Country. Full of small towns, single-lane country roads with speed limits of seventy miles per hour, and beautiful vistas formed by craggy granite cliffs, the Hill Country was truly something special. Laila and I had talked about buying a cabin out this way to better enjoy the plethora of state parks along with the culinary and shopping mecca known as Fredericksburg. Unfortunately, between the pouring rain and the thick cloud cover, I wasn't going to see much of the area's beauty tonight.

The service road teed into Route 377, and I put on my left blinker, heading east and home. I came to a stop, waiting the obligatory second while I checked for traffic coming from the west, before accelerating. Though these roads tended to be pretty isolated, a vehicle traveling at seventy miles per hour closed distance quickly. And that was assuming the driver was maintaining the speed limit—never a sure bet out in the sticks.

The Hemi's tires spun on the wet pavement as I accelerated.

Folks who are new to Texas poke fun at the natives for treating rainstorms like inclement weather. Until they've had the pleasure of driving on our slick roads. Because this part of Texas received so little rain, the dust, dirt, grit, oil, and gasoline residue all coagulated on the black-top before baking beneath the Southern sun. When it rained, the moisture turned this delightful slurry into a slippery film that rivaled black ice for its lethality.

I thought as I drove, my body on autopilot as my mind mulled over the events of the last four hours. I knew that everything pointed to Afghanistan, but I still wasn't certain what to do next. Frodo's clock was ticking, but the storm might actually help in that regard. According to the radio, the squall was part of a band of thunderstorms lighting up Texas, and I had to imagine flights were being canceled from Dallas to Houston. This meant that air travel tomorrow would be a mess, which in turn might provide me with more time to act before my best friend disappeared into the military justice system. But even with a delay working in my favor, I was no closer to answering the most critical question.

What should I do next?

A pair of lights flashed in the darkness.

I switched the wipers to high and set the defrost on full blast, trying to get a better look at what was ahead. The road edged through a sharp curve ahead, twisting to the left around a cliff face. A combination of mesquite and cedar scrub brush held the road to the right. Though my headlights couldn't penetrate the foggy murk, I remembered seeing the glint of a river on the way in—probably the Llano if my geography was correct. This must be why the flashing lights were on the left side of the road, snug against the granite cliff face.

It was a bad road to break down on anyway you looked at it, but if given the choice, I'd nestle my car against solid rock rather than a shoulder that ended with a steep drop-off. High-speed back roads made covering the vast expanse that was Texas a bit more manageable, but that convenience came with a price. Drunk drivers were a scourge everywhere, but crashes on single-lane roads in which the combined speed of the two vehicles was over one hundred forty miles per hour often proved fatal.

And a distracted driver could be just as deadly.

Even a nudge from someone texting while navigating an s-turn could send a parked car plunging down an embankment. Texas scrub brush made for great country songs, but it did nothing to curtail a five-thousand-pound hunk of metal.

I took my foot off the gas as I approached the curve, trying to get a better look at the parked car. Though road conditions were lousy, I wasn't too worried about oncoming traffic. The headlights of oncoming cars would be readily visible, and I knew the road behind me was clear for the same reason. I was more worried about accidentally forcing an unseen pedestrian off the road.

Someone like the stranded vehicle's driver.

The speedometer dropped below forty-five as I let the incline and the Hemi's mass brake for me. The disabled car was a dark-colored four-door sedan. The rock wall reflected the vehicle's flashing hazard lights, revealing an empty interior.

That was smart.

As much as waiting for a tow truck in the rain would suck, it was better than staying dry in a death trap. Parking against the rock was marginally safer than sitting on the opposite shoulder, but not by much.

I glanced to the right, checking the shoulder for pedestrians, and then eyed the car as I rolled by. I didn't see any obvious signs that the car had been in an accident. The tires weren't flat, the hood wasn't popped, and there was no visible damage to the vehicle's bumper or frame.

I accelerated into the turn, falling back on a trick I'd learned in a tactical driving class. Even though it was counterintuitive, braking in a curve was dangerous. The vehicle's center of gravity shifted upward while decelerating, making it top-heavy and more prone to skid or roll over. Even slight acceleration helped to compress a vehicle's struts, gluing it to the road. But moderation was still the name of the game. The last thing I wanted to do was to come screaming out of the turn into a slick straightaway. The Hemi's eight cylinders growled, and my headlights swept across the road's shoulder revealing . . . nothing. No rain-soaked form huddling against the downpour. No oncoming traffic.

Nothing.

Well, almost nothing.

I thought I saw something stretched across the road. My high beams played over the object for only an instant, and I didn't get much more than a sense of sinuous black. Perhaps a tree branch or maybe a stream of water running from the cliff face to the drop-off. I rolled over the obstruction about the same instant that I saw it.

My front tires burst.

The steering wheel shook.

I slammed on the brakes as my rear tires disintegrated.

Then I was hurtling toward the shoulder.

THIRTEEN

I never bought into the notion that your life flashes before your eyes before you die. I'd had more close calls than I cared to admit and never once had I experienced this phenomenon. Then again, maybe I was not a good test case. While normal people probably faced their mortality with fear or regret, I was usually consumed with a much more visceral emotion.

Rage.

Tonight was no exception.

One minute I was steering out of the turn; the next I was barreling toward a mesquite tree at ramming speed. The tree never stood a chance. Thin branches snapped like kindling and then I was hurtling down the rocky drop-off. I briefly thought that if I could keep the truck's nose pointed downhill, I might be able to maintain control of the vehicle in the same way a surfer rode a wave.

Nope.

Blown tires are no better at navigating a rock-strewn hill than a rain-slick road. I had directional control for about a nanosecond. Then a metal rim clipped a boulder and that was all she wrote. The impact ripped the steering wheel from my grip as the truck skidded sideways like a drunk hippopotamus on skis.

Then I was airborne.

The terror burned through my rage as black sky filled the windshield. Then the truck slammed into the ground, thrashing me against my seat belt. The good news was that I was no longer hurtling through the air. The bad was that the truck was now rolling down the hillside with equal vigor. I somehow stayed conscious for the first rotation or two though the terrified sounds that left my lips were probably not befitting of a former Army Ranger.

Then my head cracked against the doorframe, and I stopped caring.

About anything.

When I came to, I was hanging upside down from my seat belt as the truck slowly flooded. To be fair, the whole *slowly* part was a matter of interpretation. While the water wasn't pouring into the cabin like in a submarine that had sprung a leak, an inch or two covered the ceiling. The swirling eddies were getting ever closer to my perfectly coiffed hair.

In a testament to superb American engineering, the airbags had detonated. Just as important, the reinforced doors and heavy-duty cab had provided me with that all-important currency in a crash sequence—space. Like an egg carton, the truck had protected me from the worst of the multiple collisions by cocooning me in metal, fiberglass, and hardened plastic. Unfortunately, this meant that space in the truck was now cramped, and becoming more cramped by the moment as river water displaced oxygen.

I reached for the seat-belt-release button, but hesitated, my fingers hovering above the red button. As a Ranger, I'd once done an exchange tour with SEAL Team 10. The rotation had lasted only a month, and fortunately I'd emerged from the experience with no lasting degradation to my IQ. Since part of the team's mission set involved cargo ship takedowns, I had to endure two fun-filled days undergoing dunker training before I was cleared for overwater helicopter flights. While I'd spent most of the class irrigating my sinus cavities with pool water, I had learned something.

Okay, maybe two somethings.

First off, I did not regret my decision to join the Army rather than the Navy. Secondly, there was an art to exiting a helicopter that was rapidly filling with water. The obvious warning not to panic aside, our instructor had stressed the need to plan out each step of your escape before executing it. While our animal instincts were there for a reason, in this case the fight-or-flight reflexes were a detriment to survival. Fear of confined spaces triggered a primal response in a way that few other stressors did, but giving in to panic meant almost certain death.

With this in mind, I paused to consider the ramifications of unbuckling my seat belt—namely falling headfirst into a console covered with frigid river water. I reached up, grabbing the seat belt with my left hand both as a handhold and to take the tension off the locked belt. Then I unbuckled with my other hand. I still ended up wet, but I was able to ease myself out of the restraint rather than puddling onto the ceiling in a tangle of limbs.

Once I was free of the seat belt, I paused again, this time to take stock of my injuries. My face was tender and covered with grit from collisions with multiple airbags. My nose wasn't broken, which was a plus, but the skin was abraded and hot from swelling. My ribs and shoulders ached where the seat belt had locked, but aches and pains were always preferable to broken bones and dislocated joints.

I'd come out of the crash in pretty decent shape, all things considered.

Assuming I didn't drown.

My truck was resting on the driver's side with the nose angled slightly downward. This left two potential exits—the windshield and the passenger window. The world outside the truck's cabin was dark and getting darker. One of my headlights was no longer functioning and the other winked out as I righted myself in the cramped driver's seat.

Without being able to see beyond the windshield, I was loath to exit that way. For all I knew the truck had nosed into the riverbed and wiggling onto the hood would trap me between the Hemi and the muddy bottom. And that was assuming I'd even be able to exit through the windshield. The double lamination found in most windshields did a great job preventing flying pebbles from shattering the glass. Escaping that way would be a bitch.

Which left the passenger window.

Water was streaming through cracks in the doorframes, and the swirling eddies had already reached chest level. That wasn't high enough. In the truck's current orientation, the river's weight was pressing on the door, holding it closed. Even once the cabin completely flooded, I didn't think I'd have the strength to force the door open. I was going to have to shatter the window, wait for the cabin to flood, and then swim out.

Hopefully before I ran out of air.

Like every self-respecting former Ranger, I usually carried a folding knife. My Gerber was equipped with two special features—a crisis hook that could be used to slice through seat belts, and a carbide tip to etch and then shatter glass. Unfortunately, I'd removed the knife from my pocket before entering the detention facility and had left it lying in the truck's cup holder, which was now underwater.

My knife was gone.

Thankfully, there was something else I'd also removed from my person before entering the facility. Something that I'd taken more care in securing. The cloudy water had already risen over the glove box, so I had to locate the latch by feel. I slipped my fingers under the plastic and tried to spring the mechanism

No joy.

I pressed harder, thinking that the water might be gumming up the hinges.

Still nothing.

Which was when I remembered that I'd locked the glove box.

For the love of God.

The truck had a push-button ignition, so the keys were in my front pocket. Still, getting to them was easier said than done. I squirmed against the slick seats as I dug into my jeans. Finally, I gave up trying to keep my head above water. Taking a deep breath, I submerged, untangled my legs, and ferreted out the key. The tight denim resisted me at every turn, threatening to tear the key fob from my grasp. Once again, the lessons from dunker training saved the day. I kept my motions slow and deliberate, fighting the urge to panic.

Then the key was free.

I pushed off the seat, rocketing my head above water to breathe. Only a couple inches of air remained. If this didn't work, there would be no second chances. After two quick inhalations, I ducked beneath the water and fit the key to the glove box.

I twisted.

The lock wouldn't turn.

Damn it to hell.

I resisted the impulse to twist harder, knowing that if I broke off the key or jammed the lock, I was done. Instead of acting, I thought. The lock was upside down. I was trying to force the key the wrong way. My first sergeant liked to say that Rangers came in two varieties—smart or strong. I'd always considered myself one of the former.

Maybe I'd been incorrect.

I turned the key the opposite direction, and the lock disengaged. Leaving the key lodged in the lock, I slipped my fingers under the latch and triggered it.

Nothing.

I wasn't having it.

Grabbing hold of the plastic indentation with both hands, I wrenched up while channeling my anger and frustration. The cheap plastic clip broke away with a *pop* that was audible even underwater, but the glove box swung open.

Smart Ranger, my ass.

I plunged my hand into the glove box, and my fingers closed around a worn, pebbled plastic grip. Pushing off the seat once again, I burst out of the water into the shrinking pocket of air, my Glock 23 in hand. I took a quick breath, dumped the water out of the Glock's barrel, aimed at the passenger window, and started squeezing the trigger. The gun's report was painfully loud in the confined space, but I kept firing as if my life depended on it.

Because it did.

The first shot cratered the window, but didn't quite break it. The third or fourth did the trick. A column of water jetted through the window, blasting me with shattered glass. I'd had sense enough to close my eyes when I realized what was coming, but I couldn't do anything to protect my face as the window shards scored my skin. Though everything within me wanted to fight the current, I forced myself to remain still, conserving oxygen as a torrent of water turned the cabin into a makeshift toilet bowl. Until the cabin completely flooded, trying to swim out would be like battling a riptide.

After what seemed like an eternity, the invisible fists ceased pummeling my body. I opened my eyes and took stock. The window was shattered, but still largely in place, thanks to the safety glass. The hole I'd created was about the size of a baseball with plenty of jagged edges. Feeling my way down the door, I found the door handle and tried to swing it open.

Nothing.

Either the door was stuck, or the water was still holding it closed. It didn't matter which. I was running out of air, and the time for creative problem-solving was over. Flipping over, I planted my feet on the glass and kicked. The heels of my Luccheses slid across the glass without accomplishing much of anything.

The heels of my full quill ostrich Luccheses.

Assuming I lived through this, Laila was going to kill me.

Wedging my hands against the ceiling, I compressed my legs and then pistoned both heels into the glass.

The window shuddered, but held its ground.

As my lungs began to quiver, I wedged myself into place once more. Then I exploded upward, driving with my heels like I was deadlifting a refrigerator. This time the glass gave way. I followed the window out of the truck, fingers tented in front of my face. I didn't have time to clear the jagged pieces from the sill.

My vision was already beginning to tunnel.

I burst out of the truck and then took a moment to exhale, remembering yet another life lesson from the dunker—when in doubt, follow the bubbles. I saw my last bit of air heading upward in a string of silver pearls and followed. Three strokes later I broke the surface and gasped. I spent several seconds coughing up half a lung, but the pollen-laden air had never tasted so sweet. I treaded water as I restocked my oxygen supply, scanning the drop-off for bad guys.

It wasn't lost on me that swimming would be a whole lot easier without my boots, but that wasn't going to happen. My truck had survived Washington, DC, traffic and a gunfight on South Congress Street. Now it was at the bottom of a river. There was no way in hell my favorite boots were joining it.

After confirming that the woods were clear of people who wished me ill, I started a slow stroke toward the shore. Ten minutes later I dragged myself from the water. My truck, phone, and Glock were gone. I was bruised, battered, and shivering, but still alive.

Someone was about to learn that this was a lethal combination.

FOURTEEN

Qari stared at three bearded faces sitting on the floor across from him and wondered which was the traitor. That one of his comrades had betrayed him was not in doubt. Qari's arrest and imprisonment ten years earlier had not been a matter of happenstance. Though he now accepted that Allah had willed his capture in order to mold Qari into the servant he needed to become, this did not absolve the guilty party of their treachery. As Qari's former jailer had learned, sins could only be forgiven after the sinner atoned for their misdeeds.

And the wages of sin was death.

"You're looking well, brother," Ikram said in between puffs from his *shisha* water pipe.

The scrawny man never traveled with fewer than three of his ornate multistemmed hookah pipes and a supply of flavored hashish. Though the Taliban officially frowned on the use of drugs, as a member of the governing council, Ikram was immune to such edicts. Besides, he was responsible for overseeing Afghanistan's opium trade—a subject of much infighting in the council.

Hard-liners like Qari had pushed for banning the production of poppy, while Ikram had advocated for using the profits from the sale of illicit drugs to finance a government that had very little else in the way of exports. This argument had been decided in Qari's favor ten years ago. Once Qari had been imprisoned, Ikram swayed the council back to his way of thinking.

Qari didn't believe the timing of these two events was a coincidence.

"The credit goes to Allah the merciful," Qari said, knowing that he looked anything but well.

Though his garb was now laundered and the persistent smells of urine and body odor removed, Qari had refused the fresh *perahan tunban* his escorts had offered. The stains on his clothes were a badge of honor. Let his fellow commanders see the discolorations wrought from his own blood and the threadbare sections on his knees worn smooth from hours of praying. Qari had still been waging jihad even from prison.

As his companions were about to learn.

"All praise to Allah for bringing you back to us," Ikram said.

This sentiment was also one that Qari doubted. Though the four men had endured much together, they were not exactly friendly. The Taliban was an amorphous organization. To the outside world, the organizational chart that delineated the roles and responsibility of the bearded warrior scholars might seem straightforward, but the truth was far different. Though the Taliban leadership was united in the fight against Afghanistan's infidel invaders and the puppet government in Kabul, a myriad of fault lines existed just below the council's surface.

Case in point, only four faces remained where there had once been six. Attrition of the ruling class was to be expected during times of war, especially with an enemy as ferocious as the Americans. Even so, Qari couldn't help but think that perhaps he hadn't been the only victim of betrayal.

"Allah is merciful," Qari allowed, "as my presence proves. But he also expects justice."

Qari's intent had been to let the comment hang in the air, perhaps stirring the waters of worry in one of his comrades. But Ikram chose that moment to inhale deeply from his pipe. The sound of gurgling water ruined the effect Qari had been trying to achieve. Was the gesture intentional? Probably not. Then again, Ikram's *karakul* hat and *chapan* coat were of a quality somewhat at odds with his image of a man waging jihad while on the run.

"And he's delivering it," Kalan said.

The rotund man ignored the mouthpiece attached to the snaking hose connecting to the water pipe, which had been placed within easy reach. Hashish was not Kalan's vice. Instead, Kalan snared a square of *Sheer Pira* from the multitude of plates before the men. "We've captured Kabul and the Americans are fleeing with their tails tucked between their legs. Victory is upon us."

The other men made sounds of agreement even as they satisfied their carnal needs. For skinny Ikram, it was hashish; for fat Kalan, food; and for wrinkled, hairless Latif, a pair of boys waiting in the next room. Ignoring his rising temper, Qari tried to look at things from his comrades' perspective. A celebration was in order. Just as their mujahideen forebearers had routed the Soviets a generation earlier, Afghanistan's holy warriors had once again turned back the invading infidels.

And once again Afghanistan would flounder when there was no enemy left to fight. This was what Qari had believed ten years ago, and he held to this notion even more firmly now. Parwan Detention Facility had burned away everything extraneous. What remained was pure and singularly focused, like a tempered blade.

"Yes," Qari said. "Allah has delivered the infidels into our hands. Now what?"

His question jolted the men in a way in which his earlier insinuations had not. Ikram stopped with the pipe midway to his lips while Kalan abandoned the date he'd been about to devour. Even Latif stopped licking his cracked and bleeding lips in anticipation of the pleasure that was to come.

"What do you mean?" Ikram said.

"Ten years in prison gives a man time to think," Qari said, "to reflect. This is the second time Allah has given us victory over the unbelievers. We must not squander his holy gift again."

The Taliban council had been down this path before. Many times before. Prior to his capture, Qari had labored for months gathering support for an exploratory meeting with a potential partner who was crucial to Qari's vision for Afghanistan's future. The same meeting during which Americans dropped from helicopters to capture him. Two of the council members who'd supported his plan had also vanished in the ensuing years.

Perhaps prison had been beneficial in more ways than one.

"We have been through this," Kalan said, balancing a plate of *Gosh-e Fil* on his ample belly. "Ikram believes that our thriving opium trade will finance our endeavors until the rest of the world accepts the inevitability of our rule. You do not. Ten years ago, you presented the council with a viable alternative. That alternative no longer exists."

"That's where you're wrong, brother," Qari said.

This time no one interrupted the ensuing silence.

Though he'd never been fond of hashish, Qari took a pull from his pipe. Until he could identify the traitor, he intended to cultivate each of these men as allies.

Just as he'd done with his jailer.

"After giving praise to Allah for my freedom, the first thing I did was to place a call," Qari said. "A call to our potential partner."

"Surely their offer has expired," Ikram said, the pipe resting between two nicotine-stained fingers.

"It certainly has," Qari said. "Our proposed price was far too generous ten years ago. The world has changed. Today, our partner is hungrier for what we have to offer than ever before. I quoted him a price that was double the old."

Now Qari had the room's undivided attention. The first deal had been for three billion dollars. Six billion would go a long way toward financing a council that for all its claims of Islamic piety had no intention of subsisting on prayers alone.

But the best was still to come.

"Six billion dollars is substantial," Latif said, rubbing his hands together. "We could do much with that sum."

"Six is just the down payment," Qari said, dusting off his fingers before selecting a pastry. "Our partner would be expected to contribute a yearly percentage of production. I set the minimum payment at two billion."

"Impossible," Kalan said, powdered sugar falling from his quivering lips. "They would never agree to this."

"They already have," Qari said. "Our new partners are arriving in-country as we speak to finalize the arrangement."

"How?" Ikram said. "How have you managed this?"

"I am in possession of something they want," Qari said, "something even more valuable than our nation's vast natural resources. Is there more of this?" Qari pointed at the *Gosh-e Fil*.

"Forget the food," Kalan said. "What have you discovered?"

"A way to identify each and every enemy," Qari said with a smile, "both American and Afghan. The traitors who fought against us will not be able to scurry away while we consolidate power."

"And the Americans?" Latif said.

Qari smiled. "We will be able to identify every American who set foot in this country. This is what brought our foreign partners back to the negotiating table."

Ikram, Kalan, and Latif stared at him in wonder. Qari eyed each man in turn, wondering if he'd been naïve before. Perhaps there wasn't one traitor in the room.

Maybe there were three.

"Is such a thing possible?" Ikram said, his voice a whisper.

"We will know by this time tomorrow," Qari said. "Now, who would like more *Sheer Pira*?"

This time, everyone reached for the plate.

FIFTEEN

Turns out that locating a pair of Army CID agents isn't as hard as you might think. Especially if you've worked for a federal bureaucracy, have experience tracking people who don't want to be found, and are spoiling for a fight. Okay, so that last quality isn't a hard-and-fast requirement, but I've found that a little aggression can go a long way toward righting the world's wrongs.

Right about now I had plenty to choose from.

I eyed the establishment in front of me, considering how I wanted to play this. Correction—how I *should* play this. Aggression was great at getting the blood pumping, but battle lust always needed to be tempered. As much as I hated to admit it, sometimes the situation called for a subtle approach.

"You coming or going?"

But not tonight.

The old man asking the question was standing by a meat smoker the size of my kitchen, about to feed a log into the gaping firebox. He was African American and in his late seventies or early eighties. His hair was mostly gray fuzz, and his face was a web of wrinkles. But the hand holding a knobby length of mesquite looked sturdy enough.

He eyed me with the look of someone who knew trouble when he saw it.

He was right.

While I was no longer dripping river water and covered in mud, neither did I look like I belonged at the present establishment. After climbing up the river's steep embankment, I'd managed to flag down the driver of a beat-up pickup truck. That he'd stopped at all was a testament to the good folks who called Texas home.

Or the Colt 1911 he'd been wearing open-carry style in a leather holster on his waist.

In any case, the driver had given me a lift into town absent too many questions. From there, I'd used the credit card in my waterlogged money clip to procure a burner phone at a truck stop, logged into my Lyft account, and ordered transportation. While waiting for my ride, I'd made liberal use of the hand dryer and paper towels in the men's room and planned my next move.

Though *next move* lent a far-too-sanitary connotation to what I was planning. While there'd been no one waiting for me at the top of the embankment, I'd still found evidence confirming what I'd suspected. The driving rain had washed away any trace of what had been stretched across the dark pavement, but the road's shoulder provided me with a much-needed clue.

After walking along the brush opposite the direction I'd been traveling, I'd found a flurry of footprints sunken into the mud along with a serpentine impression. The footprints centered around a narrow length of steel that had been driven into the ground.

The anchor point for whatever had blown out my tires.

The six-inch-long rod was about the diameter of my thumb—the perfect size to shove in my pants pocket. The bulge wasn't nearly as comforting as the Glock still sitting somewhere in my flooded cab, but it would do.

"No loitering," the old man said. "Either getcha inside or move along."

His establishment was single story, windowless, and crafted from river rock. The entrance consisted of rusted steel mesh that hung slightly askew from its frame. The mesh protected a second door, also steel, by the look. Paint peeled from the door in long strips, exposing a pitted surface stained by the elements and who knew what else. The hand-painted sign above the door read **Bubba's BBQ and Beer**. This late at night, I figured Bubba was probably selling more beer than barbecue. But unless you counted the fast-food joint at the truck stop, it was the only restaurant in the one-stoplight town.

So that's where I'd headed.

Bubba's place was also within walking distance of the sad-looking hotel across the street. A hotel that offered the government lodging rate and was within the allotted travel mileage to the detention facility. Like I said, tracking a pair of CID agents wasn't too difficult if you understood the games their federal bureaucracy forced them to play.

I'd already been by the hotel to conduct a recon of the parking lot. Besides a couple of trucks that had been in their prime two presidential administrations ago, I identified two likely candidates—a pair of four-door sedans that were of American make. A federal employee's work car had to be American made. If it hadn't been almost midnight, I could have used some DIA IT support staff to confirm the registrations associated with the cars' license plates to further narrow down the culprits. But that was fine. I was after the CID agents themselves, not their car.

Which lead me to Bubba's.

"You Bubba?" I said to the old man.

"Might be."

I walked over to the neatly stacked pile of wood adjacent to the smoker and grabbed an armload. "I'm looking for some friends," I said as I replenished the man's wood supply. "I was hoping you could tell me if they're inside."

"Call 'em," Bubba said.

He added his log to the firebox and shoved the coals around with an iron poker. Then he turned to face me, thick fingers still gripping the fire tool.

"I wanted to surprise them," I said, feeding a chunk of mesquite to the flames.

"You a cop?" Bubba said.

"No, sir. More of a concerned citizen."

Bubba snorted, but he nodded toward the firebox. "Hickory."

I selected a length of hickory and placed the log into the firebox.

"Too much mesquite makes the meat taste bitter," I said. "I like to balance the flavor with fruitwood."

"You know BBQ?" Bubba said.

"A little," I said.

Bubba speared the coals with the poker, arranging the fresh wood with deft, quick movements.

"Your friends," Bubba said, turning back to me, "they a beefy white dude and a Hispanic girl?"

I nodded.

"They come in about thirty minutes ago. Sitting in the corner. By the bathroom."

Which is exactly the booth I would have taken.

"Thank you," I said. "Is there an entrance behind the building?"

Bubba gave a slow nod.

"Unlocked?"

Another nod.

"Is the kitchen back there?" I said.

"Yep."

"Thanks," I said.

"I don't want no trouble."

"Me neither," I said, "but sometimes trouble still finds us."

"Any rough stuff and I'm calling the cops," Bubba said.

"I just want to talk," I said, "nothing more."

Which was true.

Unless of course the two agents who'd arrested Frodo tried to kill me.

In that case, I'd start with rough stuff and go from there.

"You don't look like much of a talking man," Bubba said.

I answered with a wink.

SIXTEEN

Believe it or not, the rear of Bubba's establishment wasn't a huge improvement on the front. A steel structure held a large dumpster while a second shed was stocked with wood. A spare smoker sat nearby, a metal monstrosity that looked capable of cooking an entire elephant with room to spare.

As promised, the bar's back door was unlocked.

I edged it open and slipped inside.

Blaring music washed over me as I paused, allowing my eyes to adjust to the semidarkness. I was standing in a narrow hallway with a single bathroom to my left and a swinging door leading to the kitchen to my right. A waitress hurried from the dining room, holding a tray piled high with dirty dishes. She slowed as she saw me, and I pressed my back against the wall and motioned her past me. She smiled, and I snagged a half-full glass as she went by.

"Wasn't quite done with this one," I said.

"I can get you a clean one, sugar," she said.

"No need," I said with a smile. "This will do just fine."

"Suit yourself."

The waitress pushed into the kitchen, calling out an order as she entered.

I waited for the door to swing shut before meandering down the hallway, careful not to spill what remained in the glass. The sudsy liquid was probably a Shiner, and I had mixed feelings about what was going to happen to the remnants.

A Texas beer deserved better.

While I was certain that the two CID agents knew more than they were letting on, I was not as sure that they were responsible for sending me into the river. This was why I was approaching them in a public place instead of visiting them in a more intimate environment.

Like their hotel rooms.

I edged up to the corner of the hallway and found my favorite couple sitting in the exact booth Bubba had described. The meathead male agent, Fred, had his back to the wall. His Hispanic partner, Julie, was positioned across from him.

Good.

I wasn't crazy about hitting girls. Call me old-fashioned, but it's the truth. Popping Fred, on the other hand, was going to be downright enjoyable. Both agents had the remains of a meal in front of them, and judging by the empties, Fred was on at least his second beer. A bottle of Topo Chico sat in front of Julie, meaning that her reactions would be considerably faster than her partner's.

Noted.

Julie's eyes flicked from her partner to me as I strode

out of the darkness; they widened as she recognized me. Perfect. I chucked the contents of the beer glass at her even as I mentally apologized to the fine men and women of Shiner, Texas. The beer burned as beer does, and Julie's hands instinctively went to her face.

Not the pistol holstered at her waist.

Fred was turning toward me as I slid into the booth next to him. I rewarded his curiosity with an elbow strike to the temple. Not a full-on blow meant to drive the thin bone into his skull, just a little something to get his attention. His head bounced off the wall, which gave me more than enough time to strip his pistol from his waist holster and shove it into his ribs.

"I wouldn't," I said as Julie's manicured fingernails moved toward her gun. "Nothing but a little pride has been hurt so far. Whether that remains true is up to you."

I shoved the pistol deeper into Fred's side, eliciting a grunt from him and a look of comprehension from his partner.

"What do you want?" Julie said.

"Hands on the table. Now. Then we talk."

Julie stared at me, her dark eyes calculating.

"Seriously," I said. "Don't. I'm assuming your boss also gave you a copy of my file, right?"

"A summary," Julie said.

"What did it say?" I said.

"That you were . . . capable."

"I am," I said. "Very. The kind of capable that doesn't kill people in a crowded bar. I'm here to talk."

By now Fred had recovered enough of his wits to realize he'd been outsmarted. Embarrassment quickly followed on the heels of this realization. In my experience, men with tree trunks for necks don't handle embarrassment well.

Fred was no exception.

He made a grab for his pistol.

That was a mistake.

I headbutted him in the face. Not Jack Reacher hard, but with more than enough force to set his eyes to watering and ring his bell. Then I edged out of reach while keeping the pistol leveled at his rib cage.

"Now that we've got the nonsense out of the way, you ready to talk?" I said.

I directed the question to Julie.

She nodded.

"Good," I said. "Tell old Fred here to stand down. He'll get his pistol back once we're through."

Fred opened his mouth, undoubtedly to say something unwise, but Julie intervened.

"Give it a rest, Fred," Julie said. "He's not going to kill us here. Get it?"

Fred slowly nodded, both hands pressed to his nose. He didn't speak, but the gaze he leveled at me wasn't exactly rainbows and unicorns. Whatever. As my Ranger Regiment first sergeant used to say, if you're gonna be stupid, you'd better be tough.

"Fantastic," I said. "First question—why did you try to kill me?"

I've spent almost ten years as a handler—espionage speak for someone who persuades other people to betray their countries or ideologies for a living. I run and recruit spies. One does not succeed in this endeavor without be-coming a good judge of character. It wasn't that I consid-ered myself a human polygraph machine—my FBI brethren don't call us professional liars for nothing—but I'm pretty good at deciphering reactions. Especially reactions to the unexpected. Julie might have thought I'd say a number of things, but my accusation had caught her flat-footed.

Her confused expression was genuine.

"What are you talking about?" Julie said.

"The spike strip on the eastbound lane of Route 377. Great placement by the way. I came out of the turn blind, and all four tires popped. Before I could blink, I was over the embankment and into the river."

For the first time Julie seemed to notice the discolor-ations on my face and the crusted scab on my lip. Her eyes widened as she took in my still-damp clothes.

"You crashed into the river?" Julie said.

"My truck's still at the bottom," I said. "Want to tell me why?"

"I don't know," Julie said, "or at least not in the way you think."

Progress.

"Explain," I said.

"Julie," Fred said, "don't."

"This is still an adults-only conversation," I said.

"Sit still and keep your mouth shut," Julie said.

I'm not sure who Fred responded to, but he clamped his lips together. I considered that a win. Even so, the murderous look on his face suggested that even if he wasn't responsible for the spike strip, he was taking notes for next time.

Get in line, jack wagon.

"The arrest tasking came from headquarters," Julie said. "We're stationed at Fort Hood, so we caught the lead. It was supposed to be a simple arrest, nothing more."

"But?" I said.

"But I did my due diligence before driving down to Austin. Or at least I tried to. The case file was restricted."

This was starting to sound all too familiar.

"Is that normal?" I said.

"Yes and no," Julie said with a shrug. "It's certainly not unusual for a case file to be restricted. We have the same security concerns as other federal investigative agencies. The odd part was that it was restricted from me."

"You personally or you as an investigator?" I said.

"The latter. Even if it's only temporary, an investigator is always granted access to the case file so that you can familiarize yourself with the case before making an arrest. This is done both from an officer-safety standpoint as well as to prepare the investigator in case the subject says something germane during the arrest."

I wasn't a cop, but what Julie said was logical. Arresting an unfamiliar subject could be dangerous business. It made sense to me that you'd want to know whether the person you were taking into custody was a violent offender or had the potential to become one.

"You tried to review that case file and couldn't," I said. "Then what?"

"At first I thought it was a mistake," Julie said, "so I called headquarters for clarification. That's when I got word that we weren't permitted to view the case file's contents."

"What did you think about that?" I said.

"That it was bullshit," Julie said. "I've been doing this a long time. I've investigated and made arrests for every violation from child pornography to espionage. I've never been restricted from the originating case file. I called in a couple of favors to see what I could learn. I still hit a brick wall, but a friend forwarded me a redacted summary."

"And that was enough to give you pause?" I said.

Julie nodded.

"The redacted summary didn't provide much more than Frodo's arrest warrant," Julie said, "but it did mention another lead."

"Another arrest warrant?" I said.

Julie shook her head. "No, this lead instructed a team stationed at Fort Bragg to conduct an interview of a person of interest."

"Who?" I said.

"Fletcher Spies."

The name didn't mean anything to me.

"Why's he important?" I said.

"Because he's dead."

SEVENTEEN

"Dead how?" I said.

"Car accident," Julie said. "I ran his name through Google and came up with an obituary from a local newspaper. Nothing specific. Just that his death had been the result of a single-vehicle crash."

"Got a picture of Mr. Spies?"

Julie passed her cell across the table. I'm pretty good with faces. You have to be in my line of work. The balding middle-aged man looked familiar, but I couldn't place him. I swiped past the image to the article, thumbing through to see if they had any more pics of him.

They did.

This one was from eight years ago and showed Spies in uniform. The middle-aged chubbiness in his cheeks was gone, replaced by an operator beard and the shaggy hair to match. Now my spider senses were really tingling, but I still couldn't put a name to the face. I looked at the flash on his beret—3rd Special Forces Group.

Son of a bitch.

The same Special Forces Group Frodo and I had briefly embedded with in Afghanistan. I stared at the face again, racking my brain. Was he on Jason's ODA? I still wasn't sure. There were four battalions in 3rd SFG and each battalion had twenty or more ODAs. Just because Fletcher and Jason had served in the same Special Forces Group didn't mean they'd been on the same ODA.

"Do you know which ODA Spies was assigned to?" I said.

Julie shook her head. "We don't have any information on his military service beyond this photograph."

I filed that information away with a mental note to investigate a possible link between Jason and Fletcher.

"Did Fletcher die before the CID team got to him?" I said.

"Yes," Julie said, "about a week prior. All the arrests were to occur last week."

"Then why wasn't Frodo arrested last week?" I said.

"He was supposed to have been," Julie said. "The original lead went to the Washington, DC, office, but they couldn't locate Frodo."

"Because he was here," I said.

Julie nodded.

"A CID analyst did a manifest search and hit on his plane ticket to Austin. That's when we caught the lead."

I didn't bother asking how Julie and her partner had found us in the Twilight Wrangler. Julie seemed competent, and finding people who didn't want to be found was bread and butter for a federal investigator. Besides, it wasn't like we were trying to mask our digital footprints. Laila and I had been planning for Katherine and Frodo's Austin visit for a month. If a pair of investigators with the full resources of the federal government couldn't locate a single man on vacation, we were in trouble.

"Did you see any other names in the redacted summary?" I said. "Subjects, people of interest, anything?"

"No," Julie said. "The only other name I saw was . . ."

"Mine," I said, finishing her statement.

Julie nodded.

"Am I a subject or person of interest?"

Julie shook her head.

"You're mentioned as Frodo's close associate and that we should effect the arrest without you present if possible. You're characterized as . . . unpredictable."

Based on the way Julie had struggled for the word *unpredictable*, I had a feeling that the case file's characterization of me had been a whole lot less charitable. They were right. When it came to defending the ones I loved, I was a honey badger. The more people both inside and outside our government who knew this, the better. But honey badger or not, Frodo was still sitting in jail, and I was no closer to understanding why.

"Okay," I said, getting to my feet. "Thanks for your help."

"Wait. That's it?" Julie said.

"For now," I said. "My best friend is still in prison, and you two put him there."

"We were just doing our jobs," Fred said.

"I know," I said. "That's why we're having a pleasant conversation instead of something else. Look, if you haven't done so already, read Frodo's service record. Even the parts that aren't redacted should tell you that you've got the wrong guy. He was awarded a Silver Star. He's not a murderer."

"I already read it," Julie said, "but it doesn't matter what I think. We're not the case agents. We just caught the arrest. There's nothing I can do."

"Actually, there is," I said. "I need time. Time to figure out what's really going on. You and I both know that once he disappears into the military justice system, he's gone. It wouldn't be the worst thing in the world if car trouble or maybe even a bad hangover kept you from transporting him to Bragg tomorrow."

"No way," Fred said. "We've got—"

Julie silenced her partner with an upraised hand.

"Let's say we got you some time," Julie said. "A day or two maybe. What would you do with it?"

"What I do best," I said. "Hunt down the bad guys."

I placed Fred's pistol on the bench and exited the bar the same way I'd come in—the back door. I could feel Julie's eyes tracking me as I left. She hadn't said yes to my proposal, but neither had she said no.

I could work with that.

EIGHTEEN

Can you turn that up, please?"

My Lyft driver dutifully complied, spinning the volume dial on the radio. I had a feeling most of his nighttime fares didn't involve a sober man who appreciated listening to twenty-four-hour satellite news. Then again, my clothes still stunk of river water, so I probably wasn't in the running for perfect passenger either.

"Things in Afghanistan have taken an ominous turn," the announcer said, doing an admirable job of stating the obvious. "Taliban formations have now completely encircled Kabul. The US embassy staff is evacuating."

I closed my eyes as the words hammered into me, surprised at the almost physical pain they provoked. My father had been too young for Vietnam, so while the iconic shot of the last Huey departing from the embassy made me feel disgusted as an American, I'd never had a personal connection to the tragedy.

Until now.

"Did you serve?"

I opened my eyes to see my driver staring at me from the rearview mirror. Normally this was a question I dodged. I prepared to answer with my standard denial, but hesitated. This was a guy I didn't know and would probably never see again. From an operational security standpoint, the risks inherent with telling him the truth were minimal. Besides, I had a feeling I knew why he was asking.

"Yeah," I said. "You?"

The driver nodded.

"Who with?" I said.

"The 82nd. One tour in Iraq. One in Afghanistan."

"When were you in Afghanistan?" I said.

"2007."

I nodded.

"What about you?" he said.

"The Ranger Regiment in Afghanistan," I said. "Twice."

"No shit?" he said. "My squad leader went to Regiment after we got back from Afghanistan. Mike Vohl. Know him?"

The Ranger Regiment was a small community, but it still consisted of three battalions stationed at three separate Army posts. The odds that I'd know the driver's friend were minuscule. But somehow I still did.

"Of course I know Mike," I said. "Hardest-working platoon sergeant I ever had. Great Ranger."

The driver smiled when I answered, but then his grin faded as he asked the question I'd been dreading.

"Were you there when he . . ."

"Yeah," I said, staring out the window into the darkness. "Hell of a thing. His platoon had been on more hits than I could count. They were absolutely slaying the

Taliban, but somehow Mike still brought every Ranger home after each mission. The final Op before our redeployment was more of a right-seat ride between us and the 2nd Batt guys who were replacing us. Mike wasn't even supposed to be on the objective. But when the ambush happened, he ran toward the sound of the guns, just like always."

The ensuing silence stretched as the announcer droned on. I lost myself in the night as I relived the ramp ceremony. Sixty Rangers standing at the position of attention in the pouring rain as we loaded Mike's flag-draped coffin onto a C-17 for the long flight home. Four more days and Mike would have been kissing his pregnant wife and holding his toddler son at the welcome-home ceremony in Savannah.

Four.

More.

Days.

Fuck me.

"You were an officer?"

"Yep," I said. "Mike's company commander."

"Tell me something, then," the Lyft driver said, his eyes burning into mine. "Was it worth it?"

Until recently, my answer would have come reflexively. Of course it was. It had to be. We'd dumped too much blood and treasure for too many years into Afghanistan for it not to be worth it. Truthfully, I'd never really entertained the alternative. Now it was slapping me in the face. Looking back at my driver, I answered the only way I could.

"I don't know anymore."

NINETEEN

The vast majority of people who fly into Austin do so via Austin–Bergstrom International Airport. As airports go, it's pretty good. The facility gives visitors a decent preview of their coming experience in the home of the weird. Breakfast tacos abound, food trucks sell Austin's famous coffee, and a live-music venue showcases local musicians. The bars carry Austin beer and the stores are full of Austin knickknacks.

I think it does my home city proud.

But Austin–Bergstrom isn't the only airport in town.

Drive about thirty minutes north and you'll find a second airfield. Aptly named Austin Executive Airport, this facility is geared toward the crowd that doesn't fly commercial. Its one hundred thirty thousand square feet of hangar space caters to the kinds of private jets and turboprop airplanes that star in music videos. The clean, modern facility does bustling business transporting the collection of tech giants, start-up mavens, investment fund gurus, rock stars, and A-list actors who call Texas's once sleepy capital home. While I did not fall into any of the aforementioned categories, my Lyft driver still dropped me off at a discrete hangar set apart from the glitter and glam that made up the Henriksen Jet Center.

"You sure this is the right place?" my driver said.

"Positive," I answered.

His skepticism was certainly justified. While the metal structure appeared sound, nothing about it was particularly inviting. No signs adorned the siding and no windows looked out onto the starry Austin night. The exterior was rust free, but painted a drab gray. Other than a single security camera, partially hidden by a fake ventilation duct, there was nothing to suggest that the building was anything more than what it appeared to be—a private hangar available for rental.

Which was exactly the point.

I opened the door, but paused before I climbed out.

"Hey," I said. "What's your name?"

"Josh. Josh Hood."

"Do you have someone to talk to, Josh?"

"My wife loves to talk," Josh said with a chuckle. "I'm usually looking for some quiet."

"I'm serious," I said. "I've lost too many good friends to bullets and bombs. I don't want to lose any more to ghosts and regrets."

Josh's smile faded.

"Yeah, man," Josh said. "I'm all good."

"Maybe that's true and maybe it isn't," I said, "but if Afghanistan goes the way I think it will, you're not going to be all good for much longer. This is my number—call me."

I scribbled down my cell onto a scrap of paper and passed it to him.

"Thanks," Josh said. "You really think it's all about to go down the shitter?"

"Yes," I said, holding his gaze.

"Man, I hope not."

Josh squirreled the paper I'd handed him in a pocket.

"When it gets bad, call me," I said.

"Okay, man. Will do."

"I'm serious," I said. "Call me."

"Yes, sir," Josh said.

I shut the door and waved. The sedan's headlights spilled across the hangar, and then Josh was just a pair of taillights fading into the darkness. I watched him go, wondering if I'd ever hear from the Army vet again. I didn't care whether or not he called me. I just wanted him to talk to someone. In 2012, veteran suicides outpaced the Americans killed in action in Afghanistan and Iraq for the first time. The numbers had been going in the wrong direction ever since. If the administration really intended to do nothing as Afghanistan devolved into chaos, suicides would skyrocket.

I shook off the morbid thought.

I couldn't save Afghanistan, but maybe I could do something about the war's veterans. People like Josh.

And Frodo.

Bypassing the sliding aircraft doors, I walked over to the hangar's pedestrian entrance. Like the rest of the structure, it wasn't much to look at. A steel door with a protruding knob in which a slot for a key was centered. I ignored the lock, instead pressing on a metal panel to the door's right. The panel swung open revealing a keypad. I punched in a seven-digit code. A serious-sounding dead bolt at odds with the lock's simple appearance unlatched with an ominous *click*.

I grabbed the handle, pulled open the door, and stepped inside.

Contrary to the hangar's external appearance, the interior was very much occupied. A series of fluorescent lights automatically ignited once the pedestrian door swung closed behind me, revealing two rather pricey toys—a Piper M600 and a Learjet 45XR. Like the hangar itself, both airplanes were functional but painted in dull schemes designed to avoid notice. Both birds also sported a couple of additional bulges on the lower fuselage if you knew where to look.

Bulges that were not exactly factory spec.

In recent years, DIA had begun to pre-position aviation assets in travel hubs across the United States. The airplanes were meant to be used when commercial travel wasn't feasible or because the operational need required the movement of people and assets clandestinely. As such, several cities now boasted these off-the-books air assets. While DIA hadn't yet procured its own air force, à la the CIA's air branch, the Agency was off to a good start. Due to its proximity to several countries of interest in Central and South America, as well as the heavy private jet traffic already associated with the field, Austin Executive Airport had made the list.

Branch Chief James Glass might have had something to do with the decision. My boss loved his newfound power to order me back to Washington at any time of the night or day, airline flight schedules be damned. Be that as it might, I wasn't complaining. The security and anonymity offered by the hangar made the structure a perfect place to store the tools of the trade I wasn't comfortable locking in my spare bedroom. The Batcave it wasn't, but the facility boasted a series of padlocked steel cages for kit, a walk-in weapons and ammunition safe, a secure internet drop, a bathroom, a small sleeping area, and a fully functional kitchen.

Not bad for nonsuperhero standards.

I crossed the hangar, passing between the two birds in favor of the kitchenette and the espresso machine featured prominently on its granite counter. The appliance was all stainless steel and protruding nozzles and looked as if it had been lifted from a fifties-era sci-fi flick. I'd received a crash course on its operation, and while I still couldn't put the multiple dials and buttons to use, I knew how to brew a fairly respectable cup of joe.

After proceeding through a series of steps that could have doubled for a checklist to launch nuclear missiles, I heard the bubbling sound of happiness. Leaving the espresso machine to work its magic, I lifted the handset bolted to the wall and pressed the speed dial button.

After the fourth ring, a sleepy female voice answered.

"Hello?"

"I need a ride."

"Where?"

"Moore County Airport, North Carolina."

"Departure time?"

"As soon as possible."

"Pax?"

"One plus kit."

"Okay," the woman said, already sounding more

awake. "I'm on the way. We should be wheels up in about sixty minutes. If you've got someone waiting on you, let them know ETA will be about five hours, depending on winds."

"Got it," I said. "Thanks."

There was somebody waiting in North Carolina, but they didn't know I was coming.

Yet.

TWENTY

Grabbing the freshly brewed cup of coffee, I headed for the gun safe, punched in the pass code, and opened the door. The shelves were lined with the kinds of toys that made boys like me smile. But as much as my fingers itched to be holding the polymer grip of the replacement Glock 23 I had oiled and ready to go, I grabbed something a little less sexy.

An iPhone.

Powering up the device, I entered the necessary pass code and then triggered an app that would clone the cell to the now deceased smartphone I'd lost in the river. I slurped coffee while the electrons did their thing and then turned my attention to the spare Glock. After doing a quick functions check, I inserted a magazine preloaded with .40-caliber hollow points and chambered a round. The Glock slipped into a spare holster that I slid inside my jeans. The still damp denim made the fit a bit more snug than usual, but that was fine. A swallow of good coffee combined with the comforting feel of a loaded pistol did wonders for my outlook on life.

The iPhone had a seizure, signifying that the imaging

process was complete. Then the cell nearly vibrated off the shelf in response to a string of missed texts. I glanced at the screen and swallowed. My hope that Laila might have gone to bed without me hadn't materialized.

Rather than waste time reading my messages, I just dialed.

She answered on the first ring.

"Matt?"

"Hey, baby," I said, pulling several other interesting items from the safe and stuffing them into a Blackhawk backpack. "I thought you were headed to bed."

"I thought you were coming home. Where are you?"

"Long story," I said, closing the safe. "I'm at the airport. I'm headed out of town."

"Because of Frodo?"

"Yeah," I said.

Dropping the bag on the floor, I opened a locker packed with clothes and inventoried my choices. Fortunately, I'd had the foresight to stock the necessities—underwear, boot socks, jeans, and pearly-snap shirts.

I could work with this.

"Why are there police outside our house?" Laila said.

I sighed.

We'd settled on an arrangement of sorts early on in our marriage. We didn't talk about what I did overseas. This wasn't because I was afraid my wife might accidentally leak operational details. We simply needed to find a way to exist without living in a constant state of worry. Being married to a spy wasn't for the faint of heart. A bad day at my job didn't equal a missed sale or a lost account. When shit went sideways, people died.

Not all of them were bad guys.

This had weighed heavily on Laila at first. More than once, she'd pressed me for details during rare phone calls while I was operational. After a tumultuous first few years, we'd arrived at a truce of sorts. My time overseas was a separate world from the life I had with Laila, and she treated it as such. This arrangement had worked out fine until my overseas life had followed me home. In the aftermath, we were still sorting out how to go forward. Transparency was one of the new rules we'd agreed upon. If my two lives crossed again, I'd promised to tell her. With my truck now doubling as a freshwater reef, I'd say that threshold had been breached.

"I asked the FBI to have Austin PD keep an eye on you," I said. "Someone tried to kill me after I visited Frodo."

"Oh my God, Matt. Are you okay?"

"Yeah," I said, suddenly feeling the cumulative effects of the last several hours. "I'm fine. Did the cops come to the door?"

"No," Laila said, "but Vinster's been acting up."

Maybe that fleabag of a dog wasn't completely worthless after all.

"I don't think you're in danger," I said. "A cruiser will be outside for the next forty-eight hours, but trust your instincts."

"On it," Laila said. "My surrogate husband is on the pillow next to me."

"I thought Vinster was your surrogate husband."

"He's still auditioning for the job. What happened to you?"

"I'm a bit banged up," I said. "But we're gonna have to go truck shopping when I get back."

"Tighty Whitey's a complete loss?"

"The Gray Ghost is at the bottom of a river," I said, ignoring her favorite dig at my ride.

"I love you, Matty, but you're hell on our insurance premiums."

"Insurance doesn't need to know just yet," I said. "Gray Ghost can stay submerged for now. Might be good for whoever's chasing me to think they succeeded."

"You're just a basketful of sunshine and roses. Okay, I'll hole up here for the weekend. Is this connected to Afghanistan?"

"Everything's connected to Afghanistan, but I'm just not sure how. The people who arrested Frodo mentioned an operation he and I were a part of back in 2011."

"Do you know why?" Laila said.

"No. But I know someone who should. The team sergeant we supported is an old friend named Jason Brown. We still keep in touch. He's in North Carolina. I'm gonna pay him a visit."

"They have things called phones, Matthew."

"I tried," I said. "He's not answering."

"Are you worried?" Laila said.

I paused, thinking about my answer. "Not yet," I said. "Jason's retired and lives off the grid. He can handle himself, but I'd be a whole lot happier if he'd answer his phone. I'll know more in a couple of hours."

"Be careful," Laila said.

"Always am. Now, let me talk to my daughter."

Laila's low chuckle sent shivers up my spine.

"You're crazy," Laila said, but I heard the rustle of clothing as she placed the phone over her belly.

"Hey, baby girl," I said. "Daddy loves you. Don't give Mama too much trouble while I'm gone."

I made a kissing sound into the phone that sounded a bit ridiculous, but that was okay. Once I met my little girl face-to-face, I knew I'd be making an even bigger fool of myself.

"Okay, cowboy," Laila said, "unless there's someone else, I'm going to bed."

"I'd give Vinster a pep talk, but that mutt doesn't listen to a word I say."

Another silvery laugh.

"He just loves me better," Laila said.

"We all do."

She was quiet for a moment, and I was content to let the silence stretch. I felt warm inside, just knowing Laila was there.

"Do what you do, Matty," Laila said, "but do it fast. I miss you."

She hung up.

TWENTY-ONE

I finally ran out of things to occupy my mind about an hour east of Austin. True to her word, the pilot had rolled into the hangar fully caffeinated and ready to rock and roll.

Literally.

Pilots are strange folks, none more so than former Army helicopter pilots. Even by those standards, the woman who came strolling through the hangar door was a doozy. She was late twenties or earlier thirties, and her blond-on-the-top-layer-and-black-beneath hair was short and spiky. She was wearing a vintage formfitting Nirvana T-shirt, black jeans rolled up over an equally black pair of Doc Martens, and black nail polish. She was already tall for a woman, probably five six or so, and the boots added an extra two inches to her height.

She could have been an audience member at an *Austin City Limits* taping.

Or a former military pilot.

She'd smiled at my reaction to her appearance, show-casing a pair of adorable dimples. She'd introduced herself as Dee Moss, call sign Bone, and informed me that she was ready for anything.

I believed her.

Together, we'd wrangled the Piper out of the hangar. Dee had preflighted while I'd stowed gear and worked some time and distance math. The M600 was a single-engine turboprop that sat four or so. It was a pretty sweet ride as smaller planes went, but nowhere near as luxurious or quick as the hangar's other resident. The Learjet was on the small side for private jets, but it was fast and had decent legs. Unfortunately, it also required two pilots and sucked down a crap ton of jet fuel.

Expensive jet fuel.

James was a pretty reasonable fellow when it came to operational expenses. I'd once dropped enough on designer women's clothing to outfit a small Iraqi militia, and he hadn't batted an eye.

Okay, that wasn't quite true.

James, along with everyone else of the male persuasion, had taken a long look at the Israeli Mossad officer I'd outfitted with my purchases, but he hadn't complained about her wardrobe's cost. She'd been dressed to catch the eye of the Chinese version of Bill Gates so that a DIA intelligence officer could take a run at recruiting him.

On the other hand, James did not tolerate boondoggles.

If spending the government's cash equated to putting bad guys out of business, my boss would beg, borrow, or steal to get the required funds. But if he thought that the

Benjamins were being wasted, Chief would come down on the offender like the wrath of God. Unlike most of our politicians, James understood that green paper did not exist in an endless supply. If his officers were blowing it on five-star hotels, some grunt in a forgotten part of the world might be equipped with one less magazine of 5.56 rounds.

That would not do.

This was why I was nestled in the Piper's passenger compartment behind Dee as we bounced through the predawn sky. While I didn't share my boss's certainty that every dollar we spent meant a dollar less for the folks actively prosecuting the Global War on Terror, I did subscribe to the belief that our nation's assets were finite. But more than that, I still didn't know whether what I was doing had an operational nexus. Frodo had been arrested for murder, someone had tried to kill me, and the same someone might or might not have already succeeded in killing a Green Beret named Fletcher Spies. A Green Beret who had served in 3rd SFG.

Just like Jason.

Coincidence?

I didn't think so.

In a break with what many of his comrades in arms did after hanging up their rifles, Jason had not disappeared into a three-letter agency or joined one of the many military contractors located just outside Fort Bragg's Fayetteville gate after his retirement. Jason had decided that he was done with government service altogether. He and his wife had purchased twenty acres of pine forest about an hour west of the greater Fort Bragg area. With a grit that would have done his pioneer ancestors proud, Jason had set about clearing five of those acres for a house and farm.

A goat farm to be precise.

Yep.

Master Sergeant Jason Brown, onetime Ranger and Green Beret, now raised goats and sold soap and milk. I knew this because he proudly kept me updated on the farm's progress with yearly Christmas cards. I'd grown up on a ranch outside of Salt Lake City, and the thought of spending my retirement years surrounded by herd animals set me to twitching. When I'd asked him about his choice of livestock, Jason had said that since his wife had spent her formative years on a pig farm, goats were a step up. Whatever. He'd stood on the wall for his nation. Jason had certainly earned the right to become a reclusive farmer.

In fact, Jason had purposely fallen off the map. He'd installed windmills and solar panels to generate power, pumped water from a well drilled on his property, used satellite internet, and paid for an off-brand phone service. I wouldn't have considered Jason a prepper because the word had a bad connotation. The stereotype denoted people who were convinced they'd have to fight off a Russian invasion, their own overreaching government, or perhaps both.

Jason didn't fall into these categories.

Preppers also tended to overvalue their own significance to their real or imagined enemies. Jason's concern for privacy was based on actual, not imagined, scenarios. By the time he'd retired, Jason had easily spent more time abroad than he had at home. As a Ranger, he'd been one of the faceless-nameless assaulters who'd visited death and destruction on his country's enemies.

But his tours as a Green Beret had been different.

ODAs lived and trained with the Afghans they fought alongside. Jason knew villagers' names, history, and families. He'd understood their enemy at a visceral level. More than once, Jason had ended an Afghanistan deployment with a Taliban bounty on his head. Like an FBI agent who'd spent his career working undercover, Jason had a very real reason to maintain a small digital footprint.

I pulled out my phone and dialed Jason's number, using the plane's Wi-Fi.

As per the previous three attempts, the call rang half a dozen times before going to an automated voice mail announcing the number I'd reached and nothing more. My unanswered calls were not necessarily a cause for concern. Unlike me, Jason no longer lived a life requiring him to be available twenty-four hours a day. While I was certain he had a list of numbers that would ring through the do-not-disturb setting, evidently mine wasn't among them.

Fair enough.

After two-plus decades of service, Jason had more than earned his retirement. But while my brain knew this was a satisfactory answer, my gut wasn't so sure. Or maybe sitting in the little cabin as we flew east gave me too much time to worry. I couldn't sleep, wasn't much for reading, and had had my fill of the news. At this time of the night, all the websites were simply recycling earlier stories. To get a true update, I'd have to wait until the anchors began their day in another couple of hours.

I looked outside, tried to guess where we were, and couldn't.

The darkness was absolute.

Just like it had been in Afghanistan.

TWENTY-TWO

Turns out that Tequila Tuesday was a much tamer affair than I would have imagined. Or perhaps I hadn't given Jason and his merry men the credit they deserved. To the befuddlement of the Brits, Aussies, and Kiwis, and the outright disgust of the Italians, the American Army still lived under General Order One while deployed. This meant a zero-tolerance policy of alcohol. While our allies received their daily booze ration as part of their Meals Ready to Eat and formal dinners held at their compounds usually involved a selection from impressive wine lists, the Americans were still stuck in the prohibition era.

American service members engaged in endless speculation around this topic. During the country's previous longest war, Vietnam, alcohol was part of the operational landscape. Requiring someone to spend a year away from their family while going toe-to-toe with people who wanted to kill them on a daily basis was no small ask. Most rational human beings thought that allowing a deployed service member to enjoy an after-dinner beer was the least a grateful nation could do for those who volunteered to fight a war on her behalf.

Unfortunately, the present-day general officers who set policy did not agree.

There were, however, some who regarded deployed life through a saner lens.

Like the Non Commissioned Officer Corps.

As they had been doing since their inception, the NCOs who formed the backbone of the special operations community had taken matters into their own hands. Each and every team room had a locker that was more closely guarded than the President's nuclear football. This Pandora's box contained the team's allocation of alcohol, and the libations were doled out with the reverence that they deserved.

Jason's team was no exception.

After grounding our personal gear in a wooden b-hut, Jason helped Frodo and me carry our weapons and kit into the team room, where he procured us empty cages and introduced us to the guys. There were ten Green Berets in total. Some I'd served with, some were just familiar faces, and others were complete strangers. But the special operations community is a tight-knit one. Even if I didn't know the men personally, we probably had mutual friends.

Once we'd taken care of the administrative aspects, Jason turned to the most important task—ensuring Frodo and I had our own mugs from the team room's ample supply. Then it was a splash of tequila for both of us as we sat down to discuss the pending operation.

"The target's really just outside the gate?" Frodo said.

"Damn near," Jason replied. "We're gonna fast-rope onto target for the element of surprise, but the compound is just a couple of klicks from Bagram's entry-control point. Karzai's policy banning unannounced night raids has emboldened the jihadis. When our command notifies the Afghans ahead of a night raid, some corrupt shit bag always tips off the target. Our last several hits have all been dry holes."

The policy Jason was referencing had been a bone of contention between US and Afghan leadership for some time. Bowing to public pressure, Afghanistan's President Hamid Karzai had enacted restrictions on US nighttime raids including the caveat that the mayor of the city in which the raid was to occur had to be notified ahead of any pending military operation. As could be imagined, this had led to less-than-stellar results from the American perspective. What had once been one of the most effective tools against the Taliban leadership had now become an exercise in kicking in doors to hastily abandoned houses, otherwise known as dry holes.

"What are you gonna do different this time?" I said.

"Ignore the rule," Jason said.

I looked at Jason. He stared right back, daring me to ask the question.

The psychologists charged with screening those who desired to wear the coveted Green Beret referenced a very specific mental profile. One that differed from other units composing the greater special operations community. Though Army Special Forces had been pressed into a greater direct action role since 9/11, this was not their doctrinal task. Green Berets alone learned a language as part of their training because Army Special Forces was singularly tasked with winning wars by, with, and through indigenous forces.

In laymen's terms, Green Berets were created to train and go to battle alongside foreign fighters. Triple Nickel, the men of ODA 555, was a perfect example. During the opening stages of the Afghanistan invasion, these Green Berets famously partnered with the Northern Alliance to fight the Taliban, often calling in air strikes from horseback.

Operating as part of a twelve-man element embedded with a foreign fighting force was not for the faint of heart. But beyond mere courage, a trait not exactly in short supply across the special operations community, a Green Beret possessed another critical characteristic—independence. Army Special Forces operated far from the flagpole. As such, Green Berets were staffed with men who had no issue acting without running their every decision through higher headquarters.

But sometimes that needle swung too far.

"Sure about that?" I said.

Jason shrugged.

"We're here to fight a war," Jason said, "not practice our CQB skills on empty buildings. Besides, success is the great equalizer. If we hit this compound and come back with the bomb maker, what are they going to do? Make us let him go?"

I glanced at Frodo to see if he was going to weigh in, but my bodyguard was uncharacteristically quiet. Frodo had spent the majority of his career in the Unit—home to the best of the best. His rules of engagement had differed from those used by the rest of the military, and I thought Frodo might offer Jason some advice.

He didn't.

Frodo's silence made sense after a fashion. At the end of the day, this was Jason's show. The Green Beret's strategy was tactically sound. If he had the support of his command, Frodo wasn't going to second-guess him.

"You're the boss," I said, slapping Jason on the shoulder. "We're just here to help. When's the hit? We're supposed to catch a flight to Chapman to link up with our in-country DIA rep tomorrow, but I can push that off for a day or two. Lord knows Air Force pilots don't like missing steak-and-lobster night."

Jason smiled.

Bagram's dining facility served surf and turf once a week, usually on Thursdays. It wasn't five-star quality, but it beat the hell out of meat loaf. Accordingly, Air Force shuttle flights from Bagram to Salerno and Chapman tended to develop maintenance problems with a startling regularity on Thursdays. By now everyone knew what was up, but nobody made too much noise. Happy pilots made for happy passengers. I for one didn't want someone with a grumbling stomach piloting a three-hundred-million-dollar airplane.

"That should work," Jason said. "Why don't we head over to the TOC? I can walk you through what we've got so far, and you guys can meet the rest of the team. Then we'll zero your weapons and get your kit sorted. The high-value target isn't expected to arrive for at least twenty-four hours, so we've got some time."

I was about to reply when the door to the team room crashed open, revealing a soldier who looked all of seventeen.

"Sergeant Brown," the soldier said, the words coming out between gasps, "Captain McGourthy needs you in the TOC. Now."

"On the way, Evans," Jason said, getting to his feet. "What's going down?"

"We just got a ping off the high-value target's cell phone. He's in the target compound. Captain McGourthy has trigger authority."

Game time.

TWENTY-THREE

Need some company?" Dee said.

I looked from where I'd spread my kit across the rental car's hood to my pilot.

"Thanks for the offer," I said with a smile, "but I'm not expecting trouble."

"Huh," Dee said, eyeing my kit. "Hate to see what you'd be packing if you were."

She had a point.

After landing on Moore County Airport's single runway, Dee had taxied over to the FBO, or fixed-base operations, building. Though it had an impressive-sounding name, the structure was really nothing more than a lounge for aircrews and passengers to use while they were waiting for the next leg of their flight. While nowhere near as luxurious as the Austin Executive Airport, this FBO had a commodity I desperately needed—a courtesy vehicle.

As Dee oversaw the refueling crew, I snagged the car keys from a sleepy worker and brought the vehicle around to where the Piper was parked. By then, the refuelers were gone and it was just Dee and me on a deserted tarmac in the darkness. In other words, the perfect time and place to sort the gear I'd brought but hadn't had the room to arrange in the Piper's small cabin.

The Pelican case and crew bag I'd grabbed from the hangar's locker back in Austin contained what Frodo termed an assaulter kit. Spread across the Chevy's hood was a combination plate carrier and chest rig, a ballistic helmet, night vision goggles, a first aid kit, a Persistent Systems Wave Relay radio, and an HK MP5SD outfitted with an EOTech red-dot holographic sight.

The MP5 was not anyone's idea of the weapon of choice for reaching out and touching a bad guy, but it had two major advantages. One, it was compact and fitted with a folding stock, allowing the entire weapon to be concealed in a backpack. Two, the fine engineers at Heckler & Koch had added an integrated suppressor that negated the need for subsonic ammunition. This wasn't the tool for hunting Taliban in the mountains of Afghanistan, but for silent, up-close work, the submachine gun couldn't be beat.

"I just like to be prepared," I said as I finished configuring the chest rig. "I don't need another shooter, but if you could stay up on coms and keep the bird ready to go, I'd appreciate it."

"Yeah, no worries," Dee said. "I started out as an Apache pilot and then spent some time in a special aviation unit before becoming a civilian. I know that deal."

Interesting.

"Special aviation" was slang for a US Army aviation

unit that did, well, unusual things. While not a gun-fighter per se, it was safe to assume that Dee had more than a passing familiarity with the equipment laid out on the hood. She probably also had some CQB training.

Then again, this was North Carolina, not Iraq. I was heading to an old friend's house to ask some questions and potentially pass on a warning, not jocking up for a hit. My DIA credentials, winning smile, and gift of gab ought to have been able to smooth over any interactions I might have with curious law enforcement folks on the way to or from Jason's house. Even so, that interaction could be much more difficult with two armed assaulters in the car.

"Good to know," I said. "There's a second assaulter kit in the Piper. Take what you want. I'll text you Jason's address. Welcome to the QRF."

Dee ducked her head in acknowledgment, greeting the pronouncement with the solemnness it deserved. Or rather the solemnness it deserved if I thought I needed a quick reactionary force. My decision to include Dee was more a way to say thank you for dragging her out of bed in the middle of the night and flying me halfway across the country.

While someone had certainly tried to kill me, they'd done so by using Frodo as bait. Maybe they'd even tried to get to my best friend first and failed. With him out of play, it made sense for them to set up on the detention facility and see who came to visit. If they'd known about me beforehand, they'd have interdicted me at home at a time of their choosing rather than setting a hasty am-bush on the road. But they hadn't known about me, which made me think they probably didn't know about Jason.

Even if they did, finding the former Green Beret wouldn't be easy.

Jason had been living off the grid since his retirement. While I took steps to minimize my footprint, I still paid utility bills. Jason was a ghost. I'd run his name and address through various intelligence community and law enforcement databases during the flight from Austin and come up empty. I used his address to pull up his property tax records and even those were a dead end. His farm was registered to a corporation that in turn was shrouded in some fairly respectable legalese. Given enough time I might be able to breach the digital fortress Jason had erected, but for anyone working without the benefit of a nation-state's cyber resources, he was pretty well hidden.

I still didn't know who was after Frodo, or why, and whether the "accidental" death of the other ODA team member was somehow related. But I did know that a paramilitary team's heat state rose exponentially after a kinetic operation. The folks targeting me had every reason to believe they'd been successful. This meant they'd killed once, perhaps twice if Fletcher's car crash was also their work. Logic dictated that they would have already come for Jason if they'd determined his whereabouts.

If not, the hitters certainly wouldn't be sticking around to develop the situation now.

With this in mind, I'd felt confident about my decision to drive out to Jason's farm solo, and the hour-long trip through North Carolina backcountry did nothing to change my mind. If my hypothetical direct action team even existed, logic dictated that by now they were long gone. But logic went out the window the moment my headlights illuminated a gate barring the entrance to Jason's farm.

An open gate.

TWENTY-FOUR

killed my headlights the instant I realized that the gate was ajar.

Jason's homestead stood at the top of a small rise and was surrounded on three sides by forest. He'd cleared the section facing the road and turned it into two pastures bisected by a gravel driveway leading to the main house. The land sloped gently upward in a series of hills that culminated on a plateau spanning two acres. The elevated terrain and scattered pine trees shielded Jason's house from the road.

There was nothing unique about the electronic wrought iron gate. Nothing but my feeling that someone who had gone to the lengths Jason had undertaken to maintain his anonymity would not have left their front entrance unsecure. From what I knew of Jason, I figured the gate's operation was probably controlled by his cell phone and defaulted to a closed, locked position so that his homestead would remain secure in the event of a power failure.

Or something a bit more nefarious.

In any case, neither farmers nor commandos left high-speed avenues of approach unsecured, and Jason was both. I killed the engine and dug out my cell. I tried Jason's number a final time, willing the phone to ring faster.

Once again, the automated voice mail picked up.

Killing the connection, I dialed Dee.

"Trouble?" Dee said.

"Not sure yet," I said while sliding on my plate carrier and securing the Velcro straps one-handed. "But I'd rather be safe than sorry."

"What do you need?"

"An eye in the sky," I said. "Is that bulge beneath the Piper's nose cowling what I think it is?"

"If you think it's a gimbal-mounted Star Safire 380-HD EO/IR imaging system, then you're right on the money."

"Fantastic," I said. "Got any more bulges under the wings? The kind that fire 30mm cannon rounds or 2.75-inch rockets?"

"Not on this bird," Dee said. "You sure you want a pilot instead of another shooter?"

"Positive," I said, grabbing the MP5. "Get here as fast as you can. Check in on the Wave Relay once you're overhead."

"Cranking now," Dee said. "ETA one five mikes."

"Roger that," I said. "Out here."

I squirreled the phone into my vest's front pocket, checked the Wave Relay radio, put on my Peltor headset, and jumped out of the car. It was still full dark, but the starry sky provided more than enough ambient light for my NODs. I swung the tubes down over my face and locked them into place. The world was now rendered in shades of green and white, allowing me to clearly see the gravel driveway that beckoned on the other side of the gate.

A driveway I intended to ignore.

If visitors with less-than-honorable intentions were indeed paying Jason a call, I didn't plan on strolling up to say hello. According to the Google Maps imagery I'd reviewed, Jason's largest pasture was just past the wood line off to the right. Until Dee joined the fun, I was operating blind. The pasture offered me the greatest chance of closing on Jason's house without stumbling into an ambush. With the exception of a couple of barns nearer the house, the rolling terrain was open. I'd be able to move quickly and spot aggressors from a distance.

Of course, this unobstructed view worked both ways, but I was betting that the bad guys would be focused on their target rather than empty goat pastures. Not much of a plan, but the alternative was to wait for Dee to provide me with real-time situational awareness.

I didn't have that kind of time.

I vaulted the split-rail fence one-handed, careful to avoid the thick wire running along the other side. My familiarity with goats came predominately from "Three Billy Goats Gruff," but I did know a thing or two about electric fences. Like nearly every farm kid, I'd once grabbed the live wire as part of a childhood dare.

It wasn't a mistake I intended to make twice.

I landed softly on the far side, the shin-high grass grasping my pants with wet fingers. I tested the IR laser mounted to the HK's Picatinny rail, painting the ground with the red dot visible only to my night vision goggles before releasing the push-button control. Aiming with the laser was the preferable method of employing the MP5 while wearing NODs, but if Jason's guests were similarly equipped, the dancing light would be a dead giveaway.

I started up the slight incline, holding the HK in the high-ready position as I traded stealth for speed. Jason was a good twenty miles from the nearest town and the single-lane road that passed by his driveway was lightly traveled, especially at this time of the early morning. The night was quiet with the exception of the country's ambient sounds—crickets chirping, night birds calling, and animals rustling in their stalls.

And a car door opening.

I turned my stalk into a trot, pumping my legs even as the grass whisked against my pants. The dew-coated turf would help muffle the sound of my passage, but stealth was now a secondary consideration.

The party was about to start.

A pair of buildings loomed to my front—goat barns by the looks of them. Angling behind one, I sprinted for the structure, betting that it would mask my movement. If the bad guys were competent, a sniper team would be monitoring the field I was traversing. This meant I risked running headlong into a buzz saw when I rounded the barn's corner. A little on-site intelligence would be fantastic right about now.

The low drone of a turboprop engine answered my unvoiced prayer.

"Sweet, this is Bone, over."

"Bone, this is Sweet. Go ahead, over," I said.

A SEAL had assigned me the stupid-ass call sign. I'd reflexively provided it to Dee during our impromptu mission briefing, never dreaming she'd actually have to use it. Reason 1,433 why I was less than fond of SEALs.

"Roger that, Sweet. Read you Lima Charlie. I'm on station and have eyes on objective. How's my acoustic signature, over?"

"Bone, Sweet, I can hear engine noise," I said. "It's not bad, but it will be noticeable if you hang around too long, over."

"Roger, Sweet. Skies are clear. I'm going to climb up another couple of thousand feet. That'll put me into controlled airspace, but I'll work it with air traffic control. You ready for a talk on, over?"

This girl was wasting her talents as a DIA chauffeur. With Hellfire missiles under her wingtips and a gun pod beneath her nose, I was betting old Dee Bone had been pretty popular with the boys on the ground.

"Roger, send it," I said.

I made it to the barn, took a knee, and caught my breath as I waited for Dee. My inclination was to edge around the side of the wooden structure and take a peek, but I didn't. Worst-case scenario, somebody spotted me, and I'd be forced to go kinetic. Or maybe that wouldn't be the worst-case scenario if my imaginary sniper had his sights fixed on the barn.

"Okay, Sweet, here we go. I'm designating the side of the house facing the field as green. You've got four thermal signatures approaching green side in a tactical stack. Red side at the rear of the house has one thermal signature in the wood line oriented toward the house, probably providing overwatch for squirters. White side is clear. Black side has one thermal signature, over."

I closed my eyes, picturing the layout Dee had just described. In the special operations community, building aspects were color coded. Colors were easier to remember than cardinal directions and eliminated the confusion inherent in using right or left. The black side corresponded to the section of house adjacent to the pasture. The spunky aviator had just found my hypothetical sniper.

"Sweet copies all," I said, edging to the left as I tried to put as much of the barn between me and the shooter as possible. "See any vehicles?"

"Sweet, Bone, negative on vehicles positioned near the house. Wait one while I bounce out a field of view, over."

Like all thermal cameras, the one mounted beneath the Piper had multiple fields of view. A narrower field of view provided greater resolution to a smaller section of real estate. To figure out what was going on beyond the house, Dee had to switch to a wider field of view.

"Sweet, Bone, I've got two vehicles pulled off the side of the driveway about fifty meters past the gate. Engines are still warm, so they haven't been parked long. Can't tell if they're occupied, over."

The driveway went through a series of turns as it meandered from the road to Jason's house. Parking the vehicles out of sight allowed for a covert approach to the house. This is exactly how I would have played it. Unfortunately, this was also exactly how a law enforcement fugitive recovery team might play it. I wasn't happy with the CID agents who'd arrested Frodo, but I knew they'd only been doing their jobs. I needed to confirm that these intruders were not law enforcement so that I could even the odds stacked against me by shooting first and asking questions later.

"Bone, Sweet, can you zoom in on the vehicles to see if they're cop rides, over?"

"Sweet, Bone, stand by."

While Dee conducted her reconnaissance, I thought through the tactical problem. An approach from the barn offered great concealment and cover, but I wasn't going to do Jason any good if I rounded the corner and ran face-first into a bullet. I was also having some serious buyer's remorse about the HK. The MP5 was a nail driver in close quarters, but its 9mm pistol round just wasn't meant for engagements at these distances. The tactical stack was at least one hundred meters away, and the sniper was probably double that. I needed a way to close ground without getting my ticket punched in the process.

I heard the Piper and looked up to see a window above me. The opening was too high for the goats to reach, but wide enough to vent the barn's ripe air. I let my VTAC sling catch the HK as I jumped for the windowsill and boosted myself up. A mass of animals waited on the other side.

They were big.

I'd pictured the adorable miniature variant prevalent on funny YouTube videos. These weren't them. The goats in the barn were two to three feet tall and weighed at least one hundred fifty pounds. Maybe more. A couple of them had horns—long, saber-looking lengths of bone that curled over their heads. Most herd animals were pretty docile, but dawn was approaching. My new friends would be anxious for breakfast.

With that in mind, I was hoping they wouldn't object to a visitor.

I balanced my hands on the windowsill and wriggled my chest through. The goats responded with some *baa-ing*. I ignored the commotion, concentrating instead on working my left hip over the sill. I knew what the floor was bound to be coated with, and I wanted to make my entrance carefully.

"Sweet, this is Bone, over."

I'd turned up the radio's volume to hear Dee over the goats, but hadn't realized how high I'd cranked it. Her words reverberated through my skull like a summoning from the Almighty. I jerked, lost my balance, and tumbled into the barn like a sack of wet laundry.

"Bone, this is Sweet. Go ahead," I said, trying to view the goat shit now coating my pants as olfactory camouflage.

"Roger, Sweet. I've got one sedan and one SUV. No markings visible on either. I checked both thermal or low-light spectrums. I also zoomed in on the SUV—no antenna clusters, spotlights, or the usual law enforcement vehicle add-ons."

That was interesting. Not definitive, but interesting. The more I considered it, the less I thought that the tactical team was law enforcement. A SWAT team never hit a target with just operators. The police would bring marked units to seal off the surrounding streets and run interference with bystanders. Just two cars loaded with six bad guys meant trouble.

"One more thing, Sweet," Dee said, "my spectrum analyzer is showing a spike in the eight hundred to nineteen hundred megahertz frequency band, over."

"Say that again in English," I said, herding several goats out of the way as I pushed toward the barn's entrance.

"Roger, I think the team's employing a device to swallow up cell signals."

That observation was the proverbial nail in the coffin.

I dug the phone from my vest pocket, punched the digits 911, and hit send.

Nothing.

"Okay, Bone," I said, surveying the front of the barn. "How much time before the assaulters are set?"

"Not long," Dee said. "The spectrum spiked just seconds ago. That was probably the final step before they assault the house. I'd say you've got two minutes, maybe less."

Perfect.

Or maybe not.

A growl that sounded more like a grizzly bear than a dog came from my left. The sound was so deep and low that the air seemed to be vibrating. I slowly turned and found myself face-to-face with a shaggy mound of fur that looked like a caricature of a herd dog. The thing was part sheepdog, part Great Pyrenees, and perhaps part elephant. It had to be at least one hundred twenty pounds, and the fur ball did not seem happy to see yours truly.

Apparently Jason had livestock guarding animals.

That would have been good to know.

"Easy there, girl," I said, stretching the back of my hand toward the dog's nose. "Easy."

"Sweet, this is Bone. Say again?"

"I've got a dog situation," I said. "Stand by."

While no clandestine operative ever welcomed the discovery of a canine on the objective, there was a sliding scale for such encounters. A kick dog was on one end of the spectrum in that the mutt could make a bunch of noise, but wasn't much trouble in the teeth department. On the other end was your classic fur missile—a German shepherd or Belgian Malinois.

Livestock animals, like the one currently gazing hungrily at my groin, were somewhere in the middle. They were bred to protect the herd from natural predators like wolves or coyotes, but not necessarily to attack humans. If I could convince Cujo that I meant no harm to her bleating friends, there was a better-than-even chance I'd leave the barn with my nut sack intact.

If not, Virginia was going to be an only child.

"Come on now, girl," I said, edging my gloved hand a bit closer to the pile of fangs. "I'm a good guy."

"Is that your best pickup line?" Dee said. "How in the hell are you married?"

"Never underestimate the power of pity," I said. "How much time?"

"Ninety seconds."

"All right," I said to the dog, "you're gonna have to trust me."

"You're dog food," Dee said.

I felt the same way, but that didn't stop me from closing the final couple of inches to the fur ball's snout. I couldn't afford to spend any more time messing around with Cujo. This would either work or it wouldn't. The mutt curled back her lips, revealing a set of teeth that belonged in the mouth of a velociraptor. Then the dog gave a loud huff as it sniffed my hand. She stepped closer and took another sniff, this time focusing on the goat shit covering my pants. The massive head swung back my way and an equally massive tongue snaked out, covering my wrist in dog spit. When all else fails, roll in excrement.

I'd have to file that little tactical tidbit away for use later.

"I just made it to second base with the dog," I said as I moved toward the entrance to the barn. "What's happening at the house?"

"Tactical team's fifty meters from the porch and closing. Whatever you're going to do, do it fast."

Dee's no-nonsense reply reminded me of what was at stake. A sniper still covered my avenue of approach, and a group of assaulters was about to take down my friend. I was outnumbered and outgunned. Even if I somehow managed to negate the sniper's advantage, there was no way I was taking out a tactical team of five guys without help.

Without help.

Those were the operative words.

But help was available.

I just needed a way to sound the alarm.

The baying and bleating in the barn began to crescendo as the goats concluded that I was not there to provide an early breakfast. But that didn't mean they were going back to sleep. Like livestock everywhere, once the goats decided it was breakfast time, they'd vigorously voice that opinion to the rest of the world until they were fed. As I watched, the animals began leaving the barn in twos and threes for the series of food troughs arrayed in the common area outside. Then the trickle became a flood as the barn emptied in a rush of dancing hooves, tossing horns, and dust, leaving me with the dog.

And an idea.

"Bone, Sweet, you used to fly Apaches, right?"

"Affirm."

"And you supported special operations?"

"Yep."

"So I'm guessing you've made a low pass or two in your life? Maybe so the guys could snap a cool picture of your gunship?"

"Tell me you're going somewhere with this?" Dee said.

"Low passes—yes or no?"

"I may have once conducted a flyover that was technically below the briefed minimum-safe altitude."

"That's my girl," I said, moving toward the door in a crouch. "Here's what I need."

To her credit, Dee didn't brand my plan as the dumbest thing she'd ever heard. But neither did she give it a ringing endorsement. Fine. I wouldn't have been too crazy about it if I'd been in her shoes either.

"We're gonna need to be synchronized," Dee said

when I was done. "Give me thirty seconds lead before you execute. I'll call mark once I'm over the target."

"Piece of cake," I said.

"Where have I heard that before?" Dee said.

I double-clicked the radio's transmit button in response as I prepared to do my thing.

"Ready?" I said, looking at the dog.

She didn't answer, but judging by her body language, she seemed less than impressed with my plan.

That made three of us.

TWENTY-FIVE

Goats are actually pretty friendly. Especially at feeding time. Doubly especially when their favorite guard dog was standing with them. Which was probably why they were tolerating another four-legged creature on the ground in their midst. Okay, so I technically only used two legs most days, but this morning was the exception that proved the rule.

Or something like that.

In any case, I was now crouched in the center of the herd, urging them toward the fence. This was harder than it looked. Goats are naturally curious beasts, and they trend toward cranky when a human interrupts their sleep without providing sustenance. Already the *bleats* and *baas* that had seemed so charming earlier were now taking on a more menacing tone. Several of the braver fellows had already taken test nips at my clothing and kit.

At least I hoped they were test nips.

Cujo the guard dog had nothing on a pack of omnivores that were both crabby and hungry. I was edging into furry-piranha territory. A particularly industrious goat butted his curly horns into my side after I knocked his lips away from my radio cord. My subsequent slap sent him tumbling into the dirt, but time was not on my side. The dust and dirt the herd kicked up as they moved registered as green bits of phosphorescence to my goggles, hiding my presence. But camouflage or not, forty goats all boisterously voicing their displeasure would surely catch the attention of the assaulters, sniper, or both.

That wouldn't do.

"Bone, this is Sweet. Start your forty-five clock. Call thirty and fifteen. Then give me a countdown from five, over."

"Sweet, this is Bone, roger."

If Dee found my micromanaged timeline instructions annoying, she knew better than to complain. Or maybe she was just too busy aviating. Either way, it was time to implement my half of the plan.

Four assaulters, a sniper covering the goat pasture, and another gunman on the black side to cover squirters equaled six-to-one odds. I'm good, but not that good. Fortunately, the house in question held a former Ranger and ODA team sergeant. Jason might have been retired, but after twenty-plus years in special operations, he knew his way around a rifle and probably had some serious hardware in his house. If I could get Jason into the game, we stood a far greater chance of sending the assaulters packing.

Or putting them in the dirt.

Either option would do.

The goats were still bellyaching, but I'd managed to edge them up against the fence where a small pedestrian gate permitted easy access from Jason's house to the pasture. It was secured with a simple metal latch. In the day's first bit of good luck, the metal latch wasn't locked.

Now came the tricky part.

"Sweet, this is Bone, thirty seconds."

I clicked the transmit button twice, too focused to speak. The latch articulated smoothly. The noisy goats should have drowned out any rust-induced squeaks, but I didn't want the gate wiggling back and forth as it opened. Sound could be concealed, but sight was much harder to mask. Human beings were predators, and predators keyed off motion.

Fortunately, Jason was a better farmer than I'd given him credit for. The gate swung open on well-oiled hinges. I moved out of the way, making room for the first goat to wander through. Except he didn't. Instead, the stupid creature looked at me and bleated, apparently still waiting for breakfast. I cocked back my hand and made a throwing motion, trying for the old fake-ball trick that my childhood golden retriever had fallen for every time.

That didn't work either.

Maybe goats just weren't big on fetch, or maybe the little bastards were done playing around. Either way, the only thing I got for my efforts was a pair of curly horns smacking into my thigh. I went to cuff the little shit, but he danced out of the way, still bleating up a storm.

This was going nowhere.

"Sweet, this is Bone, fifteen seconds."

I double-clicked the transmit button, even as my eyes moved from the goats to Cujo. I motioned toward the open gate, but she just stared back at me as if uncertain whether to allow this Greek tragedy to continue or go with her earlier instinct and chomp me in the nads.

No help there.

"Ten seconds."

I was preparing for a solo sprint across the field when I saw what looked like a giraffe wandering up from the back of the herd. It wasn't a giraffe. It was a llama. A goddamn llama. I'd known folks who'd used llamas to protect their herd animals, but the reviews were mixed. Llamas were great at fending off coyotes and wolves, but their utility came with a price.

A horrible temper.

The goats seemed intimately familiar with their guardian's shortcoming. The frisky bastards parted for that llama like the Red Sea had for Moses. I followed their example and moved away from the gate. The llama paused for a moment to eye me, curling her lip. I readied myself for a dose of famous llama spit, but she had other things on her mind. Like freedom. Turning, the llama marched through the pedestrian gate like a queen entering her court.

The goats followed behind her.

"Five seconds."

This was going to be close.

I let about half a dozen goats surge through the pedestrian gateway before ducking in behind them. But instead of following the four-legged Pied Piper, I cut left toward a decorative stone trough surrounded by a cluster of flowers. The lawn ornament probably doubled as a birdbath and a water dish for the dog, but it would also provide me with a position of cover from which I could take oblique shots at the tactical stack. Getting Jason into the fight was all well and good, but I had to make sure I didn't end up in the same gun line as his soon-to-be targets.

Or vice versa.

"Sweet, this is Bone, mark, mark, mark."

Dee's radio call was barely audible over the scream of a turbine engine from the darkness above me. Or what had been the darkness. I flipped up my NODs just in time to see God's spotlight shatter the night in the form of the Piper's landing lights. The trio of midnight suns illuminated the tactical stack positioned outside Jason's front door. Judging by the way they were clawing at their own NODs, my battlefield surprise appeared to have been successful.

Time to close the deal.

Leaning against stone trough, I centered the HK's holographic sight on the nearest figure and pulled the trigger. Since the assaulters were clumped close together, I'd opted for the three-round-burst setting. If I missed, the stray round stood a good chance of striking an adjacent target.

I didn't miss.

The gunman spun to the ground accompanied by a muted *clack*, *clack*, *clack* as the HK's bolt actioned. The weapon wasn't the Hollywood kind of silent, but between the roaring airplane, the bleating goats, and the assaulters' cries of surprise, it was pretty damn close. Without pausing, I panned to the next assaulter and fired another burst.

A second form tumbled to the ground.

I was on a roll.

And then the birdbath disintegrated in a cloud of dust and stone slivers.

I dropped to the ground, rolling through the thick grass as high-velocity rounds snapped by my head.

"Bone, this is Sweet," I said, scrambling toward the milling goats. "I'm taking aimed fire from somewhere. Need an immediate assist, over."

"Sweet, this is Bone, roger. Stand by."

Dee's throaty voice seemed entirely nonplussed by the situation. As if we were trading there-I-was stories over a beer instead of living one.

Then again, she wasn't the sniper's target.

The Piper screamed overhead.

Floodlights lit up the front porch and lawn to my left. I had just enough time to note that the goat herd had taken casualties in the form of several four-legged companions sprawled across the grass before Dee roared past in a blur of noise and flashing metal. This pass was a bit more aggressive than her first. And by aggressive I mean that old Bone might have given the llama a haircut with the Piper's propeller.

"Sweet, this is Bone. The shooter on the black side of the house has repositioned. He's to your left at a distance of about one hundred meters, over."

Which put him perfectly within the range of his weapon and well outside of mine.

Damn it.

"Bone, roger," I said. "How about the sniper on the white side?"

"Moving toward the front of the house. You're about to be caught between a rock and a hard place."

Story of my life.

Another round zipped past, tearing a divot from Jason's pristinely manicured lawn in a spray of dirt. This was going from bad to worse. If Jason didn't make an appearance soon, I was going to end my life covered in goat shit. I popped up, spraying a three-round burst in the direction of the sniper fire even as I screamed at the top of my lungs.

"Ranger down! Ranger down!"

I was not down.

Yet.

But I would be soon. Besides, my little white lie aside, saying those words was the equivalent of yelling *fire* in a crowded auditorium. Rangers lived by a creed. A kind of moral code encapsulated in six stanzas, one of which read in part, *I will never leave a fallen comrade to fall into the hands of the enemy.* For members of the Regiment, there was no higher calling than the directive to rescue a fellow Ranger.

If Jason was in the house, he'd come.

Unfortunately, that *if* was starting to look mighty big.

My chest rig jerked as a round missed my shoulder by a fraction of an inch, scoring fabric instead of my skin. I dropped and low-crawled toward the milling goats as bullets zipped by from at least two directions. When my time came, I'd always imagined it would happen during an asset meet gone wrong in some dusty corner of Southeast Asia.

I'd never envisioned a North Carolina goat farm.

I combat-reloaded the HK, oriented toward the house, and looked for targets.

Surviving a near ambush necessitated assaulting through the kill zone. If I could close on what was left of the tactical stack, the two snipers flanking me would have to worry about hitting a friendly. Also, in gunfighter calculus, I'd rather face two shooters than four. Unfortunately, the breaching team wasn't cooperating with my plan. The two men I'd drilled were down, but the remaining pair had taken cover beside a set of concrete flower planters flanking Jason's front porch.

For a former Ranger, Jason had an uncomfortably large collection of potted plants.

I panned the EOTech's multipointed red circle onto a crouching figure to the left of the porch and fired. Concrete splinters filled the air. The assaulter jerked his leg behind the structure. I might have winged him, but his answering volley proved that he was still in the fight.

I proned out as a trio of goats toppled. The assaulter's rifle was not suppressed and an AK-47's familiar retort echoed from the house. The goat herd's collective mind decided that discretion was indeed the better part of valor. The animals trotted back toward the pedestrian gate, clumping together as the herd of forty jostled through an opening meant for a single person.

A heavy *thud* sounded from my left.

The llama was down. Her spindly legs thrashed twice and then went still. I crawled toward the fallen animal even as rounds kicked up earth to either side of me. I was caught in a cross fire with only a dead llama for cover.

My goose was cooked.

"Sweet, this is Bone. You've got a second thermal signature closing in from the black side, over."

Fantastic—more shooters.

Just what I needed.

I was keying the radio when massive floodlights mounted to either side of the front porch ignited.

Then all hell broke loose.

The front porch planters detonated in clouds of cement and dirt, and the remaining assaulters crumpled. At the same time, the distinctive chatter of 5.56 gunfire echoed from the black side of the house.

"Sweet, this is Bone. The new shooter on black side is getting some. The sniper's down. He's rounding the corner of the house, heading for green side, over."

Jason.

Spinning to my left, I dumped a magazine at the remaining sniper. Though I tried to keep the red dot centered on his prone form, I didn't have much of a prayer of hitting him at one hundred plus yards. That was fine. I just needed to keep him occupied until someone else ended the engagement.

My fellow Ranger.

But it wasn't Jason who caused me to jerk my aimpoint to the right, sending the last three-round burst into the wood line. That honor belonged to Cujo. One moment the sniper was hammering the llama's carcass. The next he was fighting for his life as Cujo clamped her massive jaws across the base of his neck.

"Holy shit, Sweet," Dee said. "You seeing this?"

"If by *this* you mean Cujo shaking that sniper like a rat, I sure am," I said. "Where's Jason?"

"Ranger coming in!"

I'd never heard three more amazing-sounding words.

At least not in the middle of a gunfight.

"Clear," I said, rising to a crouch even as I kept the HK oriented on the last gunman and final threat.

I wanted to give Cujo a hand, but the fog of war was already pretty thick. Better to stay put than present Jason with another possible target. A moment later, my Ranger brother eased out of the dark, and I suddenly felt damn near invincible. With a fellow Batt Boy on my right flank and a weapon in my hand, there wasn't a enemy alive who could stand against us.

"Is that the last shooter?" Jason said, gesturing toward the limp form Cujo was still worrying.

"I think," I said. "Wait one. Bone, this is Sweet. We got any other players, over?"

"Sweet?" Jason said.

"You don't want to know," I said.

"Oh, but I do."

"Sweet, this is Bone. That's a negative. I've done two full sweeps of the property—one manually and one with the sensor's algorithms. Nothing but the two of you and the dog's chew toy, over."

"Roger, Bone," I said. "Go ahead and RTB. Refuel the bird and stand by. I'll be in touch. Thanks for the help."

"Roger that, Sweet. Returning to base. Bone out."

"We're clear," I said.

Jason nodded. He lifted what looked like a thin reed from where it was hanging from a cord around his neck, put it to his lips, and blew. I heard a soft hiss, but nothing else. Cujo seemed to hear plenty. The massive dog dropped the shooter, backed off several paces, and obediently sat.

In one smooth motion, Jason brought his M4 to his shoulder and fired.

The limp figure jerked.

"Safe always beats sorry," Jason said.

"So I've heard," I said.

TWENTY-SIX

'm delighted you joined the party," I said, "but maybe next time, don't take so long getting dressed."

It had been years since I'd last seen Jason, but the smile I'd expected was nowhere to be found.

"Never went to bed," Jason said. "Been watching the news."

At first I didn't understand.

Then I did.

"Afghanistan?" I said.

He nodded.

"How bad?"

"Bad," Jason said. "The shit happening there makes this look like a misunderstanding."

He waved his hand as he said *this*, the gesture encompassing the carnage scattered across his lawn. We were walking side by side toward the sniper Cujo had savaged, the grass tracing wet fingers across our pant legs. Jason was dressed in commando casual—hiking boots, range pants, and a worn T-shirt beneath his plate carrier.

Not exactly what I wore while watching late-night TV, but to each his own.

Jason was sporting the obligatory operator facial hair, now more gray than brown. His eyes were bloodshot and his face looked drawn. Thinner somehow. He'd lost weight, and while he still looked fit, the wide shoulders and barrel chest I remembered had morphed into a smaller frame.

Something less.

"Was Claire sitting up with you?" I said.

Jason looked at me and then shook his head. "She died six months ago. Cancer."

"Jesus," I said. "I'm sorry, brother."

Jason nodded without breaking stride, his eyes fixed on something in the distance.

Something I couldn't see.

"It happened real sudden," Jason said. "Started in her pancreas and spread from there. The disease just ate her up. I'm thankful she went quick."

I squeezed Jason's shoulder, saying nothing. But he heard me all the same.

"Thanks," Jason said. "So what's this shit about?"

He pointed at the limp sniper.

"Not sure," I said, switching gears.

Clearly Jason was hurting, but just as clearly he wasn't ready to discuss Claire. I understood. Men in our profession feared the death of loved ones above all else. It was the one enemy you were powerless to fight. Even so, I'd be ready to listen when Jason was finally ready to talk.

That's what brothers did.

"Do you know a Green Beret named Fletcher Spies?" I said.

Jason nodded. "Sure. We were on the same ODA."

Fuck.

"Was he on the team back when Frodo and I helped you with that Op in Afghanistan?" I said.

"Yes," Jason said. "Why?"

"He's dead," I said. "I think these guys may have had something to do with it."

"What do you know?" Jason said, his eyes hardening.

"Not much yet," I said. "I'm hoping they'll help me start connecting dots."

"Let's see what we've got," Jason said.

He grabbed the sniper's body and turned the man onto his back, providing me with my first look at one of the men who'd been trying to kill me. I sucked in a breath.

The sniper was Asian.

"Interesting," Jason said as he searched the body with quick, efficient motions.

I pulled out my cell phone while he worked, snapping a couple of pictures of the shooter's face. Jason's bullet had struck the sniper in the right torso, causing a horrific exit wound but leaving the man's face untouched. While I wasn't expecting to recognize the gunman, his race still threw me for a loop.

I'd expected him to be Middle Eastern or maybe Caucasian. Between my work in Iraq and the 'Stans, as well as some run-ins with Russian operatives, I'd made more than my fair share of enemies. Even so, Asia was a new addition to the I Hate Matt Drake Club.

"His gear's generic," Jason said, even as he dumped the contents of the man's pockets on his chest. "He's running an AK, but so are the majority of the world's bad guys. Wait a minute—what have we got here?"

Jason opened up what looked like a wallet and passed it to me.

It was a set of credentials conferring diplomatic immunity upon the holder.

The gunman was a diplomat.

A Chinese diplomat.

"Well, shit," I said.

"Yep," Jason said. "What now?"

"Time to bring in the artillery."

TWENTY-SEVEN

G lass."

The voice coming through my handset carried the usual amount of gruff I expected from my boss. But there was something else in James's one-word salutation not usually present. Something I couldn't quite place.

"Chief, it's me," I said, putting a finger in my left ear to mute the ambient noise. My AirPods, like my phone, were at the bottom of the river. As with my Luccheses, they'd been a gift from Laila.

There was going to be hell to pay when this operation was over.

"Matthew? Where are you, son?"

Son.

That was new.

While I had no doubt that James cared about me, he did so in the same manner a Ranger platoon sergeant cared for a new private. More tough love than warm and fuzzy. I could count on one hand the number of times James had called me *son*.

"North Carolina," I said. "Why?"

The words had no sooner left my mouth than I had a

thought. The kind of thought that torments parents when their phone rings in the middle of the night.

Frodo.

"Thank God," James said. "I was afraid you were going to say Afghanistan."

Okay, so I hadn't seen that coming. To be fair, I did have a reputation for doing my own thing. Some may say a deserved reputation. But even I had never hopped a plane to a combat zone without informing my boss.

Yet.

"Did something happen to Frodo?" I said, unable to put the nagging worry to bed despite James's odd response.

"What? No. Last I checked he was still in the Texas detention facility. Why?"

There it was again. An odd inflection to James's voice that was strange yet somehow familiar. Then I understood. Worry. I was hearing worry in my boss's tone. That set my heart racing for an altogether different reason. Over the course of my employment with the Defense Intelligence Agency, I have gotten into more than my fair share of trouble. In response, I've heard James express a variety of emotions, including anger, frustration, and, on rare occasions, bewilderment.

But never worry.

"You sound concerned, Chief," I said.

"I am. You watching the news?"

"Sorry," I said. "Been busy."

If I was engaged in a conversation with a normal human being, I might have referenced the predawn hour. With James, I didn't bother. When it came to my boss, most of the conventions associated with normal human beings did not apply. Truth be told, James's relationship with work couldn't be termed *healthy* in any sense of the word. In addition to his eye, his time as an ODA team sergeant had cost him two marriages.

With James, the mission came first.

Always.

He'd brought this same mentality to the DIA. In a culture that celebrated workaholics, James was in a class all his own. Most Senior Executive Service members kept a spare suit in their office's closet. Not James. His closet held a collapsible cot. On more than one occasion, I'd come in at daybreak to find him wrapped in a poncho liner and snoring. James routinely worked late, but shuffling papers at three in the morning was a new one even for him.

"We're about to lose Afghanistan," James said, his voice catching on the word.

"How long?" I said, getting the words past a lump in my own throat. "How long till it falls?"

"Don't know," James said. "We've shifted to full-fledged evacuation mode."

"We're not going to try to stop the Taliban?" I said.

"We don't have the political will. The President campaigned on ending our involvement in Afghanistan. He hasn't changed his mind."

I ignored the sense of helplessness that accompanied James's answer. If my boss was still at the office, there was still hope. James might be the most difficult supervisor I'd ever worked with, but when push came to shove, he made shit happen.

"Then what are you doing?" I said.

"Planning contingencies, Matthew," James said. "I might not be able to change the President's mind, but I want to have operational plans ready to go in the event that someone more persuasive than me can. Why in the hell are you in North Carolina?"

For a long moment, I thought about how to answer.

Then a *beep*, *beep*, *beep* did the job for me.

"What is that?" James said.

"A backhoe," I answered. "It makes that noise when it backs up."

"What are you doing with a backhoe?"

"Digging a hole."

The silence that followed my answer was brief, but meaningful.

"Can you go secure?" James said.

"Negative," I said. "My work phone is at the bottom of a river."

"I see. I'm texting you a link to an ad hoc secure network. Click it. Then tell me everything."

I did.

"Holy shit," James said, ten minutes later. "Ho-ly shit. You never do anything by half."

"Give me a break, Chief," I said. "They drew first blood. Not me."

"Did you just quote Rambo?"

"Seemed appropriate."

Another series of beeps temporarily interrupted our phone conversation as Jason opened more ground. Burying six dead shooters and two cars required a pretty big hole.

"Okay," James said, resignation replacing exasperation. "Let me run the pictures you sent of the dead shooters. The Chinese diplomat is a no-brainer, but the Hispanics might take some doing. The obvious answer is that they're cartel, but that makes zero sense. I'm assuming Jason isn't breaking ground on a new pool?"

In another surprise, the remainder of the shooters had been Hispanic, not Asian. But they didn't have the look of gangbangers or tatted-up street muscle. Nor had they fought like criminals. Thugs with guns don't use tactical stacks or snipers. The gunmen were military.

"I can call local law enforcement if you want," I said. "Or better yet, I can give my favorite special agent a ring. DC's only a couple of hours by plane. I'm sure HRT will sort this out in a jiffy."

"No reason to be a jackass, Matthew," James said. "Just make sure the bodies are bagged, and Jason doesn't forget where he put them."

Not much chance of that.

On the positive side of the ledger, Jason's rural property was isolated from civilization. We were working on the back half of his property, where both the wood line and his house kept our activity from view. On the negative side, Jason had dredged up a big section of his yard. It wouldn't take Sherlock Holmes to find the bodies if someone came looking.

And someone would definitely come looking.

"Smart thinking with the backhoe," James said, grudgingly. "You can stash a body or two in an industrial freezer. But six is pushing the limit."

This time I was the one who was silent, waiting for James to laugh.

He didn't.

"Want me to come in?" I said, my thoughts returning to Afghanistan.

"No," James said. "I've already got one of my boys in the clink. Get gone and take Jason with you. Give me some time to work this."

"Where?"

"Home, Matthew. Hug your pregnant wife and wait for my call."

James had never sent me home. Ever. Either Afghanistan really was about to collapse or the end of times was near.

Or maybe both.

TWENTY-EIGHT

AUSTIN, TEXAS

"This your place?"

It was the way the woman asked the question more than her actual words that jerked me awake. I opened sleep-crusted eyes and blinked, trying to make sense of my surroundings. At first, I couldn't figure out what had prompted my Uber driver's cautious tone. Then I realized I was eyeing the wrong side of the street. Stifling a yawn, I turned my head to look through the opposite window.

And was instantly alert.

"Yep," I said, swinging open the door.

"Y'all be careful," my driver said.

Her name was Terri. She was a sixty-something widowed woman who'd moved to Texas from New Orleans to live with her daughter and son-in-law. She drove for Uber to provide some much-needed separation between her and her extended family. In the manner of ride-share drivers, she'd willingly supplied all these details within moments of picking me up from Austin Executive Airport.

Dee had offered me a ride, but after flying me cross-country twice and saving me from a team of shooters all within the last twelve hours, I thought she'd done enough. I'd sent the spunky pilot home with instructions to grab some rack time, but to stay close to her phone.

Jason had come to Austin too.

The former Green Beret had wanted to go to war on his own, but as a veteran of many one-man rages, I'd talked him out of that plan. I was all about vengeance, but first we needed to understand who had targeted Jason and why. He'd reluctantly agreed, and I sent him off to a downtown hotel with a front company's credit card and instructions to wait for my call.

Then I'd hopped in with Terri and fallen asleep to her Cajun accent.

Now I was regretting that decision.

I smiled politely at Terri as I closed the car door, but my heart was pounding. Two Austin PD cruisers were parked adjacent to my driveway.

That was the good news.

The police presence was proof that, unlike some cities, Austin local law enforcement and the Federal Bureau of Investigation got along just fine. The not-so-good news was that two officers were talking to a man in my driveway.

A man who was not one of my neighbors.

The gentleman in question was dark-complected with thick black hair and a spare build. I pegged him as late forties or early fifties. He had a pianist's long, thin fingers, the stooped shoulders of someone who spent a lot of time in front of a computer, and a set of Buddy Holly–style glasses. He was not the kind of person who would set your adrenaline spiking in a dark alley. On the other hand, some of my most dangerous enemies would have looked right at home in an elementary school's parent-pickup line.

I crossed the street at a jog that immediately garnered the attention of the closest officer. He moved to intercept me. His body language was polite but assured. This was his street, and he would decide who graced it.

"Can I help you, sir?"

The officer was young, probably mid to late twenties. His wide shoulders tapered to a narrow waist. He probably subsisted on protein shakes and tuna. His name tag read PRUITT in large block letters.

"This is my place, Officer Pruitt," I said. "I'm Matt. Matt Drake."

I didn't offer a handshake, not because I wasn't trying to be friendly but because I had a pretty good idea it wouldn't be returned. Officer Pruitt was standing with his hands folded chest high as he took my measure. This was known as the interview stance precisely because while Pruitt's body language was nonthreatening, his hands were up and ready to defend his face. Something hinky had just gone down, and Officer Pruitt was trying to determine if I'd had a hand in it.

"Good to meet you, Mr. Drake," Pruitt said. "Where you coming from?"

"The airport," I said.

Officer Pruitt gave a slow nod even as his cop eyes marked my rumpled, stained clothing and lack of luggage. Good cops have an innate bullshit detector. Unfortunately, spies sling bullshit for a living, and the residue always seemed to trigger a cop's spider senses.

Or maybe he was keying off the goat shit I'd rolled in a few hours earlier.

It had been a day.

"Can I see some ID?" Pruitt said.

"Sure," I said. "You can also give Special Agent Rawlings from the Austin RA a call. He'll vouch for me."

"A driver's license will be fine," Pruitt said.

I nodded. "I'm about to hand it to you, but from an officer-safety perspective, I also want you to know that I'm carrying a concealed Glock 23."

Pruitt's easygoing smile never wavered, but his eyes hardened.

"I thought you came from the airport?" Pruitt said.

"I did."

Pruitt paused as though waiting for me to explain this contradiction. I did not. Instead, I pulled out my money clip and handed over my license. Silence is a great technique for interrogating criminals, but it doesn't do much to spies. Pruitt took the license, compared me to my smiling mug, and handed it back. His bunched shoulders loosened, but his stare didn't. He was miffed that I wasn't being more forthcoming.

Welcome to the club.

"Okay, Mr. Drake," Pruitt said. "You can go on up to the house."

"Thanks," I said, "but I'm more interested in the fellow in my driveway."

"Nothing to worry about," Pruitt said. "Just police business."

"Look," I said, trying to sound reasonable, "I'm one of the good guys. If you don't know my story, ask around.

Or better yet, call Rawlings. I don't mean to be a jackass, but it's been a long day. You can tell me what's going on, or I can make a couple of calls. Then someone is going to give you a call with the same instructions, only they're not going to ask as nicely. What's it gonna be?"

Pruitt looked at me for a beat before sighing.

"He rolled up to the house just before you arrived. We're questioning him."

"Did he say who he was?" I said.

"Family. Your wife's distant cousin."

This time I sighed.

"Let me talk to him."

Ten minutes later, we were sitting at the kitchen table. Or at least the man and I were sitting. Laila was eyeing us from the other side of the island. She was supposedly making coffee, but I knew my wife better than that. While her hands were indeed fiddling with a stainless steel monstrosity that could render coffee beans and milk into a thousand different caffeinated beverages, her shimmering eyes told the true story. Laila was on the other side of the island because she didn't trust herself not to throttle our guest.

"Tell me what you know," I said to the man seated across from me. "I'll do what I can."

I purposely did not look at my wife as I spoke, but she made her presence known all the same. A rush of hot air escaped the espresso machine with a long reptilian *hiss* that sounded like Godzilla belching. Laila's eyes were not the only window into her temperament.

"It's been over twenty-four hours since I last heard from her," the man said, his words heavy with emotion.

The man's name was Gharib, and the *her* in question was his daughter, Ferhana. The same foolish girl who'd jetted off to Afghanistan without permission to attend a childhood friend's wedding. In her earlier appeal, Laila's mother had made Ferhana out to be next of kin, but it was clear that this was not the case. Laila and Gharib had never met, and my wife certainly didn't know his daughter.

"Look," I said, "I'm not a father—"

Laila placed two coffee cups on the table with a bit more force than was strictly necessary. Brown liquid foamed over the lip of mine, spreading across the table and narrowly missing my fingers.

"Yet," I said with a pleading look at my wife. "I'm not a father yet, and I can't imagine what you're feeling. But just because Ferhana's been out of contact for a day doesn't mean the worst. She's on an adventure in a foreign country. Maybe she's just being a typical teen."

"I said the same thing to Ferhana's mother," Gharib said, coffee untouched, "so she wouldn't worry. This is what I haven't told her."

Gharib pulled a phone from his pocket and set the device down on the table. A young girl stared at me from the phone's screen saver. Lanky with curly black hair, sparkling brown eyes, and a mischievous smile. She looked about eighteen and was on the cusp of the transition from girl to woman.

"Ferhana," Gharib said, touching her face with an index finger. "This was before her mother and I divorced. Back when she was happy."

Laila abandoned her island redoubt to join us, her hand resting on my shoulder. To someone not married to her, Laila's gesture would have seemed unconscious. A wife seeking solace in her husband. I knew differently. Laila's slender fingers sought my shoulder as an anchor. A physical connection to what really mattered—her and baby Virginia. I squeezed her hand so that she knew I understood.

Laila and Virginia were my life.

"Sorry," Gharib said, clearing his throat. "I've never felt so helpless. I'm her father. Fathers protect their little girls."

Gharib swiped through pictures until he found a video.

Then he pressed play.

It was hard to watch for more reasons than one. The movie had the jerky quality of a cell phone video. One taken as the photographer was moving. In this case, the videographer was dancing, as were the rest of the people in the frame. As a first-generation American, Laila hadn't been much for traditional Afghan or Pakistani customs when we'd married. We'd said our vows in a church with a pastor officiating, but in a bid to please her mother, Laila had consented to some traditional aspects during the ceremony and the reception.

Many of the attendees from Laila's side of the family had worn full Afghan and Pakistani regalia. With this in mind, I figured the video had been taken after the wedding's conclusion. The point at which the day's solemnity had largely ended. Now the twentysomethings who made up the bulk of the crowd were free to let their hair down and forget their worries. They did so in the manner of twentysomethings everywhere—by dancing and drinking.

In a testament to how much smaller the world had grown in the years since 9/11, the wedding party was dancing to "I Gotta Feeling" by the Black Eyed Peas, much to the chagrin of their dour-faced elders standing at the crowd's edge. The thought of Afghan kids jamming to Fergie almost brought a smile to my face.

Almost.

I knew how this was going to end.

Midway through the song's second chorus, the doors to the dance hall swung open, revealing a cluster of men. Taliban. With a heartlessness that was difficult to watch, the Talibs set upon the crowd, wielding their clubs with brutal effectiveness. While the enforcers were equal-opportunity practitioners when it came to the targets of their rods, the men seemed to reserve special ire for the women and girls. With thunderous shouts of rage, the thugs clubbed the beautifully dressed females with vicious blows, eliciting cries of agony.

I wanted to look away.

I couldn't.

While I didn't believe that evil would someday vanish from the world, I knew that wickedness was often unwillingly facilitated by men and woman who averted their gazes. I would watch this horror to its conclusion.

It was the least I could do.

The video ended in a predictable, if not heartrending fashion. A cudgel-wielding caveman locked in on the cell phone's holder from across the room. With a shout, he rounded on the videographer, stick lifted above his head, face frozen in a mask of hatred. The imagery ended with a still shot of the Talib's face, lips curled in snarl, beady eyes burning with unholy fire.

"The wedding was livestreamed on Facebook," Gharib said, his voice sounding dull, shell-shocked. As if his mind was trying to divorce itself from the video's horrible truth.

"You're sure your daughter was there?" I said.

Gharib nodded, shoulders slumping.

"She posted several selfies before the Taliban overran the wedding. Nothing since."

Laila's fingers dug into my shoulder, her fingernails scoring my skin. I understood, but I asked a question anyway.

"Have you been in contact with anyone from the wedding?"

Another slow nod.

"Yes. One of Ferhana's friends managed to escape, but she saw what happened next. After they grew tired of clubbing people, the Taliban separated the men and women. The men were taken out in the courtyard, lined up against the wall, and shot."

Laila sucked in a breath, even as she collapsed into the chair next to me. Her left hand cradled her belly even as her right remained clutched on my shoulder.

"And the women?" I said.

For the first time, Gharib shifted his gaze from the phone to me.

I could see the answer in his eyes.

"The women were herded into waiting trucks like cattle and driven away."

"Why?" I said.

Gharib shrugged.

"I don't know for sure. It's rumored that they're being set aside as brides for Taliban fighters. I'm going to Afghanistan. I've already purchased my ticket."

"What are you going to do?" I said.

"Whatever I can," Gharib said, the simple words spoken without bravado.

I looked from the cell phone with the cracked screen to the broken man holding it.

Whatever I can.

The truth was that Gharib would be able to do very little. He was a computer programmer, not a warrior. His soft frame spoke to an accommodation reached with middle age—a pledge not to do anything stupid with cheeseburgers in exchange for a promise not to embark on a second career as a powerlifter. I'd have been surprised if Gharib had partaken in any exercise more rigorous than a daily walk to the mailbox in years. Neither did he have the financial resources to ransom his daughter or the political weight to motivate the State Department's bureaucrats.

He was simply a father with a missing daughter.

"Look," I said, choosing my words carefully even as Laila dug her fingers deeper into my shoulder, "I—"

"Matt," Laila said, the pain in her voice evident.

"I know, baby," I said, squeezing her hand. "I won't—"

"Matt—it's the baby."

I turned to see my wife bent at the waist, both hands wrapped around her stomach.

In a heartbeat I was out of my chair, kneeling at her feet.

"You okay?" I said.

Laila lifted her head, and my stomach dropped.

This time, her emerald eyes reflected another emotion.

Fear.

TWENTY-NINE

watched the green line bounce on the electronic display, willing it to continue its merry dance even as the fear gripping my heart whispered that each wobble would be the last. Actually, there were two green lines. One cycled much slower and belonged to Laila.

The other was Virginia's.

"She's doing fine. They both are."

I looked from the EKG monitors to the shift nurse standing in the doorway. Her short hair had more gray than black, and her laugh lines had deepened to furrows, but her blue eyes still shone like those of a woman half her age. She projected competence and compassion in equal measure—part medical technician and part grandmother.

A comforting combination.

I eased my hand from beneath Laila's and stood, moving toward the nurse with slow, deliberate motions. Laila had kept it together the entire way to the hospital, even making it through the first round of examinations without so much as a word. Only once the contractions had ceased and the doctor had assured her that the baby was okay did the emotion she'd kept hold of so tightly break free. My wife had wept with abandon, and I'd held her until the tide receded.

Then she'd fallen asleep.

Not me.

"What's *fine* mean?" I said, whispering the question.

"It means that your baby girl isn't coming today."

"What about tomorrow?" I said.

"The doctor will have more to say about that."

"I'm asking you," I said.

The woman paused as her blue eyes took stock of mine.

Then she nodded.

"I suspect the doctor will want to admit your wife for the next twenty-four hours to ensure the contractions don't return. After that, I imagine she'll put her on bed rest. Your wife is at sixteen weeks. We need to keep that baby inside her until at least thirty-two."

I nodded. This tracked with what I'd been able to google, but hearing the prognosis delivered in the nurse's no-nonsense voice was reassuring.

"Why is this happening?" I said.

The nurse softly sighed.

"That's the million-dollar question. It could be any number of things. The truth is, we just don't know. Some women have trouble carrying to term. Others don't. I'm afraid there's no rhyme or reason."

"Could it be stress?" I said.

The nurse's eyes hardened.

"We're not having any of that," she said, steel in her voice.

"Any of what?" I said.

"Any of you blaming yourself. I don't know you, Mr. Drake. But I know your type."

"My type?"

The nurse nodded.

"I'm married to a hard man too. He runs into burning buildings for a living. A man like that never sees the good he does because he's too busy chastising himself for the ones he couldn't save. You've got my husband's look, Mr. Drake. The look of someone who goes into harm's way while carrying the weight of others on his shoulders. What happened to your wife is not your fault. The sooner you come to terms with that, the sooner you'll stop feeling sorry for yourself and start being useful to her."

I didn't know what I'd been expecting her to say, but that wasn't it. My face must have reflected my shock, because the nurse tempered her next words with a smile.

"Don't be getting all sensitive on me," the nurse said, squeezing my biceps. "The world needs hard men. Without the likes of you, evil would triumph. But right now I need you to let that go and just be with your wife. Okay?"

I nodded, not trusting myself to speak.

"You're a good man, Mr. Drake," the nurse said, gripping my hand in both of hers. "Now go be a good husband."

With that admonishment, she walked out of Laila's room, trailing a cloud of Chanel No. 5. As someone who'd grown up going to church, I'd heard the phrase *God works in mysterious ways* more times than I could a count. Over the course of my paramilitary career, I'd certainly felt the Almighty's presence. That said, a guardian angel who wore my mother's perfume was a new one. I watched her stride down the hall, half expecting a chariot of fire to collect her, when my phone buzzed.

I pulled the device from my pocket and looked at the caller ID.

James.

I'd spent the last several minutes listening to an angel. Now it was time to give the devil his due.

THIRTY

"Drake," I said into the handset.

I stepped into the hallway, easing the door closed behind me. While I'd managed not to disturb Laila during my conversation with the angel-turned-nurse, I knew better than to try that with James.

My boss did not do quiet.

"Matthew—where are you?"

"The hospital."

"Christ," James said, his voice thundering from the handset. "Who did you kill this time?"

A candy striper pushing a cart full of books gave me a sharp glance.

I answered with my brightest smile.

He didn't reciprocate.

Taking James's comment as an indication for how this conversation would go, I looked up and down the hall, searching for somewhere close to Laila's room that would offer me the opportunity to talk in private. Aside from the rows of patient rooms, my only option was an unmarked door next to the bathroom across the hall.

"Wait one," I said to James as I hurried to the door.

The lockpick set I kept in my truck's glove box was inaccessible, but my shoulder functioned just fine. After ensuring the candy striper wasn't returning for a second look, I prepared to slam my body into the door.

Then I had a startling thought.

I grabbed the door handle and turned it.

Unlocked.

Who said you couldn't teach an old dog new tricks?

"Okay, Chief," I said, closing the door behind me. I was in some sort of broom closet and it took a bit of fumbling before I found a light switch. "I can talk."

"How many more bodies did you add to your tab?" James said.

"I didn't kill anyone," I said. "It's Laila. There's trouble with the baby."

"Shit," James said, his tone instantly one of contrition. "Is she all right? Is baby James all right?"

I had explained to my boss that we were having a girl about a dozen times. James either didn't believe me or didn't care. Rather than correcting what I'd corrected countless times before, I devoted my energies to a more fruitful task—finding someplace in the crowded maintenance closet to sit. Shelves containing cleaning supplies and other odds and ends lined one wall while an industrial sink took up most of the other. The rear of the room was cluttered with plungers, mops, brooms, and other tools of the trade, leaving me to believe that the tiny bit of floor space I currently occupied was my best bet.

Surrendering to the inevitable, I took one of the large buckets from a hook on the wall and spun it upside down. A rubber doorstop dropped onto the floor. After wedging the stop beneath the door, I sat down on the bucket. Few things did a better job of reminding you of your place in the world than planting your backside on a dirty mop bucket.

"The baby's fine, boss," I said, stifling a sneeze. "Laila is too. Though I think the doctor's gonna want her on bed rest."

"You need some time?"

I sighed. That was the million-dollar question. Should I take some time off to be with my wife? Yes. Could I afford to do so right now? Probably not. Between Frodo, the hit team, and now Gharib's daughter, Ferhana, time wasn't something I had in large quantities.

"I'll talk to Laila," I said, hedging with both James and myself.

While this was true, I also knew the notion of being waited on by her mother was not one my wife would relish. I'd cross that bridge once I came to it. First, I needed help from my boss. The kind of help that only James Glass could provide.

"Good," James said, "because I need you back here pronto."

That sounded encouraging.

"You got a lead on the shooters?"

"If by *lead* you mean, did everyone from the Director on down call to ask why I was flagging a credentialed foreign intelligence officer with our search engines, yes. Yes, I did. The Chinese diplomat you bagged was a suspected Ministry of State Security operative. The other shooters are Mexican Zetas. Foot soldiers to be sure, but they are without a doubt cartel. Before you ask, no one knows why Zetas are palling around with a Chinese intelligence officer, much less why they targeted a former Green Beret. As usual, you managed to kick over an anthill, Matthew."

I bit my tongue to refrain from pointing out that I'd made the shooters' acquaintance only *after* they'd tried to kill me. I knew that this was James's way of venting and that he would spool down eventually. Still, enduring a dressing-down for having the temerity to live through an assassination pissed me off. But getting angry about James's lack of empathy was about as useful as yelling at a dog for watering a fire hydrant.

Things were what they were.

Besides, from a tactical perspective it made sense that the Hispanic shooters were Zetas. The Zetas were unique among Mexican cartels in that many of their founding members were former soldiers, some of whom had benefited from special operations training when they'd still been employed by the Mexican government. This did much to explain the tactics employed by the hitmen. But it did little to explain why one of Mexico's most notorious narco organizations was working with a Chinese intelligence officer.

"There are two teams of shooters," I said as a particularly ferocious-looking black spider emerged from a pile of washrags to my right. "Maybe more. I took a private plane from Austin to North Carolina and the operatives intent on bagging Jason beat me to his house. Unless they had a Concorde on standby, there's no way the guys now fertilizing Jason's tomatoes also put me in the river."

"Seriously, Matthew," James said, "there are some

things we don't talk about. Even on a secure line. You're probably right, but that's no longer important."

"A Chinese intelligence officer partnering with Zeta hitters to knock off a former Green Beret isn't important?"

The arachnid scurried off a stack of paper towels and dropped to the floor. Was it black widows that had the marking on their bellies or brown recluses? Better question—how were you supposed to inspect a spider's belly?

"Don't get all hysterical," James said. "I didn't mean your little situation isn't important. It's just not important *right now.* Hell, men from Mars landing on the White House lawn wouldn't be important *right now.* If the subject doesn't have an Afghanistan nexus, nobody in this building gives a shit."

"That's the thing, Chief," I said. "It just might."

The spider scurried closer.

I debated drawing my pistol.

If spiders and snakes weren't proof of the adage *shoot first and ask questions later,* I didn't know what was.

"Speak, Matthew."

"Afghanistan is the connective tissue between everything that's happened. Or more specifically, Afghanistan in 2011."

"Your first tour with DIA?" James said.

My boss's near photographic memory for operational details never ceased to amaze me. Ann Thelma Beaumont had been his executive assistant for almost fifteen years, and James still had trouble remembering her last name, let alone her birthday. But ask him about a debrief of a high-value target from two decades ago, and James could recite the interrogation transcript almost word for word.

My boss was Rain Man with an eye patch.

"Yes," I said. "Jason and the other dead Green Beret, Fletcher Spies, were on the same ODA."

"First off, we don't know that Fletcher's death wasn't an accident, and—" James said.

"Like me almost drowning?" I said.

"Damn it, Matthew," James said. "You've been hanging around Israelis too long. If you'd have let me finish, I'd have said that I pulled Jason's and Fletcher's service records. They were part of ODA 3324. You and Frodo didn't support that team."

ODA 3324.

How in the hell had I missed that?

"Chief, are you sure it was ODA 3324?" I said.

"Did I stutter? Of course I'm sure. Why?"

Why indeed.

"The CID agents that arrested Frodo," I said, "I had a talk with them."

"Please, God, tell me they are not also in Jason's garden."

"I thought there were some things we didn't talk about even on a secure line?" I said.

"Answer the fucking question," James screamed.

"Relax, Chief," I said. "They're still among the living. In fact, I'd say that our chat was downright friendly. For the most part."

"Matthew."

"Look," I said, "the important part is that the lead agent, Julie Soto, got a look at a redacted summary of the restricted case file. There were a couple of other people mentioned. All were veterans of ODA 3324. The same ODA that my pal Rawlings said FBI headquarters was interested in."

"I still don't see what that has to do with you and Frodo," James said. "You two never supported that team."

"Officially," I said.

The spider scurried within stomp range.

It was a clear-cut case of kill or be killed.

I flattened him.

"Matthew?" James said.

"We had a layover in Bagram," I said, "and I met up with Jason. We'd served together in the Ranger Regiment. He was a couple men short for an Op. Frodo and I pitched in."

The silence coming through the phone could have been charitably described as ominous. I toed the remains of the spider out of sight, thinking that perhaps the eight-legged assassin might have gotten the better end of the deal. At least his ending had been quick and relatively painless.

"You and Frodo took part in a direct action mission and never bothered to tell me?"

"I forgot," I said.

"Matthew."

"Look, we were all still feeling each other out back then. Frodo and I had yet to gel, and I didn't even know whether I was going to stay in the DIA. It didn't seem important then."

"It sure as shit seems important now," James said.

"Which is why I'm telling you," I said. "That operation connects everything—Frodo's arrest, Fletcher's death, the attack on me, and the Chinese and Mexican shooters. Everything."

"What did Jason say?" James said.

"That's the frustrating part," I said with a sigh. "I debriefed him on the plane flight back to Austin. He doesn't remember anything special about the operation either. But there's one more person who might."

"I thought everyone from that ODA was accounted for?" James said.

"The *Americans* from the support element that Frodo and I augmented are accounted for," I said, "but not everyone. There was also an Afghan named Zaafir. Officially, he was a 'terp, but he played a larger role than that. Zaafir was part of a trial program in which Afghans served as liaisons to American ODA teams. Zaafir interrogated high-value targets and helped to in-process them at Bagram."

"Zaafir was a shooter?" James said.

"A well-regarded one. If anyone can help us unravel this cluster, it's him."

"And Zaafir is where exactly?"

"Afghanistan," I said. "Kabul to be exact. Jason has stayed in touch with him over the years. Look, I know this is a big ask, but let me go find him. I'll hitch a ride with whoever else from our shop is flooding the zone. Give me an operational tasking—I don't care what. Just let me go. Jason gave me Zaafir's contact info. I can effect linkup and learn what he knows in a day, probably less. There's a piece we're still missing, and I believe Zaafir can help me put the puzzle together."

"Matthew—you're not listening," James said. "We're not sending anyone to Afghanistan."

"You mean, our branch isn't?" I said. "How is this not a mission for counterterrorism?"

"Not just our branch. The entire Defense Intelligence Agency. There will be no DIA employees in Afghanistan."

The door to the broom closet jiggled.

"Occupied," I said, even as I replayed James's answer, convinced I'd misheard.

"Are you in a bathroom?" James said.

"Did you just say that we're abandoning the entire Afghanistan theater?" I said.

"That's exactly what I've been saying for the last ten minutes. Come hell or high water, the administration has decided that on 31 August the only people left in Afghanistan will be Afghans."

The implications were staggering. In addition to the countless Afghans who'd helped and fought alongside us during the two decades of conflict, untold numbers of US citizens and green card holders must have also been caught unaware by the Taliban's lightning-fast advance and were likely trapped.

People like Ferhana, Gharib's daughter.

"If you're not sending anyone to Afghanistan, why do you want me to come in?" I said.

The banging on the door began again, this time more pounding than knocking.

"Almost finished," I yelled. "Shouldn't have had that second breakfast taco."

"Because your job is here," James said. "Rational

minds might still prevail. If and when we get the go-ahead to launch into theater, I want you at Andrews Air Force Base with your kit packed. Until then, we need to be sifting through the intelligence feeds, activating assets, and executing evacuation plans. Just because you aren't running and gunning doesn't mean there isn't shit to do."

What James said made sense. If we really were going to pull out, managing the evacuation would be a bitch. I could understand why James didn't want to concern himself with Zaafir, even if I didn't agree with his decision. As far as he was concerned, dealing with Jason's shooters could wait. Direct action teams operating on foreign soil don't come back for a second try. Whoever was running things from the Chinese side would know by now that the team they'd sent to Jason's farm had failed. The MSS folks would be focused on executing their exfiltration plans, not making another run at their target.

Unless I was prepared to bring in the FBI via Rawlings, the shooters would have to take a backseat. And there was no way I was going to try to explain six dead bodies to Rawlings. I had a good relationship with my Supervisory Special Agent friend, but he wouldn't sweep what happened at Jason's farm under the rug. The FBI would launch a formal investigation, and I'd be sidelined until it ran its course. Besides, the chaos enveloping Afghanistan was an all hands on deck moment the likes of which hadn't been seen since 9/11. James's request for me to shift focus was completely logical.

Except for one thing.

"What about Frodo?" I said.

The sigh echoing through the phone rattled my teeth.

"Son, you know that I'd move heaven and earth for the two of you," James said, "but there's nothing either of us can do for Frodo right now."

"So we just let him rot?" I said.

"You know damn well that's not what I'm saying. Since you seem to need a refresher, let me summarize the facts as we know them—Frodo is not being held by the Taliban. He's in jail and, for reasons we don't understand, seems rather determined to stay there. In fact, he rebuffed your offer of help. While I'm not advocating for surrender, I am saying that we need to prioritize our efforts. By this time tomorrow, Frodo will be in military confinement. It's certainly not the Ritz, but he won't be in any danger. I need you here. Now. If the answer to what's going on with Frodo really does reside in Afghanistan, then it's quite possible you might learn something of value. Either way, you're not heading overseas. No one is. Got it?"

I got it.

But that didn't mean I had to like it.

The wood bowed under the onslaught of pounding, and I scooted the doorstop out from beneath the door and pulled it open. A maintenance man and a security guard waited in the hallway.

"No worries," I said, slapping the janitor on the shoulder, "I took care of it."

"Took care of what?" The man said.

"The black widow," I said. "He scurried under the door. I followed. What's left of him is in the corner."

The maintenance worker's look of suspicion turned to something else as he peered over my shoulder.

"There really is a spider," he said.

"Well, of course there is," I said. "Why else would I be in a broom closet?"

I slid between the two men, angling across the hall for Laila's room.

I paused at the threshold, took the cell off mute, and put the device back to my ear.

"You there, Chief?" I said.

"Where else would I go?" James thundered. "Now get your ass in here. There's work to be done."

"No," I said, the word rolling off my tongue before I could stop it.

"Say again, over?"

"You heard me, Chief. I'm not coming."

"Matthew—there are times when you've defied my authority and everything has still turned out all right. This will not be one of those times. Do you read me?"

"Loud and clear," I said.

"I don't think you do," James said.

"You're probably right, boss," I said, "but I'm not much for office politics. Here's what I know—the people who need me aren't in DC."

"What do you want me to tell the Director?"

"Tell him I'm on vacation."

I hung up.

The United States of America had made its choice.

And so had I.

THIRTY-ONE

Y ou're on vacation? How fun."

The comment came from my very awake wife. Though the doctor had assured me that she was in no immediate danger, the sight of her lying in a hospital bed hit me in the gut. She looked smaller against the crisp white hospital linens.

Frail.

"You heard that?" I said, leaning over to kiss her forehead.

"I'm married to a spy," Laila said. "I've got big ears."

"Your ears were the first thing I noticed about you," I said, reaching for her as I sat down in the chair beside her bed.

"They most assuredly were not," Laila said, snaring my hand with both of hers before it could wander.

"Okay, maybe the second thing."

"You know what else being a spy's wife taught me?" Laila said as she moved my fingers to her swelling belly. "How to spot bullshit."

"Easy with the language," I said, rubbing her baby bump. "Little pitchers have big ears too."

Laila smiled, but the gesture didn't quite reach her eyes.

"Are you going make me ask?" Laila said. "Or do you want to just tell me?"

I thought about making another witty comeback, but as much as I loved the sound of my wife's laugh, it was time to come clean. I was not an accountant, and we did not pretend otherwise. Conversations about my work followed a series of ironclad guidelines. There were things Laila was permitted to know and things she was not.

"Everything that's happened is somehow linked together," I said.

"Even Frodo's arrest?" Laila said.

"Especially Frodo's arrest. It's tied to an operation he and I were part of years ago."

"Where?" Laila said.

"Afghanistan."

THIRTY-TWO

Turbine flight is REDCON 1: Stand by for Zebra, over."

I clutched my M4 closer to my chest, preparing for the stomach-dropping lurch that always accompanied an MH-6 clawing its way skyward. In some ways, I welcomed the unsettling feeling. Though I detested riding on the troop benches mounted to the Little Bird's exterior as much as the next assaulter, flying was the familiar part of the mission.

Everything else was chaos.

"Zebra, Zebra, Zebra."

The egg-shaped helicopter in front of me lifted off in a spray of water as its cyclonic downdraft churned the puddles covering the tarmac. The droplets splattered against my night vision goggles, the moisture washing out the picture like I'd driven into a fogbank. That also happened to be a fairly accurate description of my mental state. Once again, I had to keep myself from acknowledging the radio call as strange voices filled the airwaves. For the first time in my operational career, I was relegated to the backseat.

Literally.

I was on the rearmost Little Bird in our flight of four, sitting in the aft position on the starboard bench. The position occupied by the least important man in the stack. In this case, I was fine with bringing up the rear since I was still a bit iffy on the whole concept of the operation. After the runner from the TOC had interrupted our impromptu session with Jason, things had happened fast.

Really fast.

While Jason and Captain Brendan McGourthy, the ODA team leader, had congregated at the TOC for a final update, Frodo and I got acquainted with our new teammates and frantically configured our weapons and kit. Because my comrade in arms was a former Unit sniper with more deployments under his belt than most people had trips to the grocery store, Frodo had insisted that we zero our long guns before starting the long journey to Afghanistan. While any rifleman worth his salt knew that another zero would be required to account for the altitude and environmental conditions after we arrived in our new theater of operation, Frodo's HK and my M4 were more than adequate for close-range CQB work.

That was the good news.

The not-so-good news was that we would be integrating into a tactical team with which we'd never even conducted a walk-through rehearsal. While there was certainly a standard way the Army taught the battle drills associated with entering and clearing a building, every unit tweaked these techniques. Frodo's Unit brethren were considered the world's premier CQB practitioners, but just because you played football in the NFL didn't mean you could successfully jump into a high school team's starting lineup. Though Frodo and I were both deadly in our own right, our unfamiliarity with the men we were assisting had the potential to render us more liability than help.

Unless we were properly managed.

Fortunately, Jason and Frodo were of the same mind in that regard. For starters, we would be augmenting the support rather than the main effort. The target we were hitting was a typical walled Afghan compound consisting of a primary dwelling and a smaller outbuilding. According to the Fox's Afghan asset, the bomber lived and worked in the primary dwelling, leaving the outbuilding for a single elderly housekeeper. The roofs of both buildings were flat and used for communal gatherings during the stifling summer nights. Though both structures were single story, traditional Afghan construction didn't rely much on blueprints or tape measures. In this case, the outbuilding's single story was several feet higher than its companion.

This bit of happenstance made the structure an ideal location for a sniper-spotter overwatch team. Frodo and I would fill this role while the other four members of the support, or Gold, element cleared the outbuilding and secured any occupants before collapsing on the primary building to augment the Blue, assault, element. While the ODA team members conducted the kind of synchronized combat that required long hours of practice, Frodo and I would watch for squirters and provide security.

Simple.

Or at least it had seemed simple in the rushed briefing conducted in front of the team's whiteboard while we'd thrown on our kit. Now that I was on the helicopter headed toward the target, everything felt more loosey-goosey than I would have liked. Granted, meticulous mission planning and exhaustive rehearsals were hallmarks of my previous unit, but this was not the Ranger Regiment. The twelve men who made up an ODA team were senior noncommissioned officers, whereas the majority of the assaulters in my Ranger company were between the ages of eighteen and twenty. The level of maturity, experience, and familiarity Jason's teammates had with one another and the intended target made the quick turn time feasible.

Even so, there was a ton of white space between feasible and optimal.

"Gold elements, this is Gold 1, we are five minutes out. I say again, five minutes, over."

"Two."

"Three."

I listened as each member of Gold Team acknowledged Jason's radio transmission until it was my turn.

"Six," I said after keying the radio.

Though the entire Gold element sat on the same Little Bird, Jason was still using the radio to communicate. Between the howling engine, thundering rotor blades, snapping wind, and pelting rain, voice communication would have been impossible. My Peltor noise-canceling headset did much to attenuate the ambient sound, but even a casual conversation with Frodo, who was seated next to me, would have been difficult without the radio.

In a flash of realization, I understood what was bugging me about the radio calls—there were too few of them. As a company commander, I'd always had at least two radios active at the same time, sometimes more. One net was devoted to my battalion commander while the second was my company net, which I used to speak with my platoon leaders, first sergeant, and senior NCOs. Then there was the fires net, the close-air-support net, and a number of one-off radio channels I would tune to at different points in the mission. Taken in sum, the communications plan made for a lot of voices in my ear.

Not tonight.

Tonight, I was in charge of my rifle.

That was it.

The silence wasn't so much strange as eerie, and the slicing rain wasn't helping. Unlike the pilots who had a forward-looking infrared-sensor pod to help them see through the mush as well as a windshield to keep the moisture from their sensitive night vision goggles, my world was a sea of green. This was somewhat comforting since the bad guys would have a hard time shooting what they couldn't see, but the inclement weather worked both ways. If we started taking fire during the flight, I'd be hard-pressed to do anything about it. We operated at night precisely because our NODs provided us with a technological overmatch.

Tonight, Mother Nature was doing her best to even the score.

"Gold elements, Gold 1, one minute."

This time no one bothered to acknowledge Jason's transmission. At least not audibly. As per standard operating procedure, the last sixty seconds of an infiltration were pretty busy. This is when assaulters chambered a round in their rifles, performed last-minute checks on their gear, and put on their game faces. Frodo shifted next to me as he conducted his precombat inspections.

I followed suit.

I started by verifying that my M4 was on safe. Then I checked my holographic sight's illumination level in case I needed to aim without using my goggles. Next I turned on the AN/PEQ-2A laser mounted to the Picatinny rail affixed to my rifle so I could accurately shoot while wearing NODs. Finally, I ran my hands over my plate carrier, ensuring the pouches were secure and that nothing was in danger of slipping out. Once I was satisfied that I was ready, I squeezed Frodo's leg and gave him a thumbs-up. He nodded and responded with the same gesture.

Then he checked in with the assaulter to his left.

From now until we were on the rooftop, the Gold assaulters would maintain radio silence. This wasn't because we were worried about giving away our position with random radio chatter—the 425-horsepower turboshaft engine howling in each helicopter was doing a fine job of that. No, we were staying off the radios to keep the channel clear for the team leaders and the commander. We were about to learn the hard way whether we'd achieved tactical surprise.

It was the enemy's first chance to vote.

The MH's nose pitched up as the helicopter flared to decelerate. I still saw only green fog, and my sphincter tightened. 160th aviators were damned good pilots, but they were still human. Mistakes sometimes happened even to the best stick wigglers, and I was beginning to think that I might be in the middle of one. Just as I was tempted to vocalize my discomfort with a very un-Ranger-like scream, the building materialized beneath us.

The Little Bird's skids kissed the roof, and I was off the bench.

I sprinted toward the edge of the structure, running in a low crouch. As with many Afghan homes, a foot-high wall ran the perimeter of the roof, providing a guardrail against accidental falls.

I thought it would also make an excellent rifle rest.

Unfortunately, the enclosure prevented the Little Bird's downdraft from escaping over the building's side. Frothing fingers of air ripped at my face and body and sandblasted me with grit and dirt. A cot went tumbling end over end, sheets streaming behind it like a kite's tail. A single wooden leg caught the lip of the wall, and the cot cartwheeled over the side. An inverted card table slid across the wet surface before slamming into the enclosure. Then the gale became a full-fledged hurricane as the helicopter popped into the air and roared away.

The silence that followed was jarring.

It didn't last.

"Gold 5 and Gold 6 are Bluebell, over."

I could hear Frodo's baritone in stereo, his voice coming both from the radio and from where he was crouched beside me. He'd already extended the bipod mounted to the forward handgrip of his HK 417 rifle and was using the top of the wall as a shooting platform. I did the same, orienting off his right shoulder as I surveyed my assigned sector within the compound.

"Gold 5, Gold 1, acknowledge Bluebell. We are Graeters, time now."

Like every operation, significant actions were assigned radio brevity code words that followed a theme—in this case, ice cream brands. Bluebell meant that Frodo and I were in position while Graeters indicated that the rest of Gold team was beginning the task of clearing the empty building.

Or maybe not so empty.

A *thump* as the breaching charge detonated was followed by a series of *pops* behind me as the Gold assaulters made entrance. The detachable cans mounted to the assault team's rifles suppressed the reports, but certainly didn't silence the sound. The answering AK-47 fire had no suppression whatsoever. I instinctively crouched lower, trying to present a smaller target even as I resisted the urge to turn toward the sound of gunfire. Discipline was one of the hallmarks of CQB. Even though everything in me wanted to add my rifle to the fight raging within the building, the compound's courtyard was my responsibility. I had to trust the assault team to do their job just like they were trusting me to do mine. A pair of men armed with AK-47s raced from behind the garage in the courtyard below, sandals slapping the wet ground.

"Two Crows, sector alpha," I said.

"Tally," Frodo said.

Though special operators pride themselves on keeping a calm voice under pressure, Frodo was in a class by himself. I hadn't shouted my observation, but I'd be lying if I said that the pitch in my voice hadn't edged up slightly at the two men's sudden appearance.

Not Frodo's.

We might as well have been discussing the weather for all the give-a-shit his unhurried cadence reflected. I tracked my laser's red dot to the second form, but needn't have bothered.

Frodo's HK barked twice.

Both gunmen flopped to the ground.

"Crows down," Frodo said.

"Confirmed," I said, panning my laser across both crumpled forms in case either man needed a second shot.

They didn't.

Frodo had drilled both combatants in the head while they'd been running in the dark. Some people were born to compose symphonies, paint masterpieces, or write great literature. Frodo was created to kill his nation's enemies.

With him by my side, I felt immortal.

"Gold 5, Gold 1, Chicago. I say again, Chicago."

And just that quickly, my euphoria vanished.

Jason's radio transmission just signified a change in the battlefield. A change for the worse. *Chicago* was the brevity word instructing Frodo to leave his position and join the assault team. Resistance inside the structure must have been greater than we'd anticipated.

"Gold 1, Gold 5, roger Chicago."

Frodo squeezed my shoulder and headed for the door at a run.

And just like that, I was alone.

THIRTY-THREE

Frodo's departure left me with a decision to make. While you could take the man out of command, you could not take the commander out of the man. I was in charge of nothing—a notion that Jason had driven home in a kind but firm manner during our rushed rehearsal brief. I understood. When bullets started flying and the plan went sideways, there could be just one person in charge of the fight.

I was not that person.

But old habits still died hard.

Like Jason, I'd outfitted my vest with two radios. The first was tuned to the Gold internal net as he'd instructed. But the second was dialed to the command net. This wasn't because I planned on second-guessing Jason or Brendan. My decision reflected only my desire to bring what I did best to this fight, even if that capability was never needed. Frodo was a savant with a rifle. Some of that was nature and an awful lot was nurture. I was a good gunfighter, but I would never perform at his level.

My gifts lay elsewhere.

Reaching to the radio pouch fastened to my back, I found the volume dial and spun it to the right.

Like all gunfighters, I had a love-hate relationship with technology. While I loved the advantages my kit provided over the average jihadi equipped with nothing more than an AK-47 outfitted with iron sights, I was also highly distrustful of gadgets. In my experience, Murphy's Law applied doubly to technology. The moment you needed them most, GPSs were prone to lose their satellite link, optics would mysteriously go dark, and radios would cease to function.

With this in mind, I'd powered on my second radio and tested it as we'd been loading the helicopters. Once I was certain the Wave Relay radio was functioning correctly, I turned the command net's volume to zero rather than powering down the radio. This meant that the instant I spun the volume dial, a cacophony of voices flooded my ear.

I'd decided to monitor the command net for situational awareness purposes. Without Frodo, I had no one to help me keep track of the fight outside our building, and since I was now the lone assaulter providing overwatch for both Blue and Gold elements, this seemed like a critical task. Within about three seconds of listening to the command net chatter, I realized that I'd made the correct decision.

Things were not going according to plan.

"Red 1, this is Blue 1, say again new ETA, over."

"Blue 1, Red 1, unknown. I say again, unknown. We are cross-loading vehicles at this time. Our disabled truck has made route Iceberg impassible. We will flex to route

Cherry, but anticipate another ten mikes of travel time. Suggest you alert Bagram QRF, over."

Not good.

Red 1 was our liaison with a company-sized Afghan National Army, or ANA, element. While the ODA assaulters hit the target buildings and secured them, the ANA force was to provide the outer cordon. This was both for squirter control in case anyone escaped the compound and, more important, to keep any local troublemakers from joining the fight.

The Afghans rode in Hilux pickup trucks. Old, reliable, but extremely noisy. To maintain the element of surprise, Brendan had elected to stage the vehicles just inside Bagram's Entry Control Point, or ECP. This kept them out of sight of any front-gate watchers, but it also meant that the trucks would arrive at the objective approximately ten minutes after the assaulters hit the target.

Now their arrival was in jeopardy.

Motion from the gated entrance to the compound caught my eye. Shifting to my left, I pointed my rifle at the door just as a pair of fighters rushed through. I triggered the laser, centered the red dot on the center mass of the first fighter, and fired, dropping him.

His partner turned toward me, the muzzle of his AK belching flame.

I panned the laser dot onto his chest and fired twice more.

He joined his partner.

"Blue 1, this is Gold 6," I said, transmitting on the command net. "We have Crows coming in the main gate.

I say again, Crows coming in the compound's gate, over."

I sprinted for the opposite side of the walk as I spoke, praying for the best even as I prepared for the worst. The lack of an immediate on-site outer cordon was one of the riskiest elements of the plan. While I agreed with Brendan's reasoning, if this were my operation, I would have probably traded stealth for security.

This was not my operation.

In Brendan's defense, there was supposed to be a Predator overhead providing real time ISR exactly to avoid a surprise like this.

"Gold 6, Blue 1, roger that. Let me know what we've got. Pred is on station, but cannot see through the cloud cover. We also have zero coverage from the Spectre gunship for the same reason."

Oh for two.

Without the UAV or the AC-130 overhead, we had only our organic firepower to deal with the bad guys and no advance warning if they decided to try something tricky.

This operation was going south in a hurry.

"Blue 1, roger," I whispered as I drew even with the side of the building, looking out over the street. "Stand by for SITREP."

I crawled the last few feet to keep my head below the wall. In a situation like this, speed was critical, but it was also better to be slow and alive than fast and dead. I squirmed through a puddle, and the frigid water sluiced down the front of my shirt. Ignoring the icicles banding my chest, I made it to the wall and then stuck my head over the side for a quick peek.

A hail of gunfire chased me back.

"Blue 1, Gold 6," I said as I worked a pair of fragmentation grenades free from my vest, "a dozen Crows are staged outside the gate. I say again, squad-sized element staged in the road outside the main gate, over."

I pulled the grenade's pin, let the spoon fly, waited a two count, and then tossed the munition over the lip before doing the same with the second frag. The grenade's four-to-five-second fuse could be both incredibly long and terribly short, depending on the situation. While I didn't think the fighters would have enough time to scoop up the frag and hurl it back at me, I wasn't about to leave that to chance.

"Gold 6, Blue 1—"

The grenades detonated in two distinct explosions, one of which seemed uncomfortably close to my head. As I said, fuse time was incredibly subjective. Rolling to my left, I popped back over the lip and sprayed the street with several bursts from my M4.

What I saw was not encouraging.

My two frags had taken a toll, but the majority of gunmen were still on their feet. Two bodies lay sprawled in front of the gate, and I put a third fighter down with my rifle, but at least half a dozen more were now across the street. Their muzzles winked at me even as high-velocity rounds tore divots out of the section of wall where I'd last made my appearance.

If I hadn't rolled left before popping up, they would have drilled me.

I put an aimed pair into one of the fighters before his three buddies got their act together and sent me scrambling a second time. I heaved another grenade over the wall before crawling to my right, combat reloading as I moved.

"Blue 1, Gold 6," I said as I slapped the bolt release, chambering a round. "Crows have taken cover on the far side of the street. They're suppressing the roof and preparing to breach the gate, over."

"Gold 6, Blue 1, roger. I need you to—"

"Blue 1, this is Gold 1. I need an immediate medevac. One WIA urgent surgical, over."

When it rains, it pours.

"Gold 1, Blue 1, roger all. Send your remaining combat power to Gold 6's location. I'll handle the medevac, over."

"Blue 1, Gold 1, be advised we have not yet secured the objective. I say again, we have not secured the objective. Negative on shifting combat power to Gold 6."

"Gold 1, Blue 1, acknowledged—break. Gold 6, Blue 1, we are still clearing our objective. I need you to secure the main gate, over."

Of course.

"Blue 1, this is Gold 6," I said, "roger all. I've got this."

I did not have this.

Mud chunks were flying from the top of the wall as rifle and automatic weapons fire raked my measly cover. The *chunk, chunk, chunk* of a DShK heavy machine gun echoed from the street. The weapon was originally designed to swat helicopters from the sky. The crew-served weapon would make short work of the wall, not to mention the former Ranger crouched behind it.

But the machine gun's appearance was more foreboding than just the serious uptick in firepower its employment represented. The DShK weighed too much to be man portable, meaning that at least one technical, or a machine-gun-equipped truck, had joined the fray. That the machine gun was raising hell on my roof could only mean that the squad of men I'd sent scurrying for cover was now moving under the protection of the DShK's suppressive fire.

If the shooters breached the gate, we were in for a world of hurt.

For a long moment I debated popping up for a look, but didn't. As much as I wanted to get a visual on what was happening in the streets, it was no longer germane to my mission. Either I was right and the enemy was getting ready to assault through the gate, or I was wrong and they were using the technical to break contact.

Regardless of which scenario was true, my utility on the roof had come to an end.

Abandoning my observation post, I low-crawled to the side of the roof facing the compound, trying not to think about the monstrous projectiles churning through the humid air just above my head. With a speed born of equal parts adrenaline and desperation, I covered the open roof in record time. Then, before the rational part of my brain could talk me out of it, I swung my legs over the mud wall, hung by my fingers, and dropped.

Sometimes not looking down can be beneficial.

This was not one of those times.

The fall seemed to take forever, which meant that the roof was a bit higher than the ten feet I'd estimated. I resisted the urge to search for the ground, knowing that my body would follow my head. Instead, I pretended like this was just another beautiful day in the 82nd Airborne, and that I was now dangling from a beautiful silk canopy. A millisecond later, I slammed into the muddy ground and executed a parachute-landing fall that would have made a Black Hat instructor at Airborne School proud.

If he'd had a few too many and was watching a blooper reel.

I hit the ground like a bowling ball rolling off a kitchen table. My boots sank into ankle-deep mud, negating my ability to collapse into a backward roll and thereby attenuate the impact by distributing the force across my back and leg muscles. Instead, a jolt of electricity scorched through every joint, beginning with my ankles and ending at the base of my neck.

Once again, I'd be financing Dr. Kristy Clinton's spring break getaway.

My chiropractor loved me.

Gritting my teeth, I squelched out of the sinkhole and moved toward the front gate in what could charitably be described as a drunken shuffle. My brain was screaming at my body to move faster, but my legs were having none of it. Small-arms fire echoed from the target buildings to my left and right, but I was concentrated on the gate twenty meters away.

Until it exploded.

The concussion lifted me from my feet and flattened me into the muck. For an instant I lay in the mud and stared at the dark, cloudy sky, contemplating my poor life choices. Then my sense of hearing returned and with it came the rumbling of a heavy diesel engine.

The technical.

I stripped two fresh magazines from my chest harness and placed them on the ground with one hand even as I keyed the radio-transmit button with the other. I hesitated, trying to remember the correct brevity code, then just decided to go with an old standby. Hopefully someone on the net had spent time in the Ranger Regiment.

"Alamo, alamo, alamo," I said while rolling onto my stomach. "Gold 6 is Alamo."

A flood of voices answered my transmission, but they were no longer my concern. I'd done what I could to warn the team, now I was focused on just one thing.

Staying alive.

THIRTY-FOUR

The technical crashed through the remnants of the gate, sending timbers flying. Though not an armored vehicle, the dented Hilux truck still cut an imposing figure. Especially once the DShK mounted above its gray crew cab thundered to life.

It's hard to explain the devastating effect a heavy crew-served weapon has on your psyche. A plume of fire the size of a pumpkin erupted from the DShK's muzzle as the gunner went full rock and roll. He was shooting tracers. Even though I knew only every third round was coated with the phosphorous powder that caused the bullets to fluoresce, the green streaks of destruction flashing from the heavy machine gun seemed constant.

And then there was the noise.

An idling jet engine weighed in at one hundred fifty decibels while a detonating flash-bang exuded about one hundred seventy. The DShK assaulted my ears at better than one hundred seventy-two. I could feel the weapon's report in my chest, the concussive muzzle blast hammering at my body armor and rattling my fillings. The heavy machine gun was the epitome of shock and awe. Every prehistoric fiber of my being wanted to cower in the mud until the monster went away.

Unfortunately, Rangers weren't in the cowering business.

The dragon fire belching from weapon's muzzle made my NVGs useless. I flipped the tubes out of the way even as I dialed up the brightness on my EOTech sight. A crimson holographic circle appeared like an old friend stopping by to say hello. I centered the red dot in the middle of the circle on the gunner crouched behind the DShK and squeezed the trigger.

My rifle spat a three-round burst.

At least one of my shots went low, sparking off the machine gun's metal frame, but a sibling or two flew true. The gunner tumbled into the truck bed, and the courtyard was silent.

Mostly.

The Toyota's roaring diesel reminded me of another salient if unpleasant detail.

The fighters didn't need a heavy machine gun to kill me.

I thumbed the M4's selector switch to full auto, panned the red circle of death to the driver's-side windshield, and squeezed the trigger. High-velocity rounds raked the glass, spiderwebbing it in multiple places. I fired a second burst and a third, concentrating my aimpoint on the biggest cracks. As any assaulter worth their salt will tell you, shooting through safety glass was a bitch, especially with the light 5.56mm round. The bonded glass fractured the bullet while altering its trajectory in unpredictable ways. To overcome this obstacle, a shooter could either stand directly over the glass or fire a lot more bullets.

I chose the second option.

I hammered the windshield until my magazine ran dry, reloaded, and burned through another half a magazine as the truck rumbled forward. In proof of the axiom that quantity was its own kind of quality, the truck drifted to my right, slamming nose first into the outbuilding. I'd either hit the driver or poured enough lead into the cabin to distract him.

Either outcome was fine by me.

I put another burst through the truck's passenger window. Then I shifted fire to the DShK as an enterprising fighter popped up from the truck bed. I convinced him of the error of his ways, but it required the rest of my magazine. The jihadi toppled to the ground as my M4's bolt again locked to the rear.

I reloaded my final magazine.

Not good.

"Blue 1, Gold 6 is Winchester," I said, giving the brevity code for my ammunition status. "I say again, Winchester."

"Gold 6—"

Two grenades exploded, obliterating whatever it was Brendan had been trying to say. Both munitions detonated just inside the gate about twenty meters away. A chunk of shrapnel *pinged* off my helmet, adding more fire to the inferno of pain raging across my neck, but the distance saved me from more consequential injuries. My reprieve was temporary. With a roar, multiple fighters charged through the Hilux-sized hole in the gate. The jihadis fired their weapons from the hip as they advanced, but aimed fire wasn't all that important when the combatants were this close.

Since I was lying on my stomach, the initial volley passed over my head. The lead fighter realized his mistake the moment he crossed into the courtyard. His rifle's muzzle tracked downward, seeking my prone form. I fired a pair into his chest before shifting to the man standing behind him. But even as I sent a second jihadi crumpling to the ground, I knew this was it.

I was a single man on his last magazine.

There were simply too many of them.

Then someone was lying beside me.

"Can't leave you alone for a goddamn minute."

I knew who the reassuring baritone belonged to, but after resigning myself to dying in the Afghanistan mud, I wasn't quite ready to believe that salvation was at hand. Maybe I was hallucinating. Then the distinctive *thunk* of Frodo's HK joined the fray, and bad guys began to fall.

By the truckload.

"Maybe next time you could show up before I get my ass in a sling?" I said.

"Boy, you live with your ass in a sling," Frodo said.

"That's just hurtful," I said.

"But true."

The combat power an additional rifle added to my predicament was amazing. Then again, the one additional rifle had Frodo behind the optic. Where before the rush of bodies flowing through the battered gate looked like a cresting tsunami, now the flood became a trickle. Though he was undoubtedly talented enough to take out the bad guys from back to front, Audie Murphy style, Frodo had a different plan. My bodyguard shifted from attacker to attacker, dropping them like he was threshing wheat. He rarely needed more than one round per target and most of his kills were head shots.

The effect on the enemy was both immediate and consequential.

A moment ago, I'd been on the verge of being overrun. The attackers breaching the gate would have swept over my dead body before transferring their ire to the two target buildings and the Green Berets inside them.

Not anymore.

Fear is contagious.

So is courage.

My bolt locked to the rear. I was out of ammunition.

But not out of fight.

"Transitioning," I said, unholstering my Glock. Then, before the rational part of my mind could intrude, I voiced the phrase that would bind me to my fate. "Moving."

Though the word *covering* was the correct response to my pronouncement, Frodo replied with something less charitable. I didn't care. I was too focused on the dead fighter sprawled in the mud twenty feet away. Or more specifically, the AK-47 clutched in his hands. Frodo might have been a maestro when it came to slaying bad guys, but one rifle was still just one rifle.

We weren't out of the woods yet.

I covered the slippery ground in a rush without falling, which was in itself a miracle. I'd just made it to the fighter and was crouching down to retrieve his weapon when another gunman rounded the back of the Hilux. I extended my Glock with both hands, found his center mass with the stubby front sight post, and began pressing the trigger. I walked my rounds across his chest cavity and then dropped my pistol in favor of the AK-47 as the fighter tumbled to the ground.

Chest pounding, I scooped up the rifle and sprinted the rest of the way to the Hilux. With my side pressed against the metal body, I edged around the rear bumper, leading with the rifle. I displayed a bit more caution than the dead jihadi, and my restraint saved my life.

A cluster of fighters had regrouped on the far side of the wall.

Fighters armed with RPGs.

"We need to work on your movement technique," Frodo said, now beside me.

I almost jumped out of my skin.

How in the hell does he keep doing that?

"Seriously?" I said, trying to hide my surprise. "I was moving like greased lightning."

"You were moving like my grandma," Frodo said, "and she uses a cane."

He brought his HK up to his shoulder as he spoke, and the rifle barked. In a first for the day, Frodo missed, but his shot still sent the fighters scurrying.

"They've got RPGs," I said, firing a burst from my AK at their retreating forms, "and this truck makes a really big target."

"Agreed," Frodo said. "What's the play?"

"You're asking me?" I said.

"You charged up here like a hero. I assumed you had a plan."

"You know what happens when you assume," I said.

The football-shaped warhead of an RPG peeked around the corner. Frodo and I both opened up, peppering the wall even as the gunner fired. The projectile sailed over our heads and out of the compound.

"Spooked him," Frodo said, changing magazines.

"Not for long," I said. "Ready to move up to the gate?"

"Call it," Frodo said.

Left unsaid was that rushing the fighters probably wasn't going to end well for us. I'd surprised the jihadis once already. They'd be ready for us this time. Then again, we were out of options. Falling back would give the jihadis a chance to storm the compound, and the truck was an RPG magnet, so we couldn't stay where we were.

It was forward or nothing.

"Okay," I said, tucking the AK-47 into my shoulder. "I'm going on three. Three, two—"

"Gold 6, this is Gold 1, get down."

The radio transmission caught me by surprise.

I hesitated.

Frodo didn't.

Letting his sling catch his HK, Frodo grabbed my vest with both hands and jerked me down. A second later I heard the *whump* of an M203 grenade launcher firing. Then an explosion lifted me off the ground. Dirt, dust, and smoke rolled through the open gate in a hazy cloud. Coughing, I tried to get to my feet, but Frodo kept me from moving.

"Keep your crazy ass down," Frodo said.

"What?" I screamed.

A second explosion drowned out his reply.

This time I hugged the ground for all I was worth as the sound of automatic weapons fire echoed from the rooftops of both target buildings. The chattering of 5.56 rifles was a welcome counterpart to the rumble of AK-47s. The gunfight reached a deafening crescendo before dying off in a smattering of *pops*.

"All elements, this is Blue 1. Objective secure. Jackpot on the HVT. Birds are inbound. Hold position, over."

Hallelujah.

Frodo slithered past the truck's front belly until he had a clear line of sight out the gate. After waiting for him to get set, I crawled forward, joining him.

"How'd you know?" I said as sounds of helicopters thundered from overhead.

"Know what?"

"That there'd be a second grenade."

Frodo shook his head.

"You're a damn good Ranger, Matty," Frodo said, "but still a dumbass. Anything worth shooting once is always worth shooting twice."

A Black Hawk touched down behind us, the downdraft blasting us with dirt and grime. But even the filth covering me from head to foot couldn't erase the smile on my face. We were alive, the bad guys were dead, and Frodo thought I was a damn good Ranger.

Sometimes life didn't get any better than that.

THIRTY-FIVE

'm not a tactician," Laila said, "but that doesn't sound like an operation that went horribly wrong."

"Because I left that part out," I said.

As she always did on the rare occasions I could share something operational with her, Laila had listened to my story. Listened with an unnerving singular focus. She didn't interrupt, ask clarifying questions, or offer encouraging words. She just soaked up each word, her emerald eyes radiating support even as her lips stayed firmly pressed together.

"What happened?" Laila said.

"Frodo and I were paired with four other assaulters on Gold Team. One of them was shot and killed during the operation. His name was Tommy. Tommy Ledbetter."

"That's why Jason called for Frodo's help?" Laila said.

I nodded. "A second assaulter, Dan Young, was shot and killed in a follow-on operation two days later, but that was after Frodo and I had already hopped a plane to FOB Chapman."

"Which left just two from your team," Laila said.

"Yes. Jason and Fletcher Spies. Fletcher was killed in a car crash about a week ago."

"And someone just tried to kill you and Jason," Laila said. "That can't be a coincidence."

"I don't think Fletcher's car crash was an accident either," I said.

Laila was quiet for a moment, staring at the wall as she digested everything I'd told her. Then she looked back at me, her eyebrows furrowing.

"Was the bad guy someone important?" Laila said.

My wife was not an intelligence operative, but she was both smart and intuitive. In some ways her unfamiliarity with the world in which I operated was an advantage. She thought through problems without preconceived notions. When she asked questions, they were worth answering.

"No," I said, resting my ear against her belly. I turned my head to listen to baby Virginia even as I watched my wife's face. Even lying in a hospital bed, she was beautiful—midnight hair pooling about head and shoulders, skin the color of a latte, and eyes that grabbed ahold of your soul and refused to let go. "That's the horrible part. Tommy died for the capture of what was really just a midlevel Taliban fighter. Now Frodo is charged with his murder. The real kick in the ass was that we had to let the jihadi go the next day."

"What?" Laila said, her green eyes shimmering. "Why?"

"Politics. The President of Afghanistan, Karzai, had issued an edict forbidding nighttime raids unless the town's mayor was notified beforehand. The Green Berets we were helping tried to follow the rules, but corrupt politicians were using the operational heads-up to warn the raids' targets. After hitting three dry holes in a row, the team leader made the decision to hit first and let the mayor know later. Surprise, surprise, we nabbed the bad guy."

"Then what happened?" Laila said.

"A bunch of folks rioted at Bagram's main gate. Intel suggested that most of them were just paid agitators, but the demonstration got the attention of both Bagram's chain of command and Karzai. The commanding general buckled and ordered the jihadi we'd rolled up released. After that bit of nonsense, I couldn't wait to get on a plane to FOB Chapman."

"That's awful," Laila said.

I shrugged. "That's the kind of war Afghanistan was. Or still is, I guess. Anyway, there's one more person who might know what happened that night. When Jason called Frodo forward, he joined the tactical stack with Tommy, Dan, Fletcher, and an Afghan named Zaafir. Zaafir is the only person still alive who might be able to unravel this thing."

"What about Frodo?" Laila said.

"He's not talking," I said.

"Why?"

"I have no idea," I said.

Laila was quiet.

Though my wife had been valedictorian in high school and graduated summa cum laude from college, she was a self-proclaimed "Crock-Pot thinker." Unlike the DIA operative she'd wed, Laila did not blurt out the first thing that entered her head. Instead, she let her thoughts marinate before arriving at a conclusion. This led to a not insignificant amount of confusion on my part during our early years of marriage. I'd waltzed out of more than one confrontation, convinced that I'd won the argument, only to be blindsided the next day with a blitzkrieg of logic.

Now that we've been together for almost a decade, I like to think that she's learned to respond a bit faster while I've figured out how to pump the brakes. In any case, I knew not to rush Laila in moments like this. Besides, resting my head against her stomach while studying her pretty face wasn't a terrible way to pass the time.

"What's James think?" Laila said.

"That this can wait. Unless they're troops securing Kabul Airport, Americans are only traveling one direction when it comes to Afghanistan—out. With the shooters taken care of and Frodo refusing to talk, James wants me to back burner everything until the situation in Afghanistan reaches a steady state."

"You don't agree?"

I shook my head.

"There's an urgency here. I can feel it. Why would someone want to kill the surviving members of Gold Team dead ten years after that operation? Zaafir might have answers, but the window of time to get them is closing. Once we lose Afghanistan, we'll lose him."

"Then I guess you'd better go," Laila said.

I shook my head. "That's what I told James, but now I don't think so. You and Virginia are my most important people. I'm not leaving y'all in the hospital."

"I'm on bed rest, not dying," Laila said, running her fingers through my hair. "Mom can stay with me until you're back."

"What if something happens while I'm gone?" I said.

"Check it out, stud," Laila said, grabbing a handful of my hair. "Baby Virginia's Daddy does not have a normal job. She and I have accepted that. You need to do the same. This won't be the last time we face this decision. If we need you to stay, I promise to tell you, but you have to promise to believe me. Would I love for you to be here? Of course. Do I need you to be here? Not this time. Go. Save Frodo."

I could see the honesty in Laila's eyes, but I was still confused.

"When we were in the kitchen with Gharib, you wanted me home. What changed?"

Laila loosened her grip on my hair and went back to running her fingers over my scalp. It felt like heaven.

"This changed," Laila said. "For a moment, I really thought I was losing Virginia. That I'd never get to hold my daughter or see her smile. It was gut-wrenching. I've never met her, but the thought of living without Virginia almost broke me. It made me realize the desperation Gharib had to be feeling. To hold a little girl in your arms. To watch her take her first steps. To shepherd her through her teenage years only to watch helplessly as she falls into the hands of monsters. Frodo isn't the only one who needs you, Matt. If you don't help him, Gharib will lose Ferhana. What kind of person would I be if I stood between a father and his daughter?"

Laila's eyes filled with tears. I kissed her forehead, and

she threw her arms around my neck, pulling me close. Her warm skin smelled of vanilla and jasmine and her fragrant hair tickled my nose.

"Go," Laila said between sniffles. "Talk with Zaafir, but more than anything, bring Ferhana home. Whatever it takes. Do you hear me, Matthew? Whatever it takes."

"Okay, baby," I said, hugging Laila back. "Okay."

Laila's arms tightened into a crushing embrace.

Then she let go.

I kissed her once more and used the excuse of moving a strand of raven hair away from her eyes to take a mental picture of her face. What I saw surprised me. The frightened mother-to-be was gone, replaced by someone else.

A warrior.

THIRTY-SIX

MES AYNAK MINES, AFGHANISTAN

Feng Liu detested Afghanistan.

Though some of his Ministry of State Security, or MSS, comrades viewed the country's lush green river deltas, towering brown mountains, and ancient ruins with appreciation if not outright envy, Feng saw nothing of value. When he looked around him, it wasn't the countryside that Feng contemplated. Instead, he thought of a voice he'd somehow been expecting to hear every day for the last ten years.

A voice that signified Feng's greatest failure.

It wasn't Afghanistan that Feng truly detested.

It was her people.

"This is it?"

The question came from Yuze Huang, a member of the People's Liberation Army Special Operations Forces, or SOF. In a page taken from the Americans, MSS leadership had seen the value of closer integration with the PLA's contingent of paramilitary officers. This was especially true for operations like this one. Operations that did not fall into the more genteel category of traditional intelligence work. Though Feng was a member of the

International Intelligence Division of the MSS, also known as Bureau Two, he welcomed the presence of Yuze and his men. Feng was a spy, not a soldier. If Feng's previous trip to Afghanistan was any indication, the SOF contingent would be a most welcome addition. Besides, someone had to guard the convoy's contents, and that someone was not Feng.

"Yes, comrade," Feng said, holding on to the truck's frame as he stretched his aching back. "This is it. Secure the equipment and then begin your perimeter improvements. We will meet in thirty minutes to discuss what will transpire in the next forty-eight hours."

Yuze gave a quick nod, clearly suppressing his instinct to render a salute.

Though he'd never been in the military, Feng had served in his nation's intelligence service for more than twenty years. He'd held positions of authority equivalent to the Chief of Base and Chief of Station titles conferred in the American intelligence lexicon. Two of his postings included successful tours of duty in two of the most sought-after assignments—Taiwan and the United States. While he didn't hold rank in the military sense, Feng was the equivalent of a Senior Colonel and the young paramilitary officer treated him as such.

Yuze was too disciplined to inquire directly, but Feng knew the soldier was trying to make sense of him. To understand why someone of Feng's seniority would undertake such a dangerous mission. Feng understood Yuze's confusion because he felt it too. When his wife had asked a similar question, Feng had told her that he had unfinished business.

His answer made sense even if it wasn't entirely true.

The more honest response was one that Feng could scarcely admit to himself, let alone anyone else. In a stellar career that had garnered both himself and his family much honor, Afghanistan was the lone exception. A posting in which Feng's most ambitious plan had failed.

Spectacularly.

For a man accustomed to succeeding, there was no small amount of shame in knowing this to be true. Like a slowly festering splinter, what had happened ten years ago had left a scar in Feng's confidence. Since that fateful day, his triumphs were always tempered by this singular failure.

Now, thanks to a phone call from a man he'd long feared dead, Feng had been offered a chance at redemption. An opportunity to expunge the one blemish to his otherwise exemplary career. He hated Afghanistan and the cavemen who called her home. This would never change. But returning to this prehistoric nation would be well worth the inconvenience if he could right the wrong from long ago. If the man on the phone possessed what he claimed, this operation would transform Feng's greatest failure into his most successful triumph.

But that was a very big *if*.

"Is it just me, or does this place look even more desolate since we were last here?" Kai Yang said.

Feng laughed as his friend and fellow intelligence officer returned from where he'd been pissing away the three canteens of water he'd consumed on the long drive.

"If you think these buildings look old, you should take a look at yourself," Feng said.

"I'm not the one doing old-man stretches," Kai replied.

Feng smiled even as he continued loosening his tight muscles, now shifting from deep-knee bends to the opening movements of a form taken from Yang-style Tai Chi. While the quasi–martial art was typically associated with the elderly, Feng had always enjoyed the peaceful feeling the movements brought him.

Besides, Kai was correct.

Of the two men, Feng certainly looked and felt the worse for the wear. Though his lanky frame had never been hulking, what little muscle mass he'd possessed had receded, along with his hairline. Feng's bones seemed to protrude against tightly stretched skin even as white stubble replaced what had once been thick black hair. Tai Chi kept him limber, but his days of wrestling bears had retreated, if they'd ever existed.

Kai, on the other hand, was a study in aging gracefully.

The squat man still radiated strength, his hands calloused from weights and his crooked pugilist's nose giving Feng's deputy an air of menace. Kai had accompanied Feng the last time he'd been in Afghanistan, and Feng found his comrade in arm's presence comforting. Unlike Feng, Kai's career had not launched him into the MSS's upper echelons. After Afghanistan, he'd plodded from assignment to assignment, doing well, but never well enough to make the transition from agent runner to leader.

Feng had tried to bring his old friend along to his posting in America, but Kai had refused. Now the summoning to Afghanistan had provided both men with an opportunity. Feng could atone for his mistake while Kai snared a promotion and the larger pension that came with it for his looming retirement.

But first Feng had to succeed where he'd previously failed.

"I think it looks quite homey," Feng said as his eyes traveled across the orderly collection of blue-roofed buildings that comprised the Mes Aynak compound.

The camp had been constructed in the bowl formed by the Baba Wali mountains, whose towering peaks provided a natural barrier to prying eyes from the north, west, and south. A series of roads stretched to the east, leading to the small village of Mes Aynak proper. The compound could also be reached via an unimproved road that meandered through a gap in the towering ridgeline to the north, but that approach was rough going, more suitable to donkeys than the heavy-duty transport trucks loaded down with mining equipment that formed the majority of Feng's convoy.

The compound's location had been chosen both for its proximity to the mine for which it was named and for the security offered by the mountains. But nothing could protect the buildings from the ravaging effect of Afghanistan's climate. Though only forty kilometers southeast of Kabul, the modest modernity of the nation's capital was nowhere to be found. Instead, the Chinese encampment situated in the midst of the barren brown terrain could have been the home of space explorers intent on settling a foreign world.

Mes Aynak village to the east was not much of an

improvement. If the area surrounding the compound represented the prehistoric era, the Mes Aynak village with its mud-brick walls, tiered fields, and water- and electricity-less dwellings could have been torn from the Middle Ages. Advanced when compared to the dawn of single-cell organisms, but not much else.

In some cases, quite a bit worse.

"Give an old man some peace," Feng said as he stepped through the form's final movements. "The drive was fourteen hours longer than I remembered."

Kai shuffled to one side, making way for the convoy's trail vehicle. The column of trucks spiraled down the potholed dirt road to the compound's open gate. Only once the last sputtering semi was out of sight did Kai begin his own series of knee bends.

"Being here overtly has its benefits, I suppose," Kai said, his knees uttering an alarming series of pops "though hopefully we can return home via Kabul instead of Kandahar."

In accordance with the instructions Feng had received from his MSS superiors, the fifty soldiers, technicians, engineers, and geologists in his party had entered Afghanistan via Kandahar International Airfield. With the Americans long gone and the Taliban firmly in control of both the airport and the city for which it was named, KIA had been the natural infiltration point. In addition to a secure area that allowed Feng and his team to stage in private, the airfield was five hundred kilometers to the southwest of Kabul and Americans currently occupying Hamid Karzai International Airport.

Unfortunately, this secrecy came at a price.

Kandahar might have been the spiritual home of the Taliban and the epicenter of their movement, but the city was also almost six hundred kilometers of hard road to the southwest of the Chinese compound. To add insult to injury, although the Kabul-Gardez Highway was the most direct, and therefore quickest, route, the highway terminated at Kampani road, which flowed east through Kabul proper before joining the Kabul-Jalalabad Highway.

Though the Americans were fairly well occupied at the airfield, Feng had not wanted to risk discovery. Accordingly, the convoy had detoured east upon reaching the town of Ghazni before turning northeast on Sharan Road and then northwest on the Kabul-Gardez Highway. From there, the route grew ever more circuitous and treacherous, passing along back roads and through backwater villages in an effort to avoid the Americans' notice.

True to their word, the Taliban had provided safe passage, in some places guiding the convoy through the trickier interchanges, but the indirect route had taken time. From touchdown at Kandahar to arrival at the compound, what should have been a ten-hour trip had lasted closer to twenty.

Feng's tired body had felt every single minute.

But now they were here.

"I hope for that as well, my friend," Feng said, watching as the paramilitary officers dismounted from their vehicles and began emplacing crew-served weapons, cameras, and other security measures while the technicians started unloading earthmoving equipment. Young or not, Yuze seemed to know his business. "The Americans have conveniently announced the precise day on which they will depart. Yankees are nothing if not punctual."

Kai laughed, the sound bellowing from his burly lungs.

"They might be punctual and at times foolish," Kai said as his chuckle subsided, "but they are also an enemy not to be underestimated."

Feng was not offended at the undertone in Kai's statement. Though the barb could have been aimed at him, he thought it was not.

"Do you refer to the operation in America?" Feng said.

Kai spat rather than answer, proving that Feng's mouth wasn't the only one filled with grit from the dusty road. Or perhaps the operative was using the gesture as an excuse to gather his thoughts. The two men had been friends and colleagues for many years, but in their line of work, failure was not talked about and even more rarely acknowledged. After letting Feng's question hang in the air for an uncomfortable period of time, Kai slowly nodded.

"Yes, comrade," Kai said. "I knew Aiguo. We ran agents together in Hong Kong. The business in America was madness."

This time it was Feng who didn't answer, turning Kai's comment over in his mind. The conversation was quickly progressing from an innocent exchange between comrades to a critique of the Chinese Communist Party.

The MSS took a dim view of such sentiments.

On the other hand, Feng took a dim view of dying.

"You may be right," Feng said, his measured words coming slowly. "Rumor has it that Aiguo's entire team was eliminated."

"It is no rumor," Kai said, lowering his voice. "I checked the cables before we departed. Aiguo was killed alongside the Mexican cartel members."

"Have the Americans said anything officially?" Feng said.

"Not yet," Kai said. "But a highly placed agent inside the American intelligence community flagged a series of data queries containing Aiguo's identifying information. Our comrade is dead."

Feng had lobbied against the direct action portion of the American operation from the beginning, but hotter heads had prevailed. To his superiors' way of thinking, the deal Feng intended to broker with the Taliban would rub salt in old American wounds. What had been swept under the rug ten years ago would now face the brilliance of an international spotlight.

Preemptive action was the only solution.

These same geniuses had decided to off-load the actual wet work to the Zeta cartel. Chinese-manufactured fentanyl was now the most profitable drug on the black market and the Mexicans had proven to be natural distribution partners. Brokering cartel participation had not been difficult. The MSS hierarchy thought that using Zetas as the triggermen was a stroke of genius. If the Mexican assassins succeeded, so much the better. But if the narcos failed, the busted operation would be laid at their feet. No one would connect a series of random deaths in the United States to the Chinese MSS.

Unless a dead Chinese intelligence officer was discovered at the scene of the crime.

What utter foolishness.

Finding the targeted Americans had not been difficult. In 2015, Chinese hackers successfully penetrated the US government's Office of Personnel Management, the electronic repository containing the personal information of each and every American who had ever been granted a security clearance. From there, it had been a simple matter to obtain the addresses of each target. After the first American had been eliminated without a hitch, a decision had been made to interrogate the final target before he was dispatched. MSS leadership wanted to see what, if any, conclusions the Americans had drawn from the Chinese meeting with the Taliban.

This was why Aiguo had been present with the kill team in North Carolina.

This was also why the entire affair was poised to explode on the world stage.

"What lessons should we take away from that debacle, comrade?" Feng said, leaning against the truck.

"That nothing succeeds like success," Kai said. "If we close the deal with the Taliban cavemen and obtain the offered prize, we will return to China as heroes."

"And if we don't?" Feng said.

"This operation has already claimed the life of one intelligence officer," Kai said. "I don't think the MSS will lose sleep over the deaths of two more."

Feng wanted to protest, but he knew in his heart his

friend was right. Success in this endeavor was not optional, and in a country of more than a billion, Feng was hardly irreplaceable.

"Come on, old man," Feng said, climbing back into the truck. "Our Afghan partner will soon summon us. Let's ensure we're ready."

THIRTY-SEVEN

UNDISCLOSED LOCATION, TEXAS

Turns out that getting to Afghanistan without the assistance or knowledge of the United States government was a bit easier said than done. Especially since the country in question was currently devolving into a medieval fiefdom ruled by theocrats in dirty black robes. This was why I was pulling up to an unmarked gate guarding an unremarkable gravel road somewhere in the Texas backcountry that lay between Austin and Fort Worth.

Interstate 35 North was the preferred method of travel between Austin and Dallas. Though it widened from time to time, the highway was predominantly two lanes. It passed through a slew of unremarkable if quaint towns with charming names like West, Waco, Salado, and Jarrell.

I had not traveled north via I-35.

Instead, I'd ventured northwest from Austin into the land of single-lane highways and old pickup trucks. A place where etiquette from yonder years dictated that slower drivers pull to the shoulder in order to allow faster-moving cars to pass. This was the meandering but infinitely more scenic route leading to the twin-city metroplex dominated by sophisticated Dallas to the east and her more traditional sibling, Fort Worth, to the west. But as pleasing as the endless fields, pastoral ranches, and one-stoplight towns were to an Austinite like me, I hadn't traveled this path for leisure. This was a business trip.

The business of getting to Afghanistan.

"You sure this is the right place?"

Jason asked the question with a healthy amount of skepticism.

I understood why.

Gharib, Ferhana's father, had started me on this path. Along with the information I'd requested about his daughter, Gharib had texted me a link to an interview. An interview in which the man we were coming to see had spoken at length about the debt our nation owed the Afghans who had fought alongside us. Though I'd never met the man, I knew him by reputation. He was a doer and not given to idle talk. Even better, when he did speak, he had a track record of putting his considerable money where his mouth was.

I'd spent several hours working phones and schmoozing old comrades in arms to obtain his address. In some ways, the residence on the other side of the unmarked gate had reached mythical status. Everyone knew the ranch existed, but it was hard to find someone who had actually trod its hallowed grounds. Its owner had a well-known proclivity for privacy along with another trait that was much less advertised.

A propensity for helping service members in need.

Especially service members from the special operations community.

"It'd better be," Dee said, chiming in from the back-seat. "Skirts aren't really traveling clothes, and we've been driving for three hours."

"Nobody told you to wear a skirt," I said, eyeing the aviator via the rearview mirror.

"Please," Dee said with an eye roll that would have done Laila proud. "I know how this works—you guys are the operators. I'm the eye candy."

That wasn't precisely true.

I'd thought that having my entire team present during this meeting would give more credence to my ask. After her performance in North Carolina, Dee was definitely on the team. As an added side benefit, she did present a nice counterpart to Jason and me. The fellow Ranger who'd provided me with the ranch's location and the necessary introduction to its owner had offered an additional helpful tidbit—dress professionally. While the gentleman we were coming to meet was a Texan through and through, he was also a businessman.

As such, Jason and I were attired in Texas casual, which meant sport coats and button-down dress shirts that were tucked into jeans. I was wearing my second-favorite pair of boots while Jason sported a pair of highly polished leather lace-ups. Taken together, our look was functional but unremarkable.

Until you got to Dee.

I'd given her the same wardrobe instructions, but her idea of business casual was decidedly different. I'd expected the band T-shirts and rocker boots to be a thing of the past, but I wasn't prepared for their replacement. Of the grungy girl who had saved our bacon last night there was no sign. Instead, a business executive from central casting lounged in my backseat. Dee's short-cropped hair was styled in a way that was edgy but not at odds with her white blouse, tan skirt, and pumps. Her flashing dimples still gave off a girl-next-door vibe, but she'd definitely taken our pitch to the next level.

"You're the pilot," I said as I leaned out the window and pressed the red button in the middle of the call box. "Pilots are by definition eye candy, 'cause if they're not flying, what else are they good for?"

Dee replied by burying the pointy end of her shoe in my kidney through the car seat.

Still, her dimples flashed as she did it.

So far so good.

"Yep?"

The voice blasting from the speaker wasn't what I'd expected. Not by a long shot. While a person often didn't live up to the mental image evoked by their voice, I had a feeling that this instance was the exception that proved the rule. The voice was female with the unique kind of hoarseness that came from smoking a pack of Virginia Slims a day for forty years. That quantity of tobacco consumption wasn't conducive to great skin or a winning smile. I pictured a prune of a woman with a maze of wrinkles for a face and yellowed teeth still gripping an unlit ciggy.

Unlit because by now she knew that every puff took another hour off her life.

"Hi," I said, struggling in my surprise to remember the phrase I'd been given. "We're . . . ah—"

"Can y'all speak up? I'm hard of hearing."

"Sure," I said, leaning toward the speaker box as I shouted, "we're here to see Bill."

"Who?"

"Billy Bob," Jason said from beside me. "You're supposed to say Billy Bob."

"Is it too late for you to find another pilot?" Dee said.

"Sorry," I said, even as I flashed our resident aviator the one-fingered salute. "Billy Bob. We're here to see Billy Bob."

"Then welcome, Mr. Drake."

While the voice was still female, everything else about it had changed. The smoker's rasp was gone along with about four decades of hard living. This time the words carried a Midwestern accent and the no-nonsense tone of executive assistants the world over.

"That was a neat trick," Dee said.

"I think the tricks are just beginning," Jason muttered.

Though I agreed with both sentiments, I kept my thoughts to myself. The heavy-duty gate that looked formidable enough to stop a rampaging dump truck cycled open, and I motored through before the voice actor on the other end of the squawk box could change their mind. We were definitely in the right place, but I still wasn't convinced this wasn't a wild-goose chase.

Only one way to find out.

Fifteen minutes later, my teammates and I were sitting in a conference room, waiting for our host. Though the polite assistant who'd met us at the door hadn't termed the meeting as such, *audience* was the word that kept tumbling through my mind. Perhaps because our accommodations were fit for a king.

The road leading from the unmarked gate had rambled for one hundred or so meters before making a hard left to duck behind a thick grove of live oaks and mesquite trees. After disappearing into the foliage, the road underwent a major improvement. Gone was the folksy gravel. In its place was a length of sparkling black asphalt, well maintained and large enough for two vehicles to comfortably pass each other while traveling in opposite directions.

The road's condition wasn't the only change.

Now that they were sheltered from prying eyes, the grounds also underwent a startling metamorphosis. While the property still retained the feel of a rugged Texas ranch, all inferences to a typical hardscrabble homestead vanished. The multiple buildings dotting the rolling hills more brought to mind a conference center or a high-end hunting lodge than a family dwelling. The wide length of asphalt wound past a brick building housing a pair of alert-looking guards, several barns, horse pastures, and two different corrals—one populated by milling quarter horses and the other set up for barrel racing.

Once we'd left the ranch behind, the incline steepened, leading to four additional buildings located on a large hilltop. Two of the structures seemed to be garages or shops while the third was a dwelling. The final building was half again as large as the others. A paved parking lot boasted an assortment of vehicles—everything from the obligatory pickup trucks to a BMW M3.

A wooden sign with burned lettering labeled the structure **SB Ranch**.

I parked in the indicated visitor spot. Then we made our way to the building's entrance, where a young woman was waiting for us among a quartet of Adirondack chairs and a solitary firepit. After verifying my identity with a quick peek at my license, she'd led us to the conference room. I'd declined her offer of refreshments, but Jason had asked for coffee while Dee had settled on a glass of sweet tea. After fifteen minutes of twiddling my thumbs, I was beginning to wish I'd ordered something as well.

Like tequila.

"Is this gonna be like *Shark Tank*?" Dee said.

"Is that a Shark Week spin-off?" Jason said.

"Maybe I should do the talking," I said.

"That would be a fine idea."

The person who'd voiced the last statement spoke in an instantly recognizable Texas twang. Though he'd spent the last several years in semiretirement, he'd run for President as an Independent back in the eighties. A run that had garnered a respectable thirty percent of the vote. But Samuel G. Blackwood had still seen the writing on the wall. Rather than parlay his newfound fame into political currency, he'd stoically accepted the will of the American people. Leaving DC, Sam had returned to what he did best—employing thousands of hardworking men and women in his multitude of businesses scattered across the great state of Texas.

This was not to say that Sam had completely retreated from the limelight. He continued to run his privately held firms with a deftness that put many so-called Wall Street hotshots to shame. His companies did well, and his employees prospered.

For a time, this was enough.

And then on September 11th, 2001, the world changed.

In the years that followed, the true cost of that terrible day was realized in the form of the mangled bodies and broken minds of America's sons and daughters. Many celebrities and corporate rock stars formed charities or hosted telethons to raise funds for the war's wounded.

Not Sam.

He simply acted.

Disabled veterans came home from the hospital to mortgage-free houses. When a newly minted quadriplegic needed help making her residence handicap accessible, Sam's men did the work. When a Gold Star family struggled to pay for college, Sam sponsored a scholarship. The most amazing part of Samuel G. Blackwood's legacy wasn't the good that he did; it was that he accomplished his work from the shadows. He never sought the limelight in the form of flashy charitable foundations plastered with his likeness or his company's name.

Sam just got things done.

This was not to say that his work went unnoticed. In the decades since 9/11, Sam had been made an honorary member of multiple military units. From time to time, he spoke at fundraisers or cajoled fellow CEOs to do more on behalf of those who had sacrificed the most. To steal a phrase from the special operations community, Samuel G. Blackwood was the ultimate quiet professional. He acted more than he spoke, but when he spoke, he was worth hearing.

And now he was speaking to me.

"Afternoon, Mr. Blackwood," I said, getting to my feet. "Thank you for seeing us."

"Sam's fine," he said, offering his hand. "Mr. Blackwood was my daddy, and he's long since passed."

The room was arrayed so that the conference table sat facing a large TV mounted to the wall. This orientation had allowed Sam to enter the room unnoticed—something I think he used to his advantage. I took stock of the man as I returned his firm handshake, seeing what I'd expected. Despite his position as the CEO of an enterprise worth hundreds of millions of dollars, Sam had a reputation for braving the elements alongside his construction and wildcatting crews. He had the face of a Texas cowboy—leathery skin browned from the sun and toughened by the wind. His hair was mostly gray and cropped close to the scalp, but his pale blue eyes reflected the hardness of the vast Permian Basin. His hands were calloused and his build still lanky and trim without the potbelly or slouching shoulders typical of a corporate warrior in his seventies. He looked like he belonged more on a dusty cattle ranch than in a corporate board meeting.

His assurances to the contrary aside, Sam Blackwood was a man to be respected.

"I appreciate you saying that, Mr. Blackwood," I said, "but my daddy is still alive, and he raised me to use *sir* and *mister*. I'm gonna stick with that if it's all the same to you."

"Suit yourself," Sam said, releasing my hand. "How about we get started?"

Despite his nonchalant answer, I thought I saw the flicker of something in Sam's blue eyes as he and the man and woman accompanying him took their seats.

Approval.

"Yes, sir," I said, "let me introduce you to my team. The gentleman to my right is Jason Brown. He's a former Army Ranger and Green Beret. Next to him is Dee Moss. She's an Apache gunship pilot who did a stint in a Special Aviation Unit before matriculating over to a three-letter agency. I'm Matt—"

"Drake," Sam said, smoothly talking over me, "graduate of the University of Texas, which you attended on an Army ROTC scholarship. You worked three jobs to cover what the Army didn't because your family ranch in Utah barely cleared enough to put groceries on the table for your siblings. After graduating, you were commissioned as a second lieutenant in the Army. You branched infantry and attended Ranger School, where you were named the honor graduate. You went on to command a Ranger company in 1st Battalion, 75th Ranger Regiment, after which you resigned your commission and became an employee of the Defense Intelligence Agency. I know all about you, Mr. Drake. What I don't know is why you're here."

"It's Matt, sir," I said. "I'm here because I need your help."

"That's what I love about farm boys," Sam said with a nod. "They don't beat around the bush. Okay, Matt, let's hear your pitch. But before you get started, let me

introduce my associates. The lady seated next to me is
Caroline Young. She is the CFO and executive vice president of my operation. We've worked together for twenty
years. Caroline is my right hand in every sense of the
word. Garrett Smith is next to her. Garrett is my Director of Operations and Special Projects. He's a former
Navy SEAL. I trust him implicitly."

I nodded to Caroline and Garrett even as I tried to
get a sense of where things lay. In sticking with his Texas
motif, Sam was wearing a crisp white Western shirt
tucked into faded blue jeans. Caroline on the other hand
was the epitome of corporate America in her conservative
skirt and blouse. Her hair and makeup were stylishly
done, but she represented a low-key counterpoint to
Sam's larger-than-life persona. A grounded business-
woman who kept the trains running on time and the
bank accounts full, freeing up her boss to dream big
dreams.

Garrett the SEAL was a mixture of the two. He was
dressed in a button-down shirt and slacks that would
have been at home on a Brooks Brothers rack; his appearance screamed *executive* but his broad shoulders and
beard said otherwise. While Caroline had greeted me
with a polite smile, Garrett's visage wasn't quite as wel-
coming. He'd nodded during the introductions, but his
expression remained neutral. More tellingly, his eyes, like
those of his employer, were flinty.

Like all Rangers, I had a love-hate relationship with
SEALs.

Mostly, I loved to hate them.

That said, the Team Ten frogmen I had worked with

in Ukraine were top-notch commandos, even though they did use way too much hair gel. But I digress. I was coming to Sam with my hand out, so his people had every right to be skeptical. But I also made my living convincing people to betray their country.

I wasn't afraid to go toe-to-toe with a couple of corporate warriors.

"Great to meet you all," I said, making eye contact with my three adversaries. "I know your time is valuable, so I'll make this short. We need to get to Afghanistan in a manner that is unattributable to the United States government. To do so, we'd like to borrow one of your corporate jets and use your company's construction work in Afghanistan as cover."

"Interesting," Sam said. "Mind if I ask why you can't use DIA-supplied air assets or legends?"

I'd expected a question along these lines, but not with this level of sophistication. Like many operational intelligence organizations, DIA employed a number of tricks of the trade to assist employees who were operating clandestinely. These included backstopped legends for spies like me and a fleet of aircraft registered to front companies. Aircraft that could be used to shuttle operatives in and out of target countries. While this practice would be common knowledge to someone from the intelligence community, I found it unusual that a Texas oilman and philanthropist had access to this level of operational detail.

Perhaps there was more to Mr. Blackwood than met the eye.

"For OPSEC reasons, I can't go into detail," I said. "I

can say that what I'm proposing is beyond the Defense Intelligence Agency's charter."

"Bullshit."

The comment came from Garrett. I looked over at him, and he stared back in silence. His expression was still carefully neutral, but his eyes told a different story. I'd thought them skeptical before, but now I saw something else reflected in their depths.

A challenge.

"Bless you," I said, giving Garrett the smile that had softened the hearts of interrogators the world over.

"What?" Garrett said.

"Bless. You. It's an expression meant to excuse poor behavior. Like calling someone a liar without possessing the courage to actually use those words."

"Well played, Mr. Drake," Sam said, his soft Texas accent cutting through the testosterone-soaked air. "As you might imagine, I get pitched quite a bit. But you're the first person who's responded to my Director of Operations with a bluntness rivaling my own."

"In the words of someone much smarter than me, I prefer clarity to agreement," I said, still holding Garrett's gaze. "If you, Miss Young, or Mr. Smith have questions, I'll be happy to answer them. But please know that I take allegations about my integrity quite seriously."

"So do I," Sam said. "For clarity's sake, please tell us your team's precise status as it pertains to your employment by the government of the United States of America."

"Sure," I said. "Jason is retired, and Dee is a contractor. I am an employee of the Defense Intelligence Agency in good standing. However, what I am proposing is neither sanctioned nor endorsed by the DIA or any other governmental entity."

"What is your status?" Sam said. "Personally."

"It's a bit nebulous at the moment," I said. "My boss recalled me to Washington. I refused to go."

"I see," Sam said, his tone indicating otherwise. "Is this a common practice in your organization?"

"Not especially," I said.

Sam rubbed his chin as he stared at me. I could see Dee leveraging her adorable dimples with an equally adorable smile in my peripheral vision. I couldn't catch Jason's expression, but judging by his body language, I could guess. He didn't seem to care for the SEAL any more than I did and was even less diplomatic about hiding his feelings. As meetings went, this wasn't my worst performance.

But it was probably in the running.

"For argument's sake," Sam said, "let's assume I'm inclined to lend you one of my shiny airplanes. Why do you need to get to Afghanistan?"

"My best friend is accused of murder," I said, "and Afghanistan holds the proof of his innocence. If Mr. Smith here really is a SEAL, he'll recognize my friend's name."

Garrett's eyes flared, but he still asked the question. "Who?"

"Frederick Cates," I said. "But he's better known by his call sign—Frodo."

Sam glanced at his Director of Operations.

Garrett eased back in his seat, some of the wind clearly taken out of his sails.

"Never met him," Garrett said, pointedly directing his answer to his boss rather than me, "but Frodo's well known across the teams. He and another Unit sniper saved a SEAL reconnaissance element from being overrun by the Taliban. If he's a murderer, I'm Santa Claus."

"Interesting," Sam said.

Sam reached for the carafe of coffee located in the center of the table and poured himself a cup. Before taking a drink, he added enough cream to turn the liquid a light blond. This gesture told me more about Sam's character than anything thus far. A man who was less sure of himself would have been tempted to drink his java black.

Not Sam.

"I understand loyalty," Sam said, placing his mug on a coaster, "and I have no doubt that this Frodo gentleman is a hero. But I'm still not sure what this has to do with me."

"Nothing," I said, "at least not directly. But we're also going to rescue an American green card holder who's hiding from the Taliban. A teenage girl."

I pulled up the picture of Ferhana on my phone and slid it across the table to Sam.

"She's nineteen," I said. "She went to Afghanistan to attend a family friend's wedding. The Taliban crashed the wedding. Killed the men. Rounded up the women, probably to force them into becoming Taliban wives. Ferhana hasn't contacted her family since."

Sam studied Ferhana's image even as Caroline peered over his shoulder. Samuel Blackwood might have been a master boardroom negotiator, but a teenage girl's smile was enough to soften the heart of even the most hardened corporate warrior.

"Tragic," Sam said, "but how do you even know she's still alive?"

"Play the video," I said.

Sam looked at me for a long second as if weighing the mental cost of pushing play. Squaring his narrow shoulders, the Texan picked up the phone. Once again I was reminded of the qualities that had made the boy from Texarkana so successful.

Good leaders confronted hard problems head-on.

Sam was no exception.

I'd watched the video half a dozen times by now, but the sequence still hadn't lost its power. The terror and cries of pain were heartbreaking as was the casual brutality displayed by the club-wielding Taliban. The girls in the room fleeing for their lives were wearing Western-style clothing.

They could have been anyone's daughter.

They could have been my daughter.

Sam gently placed the phone back on the table.

His fingers were shaking.

"I don't know for certain that she's still alive," I said. "But if she is, the Taliban will find her." I kept my voice dispassionate. This was the time to be an unbiased commander. "When that happens, the best she can hope for is to be married against her will to a jihadi. The best. I'll leave the worst to your imagination. We're here because you had the guts to mount a rescue operation once before when no one else thought it was possible. I'm asking you to climb back into the saddle one more time."

Sam stared at me, his expression carefully blank.

The rescue operation I'd referenced was the stuff of legends in the special operations community. In 1979, two of Sam's employees working in Iran had been arrested and imprisoned. After pleading his case with the State Department and getting nowhere, Sam had taken matters into his own hands. He'd pulled veterans from across his organization into the boardroom, planned a rescue he could execute with his company's resources, and brought on a former Vietnam-era Army Special Forces officer to lead the team.

Even more telling, Sam hadn't been content to leave the dirty work to his subordinates. He'd traveled with the rescue element, even visiting his captured employees in jail before helping to stage the riot that allowed them to escape. While the entirety of the US government had tied itself into indecisive knots, Sam had acted.

As a result, Sam's employees weren't just loyal.

They would lie down in traffic on his behalf.

"The three of you are willing to risk your lives to rescue this girl?" Sam said.

"Yes, sir," I said.

"Good," Sam said. "Because I'm going to help you."

"Thank you," I said.

"You're welcome," Sam said, "but you might want to wait on the thank-yous until you hear my terms. I've got to think about the cost-benefit analysis of this operation. It seems to me that spending this much money for just one girl isn't a great use of resources."

"Sir?" I said as my blood pressure began to rise.

"If you're taking my plane all the way to Afghanistan, the least you can do is bring it back full."

"Of what?" I said.

"People," Sam said. "Americans and green card holders get first priority. Then any Afghans who helped us fight. After that, take women and children. As many as will fit in my jet, Mr. Drake. That's my price. Do we have a deal?"

For a long moment I couldn't speak. This plainspoken man was putting his reputation and hard-earned dollars on the line to rescue people he'd never met simply because it was the right thing to do. If the Defense Intelligence Agency ever decided my skills were no longer needed, Sam would be my first call. I didn't know much about construction, but I recognized a leader when I saw one.

"Yes, sir," I said, "we have a deal."

"Excellent," Sam said, a smile brightening his weathered face. "I thought we might be able to come to an agreement. That's why my Director of Operations is already packed."

"Sir?" I said, looking from Sam to the smiling SEAL.

"Sorry," Sam said, his smile growing wider. "I must have forgotten to mention that last part. This is your rodeo, Matt, but Garrett here will be along for the ride."

"Fantastic," I said.

Man, did I love to hate SEALs.

THIRTY-EIGHT

UNDISCLOSED AIRSPACE

How you doing?"

The question was innocuous enough, but hearing it asked in Katherine's voice brought a lump to my throat. That I was speaking to her via a Zoom call from somewhere over the Atlantic drove home the precariousness of the situation. My current circumstances gave new meaning to the phrase *on a wing and a prayer*.

"Better now that I'm talking to you," I said, meaning every word.

I'd worked plenty of solitary ops, but never without the support of DIA's impressive array of combat multipliers. As a member of the intelligence community, DIA could leverage the capabilities and specialties of other agencies, as my frequent collaborations with Katherine of NSA fame had proven.

And then there was Frodo.

Though my best friend had ceased being my gun-toting bodyguard years ago, he'd never abandoned his oath to watch my back. Though I missed knowing that he and his trusty HK 417 were providing overwatch from a sniper hide site, he was still my guardian angel.

Frodo now used ISR sensor packages instead of a rifle's optic.

But not on this Op.

My team consisted of a onetime gunship pilot, a washed-up Green Beret, and an angry SEAL. The Dirty Dozen we were not. Garrett stirred from where he was napping on the far side of the cabin as if he could hear my thoughts. He opened his eyes briefly, his gaze meeting mine, before closing them once more.

His lips twisted into the beginnings of a smirk before his breathing settled.

I was going to need to deal with Sam's Director of Operations, sooner rather than later. He'd been a thorn in my side since our meeting in the conference room. Between subtle attempts to undermine my authority and a never-ending supply of snide comments, I'd been tempted to eject him from the team and find another way to Afghanistan.

But I couldn't.

Dealing with people was part of being a leader, and the people who required the majority of your time were not usually the most pleasant. As much as I would have loved to leave the SEAL cooling his heels on the tarmac, I couldn't let my emotions get in the way of doing what was best for the team. Could we find other transport to Afghanistan? Maybe. But that would cost time, of which we had precious little. So I'd grinned and borne Garrett's meddling, with plans to have a come-to-Jesus with the SEAL once we touched down in Kabul. When an operation transitioned from the planning to execution phase, there could be just one leader.

Me.

"Mind if I join you?"

I turned to see Jason standing behind me.

"Sure, but you'll need this to hear," I said, taking out an earbud and handing it to him. "Jason, this is Katherine. Katherine, Jason. Katherine's my girl on the inside."

Jason took the earbud, waved at Katherine's face on my laptop, and took the seat next to me. Though the jet Sam had loaned us was certainly spacious, it came with minimal amenities. The monstrous cabin had been configured to haul cargo and cold metal flooring occupied most of the space. The setup was great for securing pallets but less accommodating to human cargo. To support our new mission, a pod of fifty airline-style seats had been secured to the front of the cabin along with a small conference table. Benches formed of cargo webbing ran beneath the windows on either side of the fuselage, completing the passenger accoutrements.

Dee wasn't rated on this bird, so Sam had also provided pilots. My aviator was up in the cockpit with them, no doubt telling flying stories. Garrett had commandeered the airline seating while I'd settled in at the conference table. I was trying not to read too much into the fact that my new team had chosen to spend the sixteen-hour flight as far apart from one another as possible, but the evidence was hard to ignore. Other than our prior service in Afghanistan and a shared desperation, we weren't bound by anything.

This was the second elephant in the room I needed to address.

"Okay," Katherine said, "let's start with the best news

first—Ferhana. She's alive, unharmed, and still one step ahead of the Taliban."

"You're sure?" I said.

"Positive," Katherine said. "We've been messaging."

I took a breath before replying, unprepared for the rush of emotions the news had elicited. Rescuing the headstrong teenager was the impetus for this entire operation. Until this moment, I hadn't even known whether the girl was still alive. That she was both unharmed and free from Taliban captivity was nothing less than a miracle. Her situation was still precarious to be sure, but this was fantastic news.

Maybe, just maybe, we were finally turning an operational corner.

"Come on, Matt," Katherine said, smiling at my expression. "You told me to get busy, so I did."

Sam Blackwell was a force of nature in every sense of the word, but he was not Superman. The jet he'd agreed to lend us had been parked in one of his hangars located at Dallas Fort Worth International Airport. It had taken several hours for us to make the drive north even as Sam's people took care of logistical matters such as pilots, fuel, and the like. I'd put the delay to good use by emailing Ferhana's information to Katherine along with a summary of everything I knew and a series of queries I wanted her to research.

Ferhana had been at the top of the list.

"Do you know where she is?" I said.

"It's easier if I show you," Katherine said.

The laptop's display changed from Katherine to a Google Maps overlay of Kabul.

"I've been localizing Ferhana's digital footprint," Katherine said, "starting with her personal data."

"I thought that WhatsApp had end-to-end encryption?" I said.

"It does, but I'm mining metadata, not messages," Katherine said. "Ferhana's been changing locations every twelve or so hours."

Katherine hovered her mouse over the section of the map with the largest number of intersecting circles. "This is the general area where she's been hiding."

"You sure it's her messaging?" Jason said.

"Positive," Katherine said. "We've done a couple video calls. She's a handful, by the way. I'd suggest assigning her a point of contact from your team. She's going to need a babysitter."

I looked at Jason and he stared right back as if daring me to ask. Fine. I wouldn't make my former Ranger buddy babysit a teenage girl. But I had a pretty good idea who might be uniquely suited for the task.

"Great work, Katherine," I said. "I've got a team member in mind. I'll get her spooled up after we finish that call. You can make the virtual introduction."

"Sounds good," Katherine said.

She made no attempt to hide the relief in her voice. Ferhana really must have been a handful. Hopefully the Afghan teen liked Nirvana.

"What else have you got?" I said.

The map vanished, and I was again looking at Katherine's pretty face.

"Unfortunately, that's what passes for good news," Katherine said with a frown. "The curtain has really come down on the government side. Everything to do with the arrest warrant and the operation mentioned in it is heavily restricted. I was able to run a couple of queries on the dead Chinese guy from Jason's place. I confirmed he's an MSS officer. Then anything to do with him became off-limits as well."

"I take it that's not normal," I said.

Katherine shook her head. "I've never seen anything like it. Someone wants this whole thing to disappear. I was able to find the redacted summary of the case file your CID agent mentioned. From there, I discovered a link to the operation's after-action review. Most of that was also redacted, but I gleaned a couple of interesting tidbits I'd like to verify with Jason."

I looked at the Green Beret, who shrugged.

"I told Matt everything I remember," Jason said, "but feel free to ask."

"Thank you," Katherine said. "I'd like to start with the detainee you captured."

"Detainees," Jason said.

"What do you mean?" Katherine said.

"There were three," Jason said. "The HVT we'd been gunning for was rolled up in the main building by Blue Team. But my element, Gold Team, bagged two more."

I stared at Jason.

"You didn't know?" Jason said.

I had not known.

To be fair, Frodo and I had been pinch hitters, nothing more. After the kinetic portion of the operation had wrapped up, Frodo and I had taken the casualty, Tommy Ledbetter, out in one bird. The rest of the team, and what I'd believed was our single detainee, exfilled in sub-sequent choppers.

Or at least that's how I'd thought things had gone down.

Now I was wondering what else I'd missed.

"Interesting," Katherine said. "The bomb maker is listed but not the other two detainees. Tell me about them."

"Not much to tell," Jason said. "I was more concerned with Tommy. A round had clipped an artery, and I was handling his medevac radio call. Fletcher and Dan took charge of the detainees."

The same Fletcher and Dan who were now dead.

"What were the detainees' nationalities?" Katherine said.

"At least one was Afghan," Jason said. "I know that."

"How?" I said.

"Because Zaafir accompanied them to the detention center," Jason said.

"To conduct the interrogation?" I said.

"Yes," Jason said. "Zaafir also would have enrolled them in the biometric database since he had an account in ABIS. That was one of his additional duties."

ABIS stood for Automated Biometric Identification System. It was a massive database administered by the US Department of Defense. Every Afghan who interacted with US forces had their biometrics enrolled in the system via ruggedized portable computers known as HIIDE, or Handheld Interagency Identity Detection Equipment. The devices were about the size of a paperback book and could capture iris scans, thumbprints, and other biometric identifiers. In a nation in which many inhabitants didn't have last names and fewer still could read or write, the ability to biometrically tag individuals had proven to be a godsend.

"Great," Katherine said. "That'll give me somewhere to start. I'll query the ABIS database with the day of the raid and Zaafir's identifier. With any luck, the results will lead me to your mystery men."

"What about the operation itself?" I said to Jason. "I was outside when the shooting went down. Frodo is charged with Tommy's murder. Is there any way he could have been the one who shot him?"

"No way," Jason said, shaking his head. "Tommy, Dan, and Zaafir were clearing the room when Tommy got zapped. Frodo, Fletcher, and I were on the opposite side of the hall when it all went down."

Jason's answer seemed pretty definitive. Maybe definitive enough to clear Frodo's name without Zaafir's testimony. But my gut said there was more here than met the eye. Between the two mystery detainees and three dead Gold Team Green Berets, I wanted to hear Zaafir's version of events.

"Fletcher keeps coming up in all of this," I said. "Assuming his death wasn't an accident, he was the first ODA member targeted. Any idea why?"

"Not on my end," Katherine said. "I've yet to establish any connection between Fletcher and the Chinese."

"I don't know if this means anything," Jason said, "but Fletcher called me out of the blue a couple weeks before he was killed."

"About what?" I said.

Jason shrugged. "About nothing. That's why I didn't mention it until now. We talked every couple of months, so hearing from him wasn't all that unusual. Anyway, he was pissed off about what was happening in Afghanistan and spent most of the call ranting. But right before we hung up, he said something about how the government betrayed us once in Afghanistan, and he wasn't going to let it happen again. He'd make sure that the truth came out this time."

"What does that mean?" I said.

Jason shrugged. "Hell if I know. Fletcher sounded like he'd already had a couple. I figured it was just the hurt talking."

When it came to Afghanistan, there was certainly more than enough hurt to go around. Every veteran I'd talked with, from friends to random strangers, was struggling. Even so, I had a feeling there was something to Fletcher's call. Something we weren't seeing.

"Let me work this," Katherine said. "I'll check everything from Fletcher's call to the operation and get back to you."

"Be careful," I said.

"I appreciate your concern," Katherine said, "but I'm just a keyboard warrior."

"I know," I said, "but this is all off the books. You'll have some explaining to do if one of your queries catches the wrong set of eyes. Besides, there's something at the bottom of this. Something worth killing for. Watch yourself, Katherine."

"Says the guy flying to Afghanistan to conduct an illegal operation," Katherine said. "I've got this, Matty."

Katherine ended the call before I could reply.

"She seems like quite a woman," Jason said.

"That's why Frodo chose her," I said.

But the more I got to know Katherine, the more I began to wonder who had chosen who.

THIRTY-NINE

KABUL, AFGHANISTAN

Y ou look well," Feng said.

It was a lie. The man standing next to him looked many things. Well was not one them. The same could be said for the line of individuals kneeling on the courtyard below him.

"I look like a man who has spent ten years in captivity," Qari said, leaning against a wrought iron railing as he peered at the prisoners.

The Taliban commander reminded Feng of a grizzled vulture. One of the older birds that was no longer as fleet of foot as its younger competitors. Qari's fingers were crooked and scarred, and his hands clutched the railing like talons. But it was his eyes more than his digits that most strongly resembled a carrion bird.

They gleamed with anticipation.

"Now you are free," Feng said, trying to ignore the moans and sobs drifting up from the courtyard, "and we can finish what we began."

Although he was no stranger to the rough ways of the dictators and strongmen China cultivated as allies, the current scene was especially macabre even by Feng's standards. Feng had answered Qari's summons, knowing how the meeting would go. Based on their handful of conversations since the Talib's release, Feng was convinced that the decade of imprisonment had fully corrupted what had already been a dark soul. The Taliban commander would attempt to shock Feng during their first in-person meeting.

Savages though they might be, the Taliban were expert negotiators. As he'd briefed Yuze and the contingent of paramilitary officers serving as his bodyguards, Feng knew that whatever depravity he witnessed today was meant to reassure him of the Taliban's resolve. But what he was witnessing sank to a new low in a nation already known for barbarity.

The meeting was being held at a school.

But not just any school.

The School of Knowledge was one of the most progressive institutions in Kabul. Here girls had studied alongside boys in classes taught by women as well as men. The institution had been a target of Taliban ire since its founding, but its administration had refused to be cowed. Rather than hiding, the school's principal had given the Western media access to the threatening letters the institution routinely received and hired private security as a bulwark against the constant death threats. Celebrities from all over the world had championed the school and many had traveled to Kabul in order to snap pictures in the iconic courtyard that formed the school's heart.

There were no celebrities present today.

Instead, bearded brutes presided over a line of kneeling men and women. Some of the captives wore the tattered remains of Afghan National Army or police uniforms, but many more were dressed in traditional garb. The school's brave administrators formed the front row, huddled on the dirty concrete as their students looked on. Feng didn't know what the madman standing next to him had planned, but he knew this would be a day to remember.

"Yes, yes," Qari said, waving away Feng's words as if the billions of dollars his organization stood to gain were of no concern. "We will conclude our business, but the terms have changed."

Feng kept his expression carefully neutral even as he seethed. The terms Qari had demanded bordered on extravagant. China's ravenous heavy industry desperately needed the ore and the rare earth metals scattered throughout Afghanistan, but the funds the Chinese Communist Party would pay were not limitless. The party elite had abandoned the Mes Aynak mine once before after deeming that the rewards were no longer worth the risk.

They could do so again.

Feng was about to relay this sentiment to his host when a bearded fighter dragged a woman from one of the classrooms ringing the courtyard. While the other prisoners certainly looked worse for the wear, the woman seemed barely alive. Her face was a mass of blood, and her nose resembled an overly ripe tomato that had burst. Her eyes were specks of black hidden in the folds of swollen cheeks and her fingers leaked trails of crimson.

Her appearance elicited a collective wail from the students.

"She was the school's headmaster," Qari said to Feng's

unasked question. "Can you imagine such a thing? A school led by a woman?"

Feng could certainly imagine such a thing, but he kept this opinion to himself. The sooner Qari concluded his object lesson, the sooner Feng could finish his business with this distasteful man in this equally distasteful country. The woman turned her undoubtedly sightless eyes toward the cries of her students. She opened cracked lips, revealing the jagged splinters of what once had been teeth. Feng held his breath, curious what the woman intended to say.

He'd never know.

As she drew a breath, the Talib standing behind her pressed his pistol against the back of her head and pulled the trigger. The woman crumpled to the filthy concrete and the children began to scream. Their cries were joined by others as robe-clad barbarians poured from the classrooms. They set upon the prisoners with reckless abandon, whipping the men and women with cables, smashing them with clubs, and stomping them with sandaled feet.

The lucky prisoners were shot straightaway.

Most took much, much longer to die.

"You spoke of new terms?" Feng said.

"Yes," Qari said, turning feverish eyes from the massacre to Feng. "Ten years ago, I was betrayed to the Americans. I wish to know who among my comrades is the turncoat."

The mayhem of violence began to subside as the prisoners were dispatched one by one, but the cacophony of sound did not ebb. If anything, the screams grew even louder. With a start, Feng realized their source.

Children.

The children were howling for their dead teachers.

"That was ten years ago," Feng said with a shrug. "What good will the information do you now?"

A lone gunshot rang out, as if to underscore the finality of Feng's words. The courtyard's slate gray stone was now a mass of scarlet, but still the rage of the fighters was not sated. The bearded fanatics stomped on the lifeless bodies as if they intended to grind them into the soil. Feng was no stranger to violence. He'd seen protestors beaten and led interrogations. On more than one occasion, he'd administered the party's justice to her enemies. But even he had never witnessed carnage like this.

"The betrayal consumed ten years of my life," Qari screamed, spit flecking from his lips. "Ten years!"

The Talib emphasized the word *ten* by poking Feng in the chest. His bony finger felt like an iron rod, but Feng showed no reaction. Beside him, Yuze stepped closer and Kai balled up his fists. Feng waved off both men.

Qari might have been a homicidal sociopath, but he was still a broken man. Though he was no longer in his prime, Feng was certain that he had enough left in him to toss the gaunt fighter over the railing if necessary. The ten-meter fall to the concrete might not kill the old buzzard, but it would do wonders to quiet his fervor.

"How would I discover this information?" Feng said.

"There are now three members of the Taliban ruling council besides me when once there were six," Qari said, his breathing rapid and shallow. "One of them told the Americans about our meeting, and his name will be in the American's biometric system. I want it. In exchange,

I will reduce the option price for the Mes Aynak mine by one billion dollars."

Feng stared at the mullah, waiting for the punch line.

One billion dollars for the name of a traitor? Afghans really did take the notion of vengeance to another level. The cost savings aside, access to the American biometric database was a large enough prize on its own to justify taking the madman's deal. Feng's MSS superiors would salivate at the thought of identifying every American agent in Afghanistan, and who knew what other useful intelligence might be gleaned? Perhaps the PLA's team of hackers could discover a back door to the American system itself.

This was the kind of intelligence coup that made a career.

Assuming that the barely literate caveman actually knew what he was talking about.

"And you have access to this biometric data?" Feng said.

"Yes," Qari said, his smile revealing rotting teeth. "I made many friends in prison. One was a prison guard. The other was the technician in charge of maintaining the backup data storage center conveniently located at Bagram. The Americans wiped the original system when they fled. My technician friend ensured the backup site did not suffer this same fate. The data center's servers are now in my possession. I assume these servers would be of interest to you?"

"Perhaps," Feng said, even as his heart pounded. "But before I convey your request to my government, I will need something."

"What?" Qari said.

"Proof," Feng said. "Proof that you have what you say."

Feng braced himself for another verbal storm, but the tirade didn't materialize. Instead, Qari reached into the folds of his robe and withdrew an innocuous-looking device. The three lenses mounted to the device's front coupled with the viewfinder on the opposite side brought to mind a ruggedized digital camera.

It wasn't a camera.

It was an American-made HIIDE portable biometric enrollment device. Feng and his fellow intelligence professionals had dreamed of getting their hands on one for years. Now the barbarian was offering it to him with the casual indifference one might show a loaf of bread.

"This is just one unit," Qari said, "but it will give you a taste. Agree to my terms, and I will provide you with access to the entire system. But don't dither. The Russians, Pakistanis, and Iranians have also been kind enough to offer their help."

With that, the Talib turned in a flourish of robes and strode down the walkway, his bony ankles peeking from beneath the stained fabric.

"What now?" Kai said once the barbarian was out of earshot.

"We return to camp and take a look at this," Feng said, turning the device over in his hands.

"And if it's what he says it is?"

Feng sighed. "Then we will take the buzzard's deal."

FORTY

I wasn't sure what I'd expected to see after talking my way into the abandoned hangar functioning as a TOC at Hamid Karzai International Airport in Kabul, but this wasn't it. The most generous word to describe the feeling pervading the cramped hangar's air was *chaos*.

Pure and unadulterated chaos.

The hangar was sectioned off into makeshift offices delineated by folding tables and hand-lettered signs. Extension cords spilled across dirty concrete like multicolored tentacles. Radios squawked from speaker boxes and dozens of people hammered away at laptop keyboards. The buzz of countless conversations filled the air, competing with a constant *thrum* from the herd of portable generators laboring just outside.

I ducked out of the entrance to make room for the stream of bodies coming and going through the structure's single pedestrian-access point. Like in most aviation facilities, the twin sliding doors could be wheeled back, opening the hangar to the outside, but they were currently closed, probably in the name of operational security. The river of human traffic brought to mind a London Tube stop during rush hour.

"Is it just me or does this look like a shit show?" Jason said from beside me.

"My thoughts exactly," I said. We'd arrived during shift change, and the mass of bodies transiting what was supposed to be a quiet spot for the planning and execution of operations battles was mind-numbing. "Who do you think's in charge?"

"Right now?" Jason said. "Nobody."

Jason's laugh softened his answer, but there was more than a little truth to his observation. We'd landed about an hour ago, and I'd taken a quick look at both the airport and the surrounding city during our descent. The view hadn't been encouraging. Hamid Karzai International Airport was located on the northern corner of Kabul proper and was surrounded by the Hindu Kush mountains. The installation had never been what you might term secure, but its current state was downright precarious.

I noticed the crowd first. The sea of people stretched across all of the airfield's entrances, obliterating any possibility of vehicular traffic. We'd had to loiter in a holding pattern while awaiting clearance to land instead of making a straight-in approach to the single runway. Even this short delay was long enough for me to gain a sense of what the Taliban had done to the city. Checkpoints littered the roads snaking toward the airfield's gates, and the Taliban's distinctive flag featuring a white background and black script was everywhere.

I'd last been to Kabul five years ago, and while Apple-
bee's probably wasn't going to open a Kabul location
anytime soon, there had been a feeling of progress. Freedom and modernity, while not yet attained, had been
realizable goals on the not-so-distant horizon.

Not any longer.

Life on the ground now more resembled Mogadishu
or Port-au-Prince. Except this time the gangs consisted
of bearded, turban-wearing thugs. But while the dress
and nationality were different, the methods of enforcing
dominance over a terrified populace were eerily similar.
Kabul was sliding off civilization's edge into a medieval
abyss. The nation was devolving right before my eyes,
and what I saw at the airport proper didn't give me any
hope that this slide into depravity could be halted.

Hamid Karzai was small for an international airport.
With only one runway, the facility didn't have much real
estate, but as we'd taxied toward parking, every square
inch seemed filled. Military transports took up much of
the apron, but a healthy contingent of civilian planes also
vied for space.

Uniformed men and women were everywhere.

But while the airfield's exterior was a buzz of activity,
the same could not be said of the other side of the fence.
Between crowds pressing toward the gates and the Taliban circling like wolves, the entire scene brought to
mind a castle.

A castle under siege.

I wasn't privy to the orders issued to whoever was in
charge, but it was clear that the military's posture was
defensive. Rather than expanding their tactical footprint

beyond the airport proper into the space that would bring soldiers, Marines, airmen, and sailors into contention with the Taliban, the Americans charged with responding to the worst foreign policy crisis since the fall of Saigon were peering over the ramparts and hoping for the best. It was impossible to win much of anything by playing defense. Then again, when it came to Afghanistan, maybe we weren't in the winning business.

I'd hoped that my initial impression of the situation was incorrect.

After entering the TOC, I realized it wasn't.

"Recognize anyone?" I said to Jason.

"A couple of familiar faces," the former Green Beret said. "Most are wearing civvies, not uniforms. I'm gonna nose around a bit. Meet you back here in twenty?"

I looked at my watch and nodded.

I'd held a planning session with the team as we'd taxied into the area set aside for commercial aircraft. While I intended to honor Sam's instructions to bring as many Americans and Afghans home as possible, I had two priority targets—Ferhana and Zaafir. Ferhana was a green card holder. She wouldn't have to worry about the bureaucratic nonsense required to obtain State Department approval to flee this death trap.

On the other hand, Zaafir had worked directly with American special operations teams for the last fifteen years. This relationship was the equivalent of a death sentence. I needed to get a bead on both targets as quickly as possible. I was hoping the almost six thousand troops hunkered down at the airport could offer assistance, but I also prepped the team to be ready to go it alone.

As such, my first order of business had been to pay a visit to the TOC with Jason in tow. Garrett had tried to tag along, but I'd intervened. I didn't need more cooks in the kitchen. Instead, I asked Garrett and Dee to conduct a reconnaissance of the airfield. I wanted to know which units in attendance might be predisposed to help us if push came to shove. We were to meet back at the jet in an hour's time while the pilots prepped our bird for departure. The tactical situation might have been relatively stable at the moment, but I wasn't counting on it remaining that way.

Garrett had reluctantly agreed.

Now the clock was ticking. I needed to put together a course of action once I understood what role the military intended to play in this human tragedy.

"Excuse me," I said, tapping a passing staff sergeant on the shoulder. "Can you point me toward Current Ops?"

Traditionally, a command post of this size was divided into two distinct cells—future and current operations. The staff in charge of planning and resourcing missions slated to occur twenty-four to forty-eight hours in the future worked in Future Ops. Current Ops held the battle captains who monitored and executed ongoing operations. I was hoping the Current Ops cell would provide me with some much-needed battle space situational awareness.

"Who are you with?" the staff sergeant said.

The name tape on the staff sergeant's MultiCam uniform read *Tucker*. She was a blue-eyed blonde who could have passed for sixteen, were it not for the bags under her eyes and the worry lines furrowing her forehead. Operations of this magnitude were hell on everyone, but the staff who planned and oversaw them paid an exceptionally heavy price. Shifts were long, the stress constant, and the demands exceptional. Regardless of what I thought of the national command authority's response to Afghanistan, people like Sergeant Tucker were still doing their best to execute their commander's intent.

"An NGO," I said. "My team just landed. We're here to help with the evacuation."

"Thank you," Sergeant Tucker said, her eyes softening. "People like you have been the bright spot in this terrible week. You a veteran?"

I nodded.

"How many tours here?"

"Three."

"Figured," Tucker said. "What's your name?"

"Matt," I said. "Matt Drake."

"Thank you for caring, Mr. Drake," Tucker said. "I don't know how this is going to end, but I'm glad veterans like you are answering the call. Current Ops is through that divider. Look for Captain Ngoy. She'll hook you up."

"Thanks," I said, "and thank you for your service."

She smiled and for a moment the carefree girl of sixteen returned. Then *Sergeant Tucker* echoed from across the room, and Tucker hurried toward the voice. Twenty years after 9/11 and America's sons and daughters were still answering their nation's call. The young sergeant was right about one thing—people were the bright spot in this terrible crisis. But the veterans or government agency types like me weren't the ones who were making a difference.

The heroes here were the kids in uniform.

Kids like Sergeant Tucker.

FORTY-ONE

Qari eyed the mining camp with more than a little envy. Though they were godless heathens, he had to admit that the Chinese knew their business. Already the compound hummed with activity. Monstrous trucks were moving back and forth from the mine shaft's entrance loaded down with rock, proof that the excavation had already begun in earnest. Men walked to and from the neatly arranged buildings roofed in sparkling blue with a sense of purpose, as if determined to make up for lost time.

But what most impressed Qari were the obvious security enhancements. The camp's entry point was staffed with hard men equipped with AK-74 rifles and crew-served weapons. A mast bearing a sensor package of some sort had been erected in the center of the camp. To the right of the tower lay a hastily dug mortar pit. Qari counted four metal tubes poking above the berm, more than enough indirect firepower to give an attacking force pause.

This time, the Chinese were here to stay.

"Thank you for coming so quickly."

Qari turned from his contemplation of the camp to the speaker, Feng. As usual, the Chinese intelligence officer was accompanied by his squat deputy and his bodyguard, a thin paramilitary officer. Though Feng had not shared Qari's long imprisonment, the experience of being arrested by the Americans was one the Chinese officer seemed determined to avoid a second time.

"You said you had results to share," Qari said.

"Yes," Feng said. "Unfortunately, they are not definitive."

Qari stared back at the intelligence officer.

He didn't speak.

He didn't need to.

The idling truck behind him spoke for him. As per the Afghan tradition, the vehicle was painted in a menagerie of different colors whose vibrance was eclipsed only by the strings of equally colorful beads hanging from the truck's bumper like a metal beard. But it was what the truck carried, not its appearance, that mattered. The servers from the data center were stacked on the truck's flatbed in hard plastic cases.

"We were able to access the biometric device's hard drive," Feng said, speaking into the building silence, "but the data is encrypted. Our engineers will eventually break the encryption, but it will take time. There is, however, an alternative."

The reed-thin Afghan standing next to Qari shuffled from one foot to the other as the intelligence officer spoke. He was the data center technician, and he'd relayed this same prognosis to Qari. That was fine. By letting the Chinese discover the obstacle, it became their problem to solve, not Qari's.

"What is this alternative?" Qari said, flavoring the question with skepticism.

"This device is keyed to several user biometric profiles," Feng said. "It has a local hard drive for storing temporary data, but it is designed to connect via Wi-Fi to the hardened US system. If you have access to one of the users stored as a profile, this person would be able to unlock not just this device, but the entire ABIS system."

Which was exactly what Qari's technician had said. As an administrator, he'd had access to the system, but not the data encoded within it. The Americans had been very careful in this regard, and rightfully so. In Afghanistan, alliances were as permanent as the shifting sand. That said, there were a few Afghans who'd been entrusted with access to the entirety of the biometric data. Afghans who served with US SOF teams and helped to process prisoners.

Qari had made the acquaintance of just such an individual ten years ago.

"This is unfortunate," Qari said with a sigh. "I'd hoped that we could work together, but perhaps the Russian scientists will have better luck."

Qari held out his hand for the HIIDE device.

"Wait," Feng said. "If you can provide us with one of the device's users, we will unlock the entire system. We could then run data queries against the contents. You would instantly know the name of your betrayer."

Qari slowly allowed his hand to fall back to his side as

if he were considering the idea. Turning to the technician, Qari asked the question he'd rehearsed.

"Do you know of someone?" Qari said.

"Yes," the technician said, bobbing his head. "As the administrator, it was my job to keep the user profiles refreshed. Most of the users fled when the Americans announced their withdrawal. But there was one man who was determined to stay. I have his WhatsApp chat information, if that's helpful."

"Give it to us," Feng said. "We will find him."

"Excellent," Qari said. "Then as a show of good faith, I will leave the truck loaded with the servers here. But my technician stays with them."

"Of course, of course," Feng said, waving away the comment. "I will call you with this man's location. Bring him to me and we will unlock the data together."

"Quickly," Qari called over his shoulder as he returned to his Hilux. "The Russians are anxious."

So was Qari.

FORTY-TWO

"Captain Ngoy?" I said.

"Yes, sir."

The person who answered was a pretty black woman in her late twenties or early thirties. Like many inside the un-air-conditioned hangar, she'd taken off her uniform top in favor of working in just her T-shirt. Even though I couldn't see her rank or name tag, I knew she was in charge. Captain Ngoy was bustling around a set of tables, previewing presentations on at least three different laptops and dictating changes to the soldiers seated in front of each computer.

"I'm Matt Drake," I said, offering her my hand. "Sergeant Tucker said you were the person to see for an orientation brief?"

"Belvina," she said. "Who are you with?"

Belvina had a lilting accent that sounded African in origin. Her handshake was firm, and the calluses on her palm went with her trim build and muscular frame. CrossFitter, if I had to guess. In any case, it was clear that Captain Belvina Ngoy had not let her physical fitness slide while assigned to a staff billet, unlike many officers.

Good for her.

"An NGO," I said, wondering if I should get a lanyard or something. "Just landed."

"You and half the veteran population," Belvina said. "Sanchez, trade out the airport graphic. Intel prepared a new one during the last battle update brief. Find it. Also, see if there's any satellite imagery of Kabul. The boss has been asking for it. Smith, go find Captain Prather. He owes me a logistics update."

"Yes, ma'am," two soldiers said in concert.

One was Hispanic and one was white.

Both were struggling to keep up with their boss's energy.

"This a bad time?" I said.

"Not really," Belvina said. "There's just no good time. Tell ya what—the BUB starts in ten minutes. Can you hold fast until then?"

"Absolutely," I said.

"Great," Belvina said. "If you head over to the far side of the hangar, you'll see a collection of chairs and a TV. That's where the contractors hang out. Let me get the boss spooled up. Then I'll find you."

I felt Belvina's pain. Like any commissioned officer, I'd done my time in the purgatory known as the S, or staff billets. As with Belvina, I'd been assigned to the S3 or operations shop. Belvina was a battle captain, which meant that she was responsible for tracking ongoing missions and providing regular updates to her leadership team. This was often done via the battle update brief, or BUB, a twice-daily summary that pulled in updates from all the staff entities. Since her boss, the actual S3, was giving the BUB, I imagined that the audience consisted of majors and above. Belvina was probably only too glad to have an excuse to duck out of the collection of field-grade officers.

Don't get me wrong. The Army's officer corps was one of the most competent collections of leaders on the planet. Unfortunately, when that many thinkers got together in one room, the good-idea fairy invariably took a spin around the place, dropping pixie dust in her wake. The last-minute tinkering to pending operations seldom added much of value, but the ensuing mission creep was hell on young staff officers like Belvina.

I was going to say something along these lines to the battle captain, but one look at her and I knew I'd be wasting my time. She was already leaning over another soldier's shoulder, dictating changes to the all-important BUB PowerPoint slides as the specialist attacked her laptop's keyboard, trying to keep up. There were many things I missed about my time in uniform.

This wasn't one of them.

I headed toward where Belvina had pointed, slipping through an increasingly diverse-looking crowd comprised of both military personnel and civilians. Traditionally, TOCs were access controlled and oftentimes guarded by soldiers who checked your ID against a roster before allowing you inside. This wasn't just because staff havens had the best coffee. The TOC was an operation's nerve center. The place where the men and women in charge formulated battle plans and monitored the ongoing fight. It was a nexus for updates from the front lines as well as instructions from higher headquarters. Oftentimes classified information was collected and reviewed in the various staff areas.

Not to mention that this was where people worked. Feverishly and around the clock. While a TOC was never going to be mistaken for a library, a staff officer reviewing her warning order for the fifth time on three hours of sleep and a diet of mostly caffeine, nicotine, and sunflower seeds appreciated a bit of peace and quiet.

But peace and quiet were in short supply.

As I moved from the set of pop-up tents holding the more secure aspects of the staff planning hub to the collection of folding chairs in the corner, I couldn't help but notice the wide range of folks I was rubbing shoulders with. Men and women in uniform were everywhere, but those uniforms encompassed all service branches. Soldiers dressed in MultiCams shared space with Marines wearing the quirky digital-print MARPAT fatigues. Sailors in their Navy working uniforms sat next to airmen in their ridiculous blue-tinged airmen battle uniforms.

But it was the folks not wearing uniforms who I studied the hardest. The bearded-to-clean-shaven ratio was probably close to three to one. Some of them were undoubtedly operators from special mission units. The kind of warriors whose wardrobe was dictated by the mission rather than military affiliation. Many more were like me—civilians or contractors.

This wasn't good.

Civilians outnumbering military was a sure sign that combat operations were not the priority.

Which made me wonder just what the priority might be.

I pushed this thought aside, trying to adhere to the guidance I'd given my team before departing the plane—talk to the people in charge before jumping to conclusions. Though the posture I'd seen thus far looked too passive for my taste, I still hoped I'd be proven wrong.

I nodded to the crowd of a dozen or so milling around the folding chairs and edged over to a small table parked in front of one of the hangar's few wall outlets. It was easy to see why a wobbly table merited such a position of prominence. Resting on the splintered wood was perhaps the greatest innovation for military staff officers since the advent of the written word.

A coffee maker.

But not just any coffee maker.

Known as the silver bullet for its unique shape and stainless steel exterior, the percolator had been the salvation of sleep-deprived service members for decades. As I approached this oasis, I noticed two things that would profoundly change my day. One, the aroma of brewing coffee filled the air. Two, the orange light on the front of the percolator was illuminated, signaling that a fresh batch of liquid happiness was ready for consumption. Snagging a white Styrofoam cup, I filled it with steaming coffee and took a careful sip.

Heaven.

Okay, so the java wasn't going to win any awards, but the coffee had two important qualities—it was both hot and strong. Maybe too strong. The stimulant contained in its murky depths hit my nervous system like a shot of adrenaline.

"Whoa," I said accidentally, doing my best Keanu Reeves imitation.

"Careful. Drink too much of that and your heart will pop out of your chest."

I turned to see a fit-looking man waiting with his own coffee-stained mug. He had longish hair, an obligatory beard, and the muscular build common to this crowd. His olive skin, dark eyes, and black hair could have passed for any number of nationalities, but the words *we the people* tattooed in flowing black script across his forearm left little doubt of his allegiance.

"Thanks," I said, "but you're about two seconds too late. What do they put in this stuff?"

"Equal parts meth and jet fuel," the man said with a smile. "The first sip hits you like a freight train, but your heart adjusts."

"Or explodes."

"There is that," the man said with a shrug, "but at least you'll die wide-awake."

I laughed and extended a hand. "Matt Drake."

"Joe Sabel," the man said. "Former Army?"

"Does it show?"

"You form coherent sentences, so you're not a SEAL, and you aren't pretty enough to be Air Force."

"What about the Marines?" I said.

Joe shook his head. "I are one, and you don't know our secret handshake."

I laughed again.

"Guilty," I said. "I was a Ranger."

"I'll try not to hold that against you. I was a Marine Raider—kind of like Rangers, but tougher."

"Said no one, ever."

Joe laughed, and I found myself chuckling along. As immature as these exchanges between rival services might seem, one-liners were part of our culture. Members of the special operations community had a deserved reputation as carnivores. The kind of people who get the call when odds are long and the chances of success slim. Living a life in which the battlefield always favored the enemy took a toll, as did the long deployments, constant absences, and the loss of brothers-in-arms.

Immature humor was one of our coping methods.

Excessive drinking was too often another.

"How long you been here, Joe?" I said.

"Long enough, unfortunately," Joe said.

"Whatd'ya mean?"

"Take a listen for yourself. Then we'll talk."

Joe pointed over my shoulder. I turned to see Belvina standing to the side of an LED screen mounted to the hangar wall. She had a green leader notebook in one hand and a laser pointer in the other. She was now wearing her blouse, and I eyed her badges. Airborne, Air Assault, and Combat Action. She turned to confer with Sanchez, who was manning a laptop, and I saw the Sapper Tab on her left shoulder.

Captain Belvina Ngoy was a go-getter.

"Okay, people," Belvina said as the television flickered to life, "we're going to get started. I know some of you have already heard my opening spiel, but we have so many new folks that I'm going to say it again. Bear with me for the first couple of minutes and then I'll transition to the update. Okay?"

Apparently it was okay, because Belvina launched straight into her brief without waiting for an answer. Once again I found myself remembering how little I'd enjoyed my time as a staff officer. To her credit, if Belvina felt the same way, she didn't show it. For the next fifteen minutes, she ran through the task organization of the military units calling the airport home, the enemy situation, potential threats, and the procedures the thronging crowds would use to gain access to the airport. She talked through the current number of Afghans, where they were being screened, and the known inbound flights as well as scheduled departures and their destinations. She even covered the weather for the next forty-eight hours. All in all, a pretty good briefing.

Except for one thing.

"All right," Belvina said as she flipped the page in her leader book, "that does it for now. Questions?"

I raised my hand.

"Yes, sir," Belvina said, nodding at me. "I'm sorry. I forgot your name."

"Matt," I said.

"Right, Matt. Go ahead."

"I apologize if I missed it," I said, "but I didn't hear you cover ongoing operations."

"Ongoing operations?"

"Yes," I said. "I was hoping we could get an overview of who's going outside the wire and when so I can sync efforts."

"Not sure what you mean," Belvina said.

I stared back, wondering if I'd somehow been unclear.

"Rescue efforts," I said. "I was hoping you could outline the rescue efforts underway. I'm assuming 'terps and folks with special visa have priority, but if you could clarify how we get names onto the extraction manifest, that would be great."

Belvina looked back at me, a flush building on her neck.

"There are no rescue efforts, Matt."

I looked from Belvina to the crowd, certain that I must have been the butt of a new-guy joke. But the expressions I saw looked just as baffled as I felt. The lone exception being Joe. The former Marine Raider's lips formed a sad smile.

"Nobody's going outside the wire to bring people in?" I said.

"Except for a couple of in extremis situations, the State Department's published guidance reads that Americans and green card holders who are stranded are to self-recover to the airport."

I opened my mouth and then closed it again. What Belvina had just said was as wrong as wrong could be, but getting angry at the battle captain with the Sapper Tab would be the epitome of shooting the messenger. She had as much say in our Afghanistan national policy as Frodo's dog. I was plenty pissed, but I'd find a target for my anger elsewhere.

"Thank you, Captain Ngoy," I said. "Tracking."

She acknowledged my comment with a curt nod, but her eyes conveyed her thanks. I'm sure she'd been on the receiving end of people's frustrations every time she delivered this briefing. Belvina answered a few more questions, which were all thankfully less loaded than mine, then concluded the briefing.

"Okay, Ranger," Joe said, "ready to talk?"

"Depends," I said, "are you planning to just sit around too?"

"Marines aren't much for sitting around," Joe said.

"Neither are Rangers," I said.

"Excellent," Joe said. "Follow me."

FORTY-THREE

take it you were a bit underwhelmed by that update?"
Joe said.

"The content was fine," I said. "It's what was missing
that has me agitated."

I'd followed the wiry Marine out the hangar doors
and into the stifling heat. Afghanistan was no Iraq, but
summers here were still less than pleasant, even at Kabul's elevation of almost six thousand feet. The conditions weren't as humid and miserable as the more tropical
Jalalabad one hundred fifty kilometers to the east, but
with temperatures hovering in the nineties, and a scorch-
ing wind scouring the flight line, it wasn't Honolulu either.

"Yeah," Joe said, his stride quickening as he angled
across the concrete, away from the hangar. "I know what
you mean. I was pretty disheartened too. Then I figured
out where the real work was happening."

"In special ops country?" I said.

"Nope," Joe said, shaking his head. "Don't get me
wrong. Our bearded brethren are doing what they can,
but neither the State Department nor the military can

figure out who's in charge. Unless there's a no-kidding American hostage situation, or an Afghan national equivalent, even the special ops folks are having a hard time getting trips outside the wire approved."

"Nobody's mounting a rescue effort?"

"Not en masse," Joe said. "But that doesn't mean one isn't happening. Step into my office."

Joe's *office* was located in a forgotten corner of the airfield. Unlike the easily recognizable modular TEMPER tents that were scattered throughout the hangar, this section of airfield featured a series of metal Conexes that had been fitted together to form an interconnected work space. But unlike traditional shipping containers, what I saw more resembled a ruggedized version of the mobile trailer often used as an office at a construction site. The huts had shingle roofs and awnings that extended from the sides, providing much-needed shade. Air conditioners sprouted from the walls and a plethora of antennas and satellite dishes grew from the roofs.

"Holy crap," I said, taking in the complex. "What's this?"

"American ingenuity," Joe said. "Welcome to Current Ops."

Joe led me toward the nearest Conex, which was also the largest. He nodded to a fellow bearded civilian, who was engaging in what was probably a highly illegal smoke break in the common area between the offices, and pushed through a series of vertically hanging rubber slats that served as a door.

We passed from one world to another.

While Captain Ngoy and her band of staff workers

were certainly busy, there was a lack of enthusiasm accompanying their efforts. Almost as if they knew that their comrades in arms were merely holding the line as opposed to going on the offensive. One look at Joe's Current Ops cell told me that was not the case here.

The far wall held an old school–style map board, on which was mounted laminated military maps encompassing Kabul and the surrounding suburbs. Operational graphics were annotated on the clear lamination in grease pencil. A woman stood in front of the board comparing the various symbols and their locations against a sheet of paper in her hand. A massive whiteboard filled with names, times, and GPS coordinates was mounted on the adjacent wall. Two large-screen TVs hung from yet a third wall. The TV on the left was tuned to Fox News while its twin seemed to be showing a text stream from an encrypted chat room.

Like in all command posts, the atmosphere felt chaotic. A bullpen formed by rows of laptop computers took up the majority of the space, and the keyboard warriors were calling out updates in real time. Encrypted Motorola radios chirped as unfamiliar voices added to the mayhem. Another cluster of civilians huddled around a third large-screen TV, this one displaying Google Maps imagery. Though the buzz of activity mirrored what was going on in the military space, the energy felt different. Every conversation and interaction seemed to be driven by an unseen urgency. I didn't know what these folks were up to, but their collective bias toward action was clear.

"This is the culmination of weeks of work," Joe said, the pride in his voice evident. "It happens tonight."

"What?" I said.

"The rescue."

Those two words gave context to what I was seeing. The graphics on the map board represented rally points, enemy locations, and evacuation routes. The massive whiteboard was a manifest of sorts with groups of evacuees sorted and tied to specific code names. I took a minute to compare the manifest to the map board and then gave up. There had to be something I was missing because the scale of the effort looked to be in the hundreds.

"How many are you trying to extract?" I said.

"Over five hundred," Joe said, his smile growing even wider.

I stared back at him, waiting for the punch line.

It never came.

"You're going to rescue five hundred people?" I said. "With what army?"

"We've been working this problem for weeks," Joe said. "It started with a former Green Beret trying to get his old 'terp to safety, and it kind of snowballed from there. We don't have the resources to get all of these folks, and the people who do have been ordered to stay behind the wire."

Joe inclined his head in the direction of the military's TOC as he spoke. There was no judgment in his voice, just resignation. If given the opportunity, I knew that Sapper-Tabbed Captain Ngoy would put together a rescue operation that would have rivaled Dunkirk. But the powers that be had decided otherwise. Rather than sulk, Joe and his fellow civilian volunteers had done what special operators do best when faced with a seemingly insurmountable problem—improvise, adapt, and overcome.

"How's it going down?" I said.

"We modeled the Op on the Underground Railroad," Joe said, pointing at the map board. "We're calling the Afghans we're rescuing passengers. They'll self-evacuate to predetermined waypoints called stations. Our guys at the stations are called shepherds. They're responsible for guiding the passengers from station to station. Communication between shepherds, passengers, and our TOC is being managed in real time via the encrypted chat feed you see over there. We've got a whole battalion of folks back in the States coordinating with our battle captains. Everyone is a volunteer and most are Afghan veterans. Once a group of passengers makes it to the airfield, they'll provide a predetermined recognition signal to the guards manning the wall. Piece of cake, right?"

The scale of what Joe was proposing was enormous, not to mention dangerous. With the resources of 1st Ranger Battalion behind me, this would have still been an ambitious undertaking. That a group of civilians was attempting the evacuation was mind-boggling.

"What's the military doing to help?" I said.

Joe's smile waned.

"What they can," Joe said. "Officially, they aren't permitted to do anything overt to assist with our operation."

"And unofficially?"

Joe shrugged.

"Everyone on that side of the tarmac would suit up and ride out with us if they could. Since they can't, the leadership is bending the rules. For instance, we're getting real-time intelligence assessments and even some ISR feeds. The military has also allowed us to liaison with the guys and girls manning the gates so that they'll know our recognition signals. We've been told in no uncertain terms that the cavalry will not be riding to the rescue tonight, but they aren't preventing us from leaving the airfield either. That will have to do."

The nonchalance with which Joe answered was striking. It wasn't the posturing of someone who had never seen the elephant. Joe was a Marine Raider. He'd been there and done that. He knew exactly what was at stake and how vulnerable he and his team would be if things went wrong. But he was still saddling up. Not for glory or money, but on behalf of the men who had gambled their lives and those of their families on the notion that an American's word was good. That we meant what we said when we promised to take care of the Afghans who'd stood by our side. After seeing what Joe and his teammates had cooked up, I'd never been prouder to be an American.

"This is incredible," I said. "Just incredible."

"Ready to jump aboard?" Joe said.

"Absolutely," I said, "but I'll need to add a couple of names to your list."

"That's gonna be tough," Joe said with a frown. "Tonight's manifest is pretty much locked down. Every name has been assigned to a shepherd. The precious cargo has been grouped by geographical location and broken into teams. We don't have the resources or time to go after singletons. Besides, your names haven't been vetted. If one of them compromises their team, we could lose the entire cell and their shepherd. I'm sorry, but it's just too risky."

"Understood," I said, "but I'm willing to put my money where my mouth is. I have a team of four. All ex-SOF. I'll give you the details on my two names. You decide which extraction is the riskiest, and my team will take it."

"I know how you feel," Joe said. "Every one of us volunteered because we share your commitment to our Afghan allies. But I can't put the entire operation at risk. We'll try to add them to tomorrow's manifest. Best I can do."

"Got it," I said, nodding, "but my folks are both time sensitive. One is just nineteen. She's a green card holder who flew over for a wedding without her parents' knowledge. The Taliban crashed the party, and she's been on the run ever since. She's just a kid. She's been lucky so far, but her luck won't last."

Joe stared at me. He was probably a terrific Marine, but he'd never make a good spy with that piss-poor poker face.

"What about the other?" Joe said.

"He served with American SOF, but that's not why he's time sensitive. The ODA team members he fought alongside have been targeted by Chinese intelligence officers working with the Zeta cartel. He's the only person left alive who might know why. We need him."

"Who's we?" Joe said with a frown.

"What I said earlier was true," I said. "I'm here as a volunteer. But I'm not retired. I'm with DIA."

"Then why in the hell aren't you guys out there making shit happen?" Joe said.

"For the same reason the 82nd Airborne Division is sitting behind concrete ramparts, twiddling their thumbs. National command authority has not sanctioned my actions, but unlike those kids in uniform, I can call in sick."

"Your boss thinks you have the flu?"

"I'm here as a volunteer, same as you," I said. "I need these two rescued. I'm willing to help get my targets, but I can't extract them both. Help me, and I'll give you something in return."

"A couple of Hellfire-armed Predators?"

"I wish," I said. "You've got to get your precious cargo to the airport. Nothing I can offer besides my team to assist with that. But if you recover my two folks, I can take it from there. Blackwell Industries lent me a big old jet with instructions to bring it home full. It seats a couple hundred. Want to help me fill it?"

"That's a helluva position to put me in," Joe said.

"War's a helluva thing. Come on, Joe. I know you're not going to abandon my two to the Taliban."

Joe looked from me to the manifest. Five hundred men, women, and children who needed a home. Gaining entrance to the airfield would be only the first step in their journey to freedom. The military birds that were landing had tremendous capacity, but many of their seats were already spoken for. And to make things more difficult, the number of countries willing to accept military transports full of Afghan refugees was limited. Put that together, and Joe was facing the very real possibility that some of the folks he rescued tonight could still be left behind after the last plane departed Afghanistan's airspace.

My jet couldn't entirely solve his problem, but it would make a pretty big dent.

"Give me the locations for your two targets," Joe said, turning back. "We'll plot them on the board. If they fall within the area of operations assigned to one of our teams, I'll add their names to the manifest. If not, they're on you. But if you decided to go it alone, I'll still integrate you into our Current Ops cell. At the very least, you'll get real-time updates on Taliban checkpoints and roadblocks. Deal?"

"Deal," I said, offering Joe my hand. "Welcome to Air America."

Joe's smile returned as we shook. "As I recall, that little airline didn't fare too well."

"That's why we're here to redeem their reputation," I said.

Air America had come to symbolize everything that had gone wrong with the Vietnam War—a halfhearted attempt by a government more concerned with optics than results. This was the opposite of that. A true coalition of the willing, staffed by men and women who'd shed blood with the Afghans we were committed to saving. In moments of great turmoil, great people often rose to the occasion. The 338,000 British and Allied soldiers saved during the Miracle of Dunkirk weren't rescued by people in uniform. Instead, ordinary citizens answered the call and accomplished the impossible. Only fools pretended to know a battle's outcome before it was fought, but I'd have bet on the volunteers on this side of the airfield any day of the week.

This was going to work.

"Matt—we've got trouble."

Or perhaps not.

FORTY-FOUR

I turned to see Dee standing behind me.

The aviator extraordinaire was back to her rock roots. While she was wearing Afghanistan's unofficial uniform of cargo pants and hiking boots, she'd traded her Nirvana T-shirt for Phish and her pixie cut was hidden behind a Foo Fighters trucker hat.

My aviator had caused quite a stir in the mostly male-populated TOC.

"Dee, this is Joe," I said. "Joe's heading up a rescue operation. He's going to add our folks to the manifest. Joe, this is Dee. She's my pilot."

"I said that I'd take a look at the probable location of your folks," Joe said. "Then we can talk about adding them to the list. Nice to meet you, Dee."

The tone Joe used to introduce himself to Dee was decidedly friendly.

Dee was a force multiplier in more ways than one.

"Likewise, Joe," Dee said, her dimples making an appearance, "and for the record, Matt got it wrong with me too. I'm not just an aviator. I'm a transportation specialist. If it moves, I can drive, fly, or sail it."

"Sounds like a useful skill," Joe said.

"Maybe you'll get a chance to see," Dee said with a smile.

"You said we had trouble," I said to Dee.

Sometimes even a good force multiplier forgets when to stop multiplying.

"Yes," Dee said, her face again serious. This girl did have a future as a spy. "Trouble with our precious cargo."

Dee had accepted responsibility for handling Ferhana with good-natured grace. She'd begun texting the Afghan girl while we were still in the air and shown me their conversation thread. My aviator had a knack for building rapport. Her comments struck the right tone by reassuring the frightened teen while also not coming across as the mother figure Ferhana had fled to Afghanistan to avoid. When it came to our wanderlust-afflicted precious cargo, we were firing on all cylinders.

At least I'd thought so.

"What have you got?" I said.

Dee cut her eyes toward Joe, but I shook my head.

"It's okay," I said. "Joe's part of the team. What's Ferhana into now?"

While I was a long way from having a teenage girl, I was already worried about how I was going to navigate those tumultuous years. Though I barely knew her, Ferhana had already nearly driven Katherine to the brink. I couldn't imagine what the headstrong girl had done to her own father *before* she'd flown off to Afghanistan on a whim and nearly been captured by the Taliban. Passing her communications off to Dee might have been the most inspired thing I'd done in the last week.

Maybe I ought to employ this same strategy with a teenage Virginia.

"It's not Ferhana," Dee said, shaking her head. "The trouble's with Zaafir."

My anxiety kicked up a notch. Besides his linguistic work, the former 'terp had taken up arms against the Taliban. If the jihadis had found Zaafir or his family, death would be the least of his worries.

"Lay it on me," I said.

"Zaafir just messaged Jason," Dee said. "Somehow, the Taliban located him. He and his family are on the run. We need to bring him in. Now."

I looked at Joe, but the Marine needed no encouragement.

"You got a location?" Joe said.

Dee nodded.

"Perfect," Joe said. "Let's take a look."

Joe strode toward the map board at the front of the room like a man on a mission. Though three or four folks were crowded around the map, using grease pencils to stencil operational graphics on the clear acetate, they moved aside for the Marine.

"Hit me with the grid, Dee," Joe said.

Dee read off an eight-digit location, and Joe moved his stubby finger along the map.

"Damn," Joe said, shaking his head. "He's beyond our reach."

"What do you mean?" I said, peering over his shoulder.

"We had to draw the line somewhere," Joe said. "With over five hundred passengers to move onto the airfield and only eight hours of darkness to do it, we had to set some geographic boundaries. Otherwise, we'd be driving all over Afghanistan just to pick up one person. I know that's a tough nut to swallow, but if we start going after singletons, we'll save the few but lose the many."

What Joe was saying made sense, but that didn't mean I had to like it.

"What about Ferhana?" I said to Dee. "Where's she?"

Dee read off another eight-digit grid, and Joe's finger once again went to work.

"Her, we can grab," Joe said. "It will take some doing, but I can add Ferhana to our manifest."

"You're sure?" I said. "She's family. Sort of."

"Warrior to warrior, I'm sure," Joe said. "But you don't have to just trust me. Saddle up with Tim. I'm sure he could use a couple more hitters. You can pick her up yourself."

"Love to," I said, "but my crew's got other plans."

Joe slowly shook his head.

"You're going after that one, aren't you?" Joe said.

"You read the Bible, Joe?" I said.

"I've cracked open the Good Book a time or two."

"Your folks are called shepherds, right?" I said.

Joe nodded.

"The Gospels of Mark and Luke both tell a story about a good shepherd who leaves ninety-nine of his sheep to find the missing one. I reckon that's us."

"I understand what you're feeling," Joe said, "but I've got a question for you."

"Shoot," I said.

"That shepherd you just referenced—is he Jesus?"

I nodded.

"Thought so," Joe said. "Do me a favor—try not to end up like him."

Dee laughed.

I didn't.

FORTY-FIVE

How we doing this?"

Jason asked the question, but I could tell from the three sets of eyes staring back at me that he wasn't the only one wondering. Four sets of eyes counting Joe. The Marine Raider had provided us with access to a small break-out room located next to the current operations cell. Apparently the price for such premium accommodations came in the form of Joe listening to our planning session from where he was leaning against the doorway.

Fine.

At this point, I needed all the help I could get. If Joe's posture of half in and half out of our space symbolized his feelings toward our operation, I'd take it. Maybe by the end of my brief I'd convince the Marine to formally join the team. Or maybe he'd run like hell and take my fledgling operatives with him.

Either outcome seemed just as likely.

"Here's what we've got," I said, referencing the map spread out on the table in front of us.

While the staggering advancements in technology had rendered paper maps an artifact for many of the younger uniformed folks, I still preferred planning an operation on an actual map. Paper maps weren't as sexy as their digital alternatives, but they were reliable and durable— two qualities this operation would need in spades.

"Our Pineapple Express friends are going to be conducting recovery operations all night long. Their area of operation covers the entirety of Kabul. Our first precious cargo, Ferhana, is well within their tactical footprint. Joe has added her to their manifest and assigned her a shepherd. Dee, I'll need you to make the digital handoff with Tim after we finish here."

"Sure," Dee said, bobbing her head.

"But Zaafir is out of luck," Jason said.

I nodded.

"Why?" Garrett said. "I thought he and his family were sheltering in Kabul."

I had to push aside the flash of irritation. While the SEAL and I had yet to become bosom buddies, he had a valid point. If he and the rest of my teammates were going to sign up for this rescue operation, they needed to understand the hand we'd been dealt.

All of it.

"Zaafir's in trouble," I said. Jason had provided me with an update prior to the meeting, but this was the first time the entire team was hearing it. "He's had to move twice in the last twenty-four hours. The Taliban almost got him at his last safe house. He only escaped because a neighbor saw the convoy approaching. Kabul is now filled with Taliban informers, so he decided to leave town."

"And go where?" Garrett said.

"Bamiyan," I said, indicating the city on the map.

"That's a good two hundred kilometers away," Garrett said. "Why there?"

"I'll take that one," Jason said. "Bamiyan fell to the Taliban weeks ago, so Zaafir thought that would be the last place the kill teams would search for him. The fighters who are nearby will be focused on people traveling south toward Kabul, not north, away from the Americans. Zaafir has a wife and two small children. He needed somewhere to lie low. Somewhere off the beaten path."

"Bamiyan isn't just off the beaten path," Garrett said. "It's damn near in another country."

That was a bit of an exaggeration, but the SEAL was correct to point out the risk.

A trip to Bamiyan would not be easy.

"It's gonna be a rough slog," I said. "Most of the drive's on the Bamiyan-Behsud Highway. The road isn't well maintained, and the terrain is challenging and full of potential ambush sites. It's at least four hours one way. Some of those mountain passes are difficult to navigate during daylight, and we'll be making the drive at night, potentially blacked out. That's the bad news."

"We have good news?" Garrett said.

"Potentially," I said, nodding at Dee with a smile. "Our transportation specialist has been working her magic."

"What kind of magic?" Jason said.

"The kind that gets us a lifeline home," Dee said. "The CIA has been conducting limited operations at night to extract US citizens in extremis situations. They're using military aviation paired with special operators to augment their ground branch teams. Since the operations fall under Langley's banner rather than the Pentagon's, the administration is allowing the missions to proceed."

"Of all the asinine things," Garrett said.

"Everyone here knows the deal," Dee said, "so let's focus on the good instead."

"Which is what, exactly?" Garrett said.

"I made friends with the CIA liaison officer," Dee said. "He gave me an overview of where they'll be working tonight. A couple of tonight's pickups are just north of the Bagram Bowl. From that area, Bamiyan is just an hour's flight due west. If we grab Zaafir and his family and head east, we could potentially meet the Agency air assets halfway."

"They'll come get us out, but won't fly us in?" Garrett said.

"The CIA has to work within the restrictions established by the administration, just like everyone else," Dee said. "Rescue operations for American citizens caught in extremis situations fall within those restrictions. Zaafir is not an American citizen."

"Then how—" Garrett said.

"Because we are American citizens who will be in extremis once we rescue Zaafir," Dee said with a smile.

"I like her," Jason said, pointing at Dee.

I also liked the idea of not driving home, but Dee's course of action came with considerable risk. If the aerial pickup didn't happen, we'd have to travel east on the Bamiyan-Charikar Highway before turning south on AH76. Not only would this detour add at least another hour to the trip, it would drag us past Bagram Air Base before funneling us through the northern section of Kabul. This leg would be littered with Taliban checkpoints, not to mention the countless other refugees heading south. But I decided to keep these thoughts to myself. Dee had done a great job working the CIA officer, and I didn't want to throw a wet blanket on what she'd accomplished. Before this was over, I had a feeling I was going to need more creative thinking from the people in front of me.

Not less.

"Well done, Dee," I said. "Any more miracles up your sleeve?"

I'd asked the question in jest, but the spunky aviator seemed determined to exceed my expectations.

"Yes," Dee said. "I secured us a pair of vehicles. SUVs with integrated low-profile armor, amped-up engines, and extended-range gas tanks. Depending on our fuel-burn rate through the mountains, we should be able to get to Bamiyan and back without touching our twenty-minute reserve."

"Damn, girl," Jason said. "Where did you magic those from?"

"The CIA officer," Garrett said.

I took the comment as more guess than fact, but Dee's blush seemed to confirm the SEAL's hunch. Perhaps she still had a bit of work to do before she was ready to run assets.

"Huh," Jason said with a smile. "My interactions with the OGA folks have never been quite as . . . fruitful."

"That's because you have the back end of a mule for a

face," Dee said. "On a totally unrelated note, if we could be back with the 'terp and his family by sunrise, that'd be great. I have a date for breakfast."

"I really like her," Jason said.

So did I.

"Okay," I said, "so far our resident transportation specialist has put all the knuckle draggers to shame. Jason—what have you got?"

"Kit," Jason said. "An old teammate of mine took the Long Walk a couple of years ago. His squadron isn't here, but he hooked me up with some friends who are. Bottom line, we've got weapons, radios, body armor, goggles, and a couple other odds and ends. Once we wrap up here, he's going to open their Conex and take a well-earned smoke break. If we need to get loud, we'll have the tools."

This was another portion of the plan I hadn't completely fleshed out. According to the gossip I'd picked up from Captain Ngoy, the US had reached an understanding of sorts with the Taliban. In the name of getting the Westerners out of Afghanistan as quickly as possible, the jihadis were not impeding our movement. Taliban kill teams were still hunting Afghan collaborators, but they didn't interfere with the US vehicles coming and going from the airfield.

This signified a couple of things, the most important being that the Taliban's leadership wasn't stupid. Though there were probably quite a few of the rank-and-file jihadis spoiling for a fight, the men in charge knew that America was on its way out. It would be foolish of them to provoke an armed conflict that might fortify the US administration's resolve to remain in-country longer.

This generation of Taliban was much more in tune with the nuances of world opinion than their predecessors had been.

On the other hand, going out as military carried its own risk, especially since our team numbered all of four. The Taliban was not the only game in town. A splinter group called ISIS-K had been steadily gaining prestige and power over the last several years. We might have a working agreement with the Taliban, but ISIS-K and any of the other terrorists subgroups were still itching to spill American blood. In fact, they might very well view the situation from the opposite end of the spectrum. Since the US was withdrawing, this might be their last chance to send Americans home in body bags.

My plan was still a long way from being finalized, and the operational clock was ticking.

"What about you, frogman?" I said to Garrett. "You bringing anything to the table besides your good looks?"

I meant the jibe to demonstrate that the SEAL was part of the team, but his annoyed expression suggested that I'd missed the mark. Garrett was proving to be about as much fun as cancer.

"Bad news, I'm afraid," Garrett said. "Mr. Blackwell's heard rumblings that things are becoming more unstable here by the minute. He wants his airplane wheels up in twenty-four hours."

"Your boss has an intelligence network in Afghanistan?" Jason said.

"Not an official one," Garrett said, "but he's got quite a few ears to the ground. Blackwell Industries has been doing pro bono construction projects in Afghanistan for some time. Schools, wells, hospitals, you name it. Mr. Blackwell cares about protecting his workers and learned pretty quickly that the State Department's advisory bulletins weren't worth much. He addressed that problem like he handles everything—head-on. Job foremen were given money to establish local sources."

"Did it work?" Dee said.

"Absolutely," Garrett said. "In the last ten years, we've had job sites vandalized but we've never lost a worker. Not a one."

"He should be giving the CIA lessons," Jason said.

"Don't think he hasn't tried," Garrett said.

"Twenty-four hours gives us time to grab Zaafir and his family," I said. "Barely. Anything else?"

Garrett shook his head.

"Okay," I said, "then get kitted and pack the vehicles with two days' worth of supplies. I'm going to coordinate our route with Captain Ngoy. I'm not expecting any official help, but her knowing where we're headed can't hurt. Rolling with two vehicles spreads us thin, but it also gives us redundancy. If we lose one, we could all pile into a single SUV along with Zaafir and his family in a pinch. It won't be fun, but it'll beat walking. We'll finalize movement plans and the manifest while we're doing our precombat checks. I'm thinking Jason as the wheelman for one vehicle with me as the TC. Dee and Garrett will bring up trail in vehicle two. In addition to rifles, I want a belt-fed machine gun in each vehicle. If you can find grenade launchers, grab one for each truck."

"What happened to the Taliban-American lovefest?" Dee said.

"Plan for the worst and hope for the best," I said. "We're going into bad-guy country with no combat multipliers. That means we need to be able to execute react-to-contact battle drills with only organic assets. I want each vehicle ready to provide suppressive fire if necessary."

"I'm just a Marine," Joe said, "but your math seems off. Whose gonna be manning the belt-fed weapon if the driver's driving and the TC is TCing? Each truck needs another shooter."

"Couldn't agree more," I said. "Do you know where I can find a few good men?"

"I know of one," Joe said with a smile. "Let me see if I can scrounge up another."

"Nobody from the Air Force," I said. "We've got a timeline to keep."

"Trust me," Joe said. "I know the perfect person."

"Fine," I said. "Tell them to kit up and meet by the vehicles in twenty minutes. I want to be rolling out the gate at sundown."

"Roger that, Skipper," Joe said. "Excited to be on the team."

That made one of us.

FORTY-SIX

Twenty minutes later, I was standing in front of our newly appropriated vehicles, dressed in newly appropriated kit, waiting to pass judgment on the newly appropriated member of our ragtag team. There was just one problem. In a first, Joe had not stayed true to his word. He had not found one additional man for our rescue mission.

He'd found twelve.

Perhaps more.

The section of ramp I'd designated as our precombat inspection/precombat check area was body to body with rough-looking men and women.

"Hey, Joe," I said, seeing the Marine at the front of the group, "who are your friends?"

Joe had the grace to look a bit sheepish.

But only a bit.

"Veterans," Joe said, "most from the special operations community."

"Great to meet you, everyone," I said. "Thanks for coming out. If you'll pardon my rudeness, I need to bend Joe's ear for just a minute. Joe?"

I pointed to a slice of concrete out of earshot from the milling group.

To his credit, Joe obliged.

The setting sun gave Joe's olive complexion a coppery burnish, but provided little relief from the oppressive heat. A steady wind swept across the flight line, bringing with it more torment. Instead of a respite, the breeze felt like a jet engine's exhaust, baking my skin and drying my eyes. The families still standing body to body on the other side of the airfield gates had to be going through hell.

"What gives?" I said to Joe, gesturing at the veterans.

"Sorry," Joe said. "Word got around. Everyone traveled here on their own dime to do something. They want to do it with you."

"I thought they were doing something," I said. "The Pineapple Express?"

"True," Joe said, "but you know how it is. Each of those folks is here to make a difference. I had three shooters in mind to round out your crew, but once people heard we were leading an honest-to-God rescue operation, hitters started coming out of the woodwork. I tried turning them down, but they wouldn't take no for an answer. At least not from me."

The unspoken implication was clear—I needed to break the news to the former warriors. I sighed as I looked over Joe's shoulder. The volunteers ranged in age from late twenties to late forties. Though most were still in shape, I could tell that more than one gut was being held in. These men and women had once been the tip of the spear, but that had been quite a few pounds and years ago.

I understood how they felt. A deep sense of sorrow ran through me too. Through every Afghanistan veteran. From my Uber driver in Austin to Garrett, my pain-in-the-ass SEAL, the feeling of helplessness united us. Even though this was shaping up to be a goat rope of an operation, I felt privileged to be standing on the tarmac as the Afghan sun slid below the horizon. At least I could do something. Countless more veterans were back stateside, watching this slow-motion train wreck from the agony of their easy chairs.

"If you're coming, we've still got room for one more shooter," I said to Joe, keeping my voice down. "Got a name?"

"Yeah," Joe said. "Kent. He's an Air Force PJ."

PJs, or pararescue specialists, were some of the best medics on the battlefield. Their rigorous training pipeline could take up to two years to complete and had an attrition rate of eighty percent. Their curriculum included many of the courses that were common across Special Operations Command with an added focus on emergency medicine. Adding a PJ to our roster would be a game changer.

"Good thinking grabbing a medic," I said. "I'm assuming he knows his way around a crew-served weapon?"

"Roger that," Joe said. "I watched him field strip the SAW we liberated from Jason's Unit friends and conduct a functions check. He's locked and cocked."

"Great," I said. "Tell Kent he's in. I'll talk to the rest of the volunteers."

"You got it, Skipper," Joe said.

I walked back to the gathered group, feeling the

weight of their collective attention. For a moment, I put myself in their place, trying to imagine the resolve they'd mustered to travel to Afghanistan with no clear idea what would happen once they stepped off the plane. Presumably they all had day jobs and most probably had families. No one had paid for their airfare, and they certainly weren't drawing a paycheck. Now they were ready to follow someone they didn't even know into harm's way because of an ethos.

A creed.

. . . I will never leave a fallen comrade to fall into the hands of the enemy . . .

The words came from the fifth stanza of the Ranger Creed, and they'd continued to shape my life long after I'd hung up my tan beret. The lives of the men and women standing before me were molded by similar words.

"I'm Matt," I said. "I'd love to take all of you with me, but I can't. We're attempting to rescue a comrade in arms at the edge of our logistical capability. We have to fly under the radar to have any shot at success. As much as I'd love to have y'all saddle up, I don't have the room."

My words had a physical effect. Where a moment ago, a group of warriors stood ready to ride into battle, now a collection of ordinary men and women looked at me. Shoulders slumped and faces fell as hope died before my eyes.

It was too much to bear.

"There is one thing you studs could still do," I said.

"Lay it on me."

One of the older volunteers had yelled out the answer.

His operator beard was long and streaked with gray, and his scalp was mostly bare. He had the wrinkled face of a man who'd spent his formative years exposed to the weather. His midsection carried a bit more padding than those of his younger peers, but his eyes still burned with passion. Bodies might deteriorate and reaction times decline, but there was one thing the ravages of time could not steal from my brothers- and sisters-in-arms.

Their pride.

"We're heading into Indian country," I said. "While I can't afford to expand my tactical footprint large enough to bring you gunfighters along, I'd feel a whole lot better if I knew you were standing ready back here."

"You want us to be the QRF?" the man said.

"No," I said, "a bunch of eighteen-year-old privates can be a QRF. I want you to be my private army. God's hammer looking for a nail. If shit goes sideways, I want you to be the cavalry coming over the hill. Interested?"

"Hell yeah," the old-timer said.

"Excellent. Then see my transportation specialist," I said, pointing at Dee. "She'll help you get coms sorted out. We're SPing in fifteen mikes. I need y'all on call from the moment we roll out of the gate until we're back inside the wire."

"On it," the old-timer said. "What's your call sign?"

I hesitated, both pissed at my best friend for his part in saddling me with a call sign I hated and missing him desperately. Though he was currently in a prison cell, Frodo would still have his fingerprints on this operation, even if it was only in the form of my detestable call sign.

"Sweet," I said.

"Sweet," the man said with a smile as the rest of the group chuckled. "Now isn't that special. Mine's Toto. I'll get our folks sorted out. We'll be ready for a commo check by the time you clear the gate."

Toto turned and began issuing instructions to his newly formed QRF without waiting for my reply. For a moment, I just watched him work, taking comfort in seeing the men and women revert back to warriors. Unlike many special operators, I wasn't big on the whole Valhalla thing, but if I was wrong and the afterlife really was populated by Vikings, I thought they'd look a lot like this bunch.

"That was well done."

The lilting accent was a dead giveaway.

"Captain Ngoy," I said, turning toward where Belvina stood behind me, "to what do I owe the pleasure of your company?"

"Word of what you're doing has been circulating through the TOC," Belvina said. "As the Current Ops battle captain, I wanted to take a look for myself."

"What do you think?"

"I think you're crazy, but I'd also give anything to go with you."

"Really?" I said.

"Really," Belvina said. "I didn't join the Army to make PowerPoint slides."

"Why did you join?" I said.

The battle captain was quiet for so long that I thought I might have inadvertently offended her. Then she spoke.

"My family came to the States from the Congo when

I was twelve," Belvina said. "We were refugees from the Second Congo War in 2003. Do you know of it?"

"Some," I said. "Jean-Pierre Bemba staged a coup, correct?"

"Him among others." Belvina said. "My father worked for Laurent-Désiré Kabila's administration. He was just a minor government functionary, but that didn't matter to the rebels. They killed anyone associated with the old regime. We fled just in time. My uncle, aunt, and cousins didn't make it."

"I'm sorry," I said.

Belvina nodded, collecting herself before continuing. "We arrived with nothing more than the clothes on our backs. My siblings and I didn't even speak English. Now, eighteen years later, I'm an American citizen and an Army officer. My sister is a doctor, and my brother is in law school. Only in America could this happen. Why did I join the Army? To give something back to the country that has given so much to me."

"You're a soldier, Belvina," I said, squeezing her shoulder. "Soldiers follow orders. I know your heart is with us."

"Not just my heart," Belvina said. "Radio connectivity is spotty where you're headed, but the cell network is pretty robust. Do you have a phone?"

I nodded.

"Give me the number."

I recited the digits. Belvina punched them into her phone and a moment later mine vibrated.

"That's my contact info," Belvina said. "I'll pass along

anything I can. Send Toto up to the TOC. I'll keep him up to speed too."

"Thank you, Belvina," I said. "I mean it."

"Rescue your 'terp and his family," Belvina said. "That will be thanks enough."

She gave me a hug and then headed back toward the TOC, leaving me alone with the sunset.

FORTY-SEVEN

We rolled out of the gate as a convoy of two, right at evening nautical twilight. While the sun had set, the ambient light had yet to fade. The sky was burnt orange and cloudless—an expression of natural beauty that seemed somehow out of place here. In another time and place, it would have been a great night to sit with Laila, beer in hand, and watch the stars appear one by one.

We were a long way from that.

Instead, I was leading five people on a mission of desperation along Death Road. If there was a more ominous way to start an operation, I couldn't think of one.

"Here come the crowds," Dee said.

My transportation specialist was driving while Jason was in the seat behind me. Ahead of us was vehicle one with Joe at the wheel; Garrett in the TC, or truck commander, front-passenger-seat position; and the newest member of our team, Kent, in the back. I'd given a great deal of thought to how I wanted to break down our little element. Since I was the TL, or team leader, it was a foregone conclusion that I would ride in the second truck. If we were ambushed, the lead vehicle would bear the brunt of it, allowing me the time and space to maneuver and plan rather than just react.

I still didn't think much of Garrett, and if I could have gotten away with it, I'd have swapped him for one of Joe's volunteers. Unfortunately, we were on a tight timeline and we still needed Sam's plane. I didn't want to start a fight that might jeopardize either. While I liked Joe and trusted his choice in Kent, in the end, I wanted the team I was most comfortable with close at hand. While no one in our convoy was a stranger to combat, I'd already gone to war with Jason and Dee.

I knew how they would react and where to best employ them.

"2, this is 1. Crowd's pretty thick up here."

It made sense that Garrett, as TC in the lead vehicle, would run the radios, but I still didn't care for the sound of his voice in my ear. So much for us behaving like adults.

"1, this is 2," I said, "roger. Keep rolling. Crowds are trying to get into the airfield, not keep us from going out. They'll get out of the way."

"2, this is 1. They're not moving, over."

I ground my teeth even as I reconsidered the battle-rostered crews. Maybe I should have swapped Jason and Garrett. I'd have to listen to the SEAL yap the entire way to Bamiyan, but at least I wouldn't be worrying about him screwing up the operation.

"1, this is 2," Jason said. "Tap the horn and rev the engine. They'll move."

A single horn blast answered Jason's transmission as Joe followed instructions. Then the taillights that had been glowing red ahead of us dimmed as the lead truck accelerated.

"2, this is 1. That worked," Garrett said. "We're through."

Dee smoothly accelerated, bumper-locking the lead truck so that the crowd couldn't flow between the vehicles and separate us.

"Sorry for jumping in," Jason said, "but I could see the vein popping out on your forehead."

"No worries," I said. "Appreciate the help."

"What's that guy's problem?" Dee said.

"He's chasing ghosts," Jason said.

Jason's response surprised me. Jason was a longtime special forces NCO, so I knew he had little patience for the kind of petty attitude bullshit Garrett radiated. I was expecting something less touchy-feely and more along the lines of *Suck it up, buttercup.*

"You know him?" I said.

Jason shook his head. "Not personally, but I did some checking. He was in the trail Chinook during the Red Wings shoot down."

Silence greeted Jason's reply.

Everyone who'd been in the special operations community longer than a minute knew the Red Wings story. Thanks to Marcus Luttrell's gut-wrenching first-person account in his memoir entitled *Lone Survivor*, a large percentage of the general population was also familiar with the events. Garrett had watched helplessly as his brothers-in-arms were blown out of the sky by a Taliban RPG. The amount of survivor's guilt he was carrying had to be monumental, even almost twenty years later.

"That would mess with anybody," Dee said.

"Yeah," Jason said, "but it doesn't give him a free pass. Everyone who's been in this business longer than a minute is carrying something in their rucksack. You have to come to terms with the fact that the past is the past and there's nothing you can do to change it. Wishing otherwise is a recipe for madness."

Jason's words hit a little too close to home. I'd spent my share of time in a dark place. My Syrian asset and his family had been executed on my watch. The survivor's guilt stemming from this tragedy and Frodo's horrific injuries had nearly consumed me. Looking back, I could see that the desperate need to somehow atone for what had gone wrong in Syria had prompted me to take some impossible chances. Were it not for Frodo and Laila, I'm not sure that I would have come out on the other side of the darkness still intact.

Or maybe at all.

"Thanks for the heads-up," I said to Jason. "I should have checked on Garrett."

"Your plate was already pretty full," Jason said. "Besides, that's what NCO's do—keep our officers out of trouble.

Truer words had never been spoken.

"Look at these people," Dee said.

Though the crowd had moved off the road, they hadn't gone far. The masses pulsed to either side of our vehicle as Dee kept rolling. I'd seen my fair share of riots, protests, and general gatherings of unrest, but this had a different feel. For one, families made up the largest demographic. Mothers and children probably accounted for seventy-five percent of the population, and the ages of the kids spanned from babies to teenagers. The sun was below the horizon, but the temperature was still above ninety. Most of the crowd had been waiting in front of the gates since sunup. The exhaustion on their faces was palpable. But there was an even more tangible emotion I could sense from the gathering.

Desperation.

As I watched, a mother tried to lift her baby up to a Marine standing on a concrete revetment above her. In his helmet, body armor, sunglasses, and camouflage uniform, the Marine looked every bit the trained killer, but something about the pain on the young mother's face reached him. Slinging his rifle, the Marine squatted on his heels. At first, I thought he was going to take the child, but he didn't. Instead, he unlatched his canteen and passed it to the woman. Then he reached into his pocket and handed her the remains of his Meal Ready to Eat.

The mother gratefully accepted both.

After taking a long drink from the canteen, she dribbled some water into her child's mouth. Then she gave the canteen back and again lifted the baby like she was offering her child to a benevolent god. The teenager took the canteen, but not the child, shaking his head. For a moment I pictured Laila in the Afghan woman's place. What level of desperation would prompt a mother to surrender her child to a stranger?

The Marine stood, his gaze moving from the mother to the sea of humanity stretched in front of him. I had a feeling that his sunglasses were doing more than just shading his eyes. The emotional toll of standing on that wall had to be incomprehensible.

"Soul crushing," Jason said. "Those kids are going to carry scars from this forever."

I wanted to say something encouraging, but I just didn't have it in me. Jason was right. Military shrinks would be working overtime after this deployment. And that wasn't the worst of it. For better or worse, everyone with an American flag on their shoulder would be boarding an airplane and heading home.

They would survive.

The prognosis for the Afghan mom and her baby wasn't nearly so rosy.

Dee turned the corner and accelerated, leaving the sorrow behind.

For now.

FORTY-EIGHT

A pulsing startled me out of a daydream as darkness glided past my window. We'd been on the road now for several hours and were traveling blacked out. Dee and Joe were both using NODs to drive. I'd just flipped mine up to do a map check and had yet to lower them again.

I opened a pocket on my plate carrier, removed the phone, and answered.

"Drake."

"Matt, it's Belvina."

My favorite battle captain's accent sounded even more distinct on the phone and the thought of her huddled out of sight with a burner pressed to her ear made me smile.

"Hey, Belvina," I said. "How are things going?"

"Fine for me, but maybe not so fine for you."

Though the first hundred or so kilometers had rolled by uneventfully, I'd been expecting a call.

This highway went by the name of Death Road for a reason.

Prior to 2004, the only safe way to travel to Bamiyan was by air. Though the remote city had the makings of a resort town with towering mountains, rushing rivers, and countless archaeological marvels, the geography that made Bamiyan special also kept the city secluded from the rest of the country. The soaring Koh-i-Baba mountains served as rugged guardians, surrounding the lush valley with jagged walls of stone that reached heights of sixteen thousand feet in places.

Enter the Italian Foreign Ministry.

As part of the Afghanistan reconstruction effort, the Italians had agreed to oversee one of the more ambitious infrastructure projects in the country's admittedly short modern history. A road connecting Kabul to Bamiyan. At only 136 kilometers in length, the effort certainly wasn't in the same league as America's transcontinental railroad or Europe's autobahns, but it was still a formidable undertaking. The highway would officially begin in Maidan Shahar, where it would wind through Wardak Province, steadily climbing upward until reaching the 12,140-foot-high Hajigak Pass.

After summiting the pass, the road would descend into the Bamiyan Valley, which at nine thousand feet was still almost double the altitude of Denver's famous Mile High Stadium. But extreme changes in elevation weren't the highway's only obstacles.

Two additional problems loomed.

Of these two, the project's program manager had pegged weather as the more manageable obstacle. This had proven to be a dangerously naïve assumption. Afghanistan's endless wars followed campaign seasons dictated by Afghanistan's brutal winters. When the temperatures dropped below freezing and the bitter winds began to blow, snow came in quantities that could see twenty-six feet of accumulation.

The Italians ambitiously proposed a series of tunnels to mitigate the inevitable accumulation of snow, but the associated cost and sheer level of effort relegated this to the ever-growing scrap heap of ideas. In keeping with the tried-and-true Italian outlook on life, the architects and engineers had shrugged their shoulders, accepting that the highest passes would remain closed in the wintertime. This had seemed to be an infinitely reasonable compromise at the time, were it not for another grave underestimation of the weather—specifically the havoc tons of snow would wreak on the road's asphalt surface.

The road's designers dictated that 2.4 inches of asphalt should suffice, completely disregarding the input of their Afghan counterparts, who'd suggested a thickness of almost twice that amount.

The Italian engineers spoke.

The construction project moved on.

And the road failed.

In a development that could have been emblematic for the entire Afghanistan reconstruction effort, the first fifty kilometers of road began to decay before the project was even complete. With another shrug of European shoulders, responsibility for the road passed from nation to nation. Construction continued on the ever-westward march toward Bamiyan even as efforts at resurfacing the existing length of road began anew. Working in Afghanistan was the definition of a Sisyphean task. Now, fifteen years later, the road was mostly complete and fairly drivable in the summertime, barring a second problem unique to Afghanistan.

The Taliban.

To be fair, the robberies, ambushes, and murders along what came to be known as the Death Highway could not all be laid at the Taliban's feet. Afghanistan was a nation of warlords and marauders. When it came to thuggery, there were more than enough bad actors to go around. Between local militias, corrupt police, the ever-growing collection of jihadis, and highwaymen, the 136-kilometer road was rife with mischief. In one four-year stretch, more than thirty people had been murdered. This statistic did not even factor in the countless "lesser" crimes in which the victims did not end up in shallow graves.

As part of their effort to rally both local and international support for their overthrow of the Afghan Army, the Taliban had promised to restore law and order while rooting out corruption. I might be a bit of a pessimist in this regard, but I figured the FBI had a better chance of ending corruption in Chicago. Only four of the last seven Illinois governors had spent time in jail, so this could be construed as progress.

Progress in Afghanistan was hard to find no matter how it was measured.

In any case, I suspected the Death Road was probably safer tonight than it had been in decades simply because the Taliban wanted to be able to show progress to a war-weary population. That said, as Belvina had pointed out during the Current Ops briefing, the Taliban wasn't the homogenous group they wanted the West to believe. Not to mention that even if the new leadership team had managed to get all the subfactions in their ranks to play nice, the Taliban wasn't the only game in town. ISIS-K was making a comeback, and the terrorists would probably like nothing more than to thumb their noses at their jihadi brothers on the world stage.

It wasn't terribly surprising that Belvina thought we were heading for trouble.

"What have you got, Belvina?" I said, as my heart rate accelerated.

"A Pred detoured to the west on our behalf for a quick look-see. It found a checkpoint set up at the Hajigak Pass. Three vehicles. Two in the road and one in overwatch."

"Tracking," I said as I fumbled with my map. "Can you give me a grid?"

"Roger—stand by."

I heard Belvina relay instructions, probably to one of her capable NCOs. I studied the imagery from Google Maps as I waited, deciding where I'd put the checkpoint. There was no shortage of good locations. The veneer of civilization along that stretch of road was very thin.

The pass was a desolate wasteland of barren ground descending from the peaks, for the most part empty of anything resembling human habitation. The road had been excavated into the side of the mountain. Sloping terrain loomed to the right side of the road while rolling hills fell off to the left. The pass was an intersection of sorts, and there were several secondary roads in varying states of repair that branched off in the other cardinal directions.

A small village lay at the base of the hills to our left. The settlement consisted of five or six single-story mud-brick dwellings surrounded by wheat fields. The epitome of a one-stoplight town.

If there'd been any electricity to power the stoplight.

The entire length of road was ripe for setting up an ambush. Towering rock on one side of the asphalt and unobstructed emptiness on the other made for perfect fields of fire. Even so, there was one stretch of pavement uniquely suited to interdicting oncoming traffic from either direction. A loop of road coiled in upon itself, entering from the northeast, briefly turning southwest, and then spiraling through a one-hundred-eighty-degree change in direction to continue northwest. The dramatic turns would force vehicular traffic to substantially decrease speed.

That was where I'd put my checkpoint.

"Ready for the grid?" Belvina said.

"Send it."

She read me an eight-digit string of numbers that confirmed my suspicions.

Sometimes I hated being right.

"Matt—one more thing. The vehicles on the road? They're Humvees."

Perfect.

FORTY-NINE

The notion of Humvees in the hands of bad guys wasn't as far-fetched as it might seem. The huge inventory of US equipment now owned by the Taliban had become a reoccurring theme in the Western media's Afghanistan coverage. Whether this transfer of technology had occurred because the kit had been left behind by Americans or captured from fleeing Afghan soldiers didn't matter. Bottom line, an astonishing quantity and variety of weapons, vehicles, and equipment that once had been solely associated with NATO countries now resided in the Taliban's armory.

Including Humvees.

"Are you certain there are no friendlies in our AO, Belvina?" I said.

This was my biggest fear. Going head-to-head with jihadis equipped with US arms and technology certainly wasn't going to be a walk in the park, but this paled in comparison to the alternative. Unlike some of our adversaries, US doctrine did not simply accept fratricide as the cost of doing business. The thought of accidentally killing a brother- or sister-in-arms had caused more than one warrior to hesitate on the battlefield, in some cases to their detriment. I needed to be one hundred percent certain that the combatants gathered on the road ahead of us were not American.

"Positive," Belvina said. "I double-checked current operations and coordinated with the special operations liaison officer. We have zero activity that far west of Kabul."

Belvina was sharp. I might have to have a conversation with her about coming over to the dark side once this was all done. The DIA could always use more smart people, and I thought James would like her.

Assuming, of course, I was still employed by DIA.

But that was a topic for later.

"Okay," I said, my brain turning. "I appreciate the eye in the sky, but I'm wondering if you have something more . . . kinetic up your sleeve."

"Thought you might ask," Belvina said. "Sorry, Matt. No can do. We don't service targets on behalf of civilians. Also, I'm going to lose the Pred's feed in about thirty seconds. The S3 isn't thrilled with all the cowboy stuff going on tonight. ISR assets are being pulled in as close to the airfield as possible. The Pineapple Express shepherds are beginning to bring in passengers."

The term *civilian* stung a bit, but I knew where Belvina was coming from. Going rogue made for good spy movies, but operating without government support was a whole lot less sexy when you were barreling down an abandoned road in the middle of the night toward a potential Taliban checkpoint. As to the rest of what Belvina said, I understood even if I didn't like it. The last thing

I wanted to do was jeopardize the shepherds as they brought their Afghans through the wire.

"Roger that," I said. "Can you tell me the number of folks manning the checkpoint?"

"Affirmative. I see three heat sources on the road and another in the turret of the overwatch vehicle. Could be more in the actual Hummers, but I can't tell."

Four fighters for three vehicles. That didn't add up. Each of the three vehicles had at least a driver and a TC, which came to six bodies. Gunner for the crew-served weapon meant seven. Worst case, an even ten. In Afghanistan, worst case tended to be the norm, which meant I was looking at ten bad guys against my six shooters.

Not exactly the three-to-one odds that Clausewitz recommended.

"Thank you, Belvina," I said. "That's a big help."

"A big pain in the ass is more like it," Belvina said. "I wish I could do more. Good luck, Matt."

Belvina hung up.

Pain in the ass was right. We were descending down a stretch of highway leading to the S-turn curve and roadblock. Sheer rock loomed to our right and a sloping series of hills led to the village on our left. The jihadis were set up at the road's lowest point with two Hummers positioned across the pavement. A third vehicle was posted in an overwatch position behind the first two, taking advantage of the rising terrain as the road corkscrewed to the right and began the arduous climb back into the mountains.

Though we were blacked out, the jihadis would soon be able to hear our engines and see our vehicles' dark forms even if they didn't have night vision devices. I had maybe a minute to tilt the terms of the engagement in our favor.

Time for an audible.

"1, this is 2," I said, keying the radio.

"Go for 1."

"Roger, 1, we've got bad guys on the road up ahead. Three Hummers—two on either side of the road forming a checkpoint and one in an overwatch position. Overwatch vehicle has a gunner in the turret. Three visible guards dismounted on the road. Assume others in the vehicles or close by. TOC confirmed there are no friendlies in the area."

"1 copies all," Garrett said. "Are we going to detour?"

"Negative," I said. "No time. Here's how this is going to roll."

I gathered my thoughts and relayed a plan I hoped was both tactically sound and would culminate with all six of us alive and on the far side of the roadblock. If I couldn't have both, I'd settle for the latter.

Tactically sound plans were often overrated.

After hearing what I intended, Garrett agreed with the strategy. Or at least he didn't second-guess my plan. Maybe he was coming around, or maybe Joe the Marine was helping to temper Garrett's cynicism.

Either way, I'd take it.

"You sure you're good with this?" I said to Dee as we rolled toward the blockade with our headlights now illuminated.

"Asked and answered," Dee said.

Her tone was matter-of-fact. Light even. Like this was just another day at the office.

Maybe we needed to change her call sign to Ice.

"2, this is 1," Garrett said. "We are in position and ready to execute, over."

"Roger that, 1," I said. "Stand by."

"Ready?" I said, looking over my shoulder at Jason.

"Just like old times," Jason said.

His answer matched Dee's nonchalance. I'd debated switching Dee out for me or Jason, but hadn't. Dee said she could handle her part, and if I second-guessed her now, she'd be second-guessing herself for the rest of the operation. That would have been dangerous. Besides, I needed my most experienced shooters in the roles Jason and I had to play.

"They don't look happy to see us," Jason said.

As per our quick briefing, Dee had triggered her bright lights before coming into view of the roadblock. Now the twin pools of light illuminated three jihadis in dirty robes armed with AK-47s. They stood on either side of the two Hummers, which had been parked in the center of the road, noses almost touching. One look at the thick glass and low riding frame confirmed my suspicion that we were dealing with the up-armored variant.

While a normal Humvee was around six thousand pounds, the heavy-duty metal plating and dense ballistic resistant glass that went into the up-armored version easily added another four thousand pounds to the vehicle's gross weight. In comparison, our Suburban weighed in at about five thousand. This made the Hummers a simple but fairly effective obstacle.

Attempting to crash through the blockade would do little more than crumple our hood, rendering our vehicle undrivable. A granite cliff face hemmed us in to the right, but the rolling hills to our left presented a possible avenue for circumventing the roadblock. This course of action assumed that the rifle-carrying jihadis and overwatch vehicle were both neutralized and that my transportation specialist could traverse the incline in our top-heavy SUV. In other words, we needed equal parts finesse and gunpowder.

Not the safest of bets.

Then again, neither was the alternative.

"Here we go," Dee said.

The fighters stalked toward us, rifles held at chest level. This far away from Kabul, I was betting that these guys were not the varsity. They were probably more accustomed to shaking down fleeing civilians than going gun on gun with two trucks of hitters.

We were about to put that theory to the test.

"1, this is 2. Prepare to execute," I said.

"This is 1, roger."

Garrett's voice was calm and collected—the response I expected from a fellow gunfighter. Despite our differences, he sounded like he was in the zone. I took in a breath, held it, and then exhaled. Next to me, Dee seemed the epitome of chill from the waist up, but her right leg was bouncing.

I reached over and squeezed her thigh.

"You got this," I said.

The aviator nodded as Jason rustled in the backseat. His window, like mine, was already rolled down, and the night's ambient sounds drifted in the cabin. I could hear the jihadis' sandals scuffing on the rock and the creak of weapons and equipment. Then the growl of a diesel engine cranking. A second later a pair of headlights ignited, lancing our comfortably dark cockpit with eye-burning brightness.

"Shit," Jason said.

The twin beams came from the overwatch vehicle parked on a rise above and to the left of the blockade. The elevated position allowed the crew-served weapon mounted to the Humvee's turret to fire over the roadblock while still raking our cabin with large-caliber rounds.

It was a masterful use of the jihadis' vehicles.

Maybe this wasn't the JV team after all.

"Steady," I said. "Nothing changes."

I made the comment as much for myself as my cabinmates. The light pouring through the windshield made our job more difficult and partially negated one of the advantages I'd intended to employ to even the odds. But that was life as an operative. The plan always changed once the enemy made their move.

Always.

"Here he comes," I said.

The three fighters separated, two approaching Dee's side, the other mine.

"Get ready," I said.

The pair of jihadis on the driver's side split again, one fighter covering the truck with his AK, while the other headed for Dee. I was hoping the gunman would roll right up to the door, but he didn't.

Instead, the fighter pointed his rifle at Dee and screamed something.

"Execute," I said.

Several things happened at once.

Dee killed the headlights and ducked beneath the door's armor plating. I drove my M4 through the open passenger window and acquired my target even as two jihadis tumbled to the ground to the accompaniment of a chattering Squad Automatic Weapon, or SAW. The fighter on my side whipped his head toward his comrades, distracted by the sight of tracers from Kent's machine gun stitching his friends. I fired a quick burst into his head, and he joined his buddies on the dirt.

So far so good.

Then the .50 cal mounted on the overwatch Humvee cut loose.

Not so good.

The Ma Deuce rocking on automatic was terrifying. The fireball at the end of the machine gun's muzzle looked like a star mid-supernova. If the 5.56 tracer rounds Kent's SAW fired looked like fairies flitting through the air, the half-inch-in-diameter bullets arcing toward us from the .50 cal could have been dinner plates. Dee reacted as briefed, gunning the engine so that our truck raced toward the roadblock and thereby cut into the gunner's sight line, but we still caught a round or two in the roof as we rolled.

Metal groaned, glass shattered, and people cursed.

I kept my cool.

"1, this is 2," I said. "I need that gunner down right fucking now."

Mostly.

"2, this is 1. Stand by."

Garrett the SEAL sounded cool as a cucumber. Of course my naval commando friend wasn't taking fire from a machine gun designed to punch holes through lightly armored vehicles. Dee had our bumper kissing the two Hummers, but if 1 didn't take out the machine gun quick, we were toast. I pressed the radio's transmit button with the intention of telling 1 what I thought of his *stand by* admonishment when a flash of light and a deep *whump* echoed from the hill.

Then the M2 fell silent.

Several more explosions bracketed the vehicles as Joe put his grenade launcher to use while Kent continued to provide suppressive fire with his SAW. I bailed out of our stricken vehicle, using the hood for cover as I panned my EOTech across the battlefield, searching for targets.

I found plenty.

The fighters who had seemed so confident earlier now scattered under our disciplined fire. I tracked the holographic crimson dot onto a jihadi running toward the burning gun truck and put an aimed pair into his back.

He fell.

I repeated the process with a second fighter attempting to use the burning overwatch Humvee for cover. If they'd taken the time to organize, the jihadis could have given us a run for our money. They didn't. Part of this was due to the devastating rifle and machine-gun fire coming from Garrett's support-by-fire position in the village downslope to our left. Though much of the engagement hadn't played out the way I'd planned, the most important aspect had come together.

By approaching the roadblock with our brights on and engine rumbling, we'd distracted the jihadis, allowing Garrett to drive unseen into the village. Joe hadn't disabled the .50 cal before it could enter the fight as planned and neither had Dee dropped the first guard with a pistol shot to the face. The longer I did this job, the more I came to believe that it wasn't the force with the best plan that carried the day.

It was the element who adapted to changing circumstances the quickest.

Training mattered.

"2, this is 1," Garrett said. "Recommend you relocate to our position. We will cover your movement, over."

Another deviation from the plan, but what Garrett was suggesting made sense. We'd beaten back the jihadis' advance, but unless Jason, Dee, and I assaulted through the objective, the engagement would quickly stalemate. Better to let Garrett's crew work the entire kill zone without the distraction of potential fratricide.

"1, this is 2," I said. "We're moving back to our vehicle now, over."

I fired a final burst at two jihadis and then jumped into the passenger's seat. Dee followed a moment later and then Jason climbed in, his M4 still rocking. Dee slammed the transmission into reverse, and the engine groaned as the shrieking sound of metal on metal filled the cabin.

"We're not going far in this heap," Dee said, spinning the wheel as she floored the gas.

I eyed the pair of Humvees, considering grabbing one of them to replace our stricken vehicle but quickly abandoned the idea. To commandeer a Hummer, we'd have to reengage the jihadis, and I wasn't willing to risk a sustained gunfight against a numerically superior force. But neither was I ready to just leave the up-armored vehicles behind and hope they didn't cause us trouble later.

"Jason, grenade launcher," I said.

Jason handed me the shotgunlike HK M320 grenade launcher. I centered the night sight on the rightmost Hummer, waited for Dee to open up space, and then squeezed the trigger. The grenade launcher slapped my shoulder as a 40mm round rocketed out of the gaping tube. A moment later the Hummer rocked as the munition detonated. I actioned the side opening breech to reload, acquired the second truck, and put a round into its chassis as well. This time the grenade went low, destroying the left front tire, but leaving the frame basically intact.

A mobility kill—good enough for government work.

Several more explosions blossomed across the engagement area as Joe pumped volleys of grenades into likely hiding places. Then we were bouncing down the side of the incline toward Garrett's element. We made it about one hundred yards before the metal-on-metal squeal became a scream and the truck ground to a halt.

"That's all she wrote," Dee said.

Fortunately, Garrett had been charting our progress. No sooner had Dee brought our truck to a stop than the second SUV rolled up beside us. With a precision that would have made a NASCAR pit crew proud, Jason and

Dee transferred our kit into Garrett's vehicle as I continued to put steel on target. I'd stopped seeing movement, but that didn't mean the jihadis weren't playing possum.

When it came to suppressive fire, safe always beat sorry.

"Let's go, Skipper," Joe said.

I lobbed a final grenade into the burning inferno, then jumped into the front seat Garrett had so thoughtfully vacated. Joe floored the accelerator and our SUV spun gravel as it launched from the village's dirt road onto the pavement. Joe handled the incline like an expert, tracking downslope of the roadblock before regaining the pavement and leaving the burning wreckage behind.

I checked the rearview mirror for pursuers.

Nothing but a trio of burning Humvees.

How very fitting.

FIFTY

What?"

Aalem ignored his commander's brusque response to the caller just as he'd ignored the ringing phone moments before. He and his two teammates had been working nonstop for the last several hours as the collection of empty Monster Energy cans could attest. Even so, Aalem prided himself on his still steady hands. Though their leadership frowned on the consumption of the caffeine-infused drinks, as with many things, Aalem and his comrades were given a pass. During the recent Taliban offensive, Aalem's unit had neutralized more high-value targets in a single month than the rank-and-file fighters had managed to do in the preceding decade.

Aalem and his teammates were killers.

But they didn't look like it.

"Where?"

Aalem almost pitied whoever was on the line. Unlike many of his fellow fighters, Aalem and his crew were educated. Highly educated. Aalem was a mechanical engineer; Gul, electrical; and Jaabir, a computer scientist. Baser, their fearless commander, had been an auto mechanic. Together, the four scrawny twentysomethings barely weighed two hundred kilos. They carried one AK-47 between them along with an ancient Russian Makarov pistol. None of the four men had ever fired a gun in anger, and their bodies in no way resembled the weathered husks of seasoned Taliban fighters.

Aalem wasn't even sure he remembered how to put their Kalashnikov into action.

But for all their lack of martial appearance, the bespectacled technicians had created one of the most fearsome weapons ever employed by the Taliban. Each member of the team had contributed his own expertise to their Frankensteinian creation.

As the mechanical engineer, Aalem had been responsible for designing and fabricating the ingenious munitions-release mechanism. It was to this finicky collection of springs, levers, and electronically actioned servos that he now devoted his attention. While the previous operation had been a success, one of the munitions had failed to deploy on command. That the munition had satisfactorily released the second time Aalem pushed the appropriate button was of no consolation. Though he was far from a traditional soldier, Aalem was intimately familiar with the fickle nature of war. Hesitation in battle cost lives, whether those hesitations were mechanical or human in nature. When it came to the portions of the weapon that were his responsibility, Aalem was every bit as demanding as the most hardened Taliban commander.

"Aalem? Aalem!"

Aalem looked over his shoulder and realized with a start that Baser had been calling his name. Though his mind was as tightly focused as ever, his body was beginning to grow weary. After a certain point, all the energy drinks in the world wouldn't be enough to combat the mental fog birthed by lack of sleep.

He needed rest.

Soon.

But not just yet.

Aalem turned back to the weapon and made a final tweak with his watchmaker's tool. Then he completed the circuit and watched the release springs smoothly action.

Perfect.

Just as it should be.

"Aalem!"

"Yeah, Baser," Aalem said, turning once again.

He needn't have bothered. Somehow Baser was now standing at his shoulder.

How had that happened?

"When was the last time you slept?" Baser said.

Aalem edged the jeweler's glasses up onto his forehead so he could see his commander more clearly. As if the answer somehow lay with Baser. Or their surroundings. With a start, Aalem realized that he wasn't entirely sure where they were. The last several days were a blur of setting up camp, executing a mission, recovering the weapon, and repeating the cycle.

When was the last time he'd slept?

"What day is it?" Aalem said.

"Friday," Baser said, running a hand over his face. "Or is it? I don't know."

"I caught a nap before the last operation," Aalem said. "Whenever that was. Why?"

Aalem knew that Baser wasn't inquiring about his well-being out of a sense of concern. Aalem hadn't seen his own reflection recently, but he couldn't imagine he looked worse than his commander. Baser's eyes were bloodshot and the skin beneath them dark and baggy. His curly hair was matted and the remains of a protein bar still powdered his face.

He looked like death warmed over.

They all did.

"We have a new mission," Baser said.

Aalem sighed.

The nonstop OPTEMPO was the price of their success. Aalem had thought his unit would get a breather once Kabul fell, but if anything, the request for support had only increased. Baser had finally put his foot down, stating in no uncertain terms that his team needed to rest and conduct much-needed maintenance on the weapon.

They'd been promised twelve hours of downtime.

Gul and Jaabir had celebrated by flopping into their sleeping bags on a section of crushed grass by the side of the road. Both men had been snoring before the engine on their Toyota station wagon had stopped ticking. The four had become accustomed to living rough, and Aalem had planned on following suit just as soon as he finished troubleshooting the release mechanism.

Surely the team wouldn't receive another tasking before sunup.

That optimism now seemed misplaced.

"Give me ten minutes," Aalem said, looking at the parts strewn across his portable workbench. "Then she'll be ready."

"You've got five," Baser said. "Pack it up. We've got to get on the road. The mission's not here."

"Where are we headed?"

Baser told him.

"Great," Aalem said, his lips forming a smile. "Gul or Jaabir can drive."

FIFTY-ONE

DEATH ROAD, AFGHANISTAN

Who's up for a little culture?" Jason asked in his distinctive North Carolina twang.

In another win for Dee, the Chevy Suburban she'd liberated from the airfield's vehicle lot was big enough to fit the six of us and our kit. Barely. The trip back to Kabul with Zaafir and his family would be considerably less roomy. Especially if we had to drive the entire three-plus hours. I was still betting on the air assets my favorite battle captain had promised, but first we had to find Zaafir.

"Me," Dee said.

Once again, our transportation specialist was to my left, driving the vehicle. Though I knew she'd seen combat as an Apache pilot, fighting in the air and fighting on the ground were two different beasts. One could certainly kill you as easily as the other, but there was something much more visceral about shedding blood in the mud. To that end, I'd been worried about Dee. Not because I doubted her abilities, but because, compared to the rest of the crew, she was untested.

She'd done fine.

More than fine, actually.

When the engagement had unfolded differently than expected, she'd both adjusted on the fly and exercised initiative. We might have lost our second ride, but if Dee hadn't made the snap decision to ram the Humvees and thereby obscure the machine gunner's gun line, we would have lost a whole lot more. After we'd put some distance between ourselves and the remains of the road-block, she'd asked to drive, and Joe had promptly obliged. She'd earned her spot on the team, and Joe was much more valuable to us with a weapon instead of a steering wheel in his hands.

My ragtag bunch of commandos might actually be coming together.

"Can we cut the cute and talk about this clusterfuck of an Op?"

Or not.

Garrett, who was seated behind Dee to my left, asked the question. The image of an angel and devil perched on each shoulder came to mind. Jason with his unabashed positivity was the angel.

And Garrett was Garrett. An executive in a highly successful company who'd leveraged his boss to get his name added to our roster. He second-guessed my every decision and ate at our team's morale like acid. He'd also watched his SEAL brothers perish in a ball of fire on an operation not too unlike this one.

I took a deep breath, suppressing the murderous rage that wanted me to reach down Garrett's throat and rip out his spleen. Garrett was partially right.

One of the things that set the special operations community apart was a rigid adherence to a process known as an after-action review, or AAR. During the AAR, rank was tabled, and everyone was free to critique the team's performance. The experience was rarely fun, but if conducted properly, it was always beneficial. Even the most switched-on teams made mistakes. Only by identifying and fixing these errors would the element get better.

But there was a way to run an AAR, and Garrett's jackassian comment wasn't it.

"You're right, Garrett," I said, speaking into the stillness that had followed his outburst. "We do need an AAR of what happened, but I want Jason to finish his thought first."

Garrett responded with a long audible sigh, but he kept his trap shut.

I'd take the win.

"Sure, boss," Jason said. "Zaafir just checked in. He saw what looked like Taliban prowling around the town, so he took his family to ground."

"Another safe house?" I said.

"No," Jason said. "This is where the culture part comes in. They're hiding in the Gholghola City ruins."

"The what?" Garrett said.

"The City of Screams," Kent said.

"Come again?" Dee said.

"It's ruins to the east of the airfield," Kent said. "A fortress Genghis Khan destroyed."

"I'll bite the bullet," Dee said, eyeing the Air Force

commando in the rearview mirror. "Why's it called the City of Screams?"

"Excellent question," Kent said.

I couldn't see the airman's face, but it sounded like he was smiling. With a head full of curly red hair, a ginger beard to match, and a ruddy complexion, Kent reminded me a bit of Prince Harry. If Prince Harry had been an American Air Force special operator with a penchant for history.

"Genghis Khan sent his grandson with part of the Mongol army to subdue the fort," Kent said. "The kid was only fifteen, but old Genghis thought he had the potential to command an army one day."

"Was Khan right?" Dee said.

"We'll never know," Kent said. "An archer took the kid out. When Genghis heard, he went ballistic. Swore he was going to raze the place."

"Crazy," Dee said.

"Oh, it gets better," Kent said.

The enthusiasm in his voice was unmistakable.

I turned in my seat.

Kent was smiling.

"Jalaladin Mingburnu, the fort's commander, had pissed off his daughter by marrying a woman from Ghazni. The daughter decided she'd fare better with Genghis than her new stepmother, so she fired an arrow at the Mongol formation with a message attached to the shaft. She promised to reveal the fort's secret entrance if the Khan agreed to marry her."

"I don't believe it," Dee said.

"I have a teenage daughter," Joe said. "Believe it."

"It's true," Kent said. "She betrayed her father and helped Khan conquer the fortress. Once Genghis secured the city, he butchered everyone inside."

"Including the daughter?" Dee said.

"Yep," Kent said. "Genghis said that if her own father couldn't trust her, why should he?"

"Terrible," Dee said.

"Karma," Joe said.

"Terrible or not, it happened," Kent said. "Supposedly the screams of the dying echoed through the valley as Khan's army went to work."

"The City of Screams," Jason said.

"What are you, a history professor?" Joe said.

"Not yet," Kent said, "but I'm almost done with my PhD. I was supposed to defend my dissertation this week, but I had to reschedule."

"Why?" Dee said.

"This," Kent said, the levity leaving his voice. "I haven't been able to concentrate on anything but Afghanistan for weeks. When I heard about folks coming over here to help, I bought a ticket. Couldn't just sit at home and watch."

"You and me both," Joe said. "You're right, Garrett. This is a pretty fucked-up Op. But it beats the hell out of doing nothing."

The silence following Joe's statement was absolute. It was like the Marine had reached into my skull and dragged out the feelings I hadn't been able to articulate. This was a fucked-up Op, no two ways about it. But the people in this car had volunteered for the same reason that each of them had endured the grueling selection processes of their respective special operations entities.

Warriors don't sit it out on the sidelines.

Ever.

"Thanks for the history lesson, Professor Kent," I said. "Jason—any more info from Zaafir?"

"Not really," Jason said. "His written English isn't stellar. We've communicated through voice messages in the past, but now he's only texting. He said that the ruins are abandoned and offer plenty of hiding places. It's the last place the Taliban will look."

"Did he say how the Taliban found him in Bamiyan?"

Garrett's question was a good one.

"No," Jason said. "I think after his near miss in Kabul, Zaafir's just playing it safe. Are there Taliban in Bamiyan? Probably. Taliban are everywhere. But are they actively hunting my 'terp? I don't know. The Taliban have limited resources. I'd think they'd be concentrating on solidifying their hold on Kabul rather than chasing one-offs like Zaafir."

"Agreed," Kent said. "Once the jihadis lock down Kabul and the US leaves, they'll have all the time in the world to round up US collaborators."

"Anyone ever been to Bamiyan?" I said.

"I've flown into the airfield a handful of times," Dee said. "There was a NATO FOB located close to the airstrip. I've seen the ruins from the air but never spent any time on the ground."

"Thanks, Dee," I said. "Anyone else?"

A bunch of headshakes.

"No worries," I said. "Here's how we'll roll."

But before I could lay out what I was thinking, a buzzing phone interrupted me.

"Sorry, boss," Jason said. "It's mine."

The Green Beret took his from his pocket and held it against his ear.

"Hello?"

Though I couldn't decipher the words, I caught the emotion behind them.

"Zaafir, hunker down," Jason said. "We'll find you."

The unmistakable sound of gunfire echoed from the handset.

"Zaafir," Jason said, his own voice rising. "Zaafir. Zaafir!"

The call dropped.

Jason punched redial and selected speaker mode. The ominous sound of a ringing phone echoed through the cabin.

Once.

Twice.

Three times.

My chest compressed with each ring. The SUV surged forward as Dee dropped the hammer even as I looked at the map and did the math. Twenty kilometers. At our current speed, that would take ten minutes. Maybe less. The speedometer needle swung to the right as Dee added still more gas. The hood vibrated. The phone kept ringing.

Six.

Seven.

Eight.

Surely it would go to voice mail soon.

It didn't.

"Jason? Jason?"

"Zaafir," Jason said, "what—"

"They're here," Zaafir said. "Hurry."

The call ended.

FIFTY-TWO

Wake up. Wake up!"

Aalem blinked heavy lids, trying to find his way out of a thick mental fog. His eyes felt gritty and his lips dry. His head ached. He had no idea where he was or the time of day or night.

Only that Baser was once again shaking his shoulder.

"Come on," Baser said.

"Okay, okay," Aalem said.

Wiping the crusty bits of sleep from his eyes, Aalem sat up and eased out of the vehicle's cracked seats. The ancient upholstery was full of jagged edges and the torn fabric was normally hell on Aalem's back.

Not tonight.

Tonight he'd fallen asleep the moment he'd tumbled into the cramped station wagon. That was the real testament to his exhaustion—Aalem had managed to nap while riding in the car's least desirable seat.

"Where are we?" Aalem said.

"Less talking, more doing," Baser said. "We have to be operational in ten minutes."

This pronouncement, more than his commander's

earlier chiding, finally cleared away the last of Aalem's mental cobwebs. He stumbled from the car to find the folding table he used as a lab bench already set up and his camp chair resting beside it. His toolbox was in place and open, illuminated by a lantern with a red light filter. Next to his tools sat an unopened can of Monster Energy, the aluminum skin glistening with condensation.

Baser could be a taskmaster, but he took care of his men.

"He's awake!"

Jaabir hissed the fake shout from his position on the far side of the table. The computer scientist's ever-present laptop was already powered on, the screen softly glowing through another light-dimming filter. Next to him Gul flashed Aalem a grin, the pimple-faced electrical engineer already fiddling with his collection of cell phones. Aalem paused for a moment as an unexpected feeling of pride swelled in his chest. Who would have thought that four nerds still in their twenties would help turn the tide of the war?

Allah truly was great.

"Quickly," Baser said, materializing out of the dark.

"Yes, yes," Aalem said.

He pulled a headlamp from his pocket, slid the fabric band over his shock of unruly hair, and activated the light. A crimson puddle appeared on the ground. Baser nodded approvingly before picking up the rusty AK-47 and striding off into the night. As the group's lone non-technician, Baser pulled security for the engineers while they worked.

Aalem was still adjusting to the idea of operational

security. When they'd first begun to work in darkness, Aalem had ruined everyone's night vision more than once by accidentally triggering the LED's white instead of red bulbs. Though he'd received a much-deserved tongue-lashing from Baser for his oversight, it was a close call with an enemy patrol that had finally driven home the need for noise and light discipline.

As Baser's approving nod showed, Aalem was becoming a soldier.

Or at least some sort of soldier.

Aalem knew he would never inspire fear in others with his physique or his prowess with a firearm. That was okay. Aalem was more than content to let his creation inspire fear on his behalf.

Opening the Toyota's hatchback, Aalem surveyed his masterpiece.

Under Baser's direction, the engineers had long since removed the station wagon's interior lights so as not to inadvertently compromise their position, but for his night-adapted eyesight, the illumination provided by Aalem's headlamp was more than sufficient. A bird of prey was nestled in the cargo area, protected by foam cutouts specially designed to attenuate the jarring bumps and jolts that came with traversing back roads. Aalem found it fitting that the weapon's smooth edges and contoured lines were bathed in red light.

His creation was an instrument of death.

Reaching inside, Aalem tenderly grabbed the fuselage and lifted the drone free from its casing. After purchasing the UAV from an agricultural company in China,

Aalem and his companions had altered the aircraft in ways that the Chinese engineers couldn't have imagined. The warbird had cost more than sixty thousand US dollars and required countless months to make the journey to Afghanistan.

More than once Baser had stood in front of his superiors to extol the potential of his *special project* even as he begged and pleaded for just a few more days as Aalem and his fellow engineers worked to make the weapon operational. Almost a year had elapsed from the time Aalem had discovered the aircraft on the internet to its maiden operational flight. Over the course of those many months, Baser had fought off countless attempts to disband his crew and roll their efforts into the work already being done by less capable men with far less capable drones. Now, as then, Aalem was privy to the meetings Baser had with the Taliban leadership, but from the sound of Baser's conversations, no one was calling for the weapon's cancellation any longer.

"Satellite link confirmed," Gul said as he adjusted the antenna to his portable terminal. "Ready to fly."

"GPS integrated," Jabir said even as his fingers continued to pound his laptop's keyboard. "Target coordinates verified. Ready to fly."

Aalem registered the men's comments even though he wasn't really paying attention. Instead, he was concentrating on his meticulous preflight checks. He'd already flexed the control surfaces and verified that the internal radios were online. Fuel and fluid levels looked fine. The sensor suite had finished initializing and had just synchronized with the onboard GPS receiver.

Image quality was good, especially considering the ambient conditions. Thermal crossover was always a problem at this time of night, but the video displayed on Aalem's Android device was more than adequate. Even the release-munitions mechanism that had given him such trouble earlier was functioning properly.

The aircraft was ready to fly.

Almost.

Walking back to the car, Aalem removed another container. This one he handled with even more care than he'd shown the aircraft. After gently placing the hard plastic case on the ground, Aalem opened the latches and pulled away the foam cutouts protecting the drone's payload. With steady hands, Aalem removed each munition, fit the ordnance to the UAV's munition rack, and armed them.

After a final, lengthier visual inspection, Aalem was satisfied.

"Ready to fly," Aalem announced.

Once again Baser appeared out of the darkness. He surveyed the loaded aircraft, the intended target coordinates, the drone's flight route, and the satellite terminal. Then he turned to Aalem and gave the command the engineer had been waiting for.

"Launch the bird."

Aalem stabbed the red button in the center of his display. The aircraft's gasoline engine roared to life and the helicopter blades began to turn. Even just meters away, the acoustically dampened rotor blades and muffled engine were surprisingly quiet. At mission altitude, the drone was nearly silent. After a final check of his instrumentation, Aalem touched a second button.

The drone shot skyward, disappearing into the black sky.

It was time to hunt.

FIFTY-THREE

DEATH ROAD, AFGHANISTAN

Dee had the RPMs redlined.

The speedometer read seventy-five, but that seemed much too slow based on how fast the trees were whizzing past. Driving under goggles was tricky in a tactical vehicle at tactical speed, which usually wasn't much faster than thirty or forty miles an hour. Dee had ūs going twice that fast. While she seemed to have things under control, we were also hauling ass through farm country in a top-heavy SUV. Getting us to the City of Screams thirty seconds quicker would be for naught if an ox decided to wander across the road.

"Back off a bit, Dee," I said. "Give yourself some reaction time. No telling what could be just around the next bend."

Dee glanced at me.

The four image-intensifying tubes sprouting from her face hid her expression, but I still guessed what she was thinking.

I don't tell you how to shoot . . . Don't tell me how to drive.

To her credit, my transportation specialist did slow down. Barely. The speedometer fell by about five miles per hour. Better than nothing. Now on to the second problem—the cold extraction that had just turned hot.

"We can't go in blind," Garrett said.

Garrett's statement was more plea than command. His quiet tone accomplished more than his sarcasm. I thought about what he must be remembering. Feeling. Once again, he was in Afghanistan, headed for a landing zone to save a comrade who was fighting for his life. This mission had to be resurrecting demons.

For all of us.

Suddenly I was riding shotgun in another SUV, this time in Syria. Frodo was behind the wheel. Behind me, Jason had to be reliving the operation that had been the catalyst for this one ten years later. I didn't know Dee, Joe, or Kent well enough to guess what they were thinking, but I had to believe their thoughts followed similar lines. Each of us had a moment we would give anything to undo, but we were all riding toward the sound of gunfire all the same.

It's who we were.

Sometimes violence of action and speed was the right choice.

The only choice.

Not tonight.

"Dee, slow down," I said. "Now."

"What?" Dee said.

"Garrett's right. We've got no air support and no QRF just thirty minutes away. We need time to see what we're up against."

Dee eased off the accelerator, dropping back to forty-five. We were still traveling at a pretty good clip, given the road conditions, but I no longer felt like we were in danger of slaloming into an adjacent wheat field. More important, the slower speed facilitated the next part of my plan.

"Kent," I said, "ready to be our eye in the sky?"

"Just because I'm Air Force, you think I know how to fly the drone?" Kent said.

"No," I said. "I thought that as our resident academic, you'd be best suited to read the directions. Or do you need a Marine to help you sound out the big words?"

"Have pictures, will travel," Joe said, reaching for the plastic Pelican case.

"Mitts off it," Kent said, unclasping the metal buckles. "I got this."

Turns out that Kent did not have this.

Judging by the chorus of voices in the back of the vehicle, it required at least three commandos to assemble and put into operation a hobby drone meant for a twelve-year-old. I spent the time trying to contact my favorite battle captain while Jason texted and called Zaafir.

Neither of us was successful.

Thankfully, my newly minted drone operators had better luck. After conducting a quick preflight consisting of powering on the UAV, establishing a GPS lock, and taking the protective caps off the sensors, we were ready to fly. Dee pulled over, Kent set the quad copter on the dirt road, and then pushed a button. The drone leaped skyward. A moment later we were back to hauling ass, and I was receiving imagery on my smartphone.

What I saw wasn't good.

The City of Screams might once have been a fortress,

but it now resembled a sandcastle that had been partially washed away by the incoming tide. The hilltop structure had been worn down by time. A single tower jutted from the remains of the citadel located at the city's pinnacle, but much of the rest of the ruins had slumped into obscurity. The defining edges and distinctive features had been softened like a partially melted wax structure.

One or two of the blobs depicted in the black-and-white thermal imagery were recognizable structures. A modern rectangular building had been erected at the base of the footpath that led into the upper ruins. It sat adjacent to a parking lot currently occupied by two Hilux trucks—the Taliban's ride of choice.

"What's with the building?" I said, drawing a box around the structure. Kent was flying the bird, but the sensor imagery could be shared in real time across several smart devices along with the graphic overlay I'd just created.

"That's for the ticket takers," Kent said.

"Ticket takers?" I said.

"Yeah," Kent said. "The ruins have become a pretty big tourist draw in recent years. The Afghan government started charging admission."

"And who said capitalism never had a chance here?" Joe said.

"Pan to the north," Jason said. "Up by the citadel."

"This was why I never wanted to be a pilot," Kent said. "Too many cooks in the kitchen."

"Amen," Dee said.

The imagery on my phone shifted, centering on the citadel itself and the crumbling tower. Then the citadel's walls, paths, and outbuildings swam into view.

Along with four figures clustered near the entrance.

"That's them," Jason said. "Zaafir and his family."

Kent dropped a waypoint at the center of the cluster, storing the GPS location in the drone's memory. Then he bounced out to a wider field of view, which showed the footpath leading downslope from the citadel to the city's remains. Once again, the original buildings were largely unrecognizable, with the exception of a long rectangular structure whose roof consisted of eight dome-like protrusions grouped in clusters of four.

A sloping path led from the domed building to the citadel's entrance.

A path occupied by ten ghostly figures.

As I watched, one of the citadel's occupants lay prone in the doorway, orienting his rifle toward the approaching figures.

Then a thermal plume blossomed from his rifle.

"Zaafir's trying to hold them off," Jason said. "He won't last long."

"Agreed," I said. "Kent, pan back to the parking lot. Let's see what we're dealing with."

The drone's imagery shifted, revealing the parking lot, the squat ticket-taking building, and the two Hiluxes.

"Scan back and forth, Kent," I said. "We need to know whether the jihadis left any security with their vehicles. Everyone else, jock up. We're gonna be rolling in hot."

The cabin exploded into motion as commandos seated magazines, activated optics, and conducted the precombat inspections that by now were second nature. The activity felt both comforting and strange. Comforting in that these rituals meant we were transitioning from the unknown to the known. The situation, vague as it had been, had now resolved into something we could deal with.

An ambush.

The earlier uncertainty was gone.

Even so, parts of this still felt strange. We were riding in a Chevy Suburban instead of a helicopter or tactical vehicle, and there was no chorus of voices in my ear. No higher headquarters providing me with a final mission update, no check-ins from orbiting CAS or waiting artillery, and no updates from secondary elements in fire-support positions. Most important, no cavalry waiting to come thundering over the hill if things went sideways.

I had the combat power contained in this SUV.

That was it.

"Got one," Kent said. "Single guy loitering by the trucks."

"Confirmed," I said, tagging the straggler on my display. "Anyone else?"

"Negative," Kent said.

"Okay, everybody," I said, tightening my plate carrier, "listen up."

Ten minutes later, we were driving up the gravel path leading to the parking area. Dee was still rolling hot, but she'd slowed for the deteriorating road conditions and our team members.

Or more specifically, our missing team members.

"One more curve and you'll see the parking lot," Jason said. "Still just one guard on the Hiluxes."

"Confirmed," I said, glancing down at the imagery on my cell.

Jason had taken over pilot duties and proven to be a natural aviator.

Or maybe the latest drones were just idiot proof.

Either way, he was locked and cocked.

"Dog, this is Sweet," I said. "Status, over?"

We were scraping the bottom of the barrel when it came to radio call signs. Since not all SOF elements awarded them, we'd had to dream up some easily memorable ones on the fly. Thus Joe, our Marine, had been christened Dog, short for Devil Dog. Kent was Professor, Jason was Duke because he sort of sounded like John Wayne, and Garrett, the lone SEAL, was Frog.

But somehow, I was still Sweet.

There was no justice in this world.

"Sweet, this is Devil Dog. Professor and I are in position. Target acquired, over."

"Dog, Sweet, take him, over."

"Sweet, roger. Stand by."

Dee crept forward, allowing the incline to slow us. This was the delicate portion of the operation. Okay, so maybe one of several delicate portions. In any case, dropping the lone sentry quietly and quickly was key to maintaining the element of surprise. I didn't want the sound of our approach to startle him into motion.

"Sweet, Dog, he's down. You're cleared into the parking lot."

"This is Sweet, roger," I said.

We edged around the curve to see an open area with

two pickups parked side by side. A man lay slumped on the ground in front of them.

"Dog, Sweet, nice shooting."

"Sweet, Dog, roger. We have eyes on multiple targets vicinity engagement area Alabama. Standing by, over."

Dee had swung our truck into a tight loop as I was talking so that the nose was now facing back down the trail in preparation for a quick egress. She killed the engine and tucked the keys in the visor. I looked behind me to see Jason passing our transportation specialist the drone's controller. He met my gaze and nodded. Beside him, Garrett made a final adjustment to his Viking Tactics sling.

Then he gave me a thumbs-up.

Showtime.

I looked out the window to get my bearings. To my right, the ticket-taker building loomed, squat and symmetrical against the fortress's run-down facade. To my left, the pedestrian trail beckoned, leading up to the citadel.

"Dog, Sweet," I said, "we are moving, time now."

"Sweet, roger."

I opened my passenger door and flowed out, the red spot generated by my laser bouncing off the fortress's rock walls. I paused for a moment until Jason exited and then formed up behind him. We moved the length of the car, him covering twelve o'clock with me pulling security over his left shoulder. At the rear of the SUV, we linked up with Garrett and Dee.

The SEAL fell in behind me with Dee bringing up the rear.

Then we tackled the incline.

FIFTY-FOUR

Aalem stared at his laptop's screen as the third Monster finally kicked in.

"Baser," Aalem said, slewing the drone's optic two degrees to the left, "are the brothers expecting visitors?"

"What do you mean?" Baser said, appearing over Aalem's shoulder.

Though Aalem was certain he no longer smelled like fresh flowers, his commander reeked. The odor was equal parts adrenaline, body odor, and perhaps fear. Baser was no more warrior than his three technicians, but he was entrusted with both the lives of his technicians and the Taliban's prize weapon.

The pressure must have been intense.

Or maybe his commander just stunk.

Either way, living in close proximity with Baser was an eye-watering endeavor.

"There's a vehicle heading up the path to the ruins," Aalem said, pointing at the thermal signature he was tracking. "Is it one of ours?"

Baser leaned closer to the screen, putting Aalem's

nose level with his commander's armpits. Aalem hadn't thought the stench could get worse.

He'd been wrong.

"Not sure," Baser said. "Why isn't the guard moving to intercept it?"

Aalem was wondering the same thing. Surely the lone sentry wouldn't just let a vehicle approach unchallenged. Unless . . . Aalem punched a button on his keyboard, toggling the streaming imagery from thermal to day TV.

"What are you doing?" Baser said.

"Checking something," Aalem said, slewing the sensor along the road.

The camera wasn't designed for night use, but it still should have picked up the approaching vehicle's headlights. His screen showed only darkness.

"It's not one of ours," Aalem said, his heart beginning to pound. "Warn the guard."

"How do you—" Baser said.

"His headlights are off," Aalem shouted. "Warn the guard!"

Baser stared at Aalem, confusion etched across his sleep-deprived face. With a curse, Aalem reached for the handheld radio clipped to Baser's shirt. His fingers closed on the device just as comprehension dawned in Baser's eyes.

"Dawoos," Baser said, ripping the radio from his pocket.

In Baser's haste, the device slipped from his fingers. This time it was Aalem who cursed. Scooping the radio from the gravel, Aalem pressed the transmit button and held the microphone to his lips.

He was too late.

The sentry was already lying on the ground.

"What happened?" Baser said.

Aalem bounced out a field of view and found the answer to Baser's question.

Two bodies were lying on an adjacent roof.

"Snipers," Aalem said. "Our men are about to be ambushed. Warn them."

This time, Aalem didn't wait for a reply.

He centered the weapon's aimpoint on the two men.

Then he released the munition.

FIFTY-FIVE

We'd made it about twenty feet up the spiraling gravel path when an explosion ripped through the night. Our tactical formation froze as the detonation echoed across the man-made canyon formed by the village. Dirt and grit tumbled from the ancient walls to either side of us, filling the air with dust. I felt like a rat in a maze. The narrow path snaking through the towering ruins made for an excellent kill zone.

Then Jason sprinted forward, all efforts at stealth forgotten.

I ran behind Jason, rifle up, laser spot flitting across my assigned sector. I was following Jason's lead, executing a react to indirect fire drill, trusting that Garrett and Dee were still hot on my tail. If not, this already lopsided engagement was going to take a turn for the ridiculous.

Quickly.

"Dog, this is Sweet, SITREP," I whispered, drawing even with Jason's shoulder.

Silence.

Garrett squeezed my shoulder, confirming he and Dee were still with us.

"Dog or Professor, this is Sweet, SITREP, over."

Still nothing.

"Dog or—"

The next thunderclap made the first explosion seem like a popping balloon in comparison. The blast wave smashed me in the back, slamming me against the wall. I kept hold of my rifle, but the impact tore the goggles from my eyes and filled my mouth with grit. As I scrambled to get my NODs back in place, two more *whumps* followed. The secondaries weren't as violent as the initial detonation, but they weren't exactly the harbingers of good news either.

"What have ya got?" I said, tapping Jason on the shoulder.

"Corridor is clear for about fifty meters," Jason said, edging around the wall. "Then it makes a ninety-degree turn to the right. Our Crows should be on the other side."

"Roger that," I said. "Keep your eyes front. Frog—you got rear security. Bone—get our drone overhead and show me the imagery."

"Copy, TL," Garrett said.

The SEAL took a knee and oriented his rifle back the way we had come.

Jason remained standing, his rifle pointing around the corner even as he used the wall to shield his torso and lower body.

Dee unfolded the Android device clipped to the center of her chest carrier. Our little quad copter had about twenty minutes of battery life remaining, so rather than call it back to the car, Dee had suggested we program the

UAV for a slow overhead orbit in case we needed the sensor for a quick look-see. Flying orbits was more power efficient than hovering, and the whine from its tiny motors was barely noticeable.

Now my aviator's foresight was about to pay dividends.

"Here you go, boss," Dee said.

I looked over Dee's shoulder at the Android's display. The sobering image felt like a hammerblow to my chest. Judging by the flaming wrecks in the parking lot, the three most recent explosions had heralded the destruction of our SUV and the two Taliban vehicles. But though the burning wreckage was the most noticeable battle damage, I was more concerned with the dome-roofed building.

The one on which Joe and Kent had been lying.

"Zoom in there," I said, touching that portion of the screen.

Dee complied, and I braced myself for what was coming next.

The image tightened.

A cloud of dust obscured most of the roof, and Dee dutifully panned back and forth even as she adjusted the drone's flight pattern, searching for a vantage point through dirt and debris. Then, like a break in the clouds, she found a spot of clarity. Her fingers moved across the control, no doubt doing something to stabilize the angle, but I wasn't paying attention.

I was too focused on the picture.

An all-too-familiar sense of despair washed over me. The thermal camera was seeing through the airborne grit, but it was not showing a white-hot human torso or head. Dee changed polarities, switching to black hot as we both searched for the cooling corpses that had once been a Marine and an airman.

"Fuck," Dee said, panning across the roof. "Fuck, fuck, fuck."

I could make out a blast crater, but still couldn't see anything that resembled a human body.

"Part of the roof's caved in," I said, pointing at the crater. "Maybe they're buried beneath the debris."

Dee dutifully tapped the screen, using the device's customized image intensifier to digitally zoom. The sensor's algorithms rendered the jagged hole in HD quality, and I squinted at the imagery, trying to find a familiar shape.

"Sweet, this is Professor, over."

"Go for Sweet," I said, even as I gestured toward where the Taliban fighters would be located off-screen.

Dee nodded even as she closed the digital zoom and bounced out to a wider field of view. Hearing Kent's voice was a gigantic step in the right direction, but I still needed to figure out what had just happened.

"Roger, Sweet. What was that?"

"Unknown," I said as Dee panned the sensor upward. "What's your SITREP?"

"We took indirect fire," Kent said. "Felt like a mortar, but I never heard it launch. Blew us off the roof. Dog took some shrapnel in the leg and torso. We are currently combat ineffective, over."

"Roger that," I said. "Do you have cover?"

"Affirm," Kent said. "We're under the remains of the roof."

Something about what Kent had said was banging around the inside of my head, but I couldn't figure out what had my lizard brain so amped up. The imagery on Dee's Android steadied, revealing a cluster of Taliban fighters. One was still facing uphill toward where Zaafir was occasionally taking potshots, but the rest were moving pell-mell around the courtyard at the base of the citadel. I agreed with Kent's assessment. The explosions had had the feel of detonating mortars, but the confusion exhibited by the Taliban coupled with the lack of the *whump* a round made as it exited the launch tube meant they hadn't fired the ordnance.

Which meant . . .

"Under the overhang," I said, grabbing Jason and pointing him toward a covered corridor to our left, "now, now, now!"

Jason spun on his heel and dashed for the crumbling section of roof. Grabbing the pull handle sprouting from the back of Dee's plate carrier, I yanked the aviator toward Jason like I was starting a lawn mower. I managed to get Dee moving in the right direction, but lost my footing in the process. Before I could fall, Garrett grabbed me beneath the armpits. The SEAL might not still be in tip-top operator shape, but he hadn't been skipping sessions at the gym either. He didn't so much lift me to my feet as carry me. I found my footing just as another explosion ripped through the corridor, sending shrapnel slicing through the sound barrier inches above my head.

That had been close.

"Where's it coming from?" Jason said as I got to my feet.

"Bone, Frog—you two good to hook?" I said.

"Just point me toward the bad guys," Garrett said between coughs.

"I'm lovely," Dee said, her voice sounding like she'd gargled with glass. "Just lovely."

"Good," I said, "because we're about to take it to them."

"How?" Dee said.

"It's time for you to do some of that pilot shit."

FIFTY-SIX

Aalem cursed in at least three languages. Maybe four. His French wasn't as good as it had been, so he wasn't sure if the last couple of verbalizations had been comprehensible or just the mutterings of a sleep-deprived engineer.

Either way, his vulgarities had hit the mark.

Which was more than he could say of the three mortars he'd just dropped.

"What happened?" Baser said. "What happened?"

The commander of the Taliban's most feared special unit touched the laptop screen, leaving a dirty smudge in its center. Normally, this breach of protocol would have earned a full-throated dressing-down from Aalem. The engineer didn't care if the offender was Mullah Omar himself; nobody touched his laptop screen.

Nobody.

Unfortunately, Aalem was in no position to express the required moral outrage at Baser's transgression. Mainly because his commander was right—Aalem had missed.

Completely.

The first miss could have been chalked up to equipment failure. Aalem had been working on the finicky munitions-release latch off and on for the last four days. He'd told Baser that the entire piece needed to be removed and replaced, but there hadn't been time nor the access to the 3-D printer required to fabricate a spare. Aalem had done the best he could under the conditions and confirmed that the latch was actuating during his preflight checks.

Unfortunately, the servo powering the latch still seemed a bit jittery.

After centering his aimpoint on the two snipers, Aalem had triggered the weapon only to watch the mortar impact significantly off target. Still, not all had been lost. Aalem had neutralized the short-term threat to his brothers. Baser, in contact with his commander, had then ordered the engineer to destroy the unknown gunmen's SUV. Aalem had adjusted his aimpoint to compensate for the latch and then released a second munition.

The results had been less than satisfactory.

While Aalem had intended the mortar to impact slightly behind the vehicle, shredding the rear tires and thereby rendering a mobility kill, he'd incorrectly accounted for the munition's drift.

Significantly.

Rather than detonate to the rear of the SUV, the munition landed dead center in the vehicle's hood. The resulting explosion threw flaming petrol in all directions, igniting one of the technical vehicles, which promptly exploded, destroying its sister vehicle in the process. Even as Aalem registered the less-than-ideal collateral damage of his intended precision strike, his analytical mind intuitively provided him with a scapegoat. Even a first-year statistics student knew that it was impossible to interpolate results with only a single data point.

Unfortunately, Baser wasn't quite so understanding.

The wiry commander hopped up and down and flapped his arms like a stringy bird attempting to take flight. But Aalem wasn't paying attention. Instead, he was laser focused on the group of hot spots moving up the incline with the intention of ambushing his comrades from the rear. Fortunately, any two points formed a straight line. With this in mind, Aalem took into account the errors from his previous strikes, adjusted the aim-point, and released the third munition.

This time, the mortar flew true.

But he still missed.

The figures fled into the cover offered by an overhang and the munition detonated where they'd been standing seconds earlier.

"The release mechanism malfunctioned, and I missed," Aalem said.

"How many rounds are remaining?" Baser said.

If he'd heard the incriminating tone in Aalem's response, Baser had ignored it.

For now.

"One," Aalem said, "but that will be plenty. To reach our brothers, the intruders must cross this open area." Aalem indicated a stretch of ruins just below the Taliban blocking force. "The roofs on these buildings are all missing, so the attackers will have no place to hide. Tell the brothers to hold their position. All will be well."

Baser's hunched shoulders relaxed, but his bony frame still radiated tension. Unclipping the radio, Baser relayed Aalem's instructions.

Then he took a phone from his pocket and dialed.

The phone he used to call only one person.

His commander.

FIFTY-SEVEN

can't find him," Dee said, frustration coloring her voice. "The clouds keep interfering with the tracking algorithm."

I looked over her shoulder as she worked, seeing nothing but wispy patches of moisture. After I'd explained what I wanted her to do, Dee had both understood and improved upon my plan. Mortars that fell silently from the sky could mean only one thing—an enemy drone. Unfortunately, the once unheard-of notion of American soldiers at risk from an adversarial air force was becoming all too common. Insurgents across the globe were adept at weaponizing the cheap, but extremely capable, hobby drones sold by Amazon and countless other retailers. With that in mind, I'd asked Dee to slew her infrared sensor skyward in an attempt to locate the aggressor.

Our drone came with a follow-me function that scoured the sensor images for moving pixels and highlighted them for the user by boxing them in white. In theory this would allow the drone to "lock onto" and follow a moving image of a person or vehicle. In this case, Dee thought it would help us to pick out the enemy drone amidst the background fog and dust.

So far, her efforts hadn't been successful.

"Any ideas?" I said.

To put it mildly, we were in a precarious position. My decision to split our force into a support and an assault element now meant that the Taliban blocking Zaafir and his family would be facing only four shooters instead of six. That aside, if we attacked now, we'd still have an advantage in that we could catch the jihadis in a cross fire between our element and Zaafir. But the longer we hid under the overhang from the enemy drone, the greater chance the Taliban would use their numbers and tactically superior position to overwhelm us.

Were I in their shoes, I'd leave one man to keep Zaafir pinned and then assault down the hill. With disciplined movement and good coordination between the element providing suppressing fire and the assaulters, the ten or so men could easily overwhelm our tenuous position.

We had to get our show on the road.

Fast.

"We need to draw the drone out," Dee said. "The mortars he's dropping are dumb bombs. Unguided. That means he's got to loiter directly over the target to hit it. If we give him a target—"

"We'll know where he's going to be," I said, finishing Dee's thought.

On her screen, the crowd of Taliban fighters was splitting into three elements. A team of two jihadis still faced Zaafir while the remaining shooters organized into a pair of fire teams. Fire teams that were now moving down the incline toward us.

Sometimes I hated being a tactical genius.

"Okay," I said, grabbing Dee's shoulder, "you're about to earn your keep."

"I thought I already had," Dee said.

"Nope," I said. "Everything before now was just the tryout. Jason—you still got the M320?"

"Yes, sir," Jason said. He unslung the HK from his back and held it out to me along with the bandoleer of ammunition. "Why do I get the feeling you're about to do something stupid?"

"Stupid would be me trying to take out those Taliban by myself. I'm not. I've got you and Garrett."

"And me," Dee said.

I shook my head. "On this Op I need a pilot, not a gunfighter."

"Calling this an Op would imply you have some sort of plan," Garrett said.

"Of course I do," I said, strapping the bandoleer to my chest. "I'm going up to the roof to cause trouble. Dee is going to do what she does. Y'all set up an ambush for the stragglers, and we'll meet in the middle. How's that grab you?"

"And they say SEALs can't plan for shit," Garrett said.

"Whatever you're going to do, do it fast," Dee said. "The Taliban's headed this way."

"Come on," Garrett said, making a stirrup of his hands, "it's about to get loud."

"You're going to be totally exposed," Jason said. "You sure?"

"I'm sure about the three of you," I said, fitting my boot into Garrett's grip. "Now stop jabbering and start killing."

Garrett stood, grunting as he thrust his hands up in something that was half dead lift, half power clean, and all muscle. It was a good thing that the frogman had come around to my style of leadership, because beating his ass might have been more strenuous than I'd anticipated.

I fairly levitated up the wall before tumbling onto the roof.

A burst of motion greeted my arrival.

I hate snakes, and Afghanistan was home to some of the world's most venomous. Then I saw the furry form and breathed a sigh of relief. I didn't much like rats either, but coming face-to-face with Jerry the mouse beat the hell out of reliving my least favorite *Raiders of the Lost Ark* scene.

I scrambled across the roof on my hands and knees, trying to keep a low enough profile that the approaching Taliban wouldn't see me while also still offering a tempting target for the drone. Playing the goat tied to the stick wasn't all it was cracked up to be.

I dropped to my belly as I approached the lip of the roof, unslung the grenade launcher, and set it beside me. Then I selected three different types of grenades from the bandoleer and stacked them next to the M320. The hairs on the back of my neck stood up as I imagined a mortar cutting through the night sky on its way to a rendezvous with my skull.

Cracking open the launcher's breech, I slid the first grenade home and checked the markings to ensure it was an HE, or high explosive. Then I snapped the action closed with a satisfying *click*, adjusted the sight based on the estimated range to the desired impact point, and waited. I wanted to ask my aviator for an update but didn't. Knowing when to relinquish control was one of the hardest aspects of leadership. Dee understood her task. Further prompting from me wasn't going to help her accomplish it any faster. Instead, I took a calming breath and waited for the advancing Taliban force to appear.

I didn't have to wait long.

One moment I was looking at a courtyard. The next a group of fighters ghosted into the empty space. I let the first five pass unmolested, waited for the second group to appear, and squeezed the trigger. The grenade launcher kicked my shoulder with vigor as the round exited in a flash of brightness and a telltale *thump*.

A second later it exploded against the gravel in a flash of white.

Then all hell broke loose.

FIFTY-EIGHT

Aalem watched the white-tinged figure crawl across the roof with glee. The fighter had popped up right where the engineer had anticipated, and now the man was trying to move undetected into a position that would let him fire upon the advancing brothers.

Aalem was not going to allow that to happen.

"Baser," Aalem said, even as he armed his remaining mortar, "look."

Baser peered over Aalem's shoulder, his phone pressed to his ear.

"Do I have permission to engage?" Aalem said.

Normally the engineer didn't worry about such formalities. Baser gave him a target, and Aalem prosecuted it. This simplistic way of doing business had netted the drone team an untold number of kills.

And not just common ANA soldiers or police.

Once Baser had demonstrated his team's capabilities, they were given sensitive high-value targets. Ranking government officials, Army and police commanders, and other prominent figures. Taking a page from the Americans, Baser and his crew of tinkerers had learned how to triangulate a target's cell phone, and they'd used this skill to decimate the opposition's leadership. As success followed success, Baser had granted his targeteer more and more operational autonomy.

But that was before tonight's less-than-stellar performance.

Tonight, Aalem thought that he could have benefited from a little more command supervision. Initiative was all fine and good, but Aalem didn't want to be held responsible for not being able to service a more lucrative target later because he'd made the solo decision to employ his final mortar now.

"One minute," Baser said before pressing the phone back to his ear.

Aalem didn't understand this mission at all. He'd received coordinates for the high-value target in the usual manner and called the man's cell phone to confirm his position as per standard operating procedure. It was only once the drone was on station and the target was in Aalem's crosshairs that things began to change. Rather than drop a mortar or two on the target, Aalem had been ordered to do nothing but keep watch until a squad of Taliban arrived.

Even after the brothers had pinned the target in the citadel, Aalem was still told to just observe. For their part, the Taliban fighters also didn't try to engage the man. Instead, they'd formed a blocking force, cutting off his escape while staying clear of his harassing fire. After more than twenty minutes, Aalem could conclude only that the Taliban commander wanted the target alive. Instead of killing him, Aalem had flown lazy orbits above the target.

Until the team of intruders had arrived.

"Baser," Aalem said, jabbing an index finger at his computer monitor.

The man slithered to the roof's edge and raised a weapon to his shoulder.

"Wait," Baser said.

The screen blossomed twice—once from the man's location and a second time as the round he'd fired detonated in the midst of the approaching Taliban. Enough was enough. Aalem offset the aimpoint and looked at the firing toggle to ensure the green LED was glowing.

It was.

The weapon was ready.

Aalem glanced back to the laptop screen and his mouth dropped open. Something had obscured his line of sight to the target. Something small, but growing rapidly larger. For a moment Aalem just stared, trying to make sense of what he was seeing.

Then he understood.

With another stream of curses, he jabbed the firing toggle.

He was too late.

The sensor feed rocked back and forth, showing equal parts sky and earth.

Then his prize creation spun earthward.

FIFTY-NINE

Sweet, this is Bone. I got him. I got the drone."

"Good shooting, Bone," I said, loading the second round into the grenade launcher. "Duke and Frog, stand by."

I snapped the breech closed and adjusted my aim, now targeting the lead group of fighters. The M320's HE round was hell on wheels, but also dangerous to employ too near friendlies. But the munition I'd just loaded had been built with close work in mind. It included a timing fuse meant to detonate the warhead at a predetermined range. I'd taken a swag at the distance while waiting for the Taliban to appear.

Now it was time to test my estimation.

I squeezed the trigger and the launcher mashed my shoulder.

When I was a kid, my daddy had an old single-shot twelve-gauge shotgun. Why anyone would have designed, much less wanted, such a thing was beyond me. But that didn't matter. We had it in our house, which meant my father was going to make sure I knew how to fire the weapon. I couldn't have been more than ten the first time I shot it. The shotgun kicked like a mule, and I'd struggled to keep the tears from running down my face. In all my time as a door kicker, I'd still never fired a weapon that had elicited as much pain as that old shotgun.

Until now.

Fortunately, the exploding munition made my aching shoulder easy to forget. The grenade detonated in a puff of red smoke followed by the buzzing sound of 115 17-grain, two-inch-long metal arrows slicing through the air.

Yep, you guessed it.

Some genius had designed a flechette round for our grenade launcher.

I wanted to kiss them.

What had once been an organized squad bounding toward Jason and Garrett was now a disorganized rabble. But I wasn't done. I slammed the final grenade home, targeted the section of courtyard closest to Zaafir, and let fly. My shoulder screamed, but my spirit cheered. This time, the munition detonated in a yellowish cloud that followed the sloping terrain toward the milling fighters.

The coughs and screams were almost instantaneous.

As anyone who's been through basic training will tell you, getting doused with tear gas isn't a whole lot of fun. Getting doused with tear gas while you're getting shot at and already disoriented is a recipe for pandemonium.

Tonight was no exception.

I could see into the churning mass of fighters, but the Taliban couldn't pierce the choking cloud quite so easily. But the best was yet to come. Per my instructions, Jason opened up with the SAW after the third grenade detonated. His red tracers scythed through the CS fog, buzz-sawing fighters into lifeless heaps. The chatter of Garrett's M4 joined the fray, a scalpel counterpart to Jason's sledgehammer. I'd just pumped a final HE grenade into a cluster of fighters and was thinking about making a run back up the incline toward Zaafir when an unexpected voice interrupted me.

"Sweet, this is Professor. What the hell's going on, over?"

Well, shit.

I'd apparently forgotten to brief the plan to two of my team members.

Maybe Garrett was onto something.

"Professor, Sweet, we are engaging the remaining Taliban, over."

"Roger, Sweet," Kent said. "What about the indirect fire from earlier, over?"

"It was a Taliban drone," I said. "Bone kamikazed it. How's Dog?"

"Dog is fine," Joe said, his voice sounding a bit woozy.

"He's not fine," Kent said, "but he's stable enough."

It had been a while since I'd undergone a refresher course in tactical medicine, but I was still pretty certain that *stable enough* was not a triage term.

"Stable enough for what?" Dee said.

With no drone to fly, my transportation specialist apparently had nothing better to do than jump on my radio traffic. Discipline in this outfit was going to shit. Who in the hell was the commander anyway?

"For me to give you folks a hand," Kent said.

A moment later I heard the *pop*, *pop*, *pop* of another suppressed M4 going to work. I looked over to see the airman atop an adjacent roof, putting lead on target. He must have felt my gaze, because he paused long enough to flash me a thumbs-up. Then he got back to the business of killing Taliban.

A thumbs-up.

Fucking Air Force.

"Sweet, this is Frog. If everyone's done jaw-jacking, I suggest we finish this, over."

Now my favorite SEAL was offering leadership tips.

Time to put a tent on this circus.

"Break, break," I said. "All call signs, this is Sweet. I'm going to put two more HE rounds into the courtyard. When the second one detonates, Duke, Frog, and Bone will assault through the objective. Professor and I will then shift fire on Duke's call. How copy, over?"

"Duke, roger."

"Frog, roger."

"Bone, roger."

"Professor, roger."

"Good," I said. "Round one is on the way."

I fired the first grenade, reloaded, and fired again. This time, I wasn't worried about shot placement. Most of the Taliban were already down, and the few who weren't would be soon. No, the exploding 40mm rounds had a single purpose—distract the bad guys as my trio of hitters assaulted across the courtyard. Laying the grenade launcher aside, I picked up my M4 and was tucking the buttstock into my shoulder when Jason broke radio silence.

"This is Duke. Shift fire, shift fire, shift fire."

I panned the EOTech's crimson to the upper edge of the courtyard and continued pressing the trigger, even though I didn't have a target. Like the grenades, the purpose of shifting fire was to keep from accidentally shooting a friendly even as your rifle report kept the bad guys' heads down.

A moment later, a trio of advancing shapes flowed in from the darkness.

The tear gas had mostly cleared out, but I still heard a few intermittent coughs mixed with the sound of suppressed rifle and SAW fire. I worked through the rest of my magazine, putting slow, controlled shots into the far wall as I tried to walk the line between wasting ammunition and still providing the assaulting force with the distraction they needed. A bloodred tracer spat from my muzzle, signaling that I was down to the last three rounds in my magazine.

"All elements, this is Duke. Objective is clear. I say again, objective is clear."

Now we were getting somewhere.

I ejected the spent magazine, slammed in a new one, and prepared to congratulate my team.

Until I heard rotor blades.

SIXTY

Sweet, this is Frog. We expecting company, over?"

That was the million-dollar question.

"All elements, this is Sweet," I said, gathering my weapons and getting to my feet. "I will identify the inbound aircraft from my position on the roof, break. All other elements link up with Zaafir and family. Then rally at the citadel's base. Professor, do you need help moving Dog, over?"

"This is Professor, negative. We're all good."

"Roger that. Stand by on the helo. Sweet out."

The heavy *whump*, *whump*, *whump* of rotor blades trying to gain purchase in the thin mountain air echoed from everywhere and nowhere. The confusing acoustics made it extremely difficult to pinpoint a helicopter's location until the aircraft was right on top of you, but the unmistakable audible signature provided plenty of advance warning.

I slung the grenade launcher over one shoulder and allowed my tactical sling to take the weight of my rifle. Flying into an LZ, or landing zone, at night was one of the most challenging aspects of an aviator's mission set.

Flying into a hot landing zone while distinguishing friend from foe was exponentially more difficult. If this had been a normal operation, I'd have been in radio contact with the inbound bird to describe the size and shape of the LZ, known landing hazards, and the method I'd use to mark the touchdown area. Since I couldn't do any of that, I wanted to look as nonthreatening as possible while the pilots were doing their initial recon.

But maybe there still was a way to make contact.

I pulled out my phone and dialed the world's greatest battle captain.

She answered in two rings.

"Matt, is that you?"

The *whump*, *whump*, *whump* seemed to be coming from the east. I adjusted the focus on my goggles and could just make out the tadpole shape of a Black Hawk knifing through the sky.

Score one for the good guys.

"Yep," I said, raising my voice to compensate for the approaching bird, "I'm here and we're linkup complete."

"Fantastic," Belvina said, the lilt in her voice making me smile. "Things are going great here too. The Pineapple Express is bringing in Afghans by the hundreds. Ferhana was in the first wave."

"She's at the airfield?" I said.

"Yes," Belvina said. "I marked her as a high priority to ensure I was notified when she arrived. I just came back from saying hello. She's in good spirits and ready to go home."

A weight I hadn't realized I'd been carrying slipped off my shoulders. Though I knew delegating Ferhana's rescue to the Pineapple Express had been the right decision, I'd still been worried. I breathed out a sigh of relief just as the Black Hawk thundered by. Afghanistan was still a dumpster fire, but Ferhana was back at the airfield, and Zaafir and his family would be joining them shortly.

We'd really done it.

"Matt? Are you still there?"

"Yeah, sorry," I said, waving at the circling helicopter with one hand even as I held the phone to my ear with the other. "Your air asset arrived right on time. They're circling overhead, time now. Can you pass them a message?"

"Air asset? I don't understand."

"Our aerial extraction," I said, now almost screaming. "The Black Hawk's here."

"Matt—I didn't send a Black Hawk."

In that moment, I realized two things. One, unlike the solid-color paint scheme American Black Hawks sported, this one featured the desert-camouflage pattern of the Afghan Air Force. Two, the helicopter's sliding door was open, revealing a man sitting behind a minigun.

A minigun pointed at me.

SIXTY-ONE

Mullah Qari Wasiq was angry.

The Chinese had delivered Zaafir's location as promised, and the rest should have been easy. As he'd explained in detail to the commander of the Taliban force responsible for securing the town of Bamiyan, he just needed the fighter to surround the ruins with his men and prevent Zaafir from escaping.

That was all.

To ensure his instructions were followed to the letter, Qari had tasked the Taliban's high-value target team to provide overwatch of the ruins with their drone while he appropriated one of the new toys the Americans had gifted them. The pilots had promised a quick flight. Within two hours Qari would have Zaafir back on the Chinese compound. Then the question that had plagued him for ten years would finally be answered.

Qari would know who'd betrayed him.

Except that absolutely nothing had gone according to plan.

"Mullah, the drone operators have lost contact with their aircraft."

"How is that possible?" Qari said, screaming into the microphone attached to his headset.

"I'm not sure. I wasn't speaking directly with the operator, but from what I can gather, they may have collided with an adversarial drone."

The man speaking was Soban—the Bamiyan regional commander. From his interactions with him thus far, Qari thought the warrior competent and not a groveling lickspittle. With this in mind, Qari was trying to temper his anger so as not to take out his frustration on the messenger, but the idiots surrounding him were making that difficult. Adversarial drones? Loss of their aircraft? Qari might not understand the technical details behind the update, but he knew incompetence when he saw it.

Much had changed during his years of imprisonment.

Much more had remained the same.

"I need to know—" Qari said, but Soban held up a hand, interrupting him.

"I'm sorry, sir," Soban said, "but the contingent of brothers on the ground is under attack."

"Attack?" Qari said, his frail head pounding with rage. "From who?"

"They don't know, sir. But they are taking heavy losses. I think—"

Soban paused and Qari could tell by the man's expression that he was listening intently. He pressed the transmit button on his toggle and his lips began to move. Since his headset was tuned only to the helicopter's intercom channel, Qari couldn't hear what the commander was saying.

Even so, the man's concerned expression spoke volumes.

"Sorry, sir," Soban said. "The commander on the ground was asking for reinforcements, but he cut off midtransmission. I can no longer raise him."

Though he wanted to demand further answers, Qari held his tongue. He could make out the city's ruins just ahead. In a moment or two, he could ascertain the situation for himself.

"Pilots," Qari said after changing channels on his headset. "Circle the ruins. Left turns."

Qari peered out of the open door as the aviators complied and the aircraft banked to the left. Though it was pitch-black, the night vision goggles he'd appropriated revealed everything—the collection of corpses where the Taliban blocking team had been, the smoking holes in the ground, and the detritus of a battle.

Someone had overwhelmed his fighters.

Someone with skill.

"Sir," one of the pilots said, "there's a man on top of the roof at seven o'clock."

Qari looked in the indicated direction and saw what had drawn the aviator's attention. A single figure stood on the roof, weapons slung, eyeing the helicopter as it circled.

As Qari watched, the fighter waved.

"Is he ours?" Qari said, directing the question to Soban.

"No, sir," Soban said, shaking his head.

"Then kill him."

SIXTY-TWO

Survival in my line of work often came down to one thing—knowing when to hold 'em, when to fold 'em, and when to run. With all due respect to Mr. Rogers, this was definitely a case of the latter.

I leaped from the roof the instant I saw the machine gun.

Then night turned into day.

Getting shot at by a crew-served weapon is never fun. Getting shot at by a GAU-17 six-barreled minigun was horrifying. The unmistakable *burp* a Gatling gun made while spitting out six thousand 7.62mm rounds per minute was terrifying. Then there was a cantaloupe-sized ball of fire formed by the six rotating barrels. But the weapon's report and muzzle flash were only warm-ups for the most terrifying component—a continuous stream of red tracers.

The lead poured out of the fire hose of a machine gun in sinuous crimson arcs.

I tumbled to the ground and rolled, seeking cover.

Any cover.

Pieces of the ancient structure fell down around me in

a cloud of choking grit. That I wasn't already torn in two had more to do with luck than skill. The line of scarlet death couldn't quite reach me. I was almost underneath the helicopter, and the gunner wasn't able to depress the minigun's muzzle far enough to stitch my floundering body.

For now.

"Taking fire, taking fire," I said even as I pulled my legs into my chest, desperately trying to become smaller.

A swarm of red fireflies tore up the gravel just inches from my toes. I pressed myself flat, trying to become one with the structure's stone wall even as the earth erupted with another burst. At this rate, the gunner wouldn't have to hit me. If he kept pouring bullets into such a confined space, sooner or later a ricochet would do the job for him. As if to drive home my point, a bullet snapped by my head, cratering the stone wall.

This was a bullshit way to die.

"Hang tight, Sweet. We've got you."

The speaker hadn't identified themself, but I was willing to overlook the lapse in radio protocol. Mainly because the stream of crimson death had just ceased. I took several deep, shuddering breaths, terrified that the steel rain would commence again at any moment.

It didn't.

Instead, I heard something even more glorious—a SAW rocking and rolling. A second machine gun joined the first. Then the two began talking—firing in alternating short, controlled bursts.

"Sweet, this is Duke. He's backing off. You're clear to the base of the citadel, over."

"This is Sweet," I said, pushing myself to my feet. "Moving."

Getting up took a bit more effort than it should have, strictly speaking. I wanted to attribute the jelly in my arms and legs to the ten-foot drop from the roof onto the hard-packed soil. But that wasn't the reason. The minigun had scared me shitless, and the adrenaline dump that had partially saved my life had also turned my limbs into wet noodles. Nevertheless, I put my head down and charged forward. The only thing more terrifying than the last couple of minutes was the prospect of enduring it again.

"Sweet, Duke, I think we tore that bird a new asshole. It just landed at the base of the city, over."

Hot damn. We might survive this nonsense after all.

"Break, break, this is Professor. I've got eyes on the bird, and I don't think he's running away. Blades are still spinning and . . . shit."

I was going to have to teach an entire class on radio protocol once this nonsense was over.

"Professor, this is Sweet. Can you be a bit more specific, over?" I said.

"Yeah, roger, sorry. The Black Hawk just unassed about a dozen fighters. They're moving up the pathway to the parking lot in alternating bounds. These guys look like they know what they're doing. Should I engage, over?"

That was a good question.

On the one hand, Kent had proven to be pretty good with his rifle. There was an argument to be made for thinning the herd now, before the jihadis could mass combat power. On the other hand, our airman extraordinaire would probably get off only a couple of shots before alerting the Taliban. If we were in for a fight, I'd rather have it on our terms with as much ammunition available as possible.

"Professor, Sweet, that's a negative," I said, huffing as I sprinted across an open area. Maybe I needed to start incorporating more cardio into my fitness routine. Falling off a building while getting lit up by a minigun really takes it out of you. "With the drone gone, you're our eyes. I don't want to give away your position."

"Roger that, Sweet. Be advised, the chopper is lifting off."

"Professor, Sweet, roger," I said. "I'm thirty seconds from the rally point. Break, break, Duke—did you effect linkup with Zaafir?"

"Sweet, this is Duke. That's affirmative. I've got the precious cargo and his family in hand. We're ready to blow this joint. Zaafir says there's a way out alongside the back side of the ruins, over."

Best news I'd heard all day.

"Sweet, this is Professor. Sorry to be a buzzkill, but we've got more trouble. A convoy of vehicles just rolled in from town. They've set up a blocking position on the north side of the ruins. I count another dozen or so fighters dismounting, over."

Fuck me running.

"Professor, Sweet, roger all," I said. "Stand by."

I put on a final burst of speed and rounded the corner.

"Ranger coming in," I yelled a moment before I burst into the open.

It was a good thing I had.

Four automatic weapons were pointing my way.

Guess I wasn't the only one feeling a little jumpy.

"What's the play, boss?" Jason said.

That was a very good question.

SIXTY-THREE

There comes a point during every mission when you are forced to confront a simple but profound question: *Why the hell didn't I listen to Mom and go to dental school?* Or maybe that was just me. Either way, stinky breath and decaying teeth were starting to sound pretty appealing right about now.

"Get everyone out of sight of the helo and ready to move," I said to Jason. "I'll coordinate the exfil route with Kent. Tell Zaafir he's got point."

The Afghan was currently helping Jason with Joe as the Green Beret worked to start an IV and push fluids into the wounded Marine. Zaafir's wife rested with her back against the dusty wall, eyes closed and a weary expression on her face. Her arms were draped around two children—a boy of about ten and a girl who was maybe seven. The boy was intently watching his father work, but the girl was staring at me. Her dark eyes met mine, and I winked.

Her little face was heartbreakingly solemn for one so young.

Then she began to cry.

"On it, boss," Jason said, snapping me back to the present, "but our window's closing."

I nodded and then keyed my radio.

"Professor, this is Sweet," I said. "What's that bird doing, over?"

"Sweet, Professor, the helo's tracking back up the hill toward your rally point. He's flying higher this time. I think he's gonna take up an orbit and play command and control for the two groups of dismounts, over."

That made sense. In my brief face-to-face with the Black Hawk, I hadn't seen the sensor pods common to American models, but that didn't mean the occupants didn't have night vision goggles or the equivalent. We'd been one step behind the Taliban the entire night. Now was not the time to underestimate their technological capabilities.

"Roger that, Professor," I said. "Does your current position offer you concealment from the bird?"

"Sweet, Professor, that's affirm. I'm set up on the top floor of a partially intact structure. The roof should keep me out of sight, and I've got windows facing both north and south, over."

Which he couldn't cover at the same time.

Kent needed another body to pick up the slack and provide security. Assuming, of course, he was actually staying in his hide site. It only made sense for Kent to stay put if we were staying put, but as the dead Taliban in the courtyard demonstrated, this was not a winning strategy.

We needed to get out of the ruins before the Taliban sealed us in.

I looked at my team, considering.

Dee had made her way over to Zaafir's wife and children. She'd offered the kids a candy bar and the mom something to drink. Next to them, Jason and Zaafir were still working on Joe. The Marine's leg had bled through his pants and Zaafir was in the process of cutting the fabric away as Jason slipped an Israeli one-handed tourniquet above Joe's thigh and began to tighten the strap.

Joe gasped even through the morphine.

I was more worried about the blood-soaked bandages on his chest. I knew enough PJs to feel confident that Kent would have said something if he'd thought Joe was critical, but shrapnel wounds could be notoriously hard to triage on a battlefield without specialized equipment like X-rays or MRIs.

Especially chest wounds.

Garrett was on the far side of the courtyard, pulling security. But he turned as if feeling the weight of my attention.

His eyes found mine.

He didn't say anything.

He didn't have to.

Between the little kids and Joe, we weren't going anywhere fast.

This was starting to feel more like the Alamo with each passing second. The Black Hawk rumbled past. The pilot kept the aircraft above the outskirts of the ruins, apparently having learned his lesson from the earlier engagement. I braced myself for another strafing run, but this time a voice, rather than bullets, emanated from the aircraft. The sound echoed across the courtyard, reverberating through the narrow alleyways and crumbling structures.

"What's he saying?" I said, turning to Jason.

But it wasn't the Green Beret who answered.

"It is message," Zaafir said. "For me. He say if I go to him, he let you go."

Jason caught my eye and nodded.

"Not happening," I said, shaking my head. "We didn't come all this way just to watch them execute you."

"No," Zaafir said, shaking his head. "He need me. Alive."

"What do you mean—" I said.

"Sweet, Professor," Kent said, interrupting me, "something's going down. The helicopter's pulling off station and the dismounts to the south are moving into the ruins, over."

"Get him up," I said, pointing at Joe, "we're leaving. Dee—you've got the mom and kids. Garrett—take point."

I could see questions in the SEAL's eyes, but he didn't voice them.

Progress.

"Professor, this is Sweet," I said. "We need to egress, time now. How we looking to the north, over?"

"Sweet, this is Professor, stand by."

Zaafir and Jason had the Marine upright, but Joe hung limply between them. Dee held the boy in her arms even as Zaafir's wife picked up her daughter. Working our way down the outside of the ruins was going to be a bitch, no two ways about it.

"Sweet, this is Professor. Dismounts to the north are holding their position, over."

Well, that was good news.

"Shit, shit, shit, Sweet, this is Professor. They're setting up mortars. I say again, northern group of dismounts is setting up indirect fire assets, over."

That made zero sense. If the Taliban truly wanted Zaafir alive, why would they risk killing him with indirect fire?

Then I understood.

"Move to the northern route," I said, "now. They're going to fire illum."

I was half right.

A trio of *whumps* announced the first volley of mortars.

The rounds ignited overhead, turning night into day as three illumination rounds drifted slowly earthward, the flares swaying under their parachutes. The sunburst caught us in the middle of crossing the courtyard, but there was nothing to be done about it. The dismounted Taliban force obviously didn't have enough night vision goggles to go around, so our aggressors were evening the odds. Not only did the 300,000 candlepower coming from each flare allow them to see better, the wash of light prevented us from using our own NODs.

These guys were smart.

But they weren't finished yet.

Another round of *whumps* heralded a second volley.

This struck me as strange since the existing flares still had several minutes of burn time before they extinguished. Lofting more illumination rounds now was a waste of ammunition.

They weren't illum rounds.

A series of explosions ripped through the citadel above us. At first I thought the gunners had missed. Then I realized the jihadis had hit exactly where they'd been aiming. The entire hillside erupted as the white phosphorus rounds ignited. Even from several hundred meters away, I could feel the intense heat radiating from the chemical fire.

But that was only half the problem.

Like a snowy river of death, thick, choking smoke poured down the incline, enveloping our group. A second volley of mortars impacted, this time at the top on the path itself. The Taliban mortarmen were driving us south.

Right into the hands of their comrades.

SIXTY-FOUR

Professor, Sweet, we need an alternate egress route. I say again, we need an alternate egress route pronto, over."

The thick white smoke was everywhere—a noxious, clinging cloud that made it difficult to see and even harder to breathe. I had to marvel at the sophistication of the Taliban's attack. Certainly large swaths of the Afghan National Police and Army had abandoned their posts and fled rather than fight the encroaching jihadists, but this wasn't the only reason the fighters had successfully taken back their country.

During twenty years of war, the Taliban had honed their martial skills while successfully licking their wounds in the sanctuary offered by Pakistan. What I was now experiencing wasn't an aberration as much as a reflection of the current state of the Taliban's fighters.

These guys were good.

"Sweet, Professor, recommend you proceed due east."

I paused, picturing the overhead imagery of the ruins I'd committed to memory. The billowing smoke swallowed my teammates, but I could still hear their coughs.

"Professor, this is Sweet," I said. "Confirm that you want us to head east. Doesn't that lead to a cliff, over?"

"Sweet, Professor, affirm, but I know another way out. I'll meet you at the eastern wall, over."

"Professor, Sweet, roger."

I charged through the smoke to find just Garrett waiting for me.

"Is Zaafir with you?" Garrett said.

"No," I answered. "I thought he was helping Jason with Joe."

Garrett coughed as he shook his head, tears streaming down his cheeks.

"He got Joe across the clearing and into the eastern corridor," Garrett said, pointing behind him. "The tourniquet came loose again. Jason and I secured it. When I looked up, Zaafir was gone."

I swore even as another volley of mortars impacted. The way we'd come was almost impenetrable. If Zaafir had stumbled into that choking cloud, it was going to be a bitch finding him.

"Okay," I said, my throat burning with smoke. "We'll—"

"Sweet, Professor, I've got eyes on Zaafir."

Garrett's bloodshot eyes widened.

"You what?" I said, coughing through my question.

"I've got eyes on Zaafir. He's walking out of the ruins toward the southern detachment of Taliban. His hands are up. I think he's surrendering, over."

"Son of a bitch," Garrett said.

"Professor, this is Duke. Can you stop him?"

The panic in Jason's voice came through the radio.

"Duke, Professor, I'm sorry, man. He's too far ahead of me. They've got him in custody now. He's on his knees."

My heart stopped as I waited for the next transmission.

The one in which a Talib put a gun to Zaafir's head and blew his brains out.

The entire reason we'd come here was now slipping through our fingers. Our chance at redemption and Frodo's innocence was now in the hands of men who threw acid on little girls and stoned women to death.

"This is Professor. The Black Hawk just landed. They bundled Zaafir on board. Now it's taking off."

I heard the Black Hawk's roar and could just make out its shadowy tadpole shape as it swept by.

"He's gone," Kent said. "Zaafir's gone."

The finality of his radio transmission broke me. I tried to keep my feelings hidden, but my facial expression must have betrayed me. Garrett squeezed my shoulder, the two of us standing as still as a grave in the swirling smoke.

"He sacrificed himself for his family," Garrett said, his voice raspy from the smoke. "For us. He took the Taliban's deal."

But as the next volley of mortars made clear, one does not make deals with the Taliban. Lightning and thunder ripped across the ruins as high-explosive warheads detonated.

The jihadis had what they wanted—Zaafir alive.

Now the rest of us were as good as dead.

SIXTY-FIVE

I turned to tell Garrett to move, but the SEAL was already racing through the clinging smoke, headed for our diminished team.

I keyed the radio and followed.

"Professor, this is Sweet. Gloves are off. The Taliban are blowing the shit out of the ruins. What's the egress plan, over?"

"Sweet, Professor, meet me at the base of the eastern wall. I'll explain in person, over."

I clicked the radio twice in response rather than trying to reply. My throat was already burning and sore. I wanted to keep as much of the toxic smoke out of my respiratory tract as possible. I ran blindly through the mess before bursting out of the man-made cloud into a bubble of clean air and the rest of my crew.

"Jason, take point," I said as I shouldered Joe alongside Garrett. "We're right behind you."

Zaafir's children were crying, and his wife didn't look much better. I didn't know if she spoke English, but her perceptive eyes found mine. The look on her face felt like a knife through my heart, but there would be time to grieve later.

After we'd survived this cauldron of blood and fire.

Jason unslung his rifle and led the way, somehow still moving like a panther despite the fact we were in the middle of Dante's inferno. The way in which he ghosted forward reaffirmed my decision to have the Green Beret lead us out of hell and into the depths of the catacombs. Between injuries and the need to assist Zaafir's wife and children, our combat power had been significantly reduced. If there was only going to be one rifle pointed at bad guys, I wanted it to be Jason's.

Garrett and I brought up the rear, holding a limp Joe between us. In addition to the ever-present smoke, I could now feel the fire's heat on my exposed flesh like a fresh sunburn. The flames howled like a rushing locomotive as the firestorm drew air into a swirling vortex. The good news was that the inferno was sucking the smoke away from us. The bad was that I was afraid the man-made furnace would soon consume all the available oxygen as well.

We had to get out of here.

Fast.

Zaafir's wife stumbled, nearly losing her hold on her daughter. Dee stabilized the woman, but it was clear the Afghan was unsteady on her feet. She swayed again, about to topple.

Then Kent appeared.

The airman stepped out from the shadows, scooping up Zaafir's wife. Then he carried both mother and child ahead at a dead sprint.

"Follow me," Kent yelled.

We weren't moving toward a break in the wall like I'd assumed. If anything, Kent seemed to be leading us deeper into the city.

"Professor, Sweet, you're heading back toward the interior of the ruins."

I'd transmitted on the radio rather than yelling, both to save my voice and so the rest of our group could maintain situational awareness.

Kent responded the same way.

"Sweet, Professor, roger. Trust me."

I clicked the transmit button twice and resigned myself to our fate. The slight breeze I'd felt earlier had turned into a sustained gust even as explosions continued to sound to our front. The Taliban mortarmen were alternating between high-explosive and white phosphorus shells. The field artillery instructor in my infantry officers' basic course had termed this combination *shake and bake*.

The joke didn't seem quite so funny now.

We turned a corner, and the heat took my breath away. I was staring into the gates of hell. Everything was on fire. Everything. Flames crawled across the stone walls, danced along the ground, and climbed crumbling steps. White phosphorus burned uncontrollably as long as it was exposed to air, and the entire ruins now seemed to be one gigantic flame.

For a heartbeat, I thought this was it.

Kent had made a mistake, and our skin was about to be broiled from our bones.

Then the airman ducked into an open door.

The structure was dim and full of choking smoke, but still Kent charged forward.

Two steps later, he disappeared.

Assuming the worst, I left Garrett to handle Joe, pushed past Dee and the Afghan family, and sprinted my way to Jason. I thought that the intense heat had triggered a structural collapse and taken Kent with the stone.

But the airman hadn't disappeared through a hole.

He'd found a staircase.

A staircase going down.

"Follow me down," Kent said, again using the radio. "Hurry."

I looked at Jason and he shrugged as if to say, *Where the hell else do we have to go?*

At this point, nowhere.

"All call signs, this is Sweet," I said, mashing the transmit button even as I ran back to Garrett and Joe. "Follow Kent down the stairway. Quickly."

Jason helped Dee and Zaafir's son into the subbasement. Then it was Garrett and me. At this point, Joe was pure deadweight, but Garrett got him down the stairs all the same. The stone steps led into a cavern of sorts, but escaping underground did little to improve our situation. While the air was noticeably cooler, dense chalky smoke had begun to flow down the steps, filling the space with noxious fumes.

Everyone was coughing and gagging.

I pushed to the front of the group, only to find Kent staring at a second set of steps.

Or at least I think they had once been steps.

It was difficult to tell since the opening was filled with water.

"Fuck," Kent said, the word a low whisper. "Fuck, fuck, fuck. I killed us. Holy shit, I just killed us."

"Slow down, brother," I said, grabbing the airman's muscled shoulder. "Tell me what I'm seeing."

Kent turned to me, his normally ruddy skin ashen.

"Remember how the citadel fell?" Kent said.

"Yeah," I said, nodding my head. "The daughter sold out her father."

"Right," Kent said. "She showed Genghis Khan a secret entrance. Archaeologists have been excavating this site for the last couple of years and a whole bunch of articles came out of their work. In one of the last publications before the Taliban shut down the dig, the lead researcher talked about finding a secret passage. Maybe even the one Khan used to gain entrance. The write-up included pictures and a map. I thought we could use it, but . . ."

"It's submerged," I said, looking at the filmy water. "Fuck me."

"Is that the way out?"

I turned to see Garrett standing at my shoulder.

Kent looked from me to the naval commando, his expression still shell-shocked.

"It was supposed to be," Kent said.

"Tell me," Garrett said.

"The city had its own underground reservoir," Kent said. "Fresh water flowed into the natural aquifer from a canal. Khan dammed the canal, and the underground channel became passable. But the water tables have shifted in the last couple of thousand years. When archaeologists excavated this passage, it was bone-dry."

"And now it's not," Garrett said. "You sure we're in the right room?"

"Positive," Kent said. "This matches the article to a tee."

"Okay," Garrett said. "Then let's see what we can see."

The SEAL began stripping away his weapons and kit, piling it in a neat stack next to the murky water as if he were getting ready for a dip in the community pool.

"What are you doing?" I said.

"Come on, brother," Garrett said with a smile. "I know Ranger Batt Boys are slow, but even a knuckle dragger like you should be able to puzzle this out. I'm going for a swim."

"You can't—" I said, grabbing his arm.

"The hell I can't," Garrett said, shaking loose my hand. "I'm a SEAL. This is what we do. Look, those steps could lead to nothing but solid water, in which case we're fucked. But there could also be an air pocket on the other side. Or better yet, we could be at a low point between two perfectly dry caverns. Either way, I'm gonna take a look. Staying here means roasting or suffocating. I'm not going out like that."

I wanted to argue.

To scream.

To tell Garrett he was wrong.

But I couldn't.

Because he was right.

"Okay," I said, nodding along with the nonsense. "Okay."

"Get everyone ready to follow," Garrett said. "Strip off any unnecessary gear and make sure the weak swimmers ditch their body armor. We may have to leave weapons behind too."

Garrett waded into the standing water even as another round of explosions shook the ground. Dirt and debris flaked loose from the ceiling, further clogging the air. The mortar rounds were hitting closer, the air was growing more foul, and the temperature was still rising. The SEAL was right—one way or another we were going into that pool.

Garrett affixed his headlamp to his face, tested the light, and then turned back to me.

"Some days I love being a SEAL," Garrett said.

Then he slid below the murky surface.

"Listen up," I said, croaking the words past my aching throat. "We're getting out of here. Ditch all your unnecessary gear. If you're not a good swimmer, leave your body armor and long guns too. Our frogman is blazing the path. When he gets back, we need to be ready. Jason, translate for Zaafir's wife. Kent—find a stimulant for Joe. He needs to be alert enough to hold his breath."

To their credit, the group obeyed.

At least for the most part.

My transportation specialist sidled up next to me as I was rearranging my own gear.

"Matt," Dee said, catching her voice at a whisper, "what about the kids?"

"We'll get them through, Dee," I said, whispering in return. "Believe it."

She nodded and began securing her gear.

Jason was engaging Zaafir's wife in a pretty boisterous conversation. While I could follow only bits and pieces, I got the gist.

She and the kids couldn't swim.

"Boss," Jason said, "we've got a problem."

"Can't swim?" I said.

Jason nodded.

"Okay, can you translate for me?"

"You betcha."

I grabbed both of the woman's hands as I looked into her tearstained face.

"I know you're scared," I said, "but we will get you out of here. I promise."

Jason translated and she gave a slight nod, her dark eyes boring into mine. Then she turned to Jason and spit out a question.

"She wants to know how," Jason said.

That made two of us.

At that moment the water parted, and Garrett emerged from the murky depths. I'd never been so happy to see a SEAL. Garrett wiped the water from his eyes and coughed, but he was smiling.

Our sour-faced naval commando was smiling.

"Good news, folks," Garrett said. "It's a bit murky, but the submerged portion's only about twenty feet or so long. Take a deep breath, kick four or five times, and you'll be there. I dropped a chem light on the far side. When you see the green light, surface. Easy."

"Does the passage lead outside?" Kent said.

"I think so," Garrett said, some of his smile fading. "I didn't have time to check, but I could feel a fresh breeze and smell manure."

You know you're in a bad spot when cow shit smells good.

"How we doing this?" I said.

I enjoyed celebrating as much as the next guy, but the air was getting harder to breathe. We needed to get this show on the road.

"It'll be a tight squeeze, but two swimmers can get through at a time," Garrett said. "Jason, you go first and pull security on the far side. Dee, you follow. I'll help Kent with Joe. Then I'll come back for Zaafir's wife and kids. Matt, bring up the rear. Good?"

"Sounds like a plan," I said. "Jason, once Dee's on the far side, scout down the passageway and see what's what."

"On it, boss," Jason said.

Without further ado, the Green Beret waded into the filmy water and submerged.

"Give him a ten count," Garrett said. "We don't want a traffic jam if he has to turn around."

Dee nodded, her eyes incredibly wide. She shucked her gear with the exception of her pistol, and stepped into the water. Garrett was a SEAL, Jason a graduate of the Army's scuba school. As a PJ, Kent had also been to dive school. Free swimming through a submerged cave wasn't their specialty, but they were a hell of a lot more suited to the task than my transportation specialist.

"Easy peasy," Garrett said, squeezing Dee's shoulder. "Take a couple deep breaths to hyperoxygenate your blood. Then go for it. You'll be on the other side before you know it."

Dee gave another short nod, took the required breaths, and slid beneath the water.

She did it so fast, I almost didn't notice her trembling shoulders.

Almost.

"Okay," Garrett said, turning to Kent, "is he up?"

"I gave him a hit of epinephrine," Kent said, "but he's barely lucid. This is going to be a problem."

"Nah," Garrett said, his expression once again all smiles. "We practiced for this in the teams."

The airman looked more than a little dubious, but he nodded anyway.

"Ready?" Garrett said.

"Let's do it," Kent said.

The three men submerged in a ripple of bubbles, leaving me with Zaafir's wife and children. I opened my mouth to say something reassuring, but didn't get the chance. A mortar detonated just outside the cavern in a flash of light and a roar of thunder.

Then liquid fire cascaded down the steps and poured into the room.

SIXTY-SIX

thought I'd experienced fear before.

I'd been wrong.

Seeing the white phosphorus waterfall down the stone steps and spill across the floor gave new meaning to the word *terror*. Don't get me wrong. Dead was dead no matter how it happened. Getting torn in two by a burst of AK-74 fire had the same outcome as piling into the earth beneath a half-opened parachute. My line of work offered a myriad of unpleasant ways to die. Even so, the prospect of being burned alive sparked a primal reaction. White phosphorus burned at greater than five thousand degrees Fahrenheit and would devour both flesh and bone. The only way to extinguish the fire was to deprive it of oxygen.

The pool of water would not save us.

The fire crawled across the floor like a smoke-spewing lava flow.

Zaafir's wife was clutching her children, which made my job easier. Enveloping all three in a massive bear hug, I leaped into the water. I found footing on the silty bottom and stood, cradling the woman against my chest as she supported her kids. I turned away from the fire, shielding the Afghans with my body, but I couldn't stay this way for long. Even though my head and neck were soaked, the heat was a physical presence. Steam was rising from my clothes and my neck was beginning to blister.

Zaafir's wife turned in my arms and looked over my shoulder. She screamed and flailed. I held on tighter, at first thinking she was panicking.

Then I understood.

She wanted me to take her children through the passageway.

Take her children and leave her behind.

"We go together," I said, bobbing toward deeper water. "Together."

"Na, na, na," she said, tears streaming down her face.

Zaafir's wife couldn't swim.

A thousand thoughts and a million faces flashed through my mind.

Laila.

Virginia.

Virginia's namesake.

Zaafir.

Zaafir, who'd sacrificed himself so his family could live.

What would I do in his wife's place?

What would any parent do?

"Okay," I said, releasing her. "Okay."

I could barely choke out the words, but that didn't matter.

She understood.

With a mother's tenderness, Zaafir's wife kissed each child.

Then she passed them to me.

"I'm coming back," I said, even as I enfolded her screaming kids. "Do you hear me? I'm coming back."

She nodded.

A hissing sounded from behind me as the white phosphorus flowed into the pool.

By the time I got the kids through the passageway, there would be nothing to come back to.

I took a deep breath and covered the kids' mouths and noses with my hands.

Then the water erupted, revealing a sputtering form.

"Need a hand?" Garrett said.

I'd been wrong before.

This was the happiest I'd ever been to see a SEAL.

"Take the kids," I said, pressing their small bodies into his muscular chest. "I've got Mom."

"Aye-aye," Garrett said.

He was still smiling.

That crazy motherfucker.

Wrapping his arms around the kids, he covered their mouths and noses, took a breath, and disappeared.

I turned to Zaafir's wife.

She tried to float out of reach, her legs and arms churning the oily water.

I was having none of it.

"You're going to live, goddamn it," I said, grabbing her.

Then I plunged us both beneath the surface.

SIXTY-SEVEN

Qari looked at the bundle of rags secured to the helicopter's bulkhead and smiled.

Tonight, his dreams would finally be realized.

"Take off his hood," Qari said, pointing at the prisoner.

"Sir?" Soban said.

"His hood," Qari said, yelling over the wind whistling through the helicopter's open doors. "Take it off."

Handing his AK-47 to the man seated next to him, Soban did as he was bidden. The rangy fighter wasn't ever going to gain a reputation as a tactical genius, but he was ruthless and courageous under fire, and he did exactly as instructed.

For Qari, that was more than enough.

Soban grabbed the burlap sack fastened over the prisoner's head and yanked. The fighter wasn't too concerned about grasping only fabric. The hood came off along with a chunk of the traitor's hair.

The man screamed, which only made Qari's smile grow wider. This man had sold his soul for American dollars. Worse than a collaborator, this *Hanzeer Bacha*

actively participated in the interrogations of his countrymen. He'd sided with the invaders over his own people,
all for the promise of money and a better life. Now he
was the one bound and Qari had command of his own
American helicopter.

Allah truly did reward the faithful.

Zaafir, the collaborator, the man who had interrogated Qari before locking him in a cage, blinked as he
looked around the helicopter's cabin.

As in keeping with the way the Americans had captured him and countless other brothers, Qari had ordered
Zaafir to be hog-tied, gagged, and blindfolded. But it had
occurred to Qari that this piece of filth was unworthy of
such a treatment. The sensory deprivation, while effective, allowed the prisoner to hide from his surroundings.
To retreat into a place of safety within his own mind.

Zaafir would not be permitted any such escape.

"Do you remember me?" Qari said, spittle flying from
his lips as he finally had the conversation he'd rehearsed
a thousand times. "Do you?"

The depth of emotion he felt at the second question
surprised Qari. His time behind bars had been transfor-
mative. A brutal sundering of everything that was im-
pure so that he could be fully devoted to the divine. It
had been as necessary to his transformation as a forge's
fire was to steel, but that did not mean the scars he bore
were any less painful.

The prisoner slowly nodded.

"Good," Qari said. "Because I want you to know who
Allah chose to be his instrument of retribution."

The look on the prisoner's face was one of resignation

rather than fear. He expected to be executed, perhaps even tossed from the helicopter, and was prepared to accept his fate. Qari felt a flash of irritation that the man could be so stoic in what he undoubtedly thought were his last moments on earth. Qari wanted to see the prisoner weep, to beg for his life.

Instead, Zaafir just stared back at Qari, his dark eyes resolute.

No matter.

The prisoner wouldn't be wearing that expression for long.

Qari swung the boom mike attached to his headset over his lips and pressed the intercom button.

"Pilots," Qari said, "stop the helicopter."

A moment of silence followed his command.

"What?" a pilot said, the bewilderment in his voice clear.

"I said, stop the helicopter," Qari said. "Now."

"Yes, Mullah," the pilot said.

The engine noise changed, growing more pronounced as the helicopter's nose rose and the aircraft bled off airspeed. After a bit of rocking, the Black Hawk came to a stop.

"We're at a hover, Mullah," the pilot said.

"Good," Qari said. "Now turn us so that I can look back the direction we came."

"Yes, Mullah."

The helicopter slowly rotated on its axis, the world spinning until Qari saw what he sought.

"Stop," Qari said, his voice filled with glee. "Hold us here."

"Yes, Mullah."

Moving the mike out of the way, Qari leaned toward Zaafir. This time, the prisoner's expression wasn't quite so stoic. The man shifted against his bonds, testing them, but to no avail. The traitor undoubtedly thought he was about to be executed.

But Qari had something much more devastating in mind.

"Do you see that?" Qari said, pointing into the distance.

The prisoner held Qari's gaze for a moment.

Then he slowly turned his head to follow Qari's finger.

Unfortunately, this idea had come to Qari too late. They were too distant for detail, but the orange stain on the western horizon was still impossible to miss.

"That is what's left of your family," Qari said, enunciating each word to ensure Zaafir heard. "After you surrendered, I had the city put to the torch. All of it. There were no survivors."

This time there was no pretense of stoicism. Zaafir screamed and lurched across the floor as if to bury his teeth into the Mullah's unprotected flesh. Qari responded with a backhand—a full-shouldered swing that connected with the prisoner's mouth and sent a spray of blood across the cabin.

This was what Qari had been waiting for.

This exact instant.

Qari wanted Zaafir to suffer.

To wish for death just as Qari had in his darkest moments.

"Bag him," Qari said, leaning back in his seat, "and

make sure he doesn't prematurely end his misery. We still have need of him."

Soban nodded and bent to the task. First he added a slap of his own to knock the fight from the prisoner; then the bag went over Zaafir's head, and his restraints were secured to metal latches on the helicopter's floor. Qari had to hand it to the Americans. When it came to designing their weapons of war, they really did think of everything.

"Pilot," Qari said, "you may continue."

"Yes, Mullah."

The helicopter's nose dipped, but the aircraft did not smoothly accelerate. Instead, the Black Hawk began to shudder as if caught by an unseen gust of wind.

"Sir," the pilot said, "we must land. Immediately. Our transmission must have been damaged earlier. This aircraft is no longer flyable."

The helicopter began descending before the pilot had even finished speaking. The maneuver was abrupt, but not a crash. As the Black Hawk's wheels made contact with the ground, Qari was still smiling. This would delay his return, but the development was an inconvenience, nothing more.

Now others would learn what it meant to wait.

Qari had all the time in the world.

Taking his cell phone from his pocket, Qari began to dial.

SIXTY-EIGHT

The helicopter slithered through the night sky. For the first time in my adult life, I felt apprehension at the sight of the Chinook's sleek shape. Just as it had been surreal to be engaged by fighters manning Humvees at the roadblock, I was having a hard time wrapping my head around the notion that the enemy now had access to Black Hawks and who knew what other airframes.

"That our ride?" Jason said, materializing out of the darkness next to me.

"I sure hope so," I said.

The Chinook made a final pass along the edge of our hasty landing zone before pirouetting in midair. With a ballerina's grace, the twenty-seven-ton machine dropped its tail while simultaneously raising its nose and sliding to the right. Whereas a moment before I would have sworn the aircraft was flying away, it now touched down on the gravel road in a rush of air and a whine of turbo-shaft jet engines.

"Has to be," Jason said. "Only Night Stalkers fly like that."

I was inclined to agree, but I was also not taking anything for granted. We were wet and filthy and missing most of our kit. Joe was muttering incoherently, and Zaafir's wife was working overtime to keep the two children's cries to murmurs. To say that we were currently combat ineffective was sort of like saying that the Pope was a little bit Catholic.

But we were alive, and I intended to remain that way.

A crew chief hopped out of the Chinook even as his comrade in arms sat hunched over the minigun, ready to bring the weapon to bear at the slightest provocation. The thought of again being on the receiving end of the GAU sent a shiver up my spine. The crew chief took two steps from the aircraft and then illuminated a red lens flashlight.

Two long strobes followed by two short ones.

Then the sequence repeated.

Exactly what Belvina and I had agreed on.

"All right," I said. "Let's go."

Jason signaled the rest of the team. Then he started for the chopper at a trot that did a good job of striking the balance between covering the distance to the waiting helicopter quickly and not looking like a suicide bomber running toward an American aircraft.

Turns out, we weren't the only jumpy ones tonight.

While I'd managed to hang on to my cell phone, we'd been forced to abandon pretty much everything else. One or two of my shooters had kept ahold of their long guns, but most everyone else was down to just sidearms. Radios, night vision goggles, plate carriers, med kits, extra ammunition, pretty much anything that gave us a force-multiplying advantage had been sacrificed to aid our escape.

Garrett and Kent followed Jason, a limp Joe between them. I touched each of my teammates on the calf as they shuffled by, ensuring an accurate head count. In the last several hours, we'd been shot at, blown up, set on fire, and almost drowned.

I wasn't going to add *left behind* to the list.

Dee and Zaafir's wife and children were next. The Afghan mother carried her little girl while Dee had her arms wrapped around the boy.

Then it was just me.

I took a quick look to ensure the area was sanitized. Or at least as sanitized as I could manage. A tracker would know that a group of people had huddled in the wheat field. The key was to make sure we hadn't inadvertently left a bit of debris that would point toward a wayward group of former warriors, a heartbroken wife, and her two children.

After finding nothing, I trotted to the Chinook and climbed up the open ramp. The crew chief touched me as I went by, ensuring his own head count. Then we were in the air. As the bird turned east, heading for the mountain pass that would lead us into the Bagram Bowl before we turned south for Kabul and the airport, I caught sight of the ruins.

From this distance, the ancient city looked like a jack-o'-lantern. Its crumbling towers and structures resembled jagged teeth and gaping eyes, while the white phosphorus–induced inferno could have been a child's candle burning from within its pumpkin husk. But as much as I wanted to pretend otherwise, I knew the ancient fortress was no Halloween decoration.

The man-made conflagration had become something more.

Something else.

As I watched, a column of swirling flames reached skyward from the citadel's peak. The superheated rock fortress was radiating air upward in the form of roiling thermals like a blast furnace even as hurricane-force winds sent replacement oxygen thundering into the fire's core from the plains below.

The firestorm was terrifying to watch, but even stranger to hear.

The City of Screams was once again screaming.

SIXTY-NINE

My phone vibrated.

Digging the device from my pocket, I saw a text from Katherine.

CALL ME.

This was easier said than done.

The MH-47 variant of the Chinook shares several distinctions that set the helicopter apart from the rest of the Army's rotorcraft. At fifty-two feet in length, it was the biggest helicopter in inventory, and with a sprint speed of one hundred sixty miles per hour, also the fastest.

It was not, however, the quietest.

"Hey," I said, waving to get the attention of the closest crew chief.

As per 160th SOP, he was kitted up in gear that made him look more like a villain in a sci-fi movie than an Army aviator. His flight helmet and night vision goggles gave him a vaguely insectoid appearance, an image only heightened by the armored mandible that enclosed his lower jaw and face. His flight vest covered his chest and doubled as an extraction harness with straps that criss-crossed between his legs. An intercom cable snaked behind him, disappearing into the Chinook's black cabin.

He looked, in a word—badass.

"Yes, sir," the crew chief said, shuffling over to where I was standing.

The Chinook's interior was heavily modified to reflect its mission of inserting and extracting special operators from hard-to-reach places. The seats had been stripped out, both to allow the helicopter to carry more passengers and to facilitate the collapsible table that could be used for minor surgical procedures in flight.

Or perhaps not so minor, depending on the seriousness of the situation.

Right now Joe was strapped to the table as both Kent and a flight medic worked on the wounded Marine. I'd checked in with the PJ. He said that Joe remained in serious but stable condition.

We were halfway through the roughly ninety-minute flight back to the Kabul airfield and the rest of my crew was scattered around the helicopter in various states of malaise. The smile that had been fixed on Garrett's face had finally disappeared. The SEAL stood watch near Kent and Joe, but said nothing. Jason sat next to the Chinook's open ramp, staring into space, while Dee was huddled with Zaafir's wife, his little boy in her lap. Zaafir's wife held her daughter and her lips were compressed into a single hard line.

Her face a mask of exhaustion and sorrow.

Not the triumphant homecoming I'd envisioned.

"I need to make a call," I said, showing my cell to the crew chief. "Do you have an adapter or something?"

I more than half expected the aviator to laugh in my face, but he didn't. Instead, he nodded and disappeared into the darkness. A moment later he returned with a separate headset attached through several connectors to a cell phone dongle along with an index card denoting the aircraft's internal Wi-Fi system.

Apparently the 160th was used to accommodating rather unique customers.

I offered my thanks, plugged the dongle into my cell, and slipped the noise-canceling headset over my ears. Then I adjusted the boom mike, made sure the cell was synced with the Wi-Fi, and placed the call.

Katherine answered on the second ring.

"Matt?"

"Hey, Katherine," I said.

"Where are you?"

"In a helicopter," I said. "Sorry about the noise. Can you hear me?"

"Yes," Katherine said. "Barely. Is this not a good time?"

That was putting it mildly.

Ferhana was safe, but other than that, my operation was a complete failure. We had Zaafir's family, but he'd been captured by the Taliban. In the short time we'd spent with the Afghan, there'd been no chance to ask him about Frodo and the raid. I was beginning to suspect more with each passing moment that Frodo's arrest was just a giant smoke screen. A diversion to obscure something else.

Which made me question whether any of this had even been worth it.

I'd been giving more thought to Jason's appearance the night I'd shown up on his front lawn. He'd come out of the house not just fully dressed, but fully kitted. In Afghanistan and Iraq, I'd seen guys rush to their fighting positions wearing just boxers and flip-flops. It didn't make sense to me that Jason would have wasted time getting completely dressed before grabbing his rifle and joining the fight.

Unless he'd already been kitted up for a different reason.

Jason's wife was dead and the singular purpose to which he'd given twenty years of his life was imploding.

I was now wondering whether my fellow Ranger had been suicidal.

Looking across the cabin at the other veterans, I didn't think Jason was the only one thinking dark thoughts. Joe, Dee, Kent, and especially Garrett were all here as part of a last-ditch effort to make a difference. Years from now when their daughter, son, or grandchild asked if Afghanistan had been worth it, they wanted to be able to look past the rubble that had once been a nation's hopes and point to something of worth.

Anything of worth.

"Matt?"

"Sorry, Katherine," I said. "It's been a long twenty years. What have you got?"

"The thread that ties this all together. And it's time sensitive."

That got my attention.

"I'm listening," I said.

"I queried ABIS like we discussed," Katherine said, "using the date of the 2011 raid and Zaafir's identifiers as search criteria. I got two hits. Mullah Qari Wasiq was one of the people you rolled up. He's a known Taliban operative and a member of the ruling council."

"Holy shit," I said. "What was he doing hanging out with a bomb maker in Bagram?"

"Great question," Katherine said. "I don't think he was. From what I can gather, Qari was using the compound as a safe house to meet with the second person Zaafir enrolled in the database."

"Who?" I said.

"This is where it gets really interesting," Katherine said. "Zaafir's initial entry didn't have a name for the second man you guys captured. It did, however, feature an ethnicity in the comments section of the enrollment form—Asian. The ABIS system is stand-alone and intended just for Afghanistan, but it also feeds a much larger database maintained by the US intelligence community. Automated queries compare every new entry into the ABIS system against the broader intelligence community's database."

"And they got a hit," I said, catching some of Katherine's excitement.

"Did they ever," Katherine said. "The mystery man meeting with Qari was Feng Liu, a known operative of the Chinese MSS."

I could hear the satisfaction in Katherine's voice, and I knew she was waiting for an attagirl, but I couldn't give it to her. Not because she didn't warrant the praise—she'd just cracked this whole thing wide open. No, I didn't pay her a much-deserved compliment for a much simpler reason—I'd lost my capacity for speech.

Learning that Feng was enrolled in the US intelligence community's biometric database wasn't a shocker. Biometrics had slowly morphed into the next battlefield over the last twenty or so years. Counterintelligence professionals spent more and more time designing schemes to harvest biometric data from officers of opposing intelligence services. That Feng had fallen prey to such an operation wasn't surprising. No, what I was still wrapping my head around was the fact that a Chinese intelligence officer had been clandestinely meeting with a member of the Taliban ruling council.

A meeting I'd known nothing about.

Until now.

"So Feng was arrested and jailed at Bagram?" I said.

"Nope," Katherine said. "His biomarkers pinged as soon as he was enrolled. He was separated from Qari and ushered out of jail the next day."

"During the riots," I said, remembering the raid's aftermath.

"Exactly," Katherine said. "The bomb maker and his crew were released to satisfy the political pressure from Karzai. Feng was turned loose at the same time."

"But Qari stayed in jail," I said. "The US administration must have struck some kind of deal with Karzai."

"Maybe not just Karzai," Katherine said. "The target

of the raid goes free, the Taliban commander goes to jail, and nobody says a word publicly about his Chinese visitor. The after-action review gets redacted and the enrollment data becomes restricted. It never happened, so everyone saves face."

"That's some bullshit right there," I said.

"Yep," Katherine said, "and I think it's also why the Chinese killed Fletcher."

"What do you mean?" I said.

"Fletcher processed the prisoners with Dan and Zaafir. He would have known about Feng."

"Okay," I said, "but you said yourself—everything got swept under the rug. Why would the Chinese kill Fletcher now, ten years after the fact?"

"Because Fletcher was about to unsweep it," Katherine said. "I targeted him with NSA's search engines—email, social media, texts, the works. My queries turned up instant messages between Fletcher and reporters as well as Fletcher's Facebook rants teasing what he called the untold story of Afghanistan—a Chinese deal with the Taliban. He was in the process of narrowing down which news organization to send his exclusive to when he died."

"You think the Chinese killed Fletcher to keep him quiet?" I said.

"And then went after the surviving members of Gold Team," Katherine said. "It sure looks that way."

Katherine was right—she had discovered the thread that tied all of this together. But as startling as her revelations were, my tired brain couldn't quite grasp the whole picture.

"Fantastic work, Katherine," I said, "but I'm still not tracking how this is time sensitive."

"Because I haven't told you the final bit," Katherine said. "Feng Liu is back in Afghanistan. He's on the phone with Qari right now."

SEVENTY

ay that again," I said, convinced that I'd misheard.

My question must have come out a little louder than I'd intended. Jason crossed the cabin to squat down beside me, and Garrett looked over, the question on his face evident.

Even Dee opened her eyes.

"You heard me," Katherine said. "Qari and Feng are on the phone right now. In addition to iris scans, fingerprints, and facial scans, the intelligence community's database also features the capacity to store a target's voiceprints. Voiceprints of Feng and Qari were both obtained surreptitiously while they were being in-processed at Bagram. The NSA's voice recognition system attributes the two voices on the call I'm monitoring as belonging to Feng and Qari with a ninety-six percent certainty. I've got them."

"Where are they?" I said.

"Qari is about sixty kilometers north of your position. Just south of the intersection of the Bamiyan-Charikar Highway and Highway AH76."

"And Feng?" I said.

"His is in the vicinity of the Chinese Mes Aynak compound."

"Where's that?"

"About forty kilometers southeast of Kabul."

Neither of those two bits of information meant anything to me without context, which prompted me to ask the question I should have led with.

"Wait," I said, feeling like an idiot. "You said they're still talking?"

"They were. The call just ended."

"What did they say?" I asked.

"Qari's helicopter had a hard landing. He wants Feng to come get him."

"Why?" I said.

"Because Qari has the guy who can unlock the entire biometric database in the helicopter with him."

I almost dropped the phone.

"Did you say helicopter?" I said. "Are you sure?"

"Lemme check," Katherine said.

I heard her pounding her keyboard as she instant-messaged the analyst.

"Confirmed," Katherine said. "Helicopter."

It had been Qari in the Black Hawk back at the City of Screams.

Had to be.

Which meant Zaafir was the person who could unlock the database.

That's why they'd wanted him alive.

"Okay," I said, my wheels already spinning. "I want you to monitor both Feng's and Qari's locations. If they move, I need to know."

"Got it," Katherine said. "Anything else?"

"Yes," I said. "Can you jam their phones?"

"Wait one," Katherine said.

Again I heard the sound of furious typing.

"Not Feng's. His is hardened. Probably something the MSS science-and-technology folks cooked up."

"What about Qari?" I said.

"Him I can do. But if I jam it, he might decide that it's not working and toss it. Then you'll lose the ability to track him."

That was a great point, but it was a risk I was willing to take. If he'd asked Feng for a ride, Qari wasn't going anywhere. But for the plan that was already starting to come together in my mind to work, Qari could not ask for help from any more friends.

"Shut Qari down," I said.

"Okay," Katherine said. "Done."

"Incredible job, Katherine," I said. "Really. You just gave us a shot. Let me know if the phones move. I've got to jump off and start making things happen."

"You're welcome, Matt. Happy to be on the team. I just hope Qari doesn't have another phone."

So did I.

SEVENTY-ONE

Mullah Qari Wasiq did have another phone.

It just wasn't his.

Qari looked from the phone in his hand to the one he'd borrowed from Soban. The cell belonging to the Bamiyan commander happily showed service bars indicating that the device was still connected to the local cell network. Qari's did not. Though he was not a technician, Qari did not consider this new development promising. Many things had changed since he'd first been imprisoned, but many more had stayed the same. Chief among them being the Americans' unrivaled dominance in all things technological.

"Soban," Qari said, "take two men and set up an observation post. Somewhere they can survey the road in both directions. I do not want to be surprised."

"Yes, Mullah," Soban said. "I'll send snipers."

The helicopter pilots had landed the Black Hawk in a wheat field adjacent to a narrow ribbon of road. In this regard, the pilots had chosen well. The nearest village was several kilometers to the south while the road to the north was clear for at least double that distance. Dawn was hours away and the deep night's quiet still enveloped the valley, but Qari felt the precarious nature of his current circumstances. The men he'd just burned to death in the City of Screams had been Americans; he was sure of it. Americans were a tenacious enemy, and even though the invaders were on their way home in disgrace, Qari did not believe they would go quietly.

Especially once word of the massacre at the ruins got out.

The traitor stirred, again testing his restraints.

Qari cuffed Zaafir in the head, careful to avoid the eye sockets he would need to unlock the biometric database. From his spot inside the Black Hawk, Qari could see Soban giving instructions to two fighters. Without being told, the Bamiyan commander was spreading the rest of the men out into a perimeter of sorts. Perhaps Soban also felt the vulnerability of being stranded.

Or perhaps he just wanted to impress Qari.

Either answer was satisfactory.

Qari checked the time on his phone. He'd finished his conversation with Feng only moments before. The Chinese spy had assured Qari he'd depart Mes Aynak immediately with a convoy of vehicles. If this was the case, Qari still had an hour to ninety minutes of waiting. Ninety minutes for the Americans to exact their revenge.

Qari powered down his phone and then turned the device back on.

Once again, it refused to connect to the cell network.

Selecting Soban's phone, Qari placed the first of several calls. Though the Taliban commanders who answered would not be happy with the orders they were about to receive, Qari did not care. When it came to dealing with the Americans, there was no such thing as having too many fighters.

SEVENTY-TWO

Okay," I said, looking at the four faces gathered around me. "We've got a chance to get Zaafir, but things are gonna get sketchy."

"Sketchy would be an improvement over the ops we've executed so far."

Garrett made the comment with a smile, but I knew there was some truth to his jest.

Okay, maybe a lot of truth.

While I still wholeheartedly believed in the adage that it was better to be lucky than good, relying solely on good fortune was a recipe for sending your team to the morgue. On the other hand, fortune really did favor the brave, and if there was one thing my band of ruffians had in spades, it was courage.

"You're right," I said, smiling at the SEAL. "That's why I want the four of you to understand what we're up against. That phone call was from my NSA teammate. I don't have time to go blow by blow, but the bottom line is this—the dude in the Black Hawk who captured Zaafir is a Taliban commander named Mullah Qari Wasiq. He got his hands on the ABIS biometric system, and he needs Zaafir alive to unlock it. Qari and his Black Hawk made a hard landing about sixty kilometers north of here. He's waiting on a convoy of Chinese paramilitary folks to give him a ride, but they're driving in from Mes Aynak. That's a Chinese encampment just south of Kabul."

"What do the Chinese have to do with this?" Jason said.

"That's another story," I said. "The simple answer is that they would also like to take a gander at our biometric system. We've got a window to make something happen, but it's closing fast."

"You just said a lot of shit, boss," Jason said, "so let me summarize. If we do nothing, Zaafir gets a bullet in his head after he unlocks the biometric system. A system that will identify every Afghan who's ever worked with us, meaning that they will also get bullets in the head. So we can either sign up for another one of your crazy-ass ops, or we issue death warrants for the three hundred thousand or so Afghans who stood with us for the last twenty years. Is that about the size of it?"

I slowly nodded.

"Thought so," Jason said. "Fuck it, I'm in."

"Me too," Kent said. "I'm gonna need one hell of an excuse for my dissertation committee. Saving Afghanistan should do the trick."

"In," Dee said. "I don't want to read about this in the newspaper and know I could have done something."

Which just left my SEAL.

Garrett's face reflected none of the forced joviality of my companions. Instead, his expression was sober. The look of someone who ran toward the sound of gunfire and still bore the scars to prove it. The last time Garrett had made a decision like this, the outcome hadn't been a Hollywood ending.

"You're sure?" Garrett said.

I shook my head. "I'm not sure of anything. I just know that I have to try."

"So do I," Garrett said. "What's the plan?"

"Still working on that part," I said. "First I have to call Belvina."

"Why?" Garrett said.

"So she can launch our QRF."

SEVENTY-THREE

Twenty minutes later, the five of us stood on the side of Highway AH76, listening as the echoes from the Chinook's *whumping* rotor blades slowly faded away. Persuading the aviators to land hadn't been easy. Only after all five of us confirmed to the pilot in command that we understood that the aviators might not be able to return did he agree to set us down.

I understood.

I thought we were a little crazy too.

Maybe a lot crazy.

The 160th aviators had dropped us off about twenty-five kilometers south of Qari's location and about twelve kilometers southwest of Bagram Air Base as the crow flew. It was jarring to think that the former bastion of American strength now represented a Taliban stronghold.

But the night was about to become stranger still.

"Here they come," Jason said.

Once again, my little team was hiding.

At three in the morning, there wasn't much stirring in the Afghan countryside. We were about thirty-five kilometers northwest of Kabul, but we might as well have been on the dark side of the moon. What little vestiges of civilization that could be found in Afghanistan's capital did not exist here. For the most part, our surroundings were swathed in darkness. A pocket of lights marked Bagram Air Base along with another faint glow denoting a town to our northeast, but these remnants of the industrial age were the exception, not the rule. Though many of Afghanistan's rural villages had access to sporadic electricity, the generators that produced it were jealously guarded. Illuminating a town at night would be a poor use of such a precious resource. This near total darkness made the column of vehicles Jason had indicated all the more prominent. Headlights played across mud compounds and farmers' fields as the sound of laboring engines filled the night air.

"At least I hope that's them," Jason said.

"Me too," I said.

"Sweet, this is Professor. Those are our boys. The lead Hilux has infrared chem lights clipped to the antenna, as briefed."

"Hallelujah," Jason said.

While I shared the Green Beret's relief, I also couldn't help but think that the appearance of the convoy turned what before had just been a CONOP into reality.

We were really doing this.

"Professor, this is Sweet," I said, keying the radio transmit button. "Any traffic behind the convoy or approaching from the opposite direction?"

Kent and Garrett were monitoring the likely avenues of approach from a rock outcropping on the far side of the road while Dee pulled security for the pair. I knew the Chinese were on their way to Qari, and I wanted to keep an eye on the competition.

"Sweet, Professor, that's a negative. Other than the three-vehicle QRF convoy, we're clear in both directions. Recommend we link up with you to get this show on the road."

I looked at Jason and the Green Beret nodded, concurring with my unspoken assessment.

"Professor, this is Sweet," I said, "roger. We'll cover your movement."

Kent replied with two clicks of the transmit button. A moment later I could see their green-tinged forms scampering down the boulders through my NODS. I flipped the goggles up as the convoy drew closer and flashed three long pulses followed by three short ones from my red-lens flashlight. The lead vehicle responded by briefly pulsing his brights. With the challenge and recognition signals complete, I moved out of the field and into the road.

Seconds later, the first Hilux truck rumbled to a stop.

"Morning," Toto said from the driver's-side window. "Need a lift?"

Ten minutes and one costume change later, we were again moving north on Highway AH76. Though my assessment of Belvina Ngoy as the world's best battle captain remained unchanged, I was also grudgingly coming around to Dee's CIA officer friend. For my plan to have any prayer of working, we needed to get close to

Qari. The kind of close that traveling on a rural highway in the middle-of-nowhere Afghanistan doesn't really support. After studying the map, I knew there was no way we could sneak up on the Black Hawk unseen.

So I wasn't going to try.

"Do I want to know where these clothes came from?" Kent said.

"No," Jason and I said simultaneously.

"'Cause mine smells like pig shit," Kent said.

"Be grateful," Jason said. "Mine has some suspicious stains around the crotch."

"I really don't want to hear it from you guys," Dee said.

The aviator's comment silenced the group.

While her CIA acquaintance had come through by providing a trio of well-traveled Hilux trucks, and what I suspected were slightly more well-traveled Taliban garb for the four of us and our QRF detachment, I'd taken Dee's wardrobe in a slightly more creative direction. Viewed from a distance, we had all the hallmarks of a jihadi convoy. Between the trucks, AK-47-wielding passengers, Taliban flags, and an obligatory DShK, I was confident we'd be able to roll up to the Black Hawk unmolested.

But that's where our advantage ended.

Rescuing a hostage was one of the most difficult operations a tactical element could execute. The assaulters who called the Unit home were the best in the world at this daunting task, and they practiced for this mission relentlessly.

We were not them.

In fact, our group of five shooters was not even up to the proficiency of the SEAL Team 10 commandos who'd helped me rescue Frodo during our Ukrainian excursion. Garrett, Kent, Jason, and I were all fine gunfighters, but we each hailed from radically different organizations and had a limited amount of joint operational experience. Attempting to conduct a conventional hostage rescue would be a recipe for disaster.

Which was why I favored an unconventional approach.

"That's it," Jason said, pointing at the windshield. "That's the Black Hawk."

My unconventional approach to saving Zaafir necessitated some changes to our team roster as well. Jason was driving instead of Dee. As the only Pashto speaker, he had the greatest chance of talking his way past a roadblock. I was in the TC slot with Garrett behind me. Kent was riding the hump and Dee was seated behind Jason.

This was not because Kent had the shortest legs.

We had plans for Dee.

"Tally," I said, following Jason's finger.

The Black Hawk was nestled in a field just to the east side of the road. It was still strange to see desert camouflage on a UH-60, but it was the minigun protruding from the open cargo door that really jolted me.

That and the collection of Taliban milling around the aircraft.

"Dee," I said, turning to my resident aviation expert, "can he still fire the gun if the bird's not running?"

"Not on just battery power," Dee said. "But if the APU's hot, he can."

"APU?"

"Auxiliary power unit," Dee said. "It's a small jet engine used to power the bird's electrical and hydraulic systems while the pilots conduct the preflight checklist. The APU doesn't burn anywhere near as much fuel as the main engines."

"How do you tell if the APU's hot?" I said. "Do the Black Hawk's blades turn?"

"No," Dee said, shaking her head. "But you can hear it."

Jason rolled down his window.

The unmistakable howl of a jet engine filled the cabin.

"I guess the minigun's live," I said.

Dee nodded.

And shivered.

This was because Dee was wearing fewer clothes than the rest of us.

Significantly fewer.

"No worries," I said, even as the minigun swung to cover our truck. "Nothing changes with our plan. Absolutely nothing."

Then my phone began to ring.

SEVENTY-FOUR

ello," I said.

"Matt? Matt!"

Belvina's French-African accent was so thick, it almost made me laugh.

Almost.

"Hey, Belvina," I said. "What's up?"

Jason steered the truck toward the helicopter, leaving the road for the field. Our tires churned through the soil, rocking the Hilux back and forth even as the Gatling gun tracked our progress.

From this distance, its six barrels looked like a single gaping maw.

"Matt—you must turn around. Now!"

A pair of jihadis moved to intercept our truck.

The AK-47s they were holding weren't pointed at us. Yet.

But I knew they would be shortly.

"Boss?" Jason said, taking his foot off the gas.

"Give 'em the jihadi wave and blow on past," I said.

We had to be close, or this was for naught. Close enough to use the pistols each of us had concealed in our tunics. Close enough to differentiate Zaafir from his captors.

Very, very close.

"Too late to turn around," I said to Belvina. "I've got five seconds—give it to me fast."

"Two convoys are closing on your position," Belvina said. "One from the north and one the south. If you turn east, I can help you circumvent the southern force by guiding you along the back roads. Get out of there!"

The Black Hawk was just fifty yards away.

The two jihadi guards less than twenty.

Could we turn around now and still escape? Probably. But if we did, Zaafir was a goner. The United States of America was abandoning Afghanistan. I couldn't do anything about that. But I could save Zaafir.

That would have to be enough.

"No can do," I said. "Have our extraction birds ready. We'll be needing them directly."

I hung up before Belvina could answer.

In my experience, desperation was a great motivator, especially for staff officers. Here's to hoping that the world's greatest battle captain lived up to her reputation.

"Anything you'd like to share?" Jason said.

"Convoys are closing in from two directions," I said. "Let's do this thing and get gone."

My phone vibrated again.

I looked at the caller ID.

Katherine.

She was probably calling with the same news. The convoy to the south had to be the Chinese. The convoy closing from the north was anyone's guess, but I knew who they weren't—Americans. Sometimes it really was good to have your back against the wall. If nothing else, it made all the second-guessing just disappear.

Jason stuck his hand out the window and gave the two jihadis a friendly wave as we rolled past. The fighters looked confused, but made no move to stop us. After all, who else but fellow Taliban would be dumb enough to play chicken with a minigun?

Me, apparently.

SEVENTY-FIVE

"Comrade, there's something you need to see."

Feng looked over his shoulder toward Yuze. The paramilitary officer was seated behind Feng and had a tablet balanced on his lap. The device was displaying imagery from a circling Laborer 1 quadcopter drone.

When his cell phone had vibrated two hours ago, Feng had considered ignoring the call. Qari had become increasingly demanding. As a longtime agent runner, Feng knew he needed to reestablish the terms of their relationship before the power dynamic irrevocably shifted. But he'd answered all the same. Unlocking the American biometric system was a prize too lucrative to ignore. He'd already sent a cable to Beijing summarizing the Taliban leader's offer. The response had been enthusiastic. Until Feng had access to the American servers, he had to answer the barbarian's every beck and call.

Even so, Feng had almost refused the mullah's request. Why should he rouse his countrymen to rescue the Afghan when the commander had the entirety of the Taliban at his disposal? But after his sleep-addled brain had had a chance to process the conversation, Feng understood. The barbarian still viewed everything through the lens of betrayal. Until Feng's countrymen sifted through the biometric data and produced the traitor's name, Qari believed he was vulnerable.

After he overcame his initial irritation, Feng saw the request in a different light. What better way to safeguard Beijing's wishes than to possess the Afghan whose iris served as the biometric system's living key? Even so, Feng was not about to ride to Qari's rescue blindly. In addition to enlisting half his contingent of paramilitary officers as an escort, Feng had instructed Yuze to monitor the Black Hawk's landing site with their quadcopter drone.

Now that decision was about to pay dividends.

"What is it?" Feng said, straining against his seat belt.

Afghan roads were challenging under daylight and downright treacherous at night. Even though Kai was at the wheel, Feng had no intention of unbuckling until his feet were firmly on the ground.

"Three vehicles are approaching the crash site just ahead of us," Yuze said, indicating three white blobs with his index finger. "Another convoy of four trucks is closing from the north. Did Qari mention this?"

The barbarian most assuredly did not mention this.

Feng took out his cell and dialed the mullah.

The call went straight to voice mail.

Frowning, Feng tried again with the same result.

Something was not right.

"How far are we from the helicopter?" Feng said.

"Two minutes," Kai said.

"Make it one."

The truck surged forward.

SEVENTY-SIX

Twenty yards to the Black Hawk.

Still too far.

A pair of fighters converged from the far side of the helicopter. I could see four figures sitting inside the cabin, which made for a total of seven, counting the jihadi manning the minigun. The two new arrivals planted themselves in our path and raised their rifles.

"Boss?" Jason said, easing off the gas.

The minigun was centered on our windshield, and the gunner's thumbs were poised above the weapon's butterfly triggers.

"Honk the horn," I said to Jason, "like you're driving a cab in New York."

To his credit, Jason didn't argue. He smashed down on the steering wheel and a series of beeps echoed through the night as we kept rolling. The jihadis stepped aside. Whether their reaction was in response to a stimulus ingrained from youth or because they couldn't fathom a bad guy stupid enough to honk his horn, I didn't know. What mattered was that the two gunmen had allowed us to pass.

Fifteen meters.

It wasn't the ten I'd been hoping for, but it would have to do.

"All units, this is Sweet," I said, keying the radio. "Execute, execute, execute."

Jason slammed the truck into park.

Three truck doors opened.

I exited the passenger's side, Jason rolled out the driver's side, and Dee followed the Green Beret.

With help.

Kent shoved her.

Hard.

Dee stumbled, unable to catch herself because her hands were behind her back.

Jason grabbed Dee by the scruff of her neck. The Green Beret steered her toward the Black Hawk as he called out a single command in Pashto.

Look.

The jihadis looked.

Dee was dressed in a *kurte*, a traditional long-sleeved embroidered robe often worn by Turkmen women.

But we'd modified the garment.

Extensively.

Strategically placed tears revealed tantalizing sections of skin that I hoped would draw the male eye. Dee's head was also bare, showcasing lengths of spiky blond hair and her beautiful face. To a religious sect that believed a woman's eyes were the only part of her anatomy fit for public consumption, our transportation specialist's appearance was equal parts scandalizing and transfixing.

Jason gave Dee a final shove.

She tumbled to her knees, head lowered in shame, hands still behind her back.

The two jihadis moved toward her.

Dee looked up.

Then her hands appeared.

They were not empty.

My transportation specialist dropped both fighters with double taps to the chest.

Then she unleashed the whirlwind.

The night exploded with gunfire. I could hear the chattering of M4s rocking as Toto and his shooters dropped the jihadis behind us, and the *pop, pop, pop* as Jason, Kent, and Garrett worked their assigned sectors with pistols. The noise was comforting, but I couldn't dwell on it. As the leader, I'd assigned myself the most dangerous target.

The minigun.

I flowed toward the helicopter in a shooter's crouch, rolling my feet from heel to toe with each step. I indexed my Glock on the gunner, verified equal height and equal light between the front and rear sight posts, and pressed the trigger. I continued forward as I fired, chasing my rounds even as the jihadi behind the GAU slumped. A blur of motion registered to my left, but I never stopped moving or shooting.

Left was Jason's sector.

This was mine.

Three more steps brought me to the helicopter's cabin. I entered, leading with the Glock. A second jihadi scrambled across the seats. He was wearing the black turban favored by the Taliban's leadership.

Qari.

His talonlike fingers reached for the minigun.

I shot him in the face.

Next, I pivoted to the helo's pilots.

A moment later it was done.

"Clear," I shouted.

"Jackpot, Jackpot, Jackpot," Jason said, his voice rising in intensity with each word.

"Jackpot," I said, acknowledging the brevity code word.

Jason had Zaafir.

We could go home.

Then a column of vehicles emerged from the road behind us.

SEVENTY-SEVEN

Sweet, this is Toto. I've got multiple vehicles rolling up. Should we engage, over?"

"Negative," I said, "but hold your position. We're returning to our truck with the precious cargo, time now. Keep the DShK trained on that column, but do not engage unless they fire first. How copy?"

"Sweet, Toto, good copy. Be advised, we're taking sporadic fire from an outcropping at eleven o'clock. Suppressing with grenades and machine-gun fire, but I recommend we get this show on the road, over."

"Toto, this is Sweet, on it," I said.

Sporadic rifle fire probably meant that Qari had kicked out a security element to keep eyes on the road while he waited for the Chinese. At least that's what I would have done in his place. I wasn't worried as much about the lone riflemen as the column from the north that had yet to make an appearance. We'd won this part of the engagement through surprise and violence of action.

Those traits wouldn't carry the day a second time.

The buzzing of a high-velocity round snapping past my head helped to order my thoughts. A moment later I heard a Dragunov's distinctive report echo from the hillside. The shooters on the rock cropping weren't just random jihadis pulling security.

They were snipers.

"Vehicles," I said. "Move."

Jason and Kent had Zaafir between them. Rather than pausing to free the Afghan from his restraints, they were simply carrying him to our Hilux. His hood had been removed, but otherwise the 'terp might as well have been a sack of potatoes. Dee was already back in the Hilux's driver's seat, which left just Garrett and me.

Garrett looked at me across the battlefield.

As our eyes made contact, he smiled.

Then he was spinning toward the ground.

The Dragunov echoed again.

"Toto, this is Sweet," I said as I sprinted for Garrett's prone form, "suppress that hillside with everything you've got. Get that DShK rocking, over."

"Sweet, Toto, roger."

An instant later the DShK's deep-throated roar filled the night, along with the *whump* of a grenade launcher, the chattering of M4s and SAWs, and the barking of AK-47s.

Everyone in our meager little convoy seemed to be hosing down the hillside.

And they were doing it two seconds too late.

I dropped to my knees beside Garrett. His shirt was a mass of red. At first I thought that the bullet must have glanced off the top edge of his plate carrier. Then I realized the wound was much, much worse. The Taliban sniper had hit Garrett in the armpit, meaning possible lung and heart damage. If the round had even nicked Garrett's heart, he'd be gone in seconds.

The SEAL's eyes found mine.

"It's okay," Garrett said. "It's. Okay."

"The hell it is," I said. "You're going home."

I spoke the words as much for my benefit as Garrett's. Grabbing the SEAL by his harness, I hoisted him into a fireman's carry, grunting with the effort. Gritting my teeth, I sprinted toward the trucks, trying to ignore warm rivulets of crimson dripping down my chest.

"Professor, Sweet," I said on the radio as I ran, "Garrett's hit. Chest wound through the armpit. He's losing blood. Fast. Where do you want him?"

"Lead Hilux. I've got my med kit in the truck bed."

I double-clicked the transmit button even as I hauled ass to the pickup. Kent met me halfway. Together we hoisted the limp SEAL into the truck bed. Kent climbed in after him and went to work.

I followed.

"It's not good," Kent said as he cut away the SEAL's uniform. "We need a surgeon. Now."

"On it," I said.

I slapped the roof twice and Dee stuck her head out of the window.

"Drive," I said.

"What about them?" Dee said, pointing at the Chinese column.

"Head for the lead vehicle," I said. "I'll do the talking."

SEVENTY-EIGHT

Feng had watched the slaughter unfold with morbid fascination.

And that's exactly what the engagement had been—a slaughter.

The gunmen had felled Qari's soldiers with an elegance that was equal parts beautiful and terrifying. Like wolves ravaging sheep, the warriors killed with a proficiency unlike anything Feng had ever witnessed. Each movement had been deliberate. Every motion a study in economy of force. The team had laid waste to the Taliban with a cold, brutal efficiency more resembling machines than men.

The decimation had ended almost before it had begun.

One moment, the trio of vehicles had been rolling up to the Black Hawk.

The next, weapons barked, and men died.

Even if he'd been of a mind to intervene, Feng could not have acted quickly enough. By the time his brain made sense of what he was seeing, the crouching figures had swept through the Taliban like a scythe through wheat. Qari alone had seemed to intuit the danger. The barbarian's talonlike fingers had been reaching for the helicopter's minigun, but the weapon had not saved the mullah.

Now the killers were headed toward Feng.

"What do we do, comrade?" Yuze said.

Feng found himself wondering the same thing.

The lead Hilux raced forward with one of the shooters riding in the truck's bed. The wind tore at the standing man's clothes, ripping away his turban. The gunman's hair was black and unruly, his cheeks unshaven. Blood stained his face, and his eyes burned with unholy fire.

In the semidarkness of the ancient Afghan plain, the man could have been Alexander the Great, leading a conquering army from his chariot. Feng instantly understood two things. One, though they'd been dressed as such, the shooters were not Taliban.

Two, death would result from crossing swords with the gunmen.

Feng's death.

The lead truck skidded to a halt.

The unkempt fighter jumped to the ground. He strode forward, halving the distance between Feng's vehicle and his own. He pointed at Feng and then the section of gravel between them.

"What does he want?" Kai said.

"To talk," Feng said.

"What will you do?" Kai said.

"Listen."

Feng opened the truck's door and stepped onto the dirt.

Though Feng wouldn't have thought it possible, the fighter looked more terrifying up close. He stood taller than Feng and was broader in the shoulders, but the gunman's physical attributes weren't what the MSS operative found most intimidating.

Looking at the gunman's face was like peering into a seething maelstrom.

"Do you speak English?" the man said.

"Yes," Feng said, keeping his words calm even as his stomach clenched. The man's appearance and accent confirmed Feng's suspicions—the gunmen were American.

"Good," the American said. "Today, I am not your enemy."

His voice was low.

Gravelly.

The sound of boulders tumbling down a mountain.

"What about tomorrow?" Feng said.

"Tomorrow may never come," the American said. "The wise warrior avoids battle. Be wise tonight. Let us pass."

Feng eyed the American, considering.

Ten years ago, Feng's career had nearly been derailed by Americans. Tonight, he stood to lose infinitely more. If violence erupted, would the numerically superior Chinese forces be victorious?

Perhaps.

Perhaps not.

Feng was too old to bet his life on a gamble. Qari was dead, but the mullah hadn't been the only Taliban council member who'd favored a closer relationship with China. The deal could still be saved. Besides, the graveyard of empires had finally crushed the Americans just like countless invaders before them.

There was no reason for Feng to fight.

Afghanistan had won the battle for him.

Turning to his men, Feng shouted a command in both Cantonese and English.

"Let them pass."

SEVENTY-NINE

What did you do?" Dee said as I jumped into the TC's seat.

"Quoted Sun Tzu," I said.

"And it worked?" Jason said from behind me.

"We're about to see," I said. "Pedal to the metal, Bone. Garrett's in trouble."

Dee stomped the accelerator and the truck surged forward, sending us bouncing along the field.

"Toto, this is Sweet," I said. "Have the gun truck break contact with the snipers and fall in behind us. We're heading home."

"Sweet, Toto, roger. What about the visitors, over?"

"They're giving us safe passage," I said. "Follow in behind us, but keep your crew-served weapons handy, over."

"Trust but verify. I like it. Roger that."

Dee shot past the Chinese convoy. The looks we received were less than friendly, but that was fine. As long as nobody pointed a weapon at us, they could flip us the bird for all I cared. I had bigger problems. A point underscored by the next radio transmission.

"Sweet, this is Professor. I need help back here, over."

"On it," Jason said.

The Green Beret wormed out of the Hilux's open window and hauled himself into the truck bed with Kent and the stricken SEAL. If the PJ was asking for help, Garrett's condition was progressing from bad to worse.

"Monitor the team internal freq," I said to Dee. "I'm bumping to the air-to-air net."

"Roger," Dee said.

Dee dropped the hammer as the Hilux's tires transitioned from dirt to road. This time I didn't bother to address her speed. If I'd thought it would make us go faster, I'd have gotten out and pushed.

Switching radio channels, I called our ace in the hole.

"Any Turbine element, this is Rough Rider 16," I said, using the call signs and frequency Belvina had provided.

"Rough Rider 16, this is Turbine 33. Go ahead, over."

A lump in my throat formed at the sound of the aviator's voice. As ground pounders are wont to do, I've given my pilot friends some good-natured ribbing a time or two. But when the shit has truly hit the fan on a dark night in the middle-of-nowhere Afghanistan, a Night Stalker's calm, steady voice was pretty close to heaven. Especially when that voice belonged to the pilot in command of a flight of two Chinooks headed my way.

"Roger Turbine 33, Rough Rider 16 is a convoy of three vehicles moving south on Highway Alpha Hotel Seven Six approximately three kilometers south of the Bamiyan-Charikar intersection. I have a head count of fifteen with one urgent surgical. Requesting immediate evac, over."

"Rough Rider 16, this is Turbine 33. Acknowledge all. Be advised, you have a convoy of six vehicles approximately one kilometer south of your location moving toward you at a high rate of speed. What are your intentions, over?"

What are my intentions?

I looked at Dee, hoping that she'd help me navigate the aviator speak. Then I realized she could do nothing of the sort. Dee was still monitoring the team internal radio channel like I'd instructed.

Fuck.

"Dee—" I said.

"Matt—I've got vehicles coming straight for us," Dee said.

I looked where she was pointing and swore. Apparently Qari had sought help from every Taliban commander in Afghanistan. I debated telling Dee to keep going in hopes of blowing right by them, but the number two Hilux ended that fantasy. The truck pulled into the opposite lane, abreast of the lead vehicle.

We weren't getting past them.

Time seemed to slow.

Turning back north meant another encounter with the Chinese, who might not be so compliant this time around. Not to mention that per Belvina's last update, a sizable Taliban force had also been closing on the Black Hawk crash site from the north. My ad hoc QRF had done a fantastic job with the very limited role I'd assigned them to play, but we weren't equipped to fight our way free against a numerically superior force. Farmers' fields lay to the east. We could attempt to evade in that direction, but the flat terrain would provide excellent fields of fire for our pursuers.

That left west.

Looking to the right, I eyed the rocky terrain leading up to the towering mountains that formed the Bagram Bowl. Most of it would be impassible.

Most but not all.

A break in the rock face just ahead revealed a narrow road.

"Right, right, right," I shouted, pointing at the road. "Follow that draw."

My transportation specialist cranked the wheel over.

Hard.

Our tires chirped and the truck swayed, but she kept us upright. The draw led deeper into the mountains, probably ending in a box canyon. That was fine. I wasn't looking for a way to escape. I just needed a defensible position to hold off the Taliban so that the Chinooks could grab us.

The secondary road deteriorated fast. In the space of twenty meters, it went from potholed pavement to gravel to dirt. I didn't care. What the terrain feature lacked in drivable amenities, it more than made up for in geographical security. Towering rock rose to either side of the narrow valley, preventing our pursuers from flanking us.

As I'd suspected, the road ended in about two hundred yards, terminating at the mountain's sheer face before widening into a relatively flat chunk of dirt. A chunk of dirt just large enough for an enterprising helicopter pilot to make a confined-area approach.

Or so I hoped.

If I was wrong, I'd just signed our collective death warrants.

Which reminded me that I'd yet to brief my plan to the two orbiting Chinooks.

"Turbine 33, this is Rough Rider 16," I said, keying the transmit button. "I need a hot exfil. LZ is a fifty-yard stretch of uneven ground oriented north-south with no obstacles. Recommend you make your approach from the north. Expect enemy contact from the east, over."

"Rough Rider, this is Turbine, roger all. We are conducting the LZ recon now. Terrain is pretty tight, so we'll have to come in one ship at a time. Say when ready, over."

"Roger that, Turbine," I said. "Stand by."

I switched radio frequencies back to team internal and keyed the radio.

"All elements, this is Sweet. We are going to conduct a hot exfil, over. Toto, have the Toyota with the DShK pick up rear security. I'll relieve the gunner momentarily. Bone, I'm passing radio coms with the birds to you. They're going to come in one ship at a time from the north. Duke, you and Toto are responsible for head count. Call me once we are PZ clean. I'll be the last one off, over."

"Stop here," I said to Dee as a series of *rogers* greeted my instructions. "Confirm you've got coms with the birds.

Dee brought the truck to a halt, steering with one hand even as she fiddled with her radio with the other. A moment later I saw her lips moving as she made contact with the helos. Then she flashed me a thumbs-up.

I squeezed her shoulder before bailing out of the truck.

The second Hilux rolled up just short of ours, offsetting to the right in a T-bone formation while our gun truck spun in a circle so that its hood and the DShK were pointed at the approaching Taliban convoy. A trio of headlights blossomed at the far side of the draw as our pursuers closed in. I waited for the DShK to discourage their progress, but the crew-served weapon remained silent.

I ran toward the gun truck even as I keyed the radio.

"Toto, Sweet, tell the DShK gunner to light up that convoy, over."

"Sweet, this is Toto. We're trying, but we've got a problem with the gun, over."

Shitfire.

"Sweet, this is Duke. Want help?"

"Duke, this is Sweet, negative. You are PZ control. Get our people on those birds. I'll handle the DShK."

PZ, or pickup zone, control was one of the most important jobs during an aerial exfil. This was the person responsible for breaking the boarding party into groups called sticks and assigning them each to a helicopter. The role was even more important now. We were under fire, at night, and had never before worked together. The possibility of accidentally leaving someone behind was real. I trusted Jason to ensure this didn't happen.

"This is Duke, roger all."

The first Chinook thundered overhead, the aerial dump truck flying just above the sloping terrain nap-of-the-earth style to utilize the greater lift generated by remaining in ground effect. Right on schedule, a series of green tracers arced up from the Taliban convoy, hunting for the huge target.

The Chinook broke off its approach.

"Sweet, this is Bone. The pilots need that convoy suppressed before they'll come in."

The Chinooks had their own miniguns and could have certainly taken a crack at the Taliban convoy, but I was glad they hadn't. We were clustered together in an extremely tight space. The chances of fratricide were simply too great.

"Bone, Sweet, I'm on it. Tell the bird to make a single orbit. By the time they're lined up for their approach, the DShK will be rocking, over."

"Bone copies all."

I didn't begrudge Dee her dubious tone. I had no idea why the machine gun wasn't firing or whether I could fix it. I did know that if I didn't get the DShK operational, we were going to die.

That wasn't going to happen.

Not today.

I covered the last ten yards at a dead sprint and vaulted into the gun truck's bed. Before my first deployment to Afghanistan as a Ranger, the Regiment's intelligence staff had taught my men a series of classes on common Russian weapons. Due to the DShK's prevalence throughout the Taliban's formations, my company had spent half a day at the range familiarizing ourselves with the machine gun. Like many Russian pieces of kit, the crew-served weapon was notoriously finicky, but I had a couple tricks up my sleeve.

"It's jammed," the gunner said as I crawled up next to him. "A double feed. Can't get it cleared."

He continued to fight with the weapon even as rounds snapped past our heads and pinged off the Hilux's metal frame. The courage displayed by my volunteer QRF was extraordinary, but all the courage in the world would be for naught if I couldn't get the machine gun operational.

"Let me take a crack," I said.

Unlike US firearms, which favored precision and accuracy, Russian weapons were designed with an eye toward ruggedness. With this in mind, sometimes it helped to treat them like the blunt-force objects they really were. Fortunately, blunt force and I were old friends. Balling up my fist, I hammered the feed tray with everything I had, putting my back and shoulder into the blow. The gunner gasped, convince I'd broken the gun, but the Russian piece of craftsmanship responded to my love tap.

The double feed broke loose.

The linkage separated.

I popped open the feed tray even as the gunner seated another belt of .50-caliber linked ammunition. I checked the ammunition's alignment, closed the feed tray, planted my foot against the tripod, and charged the bolt.

Then I pressed the butterfly triggers.

The gun roared.

"Get back to the PZ," I said, firing another burst. "I got this."

The gunner started to argue.

I summoned my best Ranger voice and reiterated my instructions.

"Get your ass moving. Now!"

This time he obeyed.

My initial bursts had gone long, so I recentered the gun's iron sights on the lead Taliban vehicle and cut loose. Green tracers slapped the truck, and I walked the rounds up the hood and into the windshield.

It was beautiful.

Glass shattered and metal buckled.

Parts of the Hilux cartwheeled into the air as steam vented from its hood.

I put another long burst into the stricken vehicle, panning the sights back and forth in an effort to catch the troops fleeing the truck like rats abandoning a sinking ship.

"Sweet, this is Bone. Keep it up. First Chinook is on the ground, time now."

"This is Sweet, roger."

The good news was that the lead Taliban vehicle was out of the fight.

Permanently.

The bad was that his two friends were still in it.

And they were pissed.

I traversed the machine gun to the left just as the DShK mounted on the number two vehicle let loose. The Hilux was still rolling forward when the Taliban gunner fired, and the bumpy terrain affected his aim. Instead of hitting me, his half-inch-in-diameter rounds tore a miniature crater out of the ground next to my right front tire.

I fired a long burst, walking my rounds across his truck.

Twenty years.

I fired again.

Twenty goddamn years and we're right back where we started.

"Sweet, Bone, first Chinook is PZ clear. Second is inbound, over."

My truck buckled under an onslaught of machine-gun fire, the rocking frame almost throwing me from my perch. I slewed the DShK to the right and fired another burst even as an incoming round sparked off the machine gun's metal frame, peppering me with bullet fragments. My position was untenable. A weapon like this could turn the tide of battle, if it was supported with infantrymen providing security and covering fire.

Absent that, the machine gun made for one hell of a target.

"Sweet, this is Bone. Second bird is on the ground. Break contact, over."

I burned through another ten rounds, alternating fire between the two remaining trucks. I was acting as a bullet magnet, but if the Taliban were shooting at me, they weren't harassing the Chinooks.

Chinooks full of people for whom I was responsible.

There would be no breaking contact.

"Bone, this is Sweet. Get that bird off the PZ. Once it's airborne, I'll escape and evade on foot. We'll link up at an alternate PZ, over."

"Sweet, this is Duke. That's a shitty-ass plan, over."

"Bone, get that bird airborne," I said, ignoring Jason. "Now. I'm about to be overrun."

I hammered the butterfly trigger once more.

Then I was flat on my back looking at the stars.

The truck shook, rounds pinging off the metal frame like hail. I wasn't even sure what had just happened. I just knew that my chest had been hit by a sledgehammer. The Hilux was coming apart around me. Pieces of metal frame were spinning through the air, but the stars were all I could think of.

Cold, bright, beautiful stars.

If this was going to be my last view of Afghanistan, at least it was a good one.

Then even that was ruined.

A black leviathan blotted out my starry window as hurricane winds thrashed the truck. Part of my mind was screaming that I needed to get up, but my sternum was on fire and every breath burned.

Maybe I should just rest for a moment.

The sky above me changed from night to day as the Chinook's miniguns erupted. The quantity of lead tearing through the air was hard to fathom as twin red lasers crisscrossed the ground.

The Night Stalkers weren't leaving after all.

That meant I'd have to get up.

Which was some bullshit.

I pushed myself upright, using the truck frame for balance, and almost passed out. It felt like someone had driven an ice pick into the center of my chest. I tried to roll over the truck frame but got stuck. If this wasn't a candy-assed way to die, I didn't know what was. I was hanging half in and half out of a Taliban truck, flopping around like a dolphin caught in a tuna net.

Then Jason was beside me.

"Come on, Ranger," he said, slinging me over his shoulder. "Time to go home."

He ran across the dirt toward the Chinook hovering just feet away, its ramp lowered and its crew chief beckoning. Jason's shoulder dug into my torso, igniting firestorms of agony with each step, but I was grateful for the pain. Without it I might have passed out, and that would have been a shame because I'd have missed what happened next. Just before he bounded into the Chinook, Jason belted out the first line of a familiar tune.

I want to be an Airborne Ranger.

Gathering the remnants of my pride, I screamed the second verse with him.

Live the life of guts and danger.

Then we were inside the Chinook.

EIGHTY

The bomb exploded as we were midway across the Atlantic.

We felt nothing.

This was because the bomb exploded almost five thousand miles away in front of the Hamid Karzai International Airport's Abbey Gate at 1750 local time. Thirteen US service members and one hundred seventy Afghan civilians were killed, many of them women and children. More than one hundred fifty people were injured.

A second bomb detonated later that evening.

Both bombs were attributed to ISIS-K, but this was only true of the first device. The second was actually an AGM-114 Hellfire II missile with an added steel-fragmentation sleeve. The air-to-ground missile had been fired by a Reaper Unmanned Aerial System. The target was a flatbed truck parked just inside the Chinese Mes Aynak compound.

A truck loaded with servers containing backup data for the ABIS biometric system.

The truck, along with several Taliban guards and two

Chinese paramilitary officers, vanished in a cloud of smoke and fire. The Chinese Communist Party did not dispute the US's characterization of the attack, just as the American government made no mention of a dead Chinese intelligence officer who'd been linked to the murder of several former Green Berets.

Realpolitik at its best.

Even so, shadow warriors on both sides of the ocean took notice. Scores would be settled, and debts honored. A new front in the ongoing skirmish between East and West had just opened.

It took an hour for news of the first bomb to reach our already somber gathering. The information came in the form of a call to my transportation specialist from her friend the CIA case officer. Dee had been sitting with Ferhana when her phone began to vibrate. Gharib's daughter had repeatedly thanked us for rescuing her and seemed determined not to leave Dee's side. But after looking at her caller ID, Dee had excused herself from Ferhana and sought an island of quiet.

She answered the phone and spoke a couple of indecipherable words.

Then her body went rigid.

One look at Dee's face and I knew.

Everything.

In addition to a quick explanation of what had occurred, the CIA officer had also provided a preliminary list of the casualties. I didn't recognize twelve of the names.

The thirteenth broke my heart.

Captain Belvina Ngoy.

"I'm sorry, Matt," Dee said. "I truly am."

The aviator gripped my hand as she spoke, and I squeezed back. My chest was a mass of black and blue. With several cracked ribs and a bruised sternum, I was in constant pain.

But I was alive.

My plate carrier had stopped the 7.62mm rounds intent on shredding my vital organs. Belvina Ngoy—refugee from Africa, naturalized citizen, and holder of the title World's Best Battle Captain—had not been as fortunate.

"She was standing on the wall when it happened," Dee said, "giving one of her soldiers a break."

This seemed appropriate.

Though I hadn't known her long, I was not surprised that Belvina had pulled guard duty on a soldier's behalf. The requirement to lead by example was instilled into every young lieutenant's head. A good officer never asked her soldiers to do something she was not prepared to do herself, and Belvina had been the epitome of a good officer. But it was the first thing Dee had said that stuck with me.

Belvina had been standing on a wall when she'd died.

Standing as a bulwark against evil on behalf of her adopted nation.

Where do we find such men and women?

"Do you want me to sit with you?" Dee said.

Unlike our flight to Afghanistan, this time Mr. Blackwell's plane was filled to the brim. In addition to Zaafir and his family, the aircraft was crammed with several hundred Afghan refugees all bound for Texas and the temporary camp setup at Fort Bliss to house them. The mood was subdued, but with this many children, quiet was hard to come by. I'd secured a rearward-facing seat by the forward bulkhead. The one next to me had been empty.

Maybe it was time for that to change.

I was in the process of saying as much when my phone vibrated.

It was a call I'd been expecting.

A call I'd been dreading.

"I'm sorry," I said to Dee. "I have to take this. Alone."

My transportation specialist nodded. Dee squeezed my hand once more and then withdrew. Taking a deep breath, I answered.

"Hello, Mr. Blackwell," I said.

"It's Sam, son. That was true before you left. It's damn sure true now."

"Yes, sir," I said. "You received my message?"

"I did. I was off the grid for a bit. Sorry it took so long to get back with you."

Sam Blackwell was apologizing.

To me.

"Sir, I'm the one who's sorry," I said. "I—"

"Let me stop you right there," Sam said, his Texas twang trampling my words. "If you want, we can have this conversation later, face-to-face. But we're not doing it over the phone. I hired Garrett right out of the military almost ten years ago. He was a fine man, but he's never been whole. He left a piece of himself on that mountain in Afghanistan with his brother SEALs. You gave it back to him, Matthew."

My eyes tracked to the corner of the aircraft as Sam spoke. The corner containing a single flag-draped coffin secured to the deck. The refugees naturally gave the coffin space. Even the children seemed to understand its sacred nature. While we'd all paid our respects to Garrett, there was one person who still refused to leave his side.

Zaafir.

Even now the Afghan stood next to the coffin, guarding his brother-in-arms. Jason and I had both tried talking to the former 'terp, but Zaafir could not be swayed. Until Garrett was back on US soil, Zaafir would stand watch over the fallen SEAL.

Alone.

"Thank you for saying that, sir," I said.

"You don't thank a person for speaking the truth, Matt. And it's Sam."

"Sam," I said.

"Glad we got that straightened out," Sam said. "I don't want to burden you with an old man's ramblings any longer. Come see me at the ranch once you're settled. We've got one more thing to discuss."

"What's that, sir?" I said.

"Your future employment."

Sam hung up before I could reply.

That was probably for the best.

I was all out of words.

EPILOGUE

—

Frodo and I were once again in a bar, but this time neither of us had to ask the proprietor to turn up the TV's volume. This was more a testament to the establishment than the employees. The bar was named the Folded Chute. It occupied the precarious market space between a watering hole for special operators and an upstanding member of the greater community with no ties to the military whatsoever.

The owner was a former Unit sergeant major named Mike Halas. Mike had parlayed a penchant for investing into a sizable nest egg. Rather than purchase a couple of rental homes or maybe a Dairy Queen, Mike had sunk his life savings into a historic brick property on the edge of downtown. His wife had an eye for interior decorating, and between the two of them, they'd revitalized the property and turned the former industrial building into a fairly respectable institution.

While the bar's name was certainly a nod to Mike's former life, there were no obvious hints as to the proprietor's true nature. Half-drunk soldiers didn't wander the floor, spoiling for a fight, and no one had ever been thrown through the beautiful glass bay windows framing the establishment's entrance. The beer was good and brewed on location, the food passable, and the service excellent. All in all, there was nothing to set the Folded Chute apart from the other vanilla mom-and-pop stores that called Main Street home.

Unless you asked for the Team Room.

This was the magic phrase that served as ticket to a completely different aspect of the bar. A short walk down a dark hallway brought you to an unmarked door beyond which lay a room large enough for four tables. I wasn't sure what the space's original purpose had been, as its windowless, drab features certainly wouldn't have made it prime office space. Perhaps a storage area or maybe even a break room. In any case, what it was *then* certainly bore no resemblance to the place *now*. The space looked more English pub than American drinking establishment. The furnishings were of dark wood and polished brass. An actual bar ran the length of one wall with pull handles for several of the Folded Chute's rotating brews.

But it was the decorations hanging from the walls that revealed the Team Room's true purpose. This was a shrine to operators past and present. Men who had given the last full measure as well as those still serving. Pictures, unit citations, framed guidons, challenge coins, all the military bric-a-brac that seemed chintzy in so many of the bars nearer to post took on an air of nobility here.

By the time I landed in the States, Frodo's arrest warrant had vaporized much like the Taliban trucks containing the backup servers for the biometric database. According to Katherine, the case file had simply disappeared. One moment its redacted version resided in the government's database; the next it had been reduced to random ones and zeroes scattered across the ether.

Her working theory was a bit cynical, even by the standards of those of us who made our living in the cloak-and-dagger world. Katherine believed that the same people who'd restricted the raid's original after-action report had flagged the surviving members of Gold Team for monitoring. That when Fletcher had begun his online rants, the Chinese weren't the only ones who'd noticed.

Katherine thought Frodo's arrest warrant was not unique. That the restricted case file from Washington Field Office had probably held warrants for all the surviving members from the Gold Team of ODA 3324. Or more specifically, the members of Gold Team who'd cleared the building and rolled up Feng and Qari. Since I'd been outside the target building the entire time and had never encountered the detainees, my name hadn't made the list.

Katherine believed that the warrants would have been used as a pretext for nameless men and women in suits to impress upon Fletcher, Jason, and Frodo the requirement to keep what had happened in Afghanistan ten years ago in Afghanistan. If past experience was any guide, these discussions would have been accompanied by one of the draconian nondisclosure agreements people in our profession were constantly forced to sign.

I suspected that her theory was correct, but I didn't know for certain.

Yet.

Assuming that I was still employed by DIA, running

that to ground would be one of my first priorities. Or perhaps I should say, assuming I still *wanted* to be employed by DIA. I'd persuaded our pilots to drop me off at Dulles so that I could catch a flight to Fort Bragg and spring Frodo. Since landing stateside, I'd endured a barrage of calls and text messages from James. I'd finally turned off my phone. Before I had anything to do with a government agency, I intended to pay Mr. Blackwell a visit.

After landing at Fayetteville Regional Airport, I'd rented a car and picked Frodo up from the Fort Bragg detention center. We'd needed somewhere to talk. Somewhere dark and quiet that offered both alcohol and privacy in equal measures. Somewhere Frodo could exorcise his demons. I'd asked Jason for a recommendation, and he'd instantly replied. Now that Frodo and I were settled in the Team Room, I understood his answer. There was no better place for an operator to unburden his soul.

"I still can't believe Afghanistan's over," Frodo said after taking a sip of his beer.

I nodded, turning my glass of Four Branches Bourbon on its coaster. Other than thanking me for picking him up from jail, these were the first words Frodo had spoken. I'd told him where we were headed and why, and he'd given a nod of assent.

The rest of the car ride had passed in silence.

That was fine.

This was why the Team Room existed.

Beers were on the honor system, so no waitstaff lurked behind the bar. The television was permanently tuned to the news, but the volume was set low and the subtitles enabled. A switch on the wall illuminated a red lamp mounted just above the closed door in the dark hallway. A lit lamp meant a Team Room occupant wanted to order something stronger than beer. Otherwise, patrons were left alone with their thoughts.

"Think we'll go back?" Frodo said.

I shrugged. "Just because we're done with Afghanistan doesn't mean that it's done with us."

Frodo nodded and took another long swallow.

On the television, talking heads pontificated about what would happen next while video showing the final C-17 taxiing to the departure end of the runway played on a loop. As historic shots went, the image of an Air Force transport thundering down the runway didn't have the same gut punch as a single Huey departing the US embassy in Saigon.

But the finality still hit home.

"I guess you're wondering why I did what I did," Frodo said.

"The question's crossed my mind," I said.

Frodo's lips twisted into the semblance of a smile, but there was no joy in his eyes.

Just a deep, abiding sadness.

"Something inside me broke," Frodo said, tracing the condensation on his glass. "I saw Afghanistan crumbling, and it suddenly called into question everything I've done over the last dozen years. Everything. All the operations that went bad. All the good men and women lost. All the innocent people killed. There was an Op in Iraq that . . ."

Frodo paused, his fingers trembling.

Then he cleared his throat and began again.

"We all know that this is an imperfect business. That we try our hardest to make sure that only bad guys end up in body bags. But it doesn't always happen that way. Between my time in the Ranger Regiment and the Unit, I've got at least a dozen deployments under my belt. I can't even begin to count how many operations that equates to. I know it's statistically impossible for all of those missions to go right. That sometimes innocent people are caught in the wrong place at the wrong time. But knowing something in your head isn't the same as feeling it in your heart. What we do carries a weight. A soul-crushing weight."

"I know," I said, because I did.

My final operation as a Ranger company commander had been to hit a compound full of high-level Haqqani network financiers. We did everything possible to take our target alive, but he decided to go out in a blaze of glory by detonating his suicide vest.

Alive bad guys were usually better than dead bad guys, especially upper-level folks who could provide intelligence about the larger terrorist organization. In this guy's case, I didn't care. He'd been a particularly heinous dude who'd made a sport out of stoning little girls to death for the crime of attending school. If he wanted to blow himself to smithereens, so be it.

But he hadn't just killed himself.

He'd taken his wife and two toddlers with him.

The sight of those lifeless, broken bodies had torn something loose in me.

"I know you do," Frodo said.

He still wouldn't look me in the eye, but his fingers found my shoulder and squeezed.

Then they returned to his glass.

"A kid died," Frodo said. "An American soldier. And I'm responsible."

The air seemed to quiver.

I wanted to rail against Frodo's pronouncement. To deride it as untrue. I didn't. He'd willingly gone to prison for a crime he didn't commit. This wasn't the time to wave away his feelings. This was the moment to be still. To listen to Frodo unburden his shame and hurt so that he didn't have to face them alone.

It was what brothers did.

"The Op we did with Jason," Frodo said, the words coming slowly as if dragged from somewhere deep within, "there's something you don't know."

"I know that two Green Berets died," I said. "One on our operation and one on the follow-up hit. Their deaths were tragic, but you had nothing to do with them."

"That's where you're wrong," Frodo said. "Tommy was a fratricide."

I shook my head, anger getting the best of me.

"Bullshit," I said. "I talked with both Jason and Zaafir. They independently confirmed that you weren't even in the room with Tommy. To have killed him, you would have had to turn completely around and shoot through the wall. That didn't happen."

"I didn't kill Tommy," Frodo said. "Dan did."

"What are you talking about?" I said.

"It was an accident," Frodo said, his voice dropping to

a whisper, "but Dan killed Tommy all the same. He told me. Afterward."

I wanted to call bullshit a second time, but something stopped me. A memory. A memory of Dan and Frodo talking quietly in the team room after the operation. At the time I'd chalked it up to a seasoned operator helping a newbie deal with a teammate's death. Everyone in special operations looked up to members of the Unit. It made sense that Dan would confide in Frodo.

But what exactly had he confided?

"Did Jason know?" I said.

Frodo shook his head.

"No," Frodo said, "but I saw it on Dan's face when we boarded the exfil bird. We had a fratricide in the Unit once. Thankfully the victim didn't die, but it fucked up the shooter pretty good. His expression mirrored Dan's. I went to find Dan after we landed. To help him process. Hell, it might not have even been his fault. Tommy was new at this too, and he could have just pushed too far forward while clearing his sector."

"So you knew you had nothing to do with Tommy's death, but you still confessed to murder?" I said.

I regretted the words as soon as they left my lips, but I couldn't take them back. Nor was I sure I wanted to. I loved Frodo like a brother, but I couldn't help but think that if he'd just confided in me, this might have gone a whole lot differently. Yes, Zaafir and his family were safe, but Garrett was dead. I was pissed that my best friend hadn't trusted me with the truth.

Petty?

Yeah.

But operators aren't any more perfect off the target than on.

"You still don't get it, Matty," Frodo said, his words barely audible.

"Then help me," I said.

"I'm guilty of murder," Frodo said, "just not Tommy's."

I stared at Frodo, waiting for him to continue.

This was bizzarro world. For a guy who made his living crawling into the heads of strangers to ferret out their deepest, darkest secrets, I was failing miserably. I shared a greater connection with Frodo than anyone but Laila, and I still had no idea what he was saying.

"Dan," Frodo said. "I killed Dan."

I shook my head. "You couldn't have killed Dan. A Taliban fighter with an AK-47 zapped him while we were at FOB Chapman, two hundred thirty kilometers away."

"A jihadi fired the shot," Frodo said, "but I'm still responsible."

Frodo reached for his beer, but the glass slipped through his fingers, spilling a sudsy tide across the dark table.

"Damn it," Frodo said, reaching for a napkin.

"I got you," I said, throwing a stack on the rapidly expanding puddle. "I wouldn't sweat it. I'm sure these tables have seen worse."

Frodo nodded, but he didn't speak. At least not at first. Instead he corralled the spilled beer with napkin after napkin until the battered wood was dry.

Then he pushed the sodden mess into a pile.

"Dan wanted to go straight to Captain McGourthy,"

Frodo said, his index finger tapping out a nervous staccato. "He was going to turn in his rifle then and there. I told him to take twenty-four hours to collect his thoughts. I said I'd seen it once before. In the Unit. He should wait for the investigation, and say his piece then. If he stepped out of the operational lineup now, he'd only be hurting his team. With Tommy dead and you and me about to leave, they were already down three men. If Dan benched himself, the ODA would be combat ineffective."

"Solid advice," I said.

"No," Frodo said, shaking his head, "it wasn't. I didn't understand how hard Dan was taking it. I should have brought him to see the chaplain or gone straight to Jason. Bottom line, Dan should have never been on the next hit."

"Wait a minute," I said. "You don't know—"

"I do," Frodo said. "Jason reached out after Dan was killed. He said Dan was sleepwalking through the hit. He drilled the shooter threatening his team, but did nothing to address the fighter who had a bead on him. Dan wanted to die, Matty."

Once again I forced myself to remain silent as I thought. Could it have gone down the way Frodo said? Yeah. It's hard when you lose a teammate and damn near unbearable when you think it might have been your fault. If Dan really had killed Tommy, it wasn't a stretch to think that he'd atoned for his mistake the only way his warrior's honor would allow.

"I never reported what Dan told me," Frodo said, speaking into the silence. "I didn't figure there was any point. As things stood, Dan and Tommy both died heroes. Nothing could bring them back, so why tarnish their memories?"

"What changed?" I said.

"Afghanistan. Afghanistan changed everything. I realized something as you and I were sitting in that Austin bar, watching our life's work turn to ashes. When there was a chance that Afghanistan might remain a semifunctioning country, I could rationalize the sacrifices. Dan and Tommy were still a tragedy, but their deaths had meaning. Purpose. But when it all crumbled, their legacies crumbled right along with it. If Afghanistan could no longer atone for their deaths, then I had to."

"Here's the thing," I said, my words pulling with them emotions I'd long ago buried. Images of a laughing Syrian toddler and her raven-haired mother. The dead wife and daughter of an equally dead asset. Testaments to my own failure. "I've sat where you're sitting. I can't tell you how to come to terms with what happened— you're going to have to walk that path yourself. What I can tell you is that you won't walk it alone."

For a time we just sat as the TV flickered and talking heads rambled. Now the quiet felt different. Less ominous and more companionable. Like the sudden stillness at the end of a free fall when your chute inflates and the ambient noise of rushing wind and roaring jet engines fades. A HAHO jump was never going to make my list of favorite things, but there was something almost magical about drifting silently through the sky beneath a canopy of silk surrounded by your brothers. That feeling of togetherness didn't make the mission any less dangerous, but maybe it did something equally as important.

It made you believe.

Believe that with rough men beside you, nothing could stand against you.

"Thank you, brother," Frodo said sometime later. "Thank you."

"Don't be getting all weepy," I said, slapping him on the back. "You're not out of the woods yet. Laila and I had planned to ask you and Katherine this together, but life got in the way."

"Ask what?" Frodo said.

"Baby Virginia is named after an incredible woman," I said, "but a name is just a start. Because of me, Laila knows things a mama shouldn't. Evil is not an abstract concept to my wife because she's experienced it firsthand. Fortunately, she also knows that there are good men and women who stand on a wall and stare down evil. Women like my baby's namesake. Men like you. We want you involved in Virginia's life."

"I've only got one good hand, so changing diapers is probably out," Frodo said. "But I would lay down my life for your baby girl. You know that."

"I do," I said. "So does Laila. That's why we want you and Katherine to be Virginia's godparents."

Frodo didn't answer right away.

When he did, his voice quavered.

"You sure?" Frodo said.

"Never been more sure about anything," I said. "You know the story of David from the Bible?"

"David and Goliath?"

"Yep. David was a warrior king and a poet. He more than any other ruler before him or since shaped the destiny of the nation of Israel. The prophet Samuel called David a man after God's own heart. I always thought that was the ultimate compliment—a man with God's heart. I don't know King David, but I do know you. I want a man with your heart to watch over my daughter."

"I'd be honored, Matty," Frodo said. "Honored."

"Good," I said. "Then finish up your beer. We've got a plane to catch."

"Where?"

"Austin," I said. "Laila wants to tell you the news in person. Act surprised."

"That's a helluva of a thing, Matty."

"You're a helluva man, Frodo."

AUTHOR'S NOTE

As with many Afghanistan and Iraq veterans, the fall of Afghanistan in the summer of 2021 left me in despair. As I traded text messages and phone calls with friends who'd also served, I knew that this horrific event would figure prominently in my next Matt Drake novel.

That was the easy part.

The hard part was reconciling the Matt Drake universe with the real one. The one in which Afghanistan crumbles. With this in mind, there are several author liberties I took with *Forgotten War*. For starters, since *Forgotten War* came out after *Hostile Intent*, in Matt's world, the Russian/Ukrainian conflict occurred *before* the collapse of Afghanistan. From a timeline perspective, I also employed some dramatic license with the sequence of events that led to our tragic withdrawal. While in real life, the capture of Bagram and Kabul happened almost simultaneously, in *Forgotten War*, I stretched these events out for dramatic effect.

This book is fictional and not meant to be completely reflective of actual events. While the Chinese did have a compound near the Mes Aynak mine, to the best of my knowledge, it was not active during the timeline covered in *Forgotten War*. Neither was the compound targeted by a US-sponsored drone strike. By the same token, while numerous civilian-staffed-and-led efforts rescued an untold number of Afghans, the operation depicted in *Forgotten War* was fictional. The Pineapple Express did exist, but I have no special insight into its members or how it functioned.

Unfortunately, the suicide bomber who killed thirteen American service members on August 26, 2021, was all too real. I spent a good deal of time thinking about whether to include this tragic event. While I'm quite proud of this book, it is just a work of fiction. That said, the sentiment that the characters in *Forgotten War* express about their service in Afghanistan is largely reflective of real conversations and text threads I exchanged with fellow veterans.

These poignant thoughts became *Forgotten War*'s thematic backbone.

With this in mind, I decided that the impact our nation's longest war had on the psyche of the volunteer force of men and women who fought it could not be understood without including the withdrawal's tragic and bloody ending. In the finest of American traditions, the thirteen men and women who gave their last full measure fell while standing for freedom. These ordinary Americans joined their respective services during a time of war, knowing full well that they would likely be sent into harm's way. Almost eight hundred thousand American men and women voluntarily served in Afghanistan over the course of a conflict that spanned two decades.

They are our nation's newest Greatest Generation.

ACKNOWLEDGMENTS

Though it's hard to fathom, *Forgotten War* is the fourth book in my Matt Drake series and my sixth published novel. I am both incredibly grateful and extremely baffled that you, the reader, have stuck with me this long. But since you're still here, let me run through some of the people who made this book possible.

As always, my incredible team at Berkley has accomplished the impossible. Really. The difference between what I submitted to my long-suffering editor, Tom Colgan, and what you now hold in your hands is immense. The Lord might have rested after the sixth day, but so far, Tom shows no sign of letting up. He's been my editor since the beginning, and I'm thankful every day for his insight and patience.

Along those same lines, marketing rock star Jin Yu has been with me from day one, and her fingerprints are on everything I do. I'm so very lucky that she's a part of team Bentley. Publicists Danielle Keir and Yazmine Hassan round out the roster of awesomeness, and I'm so thankful for their tireless efforts to introduce Matt Drake to the world. Thank you all.

Once again, the Berkley art team rendered the guts of

my novel into a breathtaking cover. Thank you to Anthony Ramondo and Steve Meditz for knocking my socks off. On that note, I'd also like to thank Jaime Mendola-Hobbie and Allison Prince for again raising the already high bar when it comes to our marketing images. If you saw a compelling advertisement leading up to *Forgotten War*'s release, chances are that these ladies created it.

The further I get in my writer's journey, the more convinced I am that it's only possible to travel this path in the company of other writers. My companions are too numerous to name, but the following folks helped keep me on the straight and narrow: Nick Petrie, Bill Schweigart, Simon Gervais, Taylor Moore, Connor Sullivan, Mark Greaney, Brad Taylor, Chris Hauty, Jack Carr, Joshua Hood, Jeffrey Wilson, Brian Andrews, Marc Cameron, Kyle Mills, Tosca Lee, Nelson DeMille, Boyd Morrison, Joel Rosenberg, and Mike Maden. Of this crew, Brad Taylor and his lovely wife, Elaine, along with Mark Greaney, were exceptionally generous with their time. Thank you all.

I'd also like to thank some folks who helped me while I was researching my last Tom Clancy novel, *Zero Hour*. Mike Reese, Doug Sanders, and Jennifer Walker from Boeing were kind enough to help an old gunship pilot get a feel for the new AH-64E Apache helicopter. As retired warrant officers and former instructor pilots, Mike and Doug bore the brunt of my questions, and they did so with the grace and professionalism you would expect of an Army aviator. Doug was also kind enough to coach me as I fumbled through a couple of simulator scenarios. Apparently, attempting to fly a thirty-plus-million-dollar helicopter seventeen years after your last flight is not at all just like riding a bike.

Who knew?

In the same vein, I'd like to thank a couple of subject matter experts for helping me with various technical and tactical aspects. Retired Army Sergeant Major and Special Mission Unit veteran Jason Beighley again helped me keep my powder dry. Along the same lines, Retired Army Colonel Kelsey Smith helped me get Afghanistan right. Kesley and I were troop commanders during my deployment to Afghanistan and he is a brother in every sense of the word. When it was time to get wet, former Navy SEAL Trevor Thompson kept me from making a fool of myself. Thank you, Trevor, and I apologize for all the SEAL jokes.

Those were Jason's idea.

From the business side of things, my agent, Scott Miller, has proven to be invaluable. Thank you, Scott, for your wisdom and savvy. I'm grateful to be working with you.

No set of acknowledgments would be complete without an ode to you, the reader. Because of you, Matt Drake exists. If you want to see more of Matt and Frodo in action, please consider leaving a five-star review on Amazon. I can't emphasize enough how important these reviews are to authors. If you want to stay connected with everything I'm working on, including my novels in the Tom Clancy universe and anything else I have up my sleeve, please visit me at www.donbentleybooks.com and sign up for my newsletter. I always love hearing from readers, and you can reach me via email at donbentley books@gmail.com or via Twitter or Facebook at @bent leydonb.

Finally, I'd like to thank my wife and kids for their support. Will, Faith, and Kelia—I'm so very grateful to be your dad.

Ang—thank you for picking me.

—DON

Ready to find
your next great read?

Let us help.

Visit prh.com/nextread

Penguin
Random
House